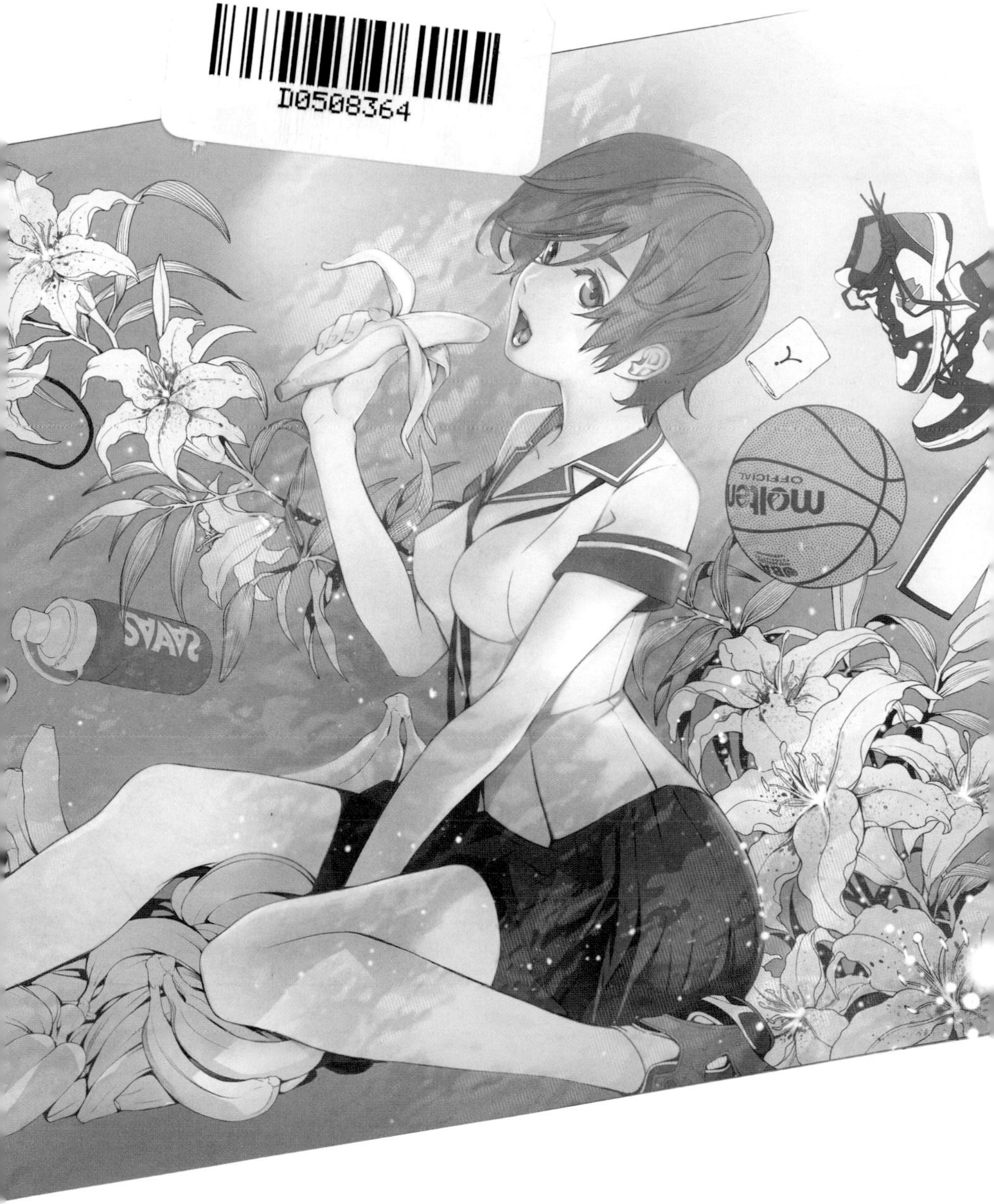

Surugamonkey

BAKEMONOGATARI

OH!GREAT

ORIGINAL STORY:
NISIOISIN

ORIGINAL CHARACTER
DESIGN: VOFAN

4

MAIN CHARACTERS

Koyomi Araragi

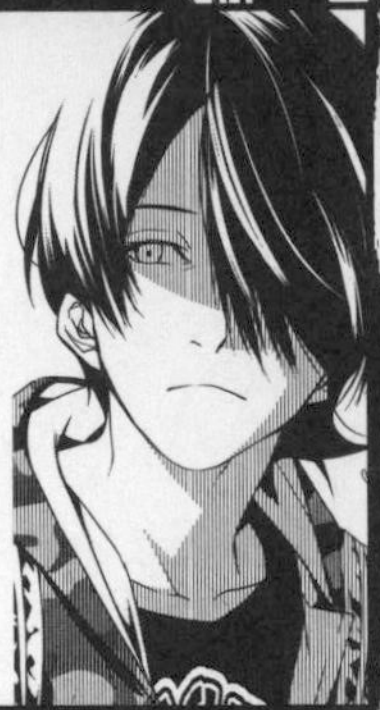

A boy who was attacked by a vampire. Accepts Hitagi's confession of love and is currently dating her.

Hitagi Senjogahara

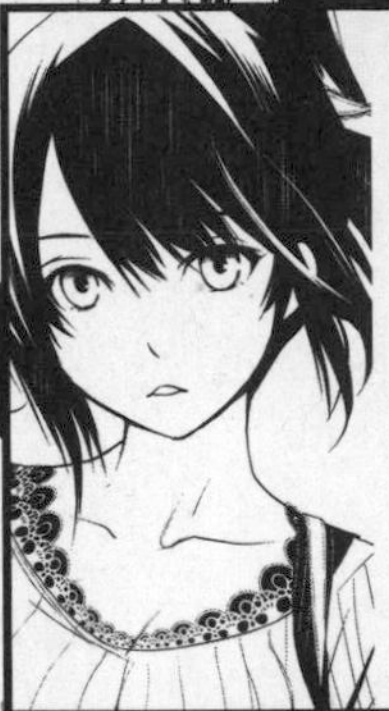

A girl whose weight was once stolen by a "crab." Tells Koyomi how she feels when they send Mayoi on her way.

Mayoi Hachikuji

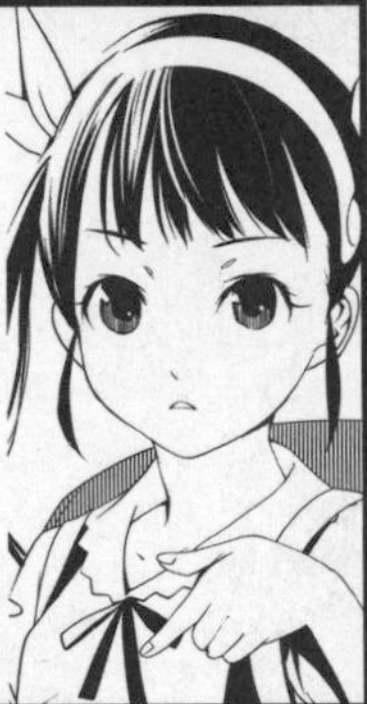

A "Lost Snail" who tries to visit her mother's house but can never arrive. Finally makes it home after Koyomi and friends save her.

Tsubasa Hanekawa

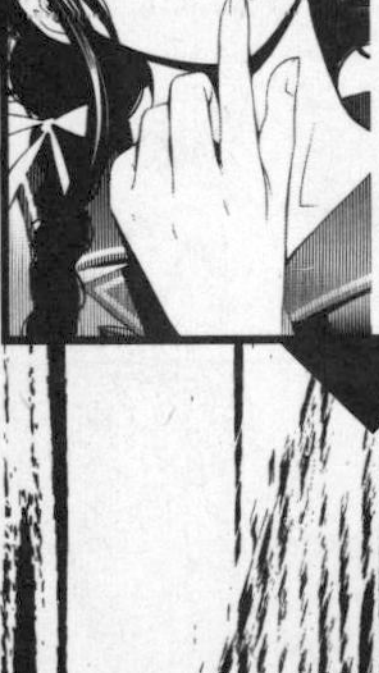

The infallible class president in Koyomi's class who was once bewitched by a "cat." Dealing with problems at home.

Karen Araragi / Tsukihi Araragi

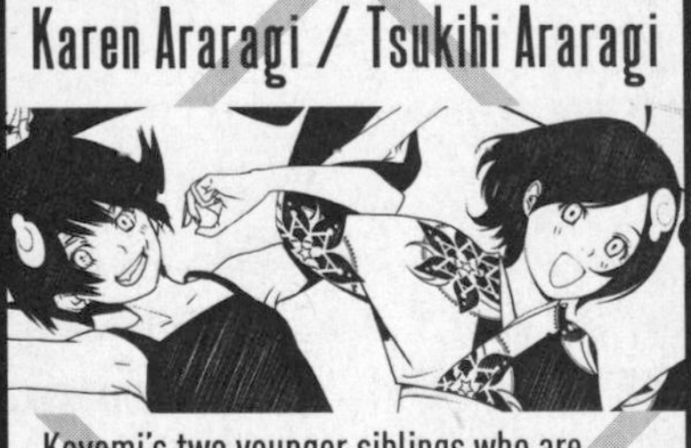

Koyomi's two younger siblings who are known as "Tsuganoki Second Middle School's Fire Sisters." Rouses Koyomi from bed each morning. Karen is the older sister. Tsukihi is the younger one.

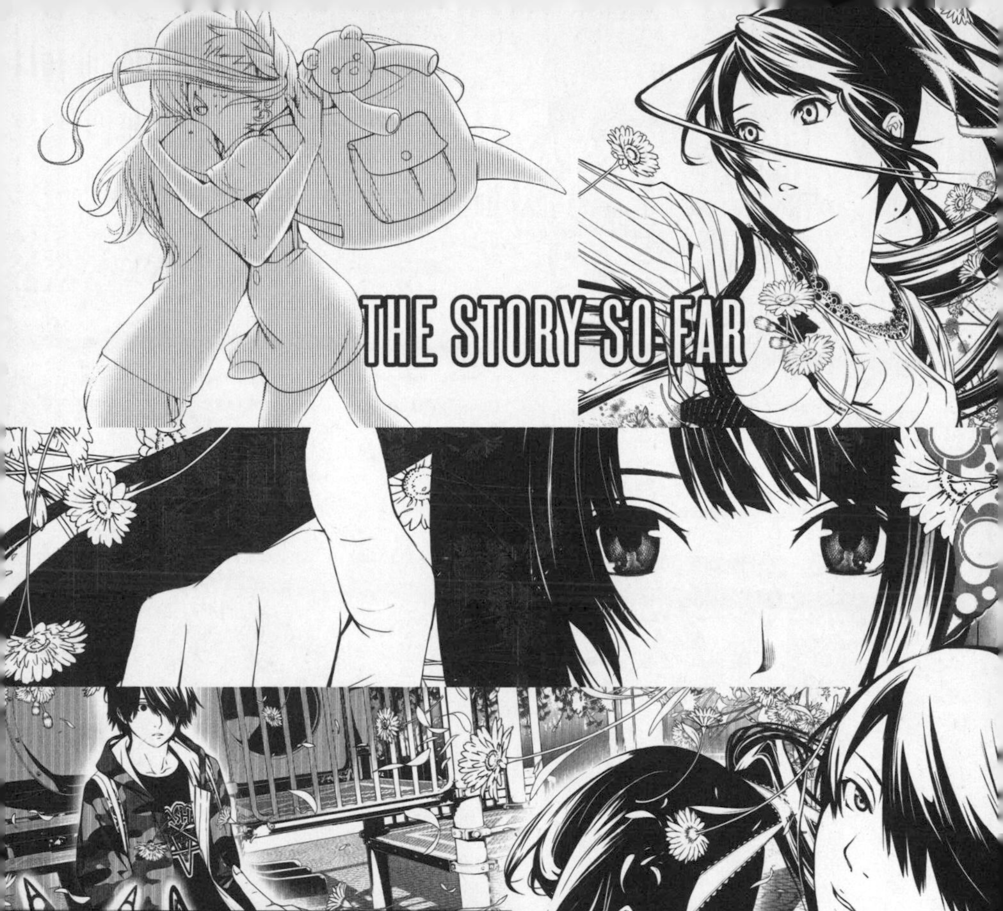
THE STORY SO FAR

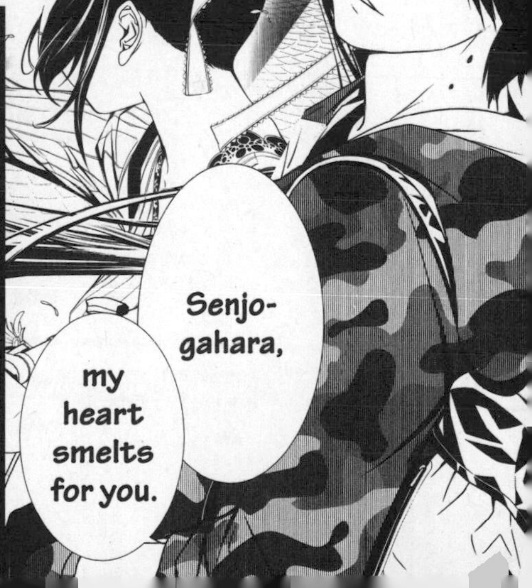
Senjo-gahara,
my heart smelts for you.

Mayoi Hachikuji is a "Lost Snail" who can never reach her mother's house. Koyomi Araragi enlists the help of Hitagi Senjogahara and aberrations expert Mèmè Oshino, and somehow manages to bring the Lost Snail back home. After that, Koyomi accepts Hitagi's declaration of love and they start going out. Now that the case has been solved and a new relationship has begun, things are finally starting to look up...

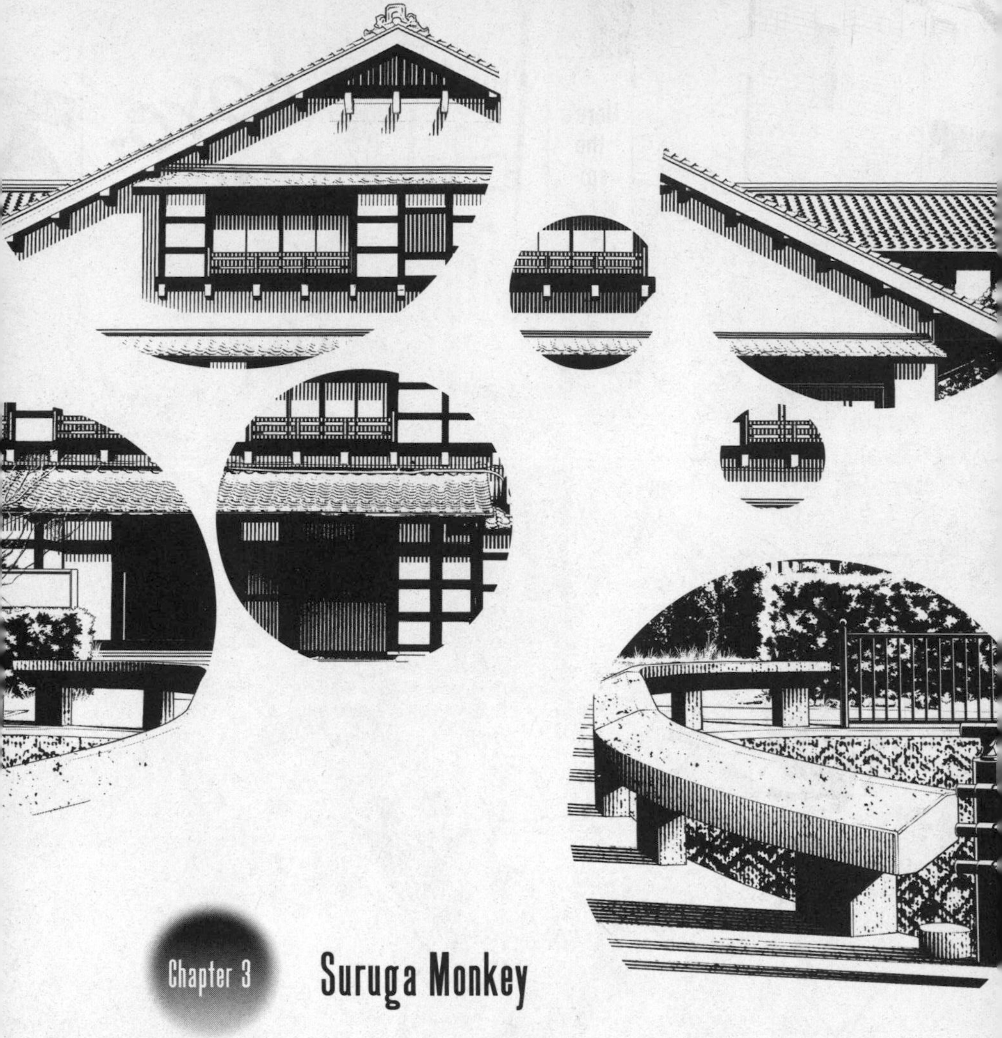

Chapter 3 Suruga Monkey

BOOK DESIGN VEIA

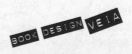

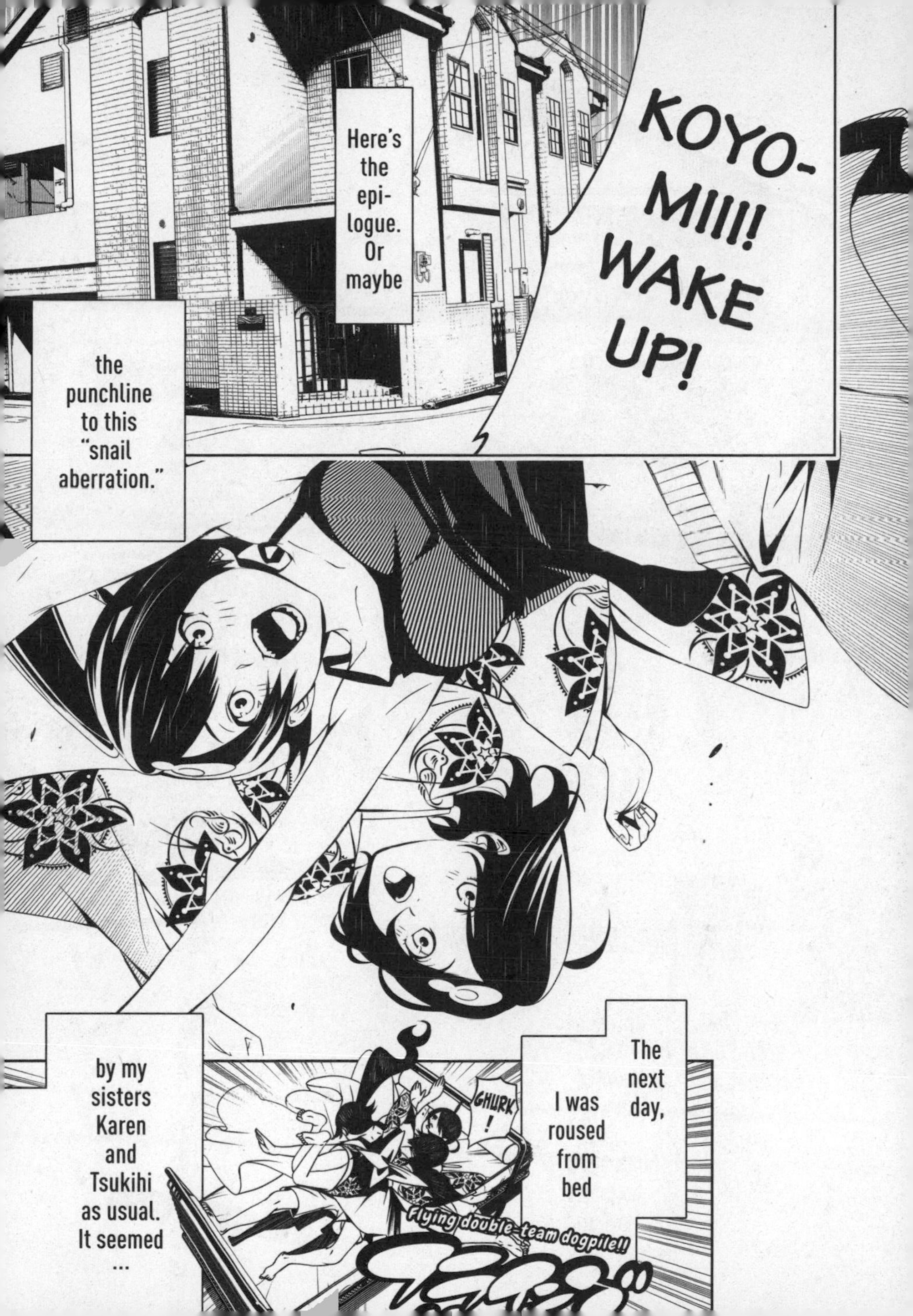
KOYO-MIII! WAKE UP!
Here's the epilogue. Or maybe
the punchline to this "snail aberration."
The next day, I was roused from bed
GHURK!
Flying double-team dogpile!!
by my sisters Karen and Tsukihi as usual. It seemed ...

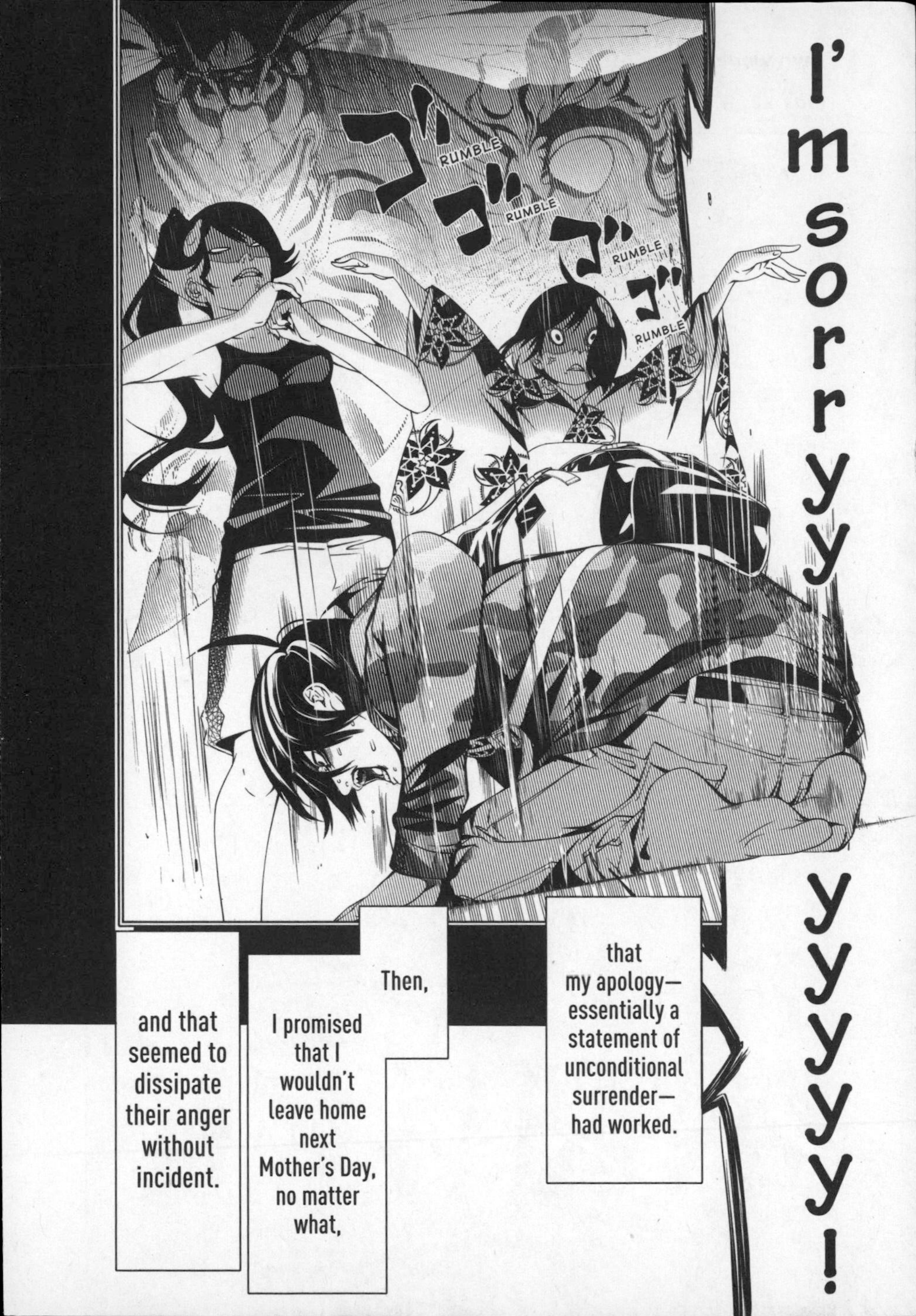
I'm sorryyyyyyyy!
RUMBLE
RUMBLE
RUMBLE
RUMBLE
that my apology—essentially a statement of unconditional surrender—had worked.
Then,
I promised that I wouldn't leave home next Mother's Day, no matter what,
and that seemed to dissipate their anger without incident.

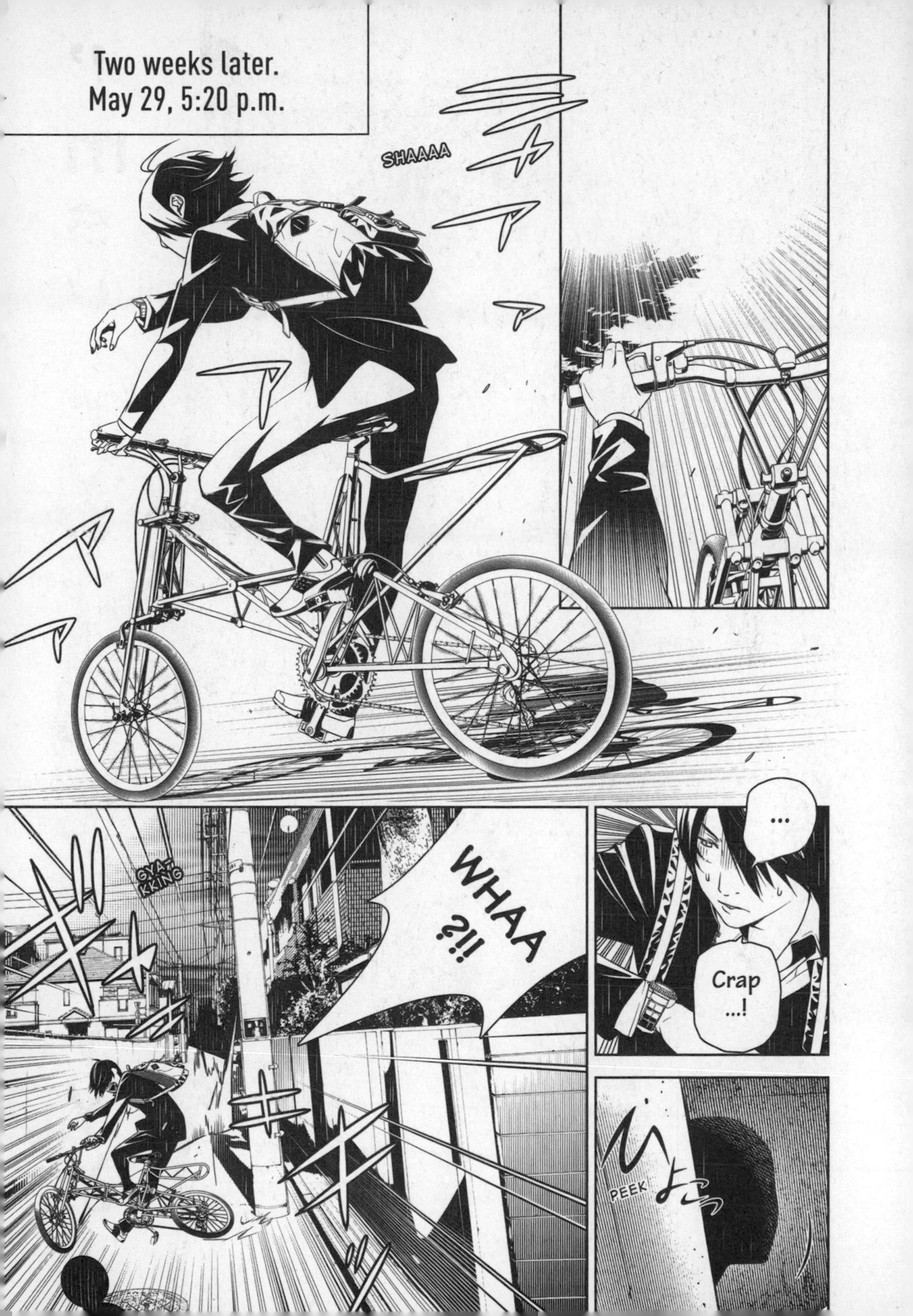
Two weeks later.
May 29, 5:20 p.m.
SHAAAA
...
Crap ...!
PEEK
WHAA ?!!
GYA-KKING

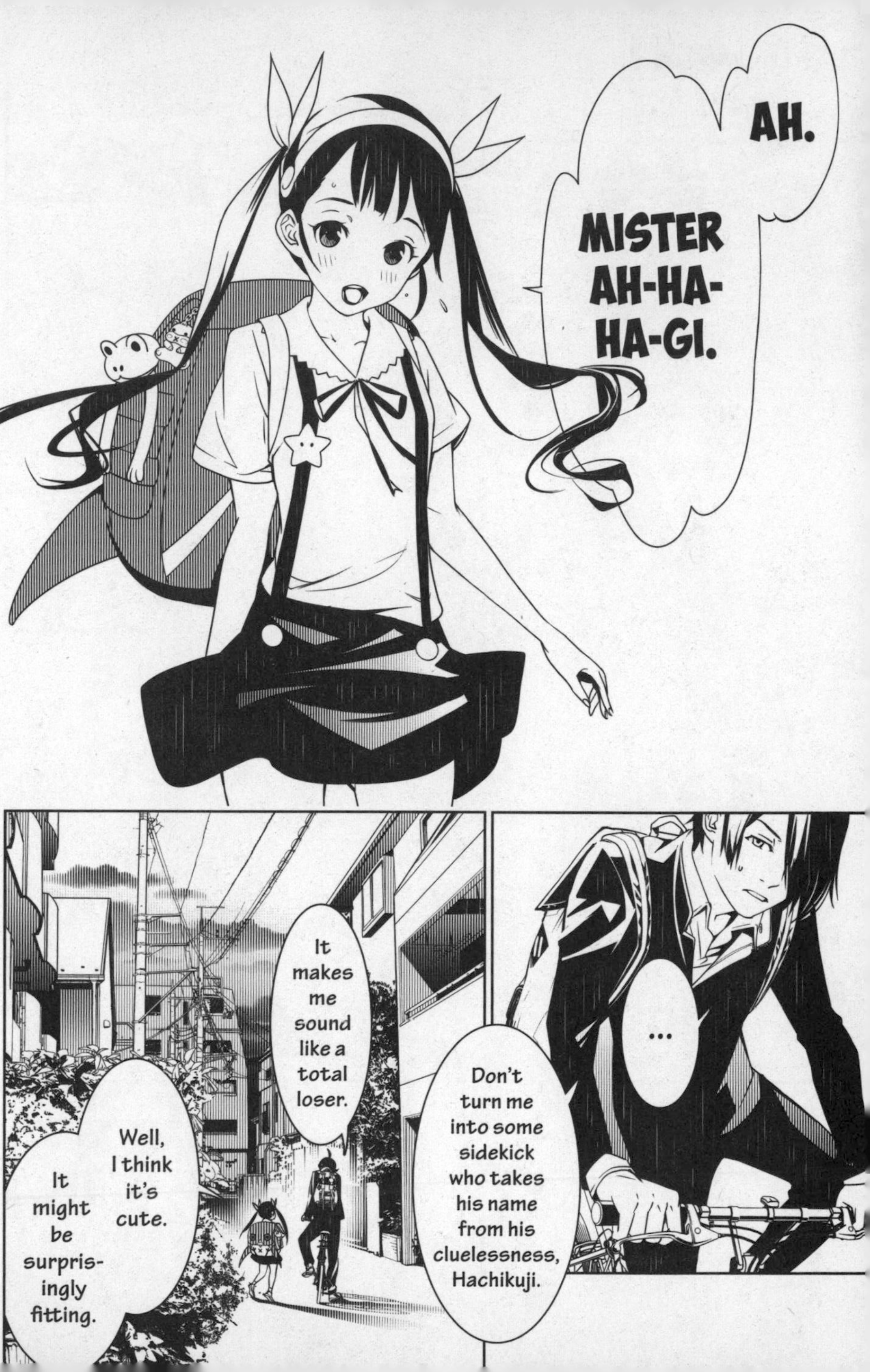
AH.
MISTER AH-HA-HA-GI.
...
Don't turn me into some sidekick who takes his name from his cluelessness, Hachikuji.
It makes me sound like a total loser.
Well, I think it's cute.
It might be surprisingly fitting.

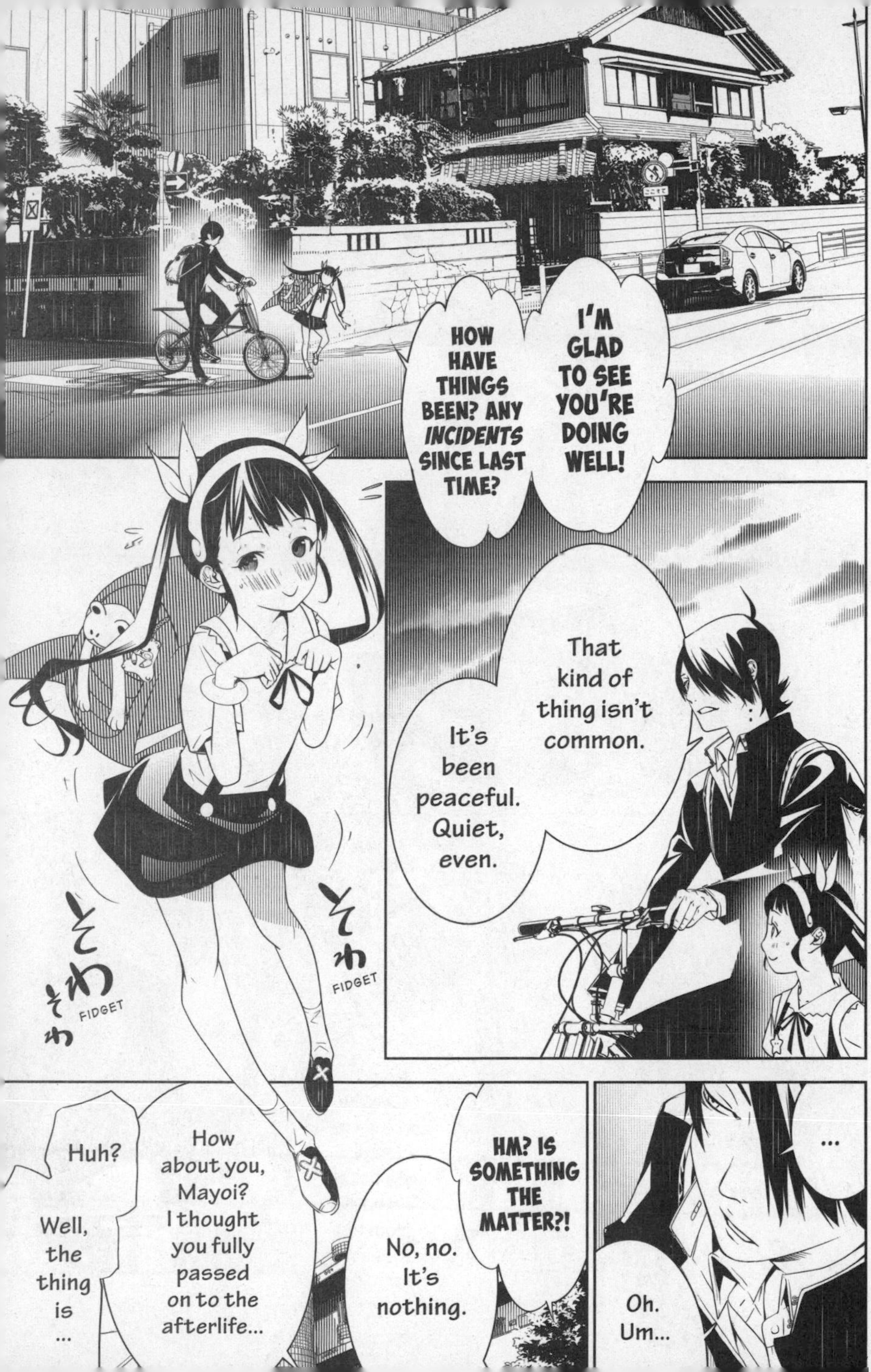
I'M GLAD TO SEE YOU'RE DOING WELL!
HOW HAVE THINGS BEEN? ANY *INCIDENTS* SINCE LAST TIME?
That kind of thing isn't common.
It's been peaceful. Quiet, even.
そわ
FIDGET
そわそわ
FIDGET
...
Oh. Um...
HM? IS SOMETHING THE MATTER?!
No, no. It's nothing.
How about you, Mayoi? I thought you fully passed on to the afterlife...
Huh?
Well, the thing is ...

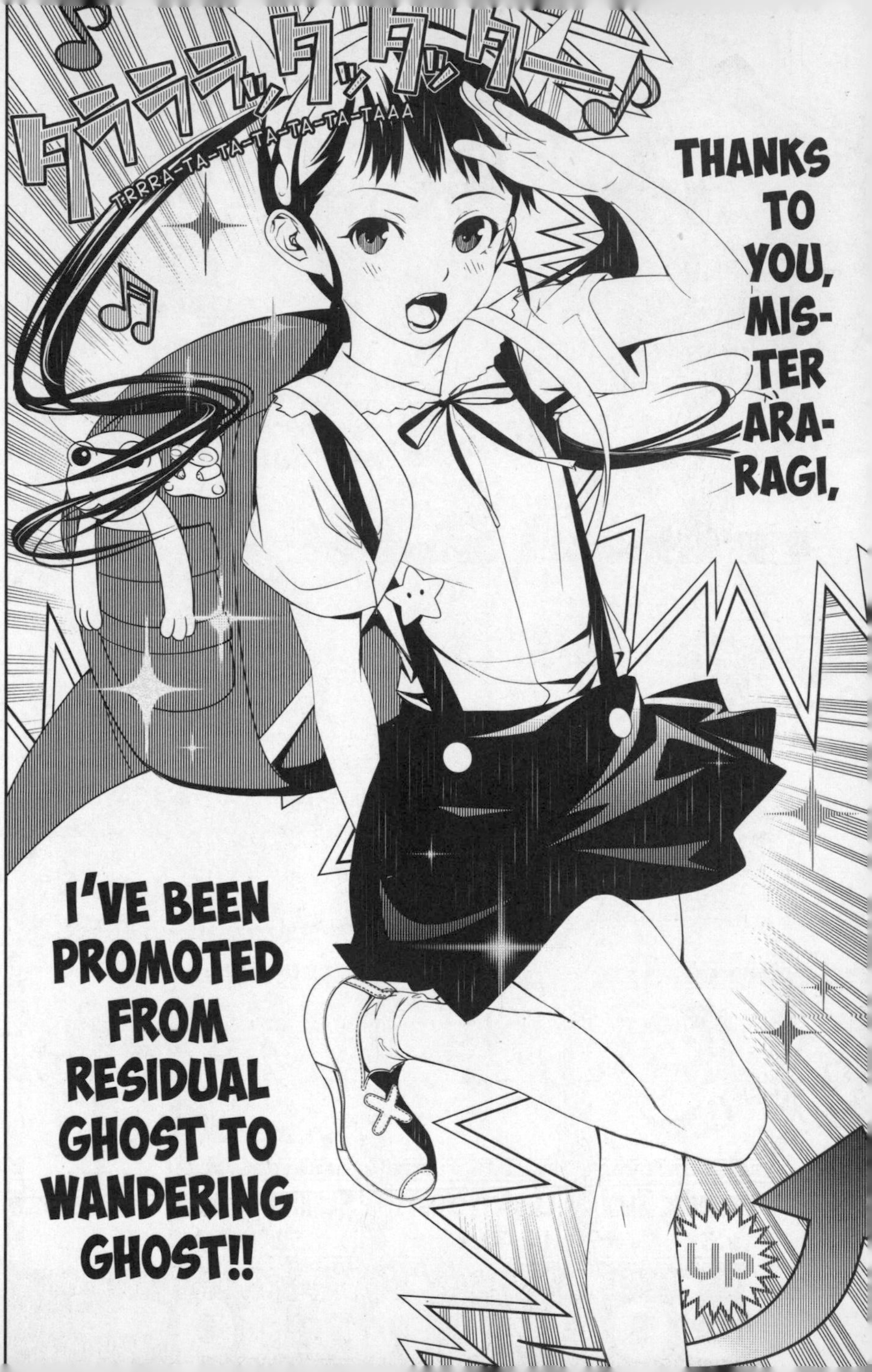
タラララッ、タッ、タッ、ター
TRRRA-TA-TA-TA-TA-TA-TAAA
THANKS TO YOU, MISTER ARARAGI,
I'VE BEEN PROMOTED FROM RESIDUAL GHOST TO WANDERING GHOST!!
Up

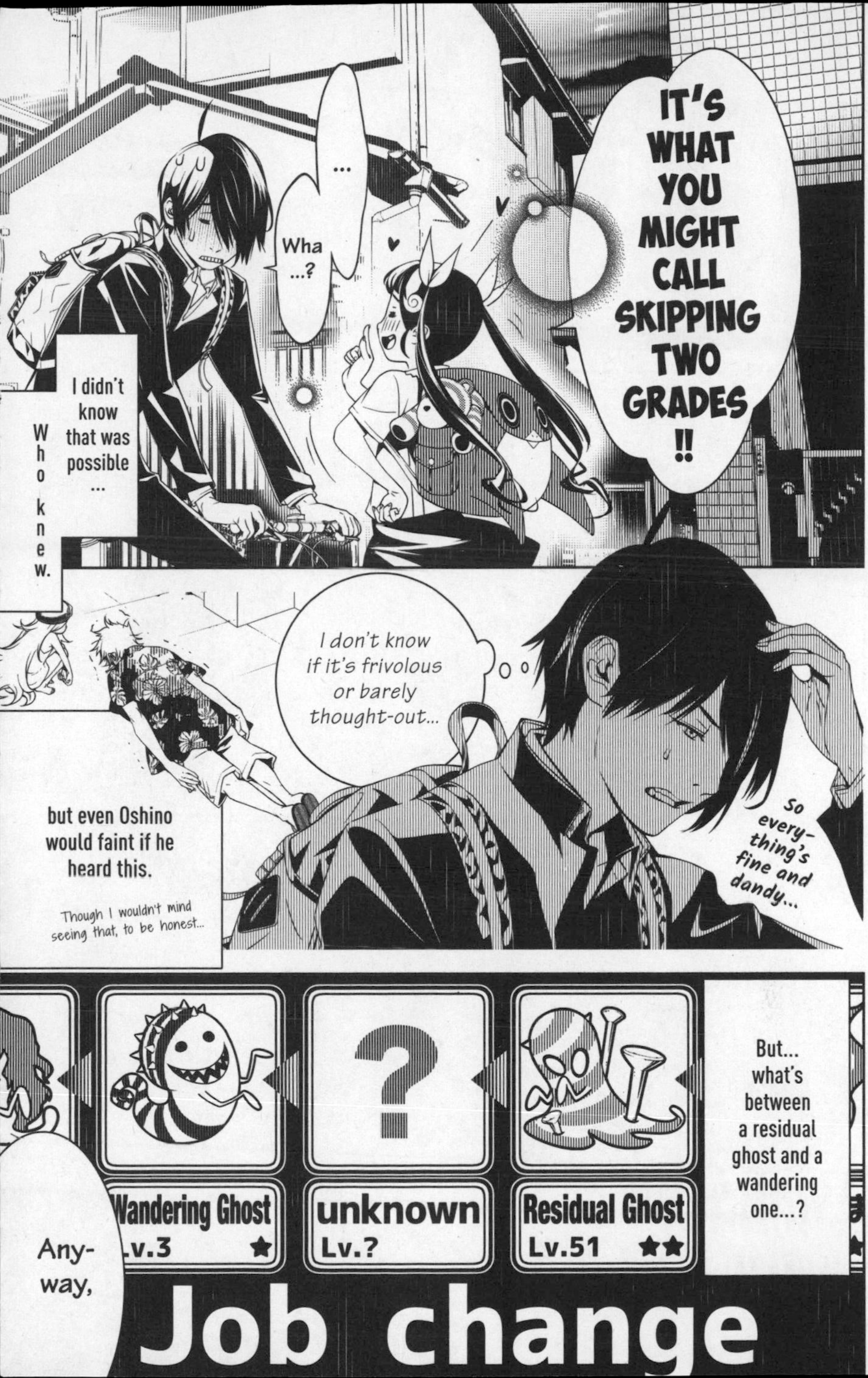
IT'S WHAT YOU MIGHT CALL SKIPPING TWO GRADES!!
...
Wha...?
I didn't know that was possible...
Who knew.
I don't know if it's frivolous or barely thought-out...
So everything's fine and dandy...
but even Oshino would faint if he heard this.
Though I wouldn't mind seeing that, to be honest...
But... what's between a residual ghost and a wandering one...?
Residual Ghost
Lv.51
unknown
Lv.?
Wandering Ghost
Lv.3
Anyway,
Job change

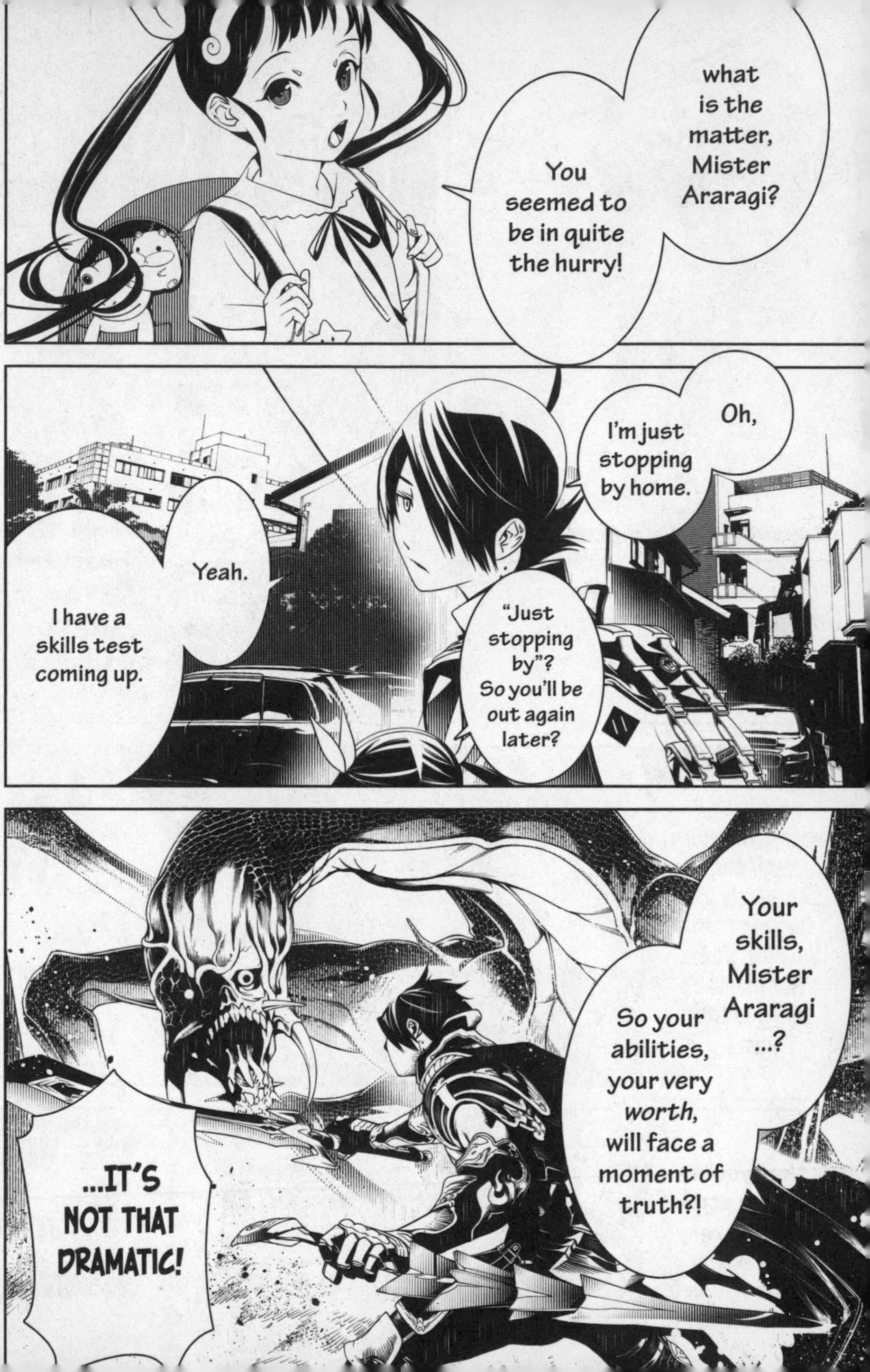
You seemed to be in quite the hurry!
what is the matter, Mister Araragi?
Oh,
I'm just stopping by home.
"Just stopping by"? So you'll be out again later?
Yeah.
I have a skills test coming up.
Your skills, Mister Araragi ...?
So your abilities, your very *worth*, will face a moment of truth?!
...IT'S NOT THAT DRAMATIC!

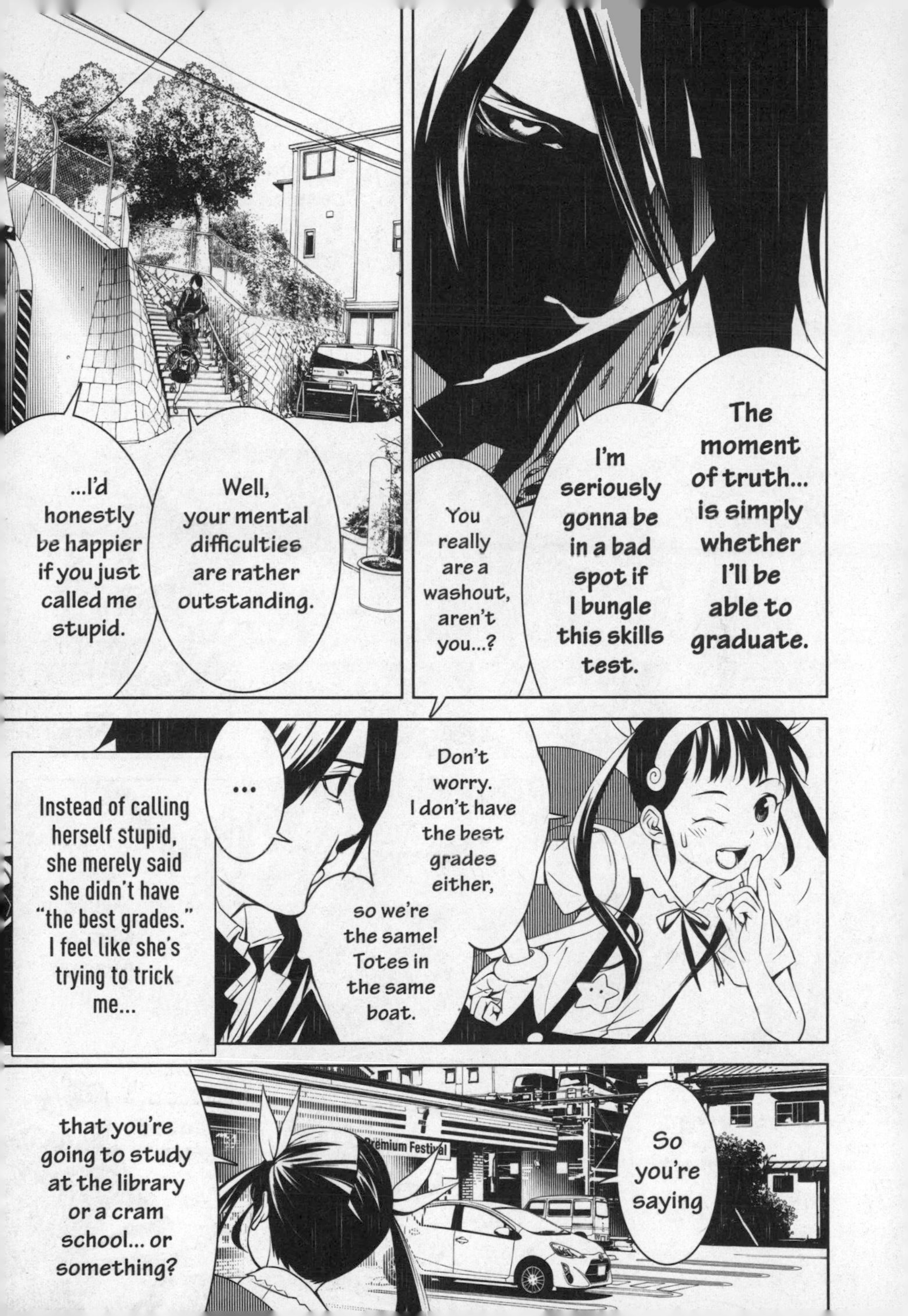
The moment of truth... is simply whether I'll be able to graduate.
I'm seriously gonna be in a bad spot if I bungle this skills test.
You really are a washout, aren't you...?
Well, your mental difficulties are rather outstanding.
...I'd honestly be happier if you just called me stupid.
Don't worry. I don't have the best grades either,
so we're the same! Totes in the same boat.
...
Instead of calling herself stupid, she merely said she didn't have "the best grades." I feel like she's trying to trick me...
So you're saying
Premium Festival
that you're going to study at the library or a cram school... or something?

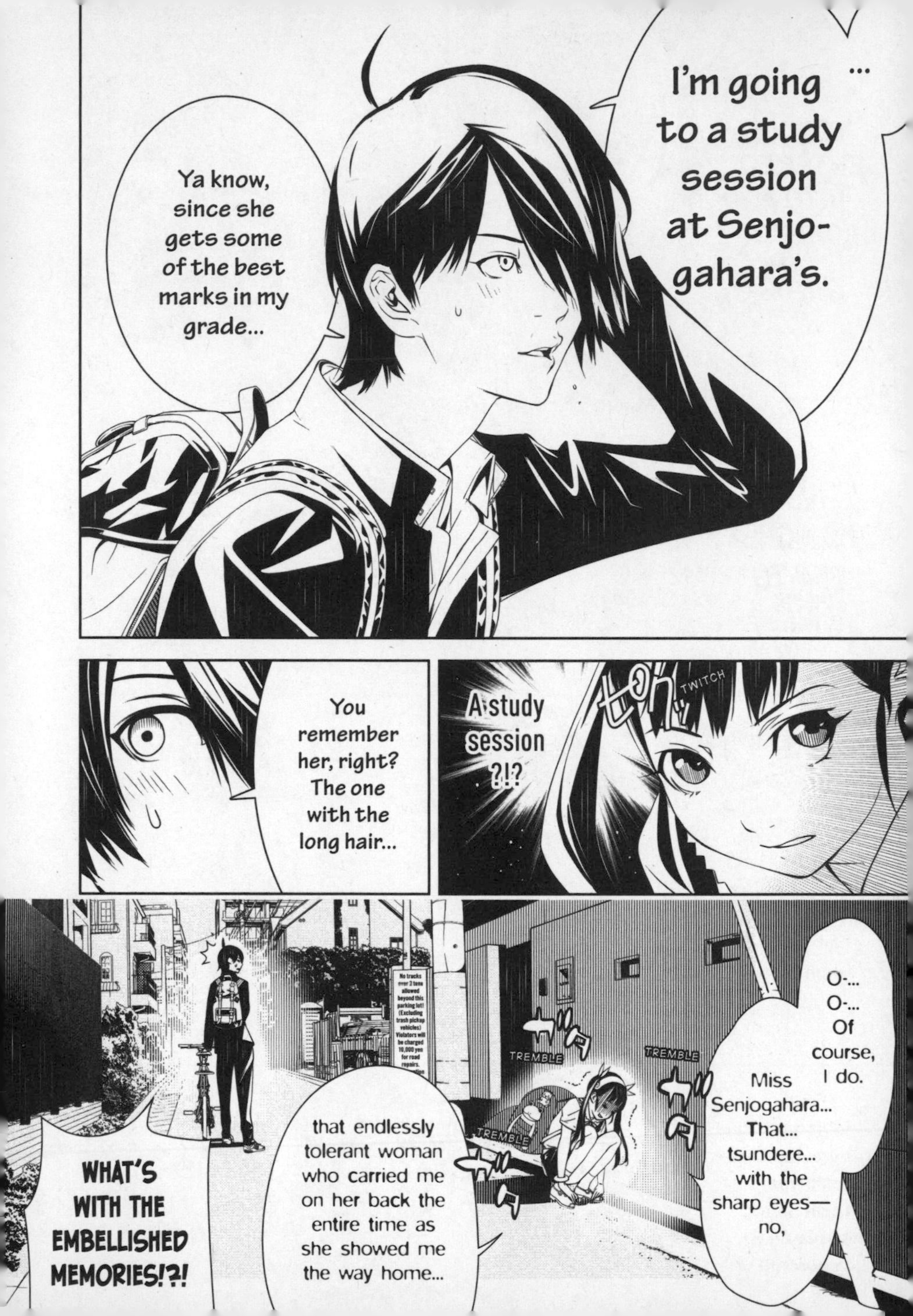
...I'm going to a study session at Senjogahara's.
Ya know, since she gets some of the best marks in my grade...
TWITCH
A study session ?!?
You remember her, right? The one with the long hair...
O-... O-... Of course, I do.
Miss Senjogahara... That... tsundere... with the sharp eyes—no,
TREMBLE
TREMBLE
TREMBLE
that endlessly tolerant woman who carried me on her back the entire time as she showed me the way home...
No trucks over 2 tons allowed beyond this parking lot! (Excluding trash pickup vehicles) Violators will be charged 10,000 yen for road repairs.
WHAT'S WITH THE EMBELLISHED MEMORIES!?!

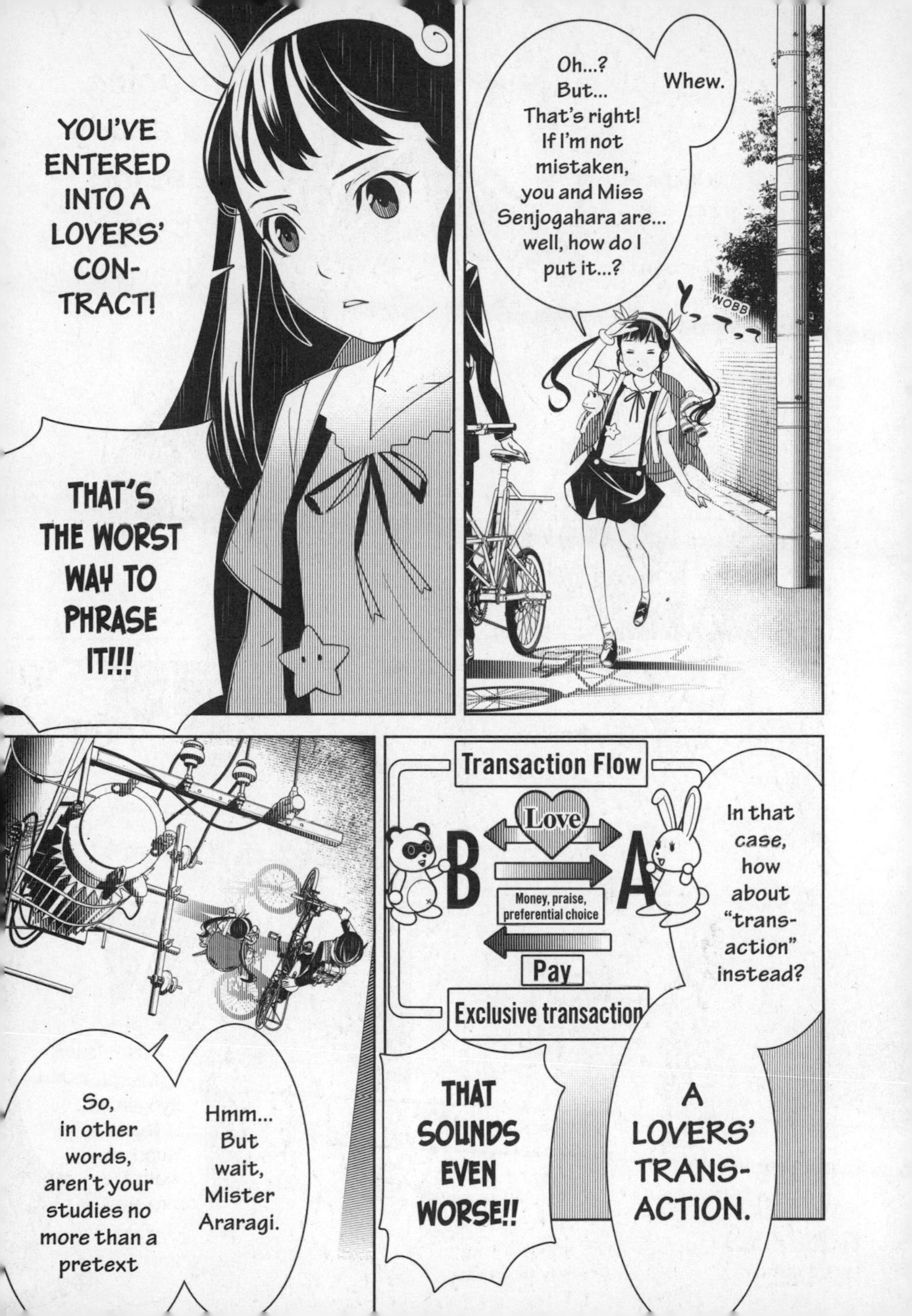
Whew.
Oh...? But... That's right! If I'm not mistaken, you and Miss Senjogahara are... well, how do I put it...?
WOBB
YOU'VE ENTERED INTO A LOVERS' CON-TRACT!
THAT'S THE WORST WAY TO PHRASE IT!!!
Transaction Flow
Love
B
A
Money, praise, preferential choice
Pay
Exclusive transaction
In that case, how about "trans-action" instead?
A LOVERS' TRANS-ACTION.
THAT SOUNDS EVEN WORSE!!
Hmm... But wait, Mister Araragi.
So, in other words, aren't your studies no more than a pretext

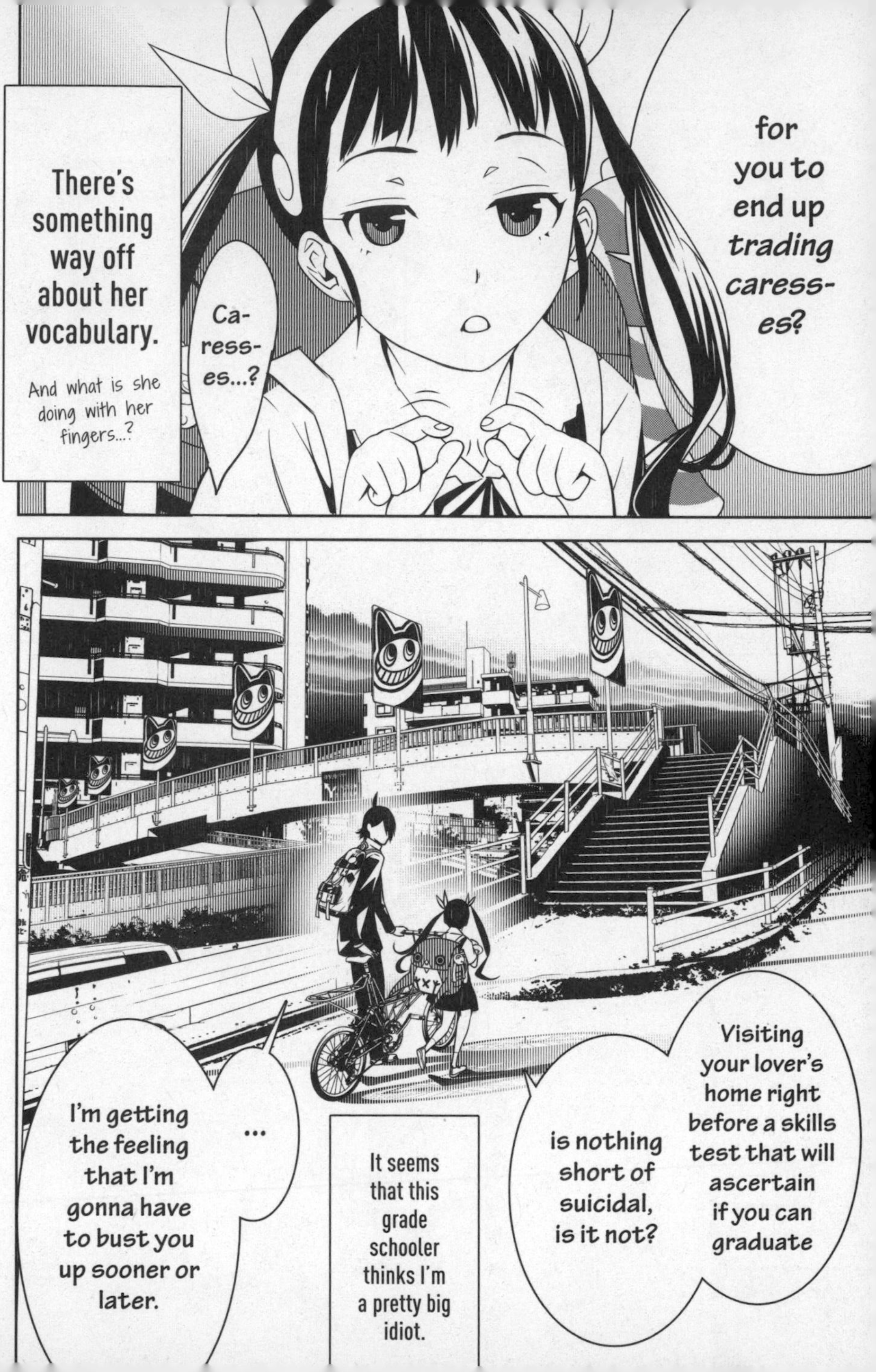
for you to end up trading caress-es?
Ca-ress-es...?
There's something way off about her vocabulary.
And what is she doing with her fingers...?
Visiting your lover's home right before a skills test that will ascertain if you can graduate
is nothing short of suicidal, is it not?
It seems that this grade schooler thinks I'm a pretty big idiot.
...
I'm getting the feeling that I'm gonna have to bust you up sooner or later.

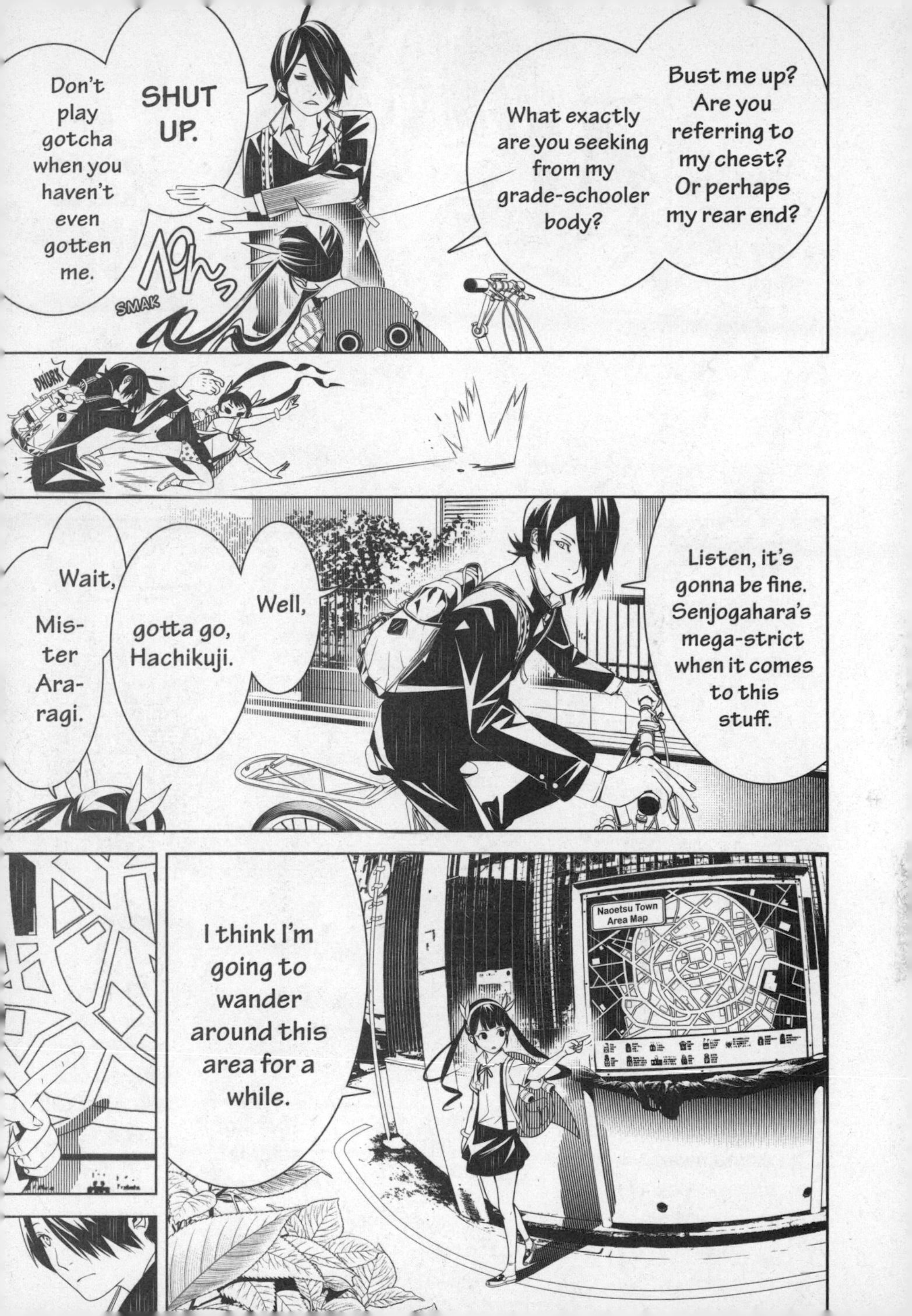
Bust me up? Are you referring to my chest? Or perhaps my rear end?
What exactly are you seeking from my grade-schooler body?
SHUT UP.
Don't play gotcha when you haven't even gotten me.
SMAK
DHURK
Listen, it's gonna be fine. Senjogahara's mega-strict when it comes to this stuff.
Well,
gotta go, Hachikuji.
Wait, Mister Araragi.
Naoetsu Town Area Map
I think I'm going to wander around this area for a while.

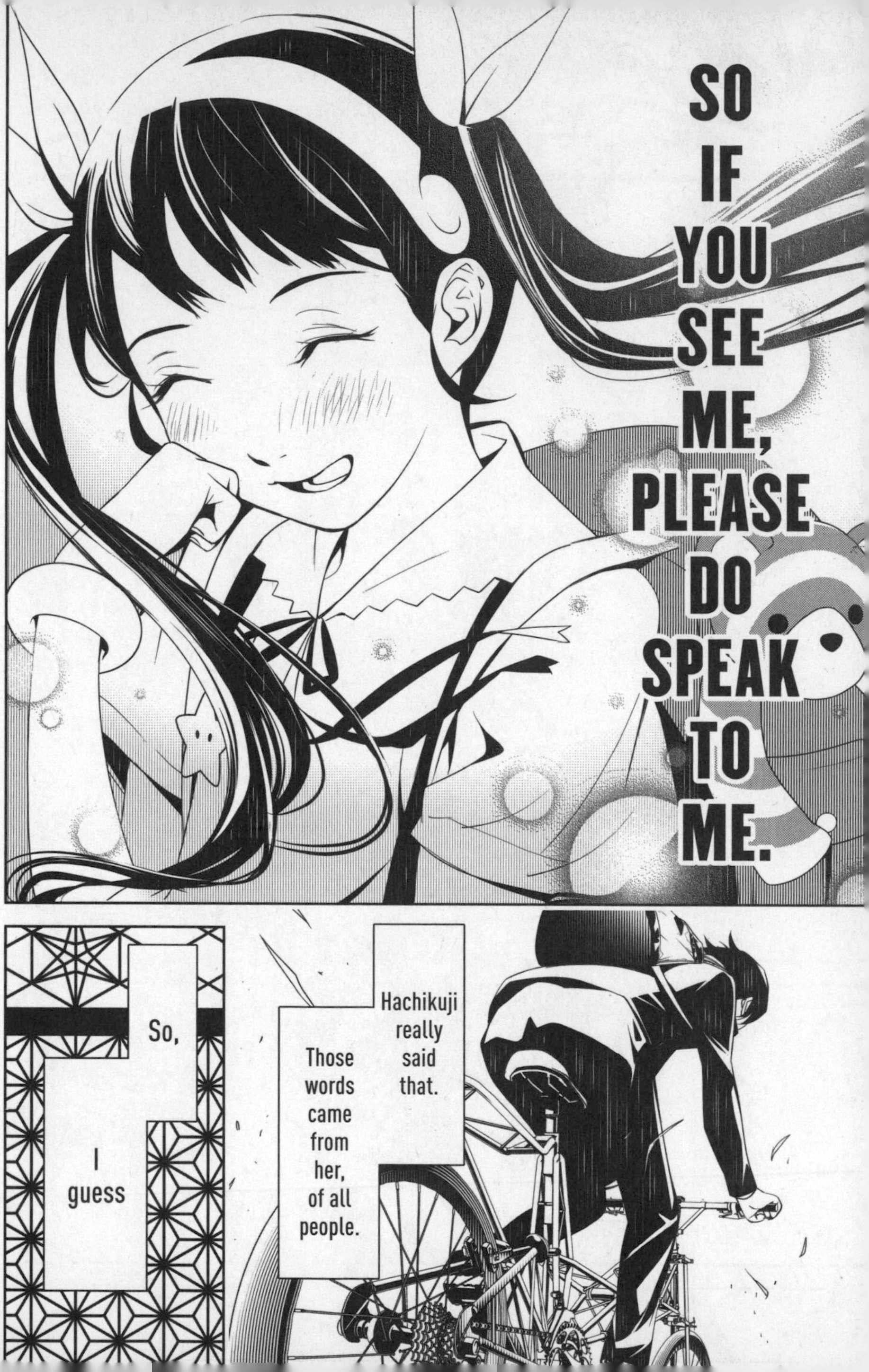
SO IF YOU SEE ME, PLEASE DO SPEAK TO ME.
Hachikuji really said that.
Those words came from her, of all people.
So, I guess

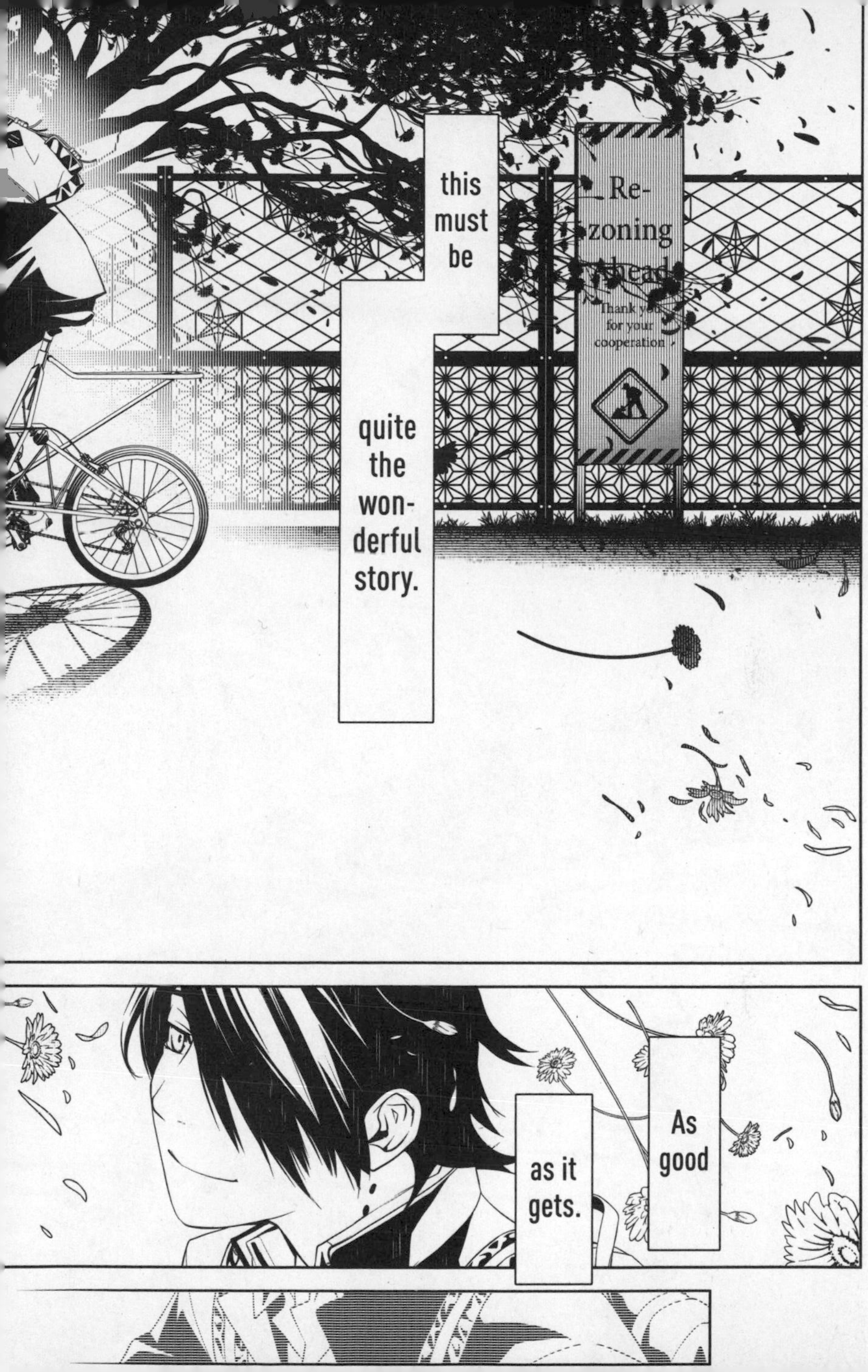
Re-zoning Ahead
Thank you for your cooperation
this must be quite the wonderful story.
As good as it gets.

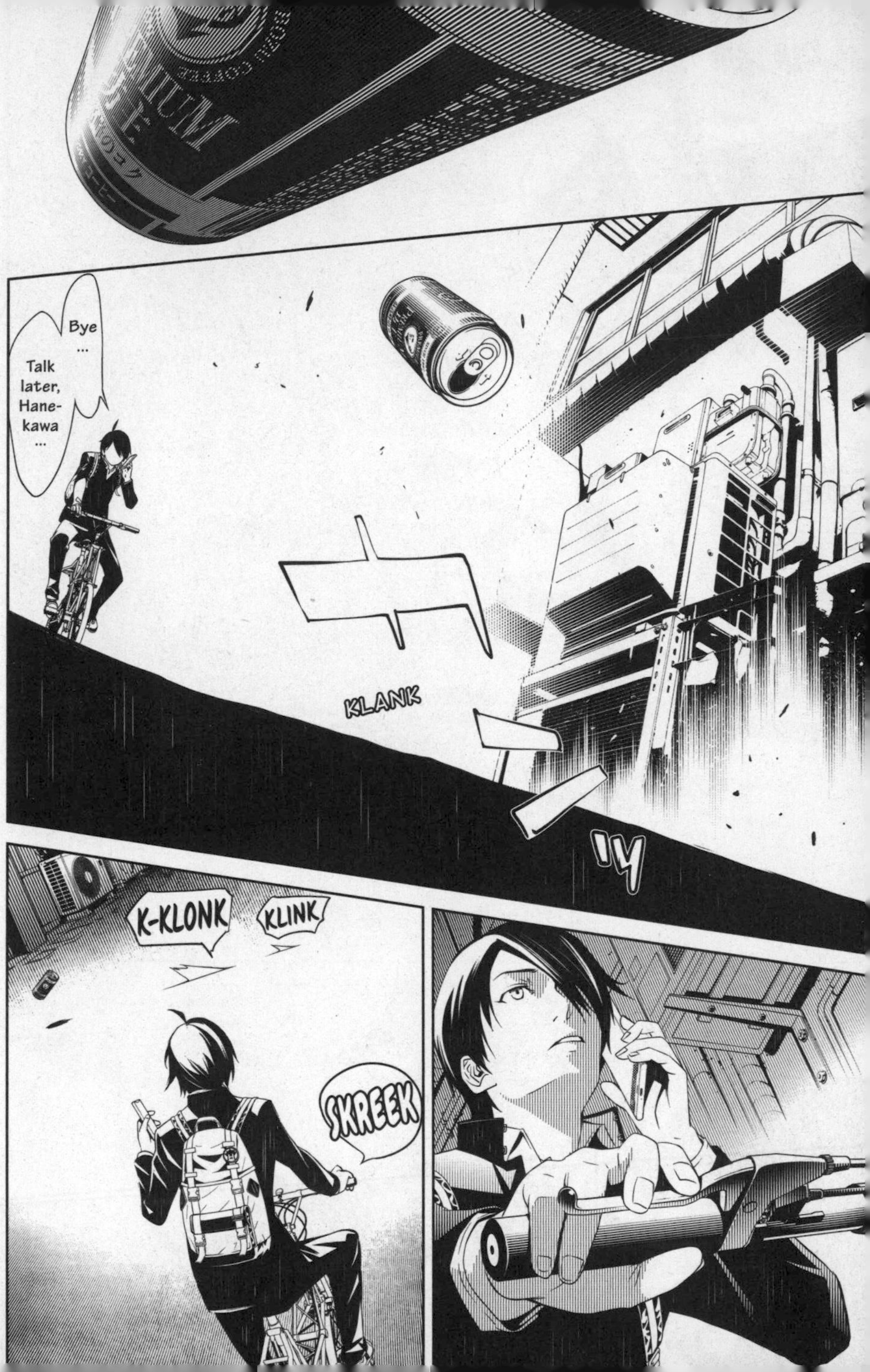
Bye ... Talk later, Hane-kawa ...
KLANK
KLINK
K-KLONK
SKREEK

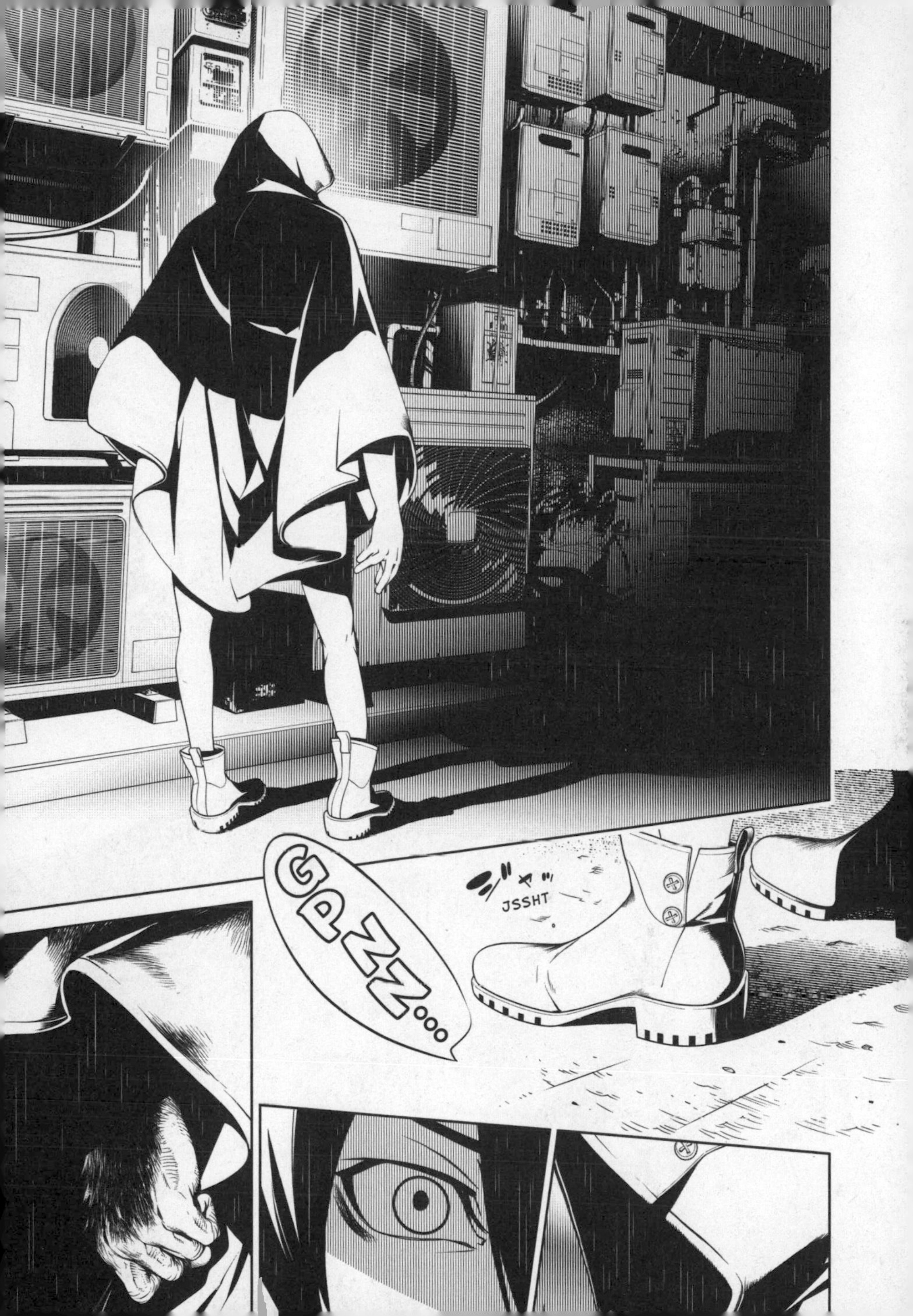
JSSHT
GPZZ...

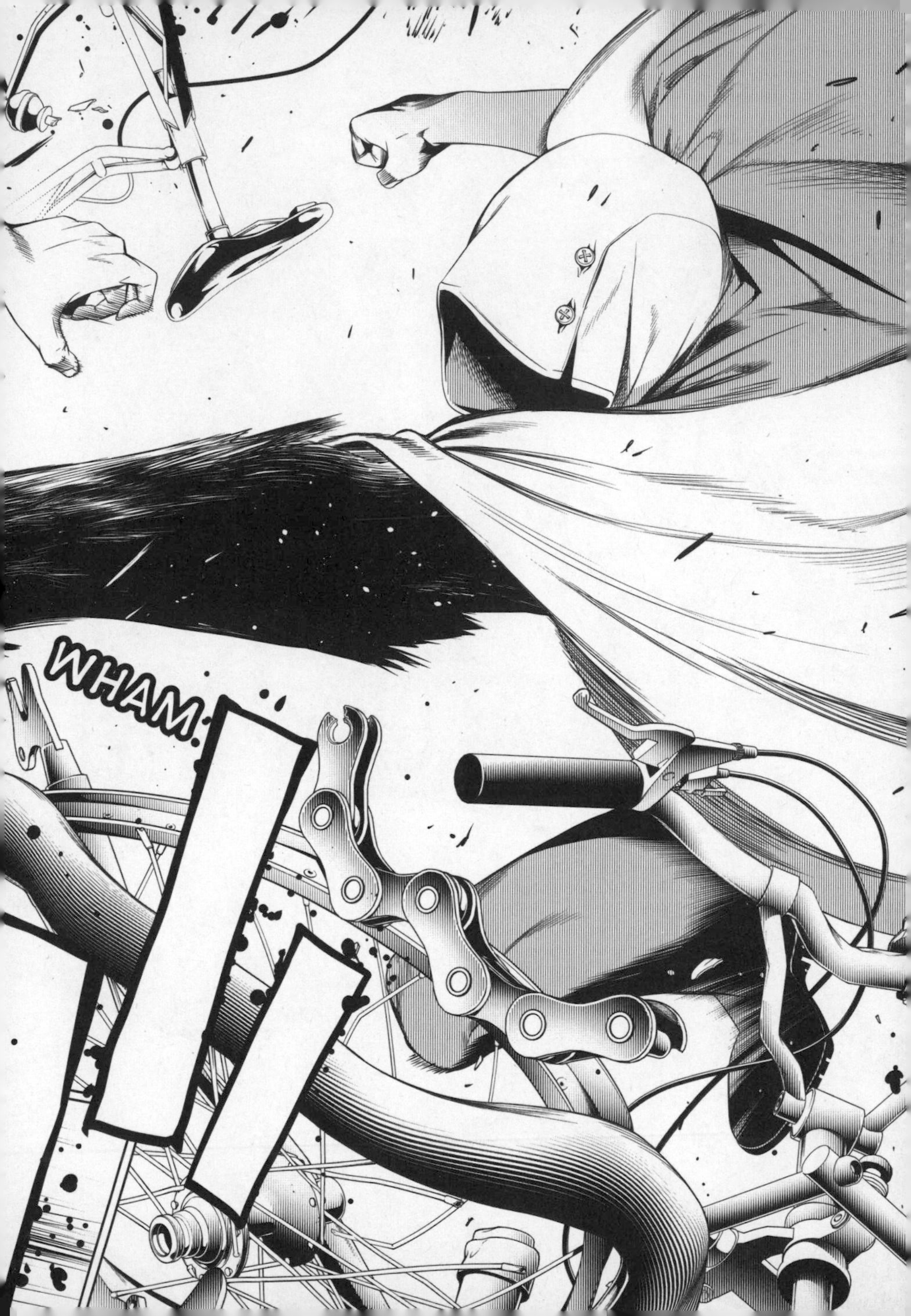
WHAM!!

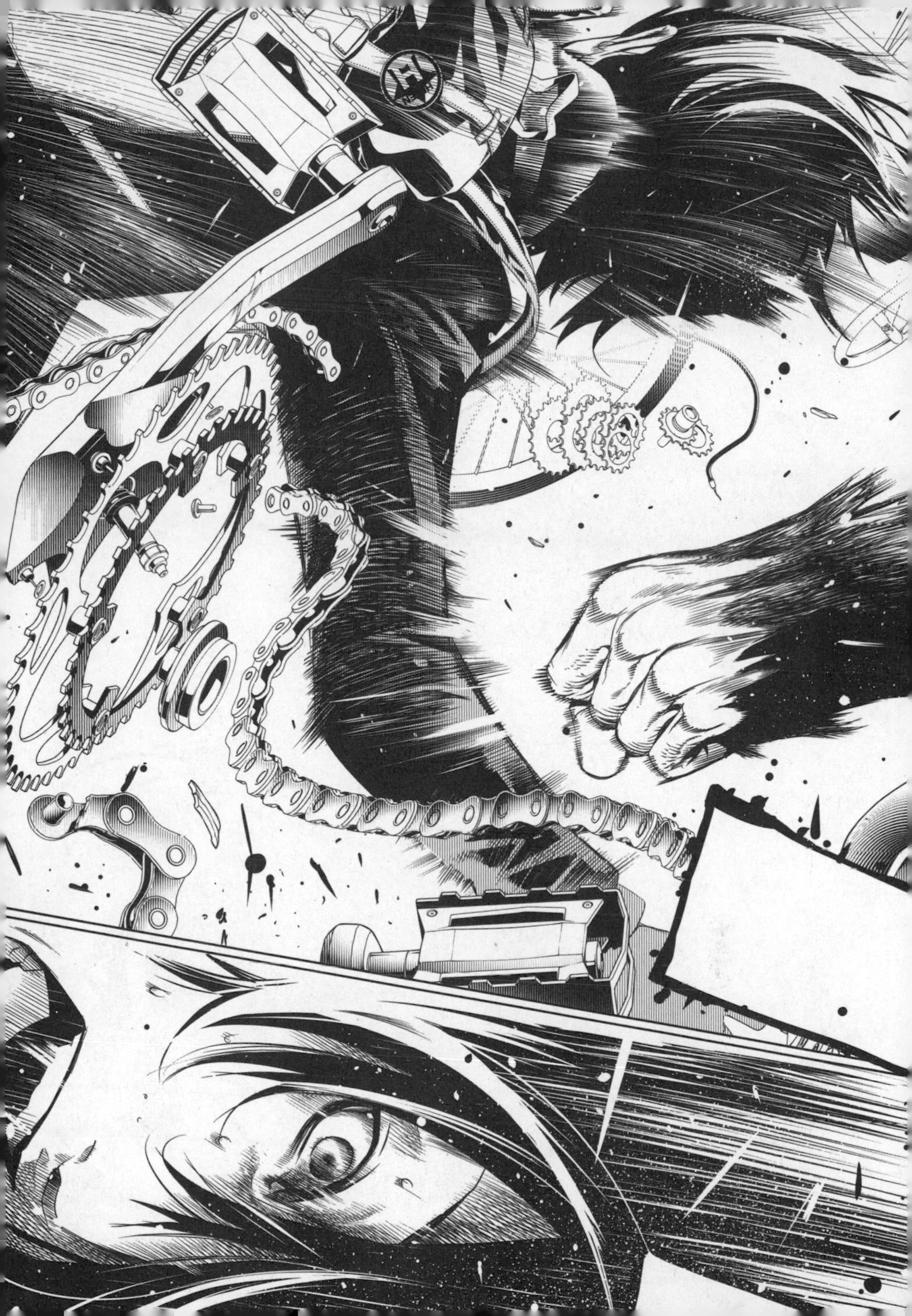

BAKEMONOGATARI

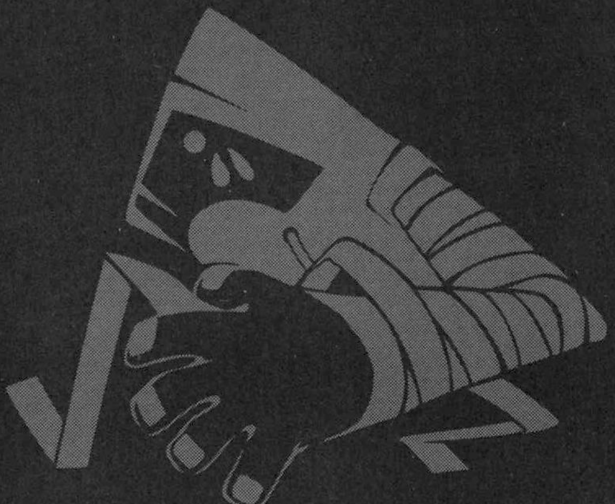

03: Suruga Monkey

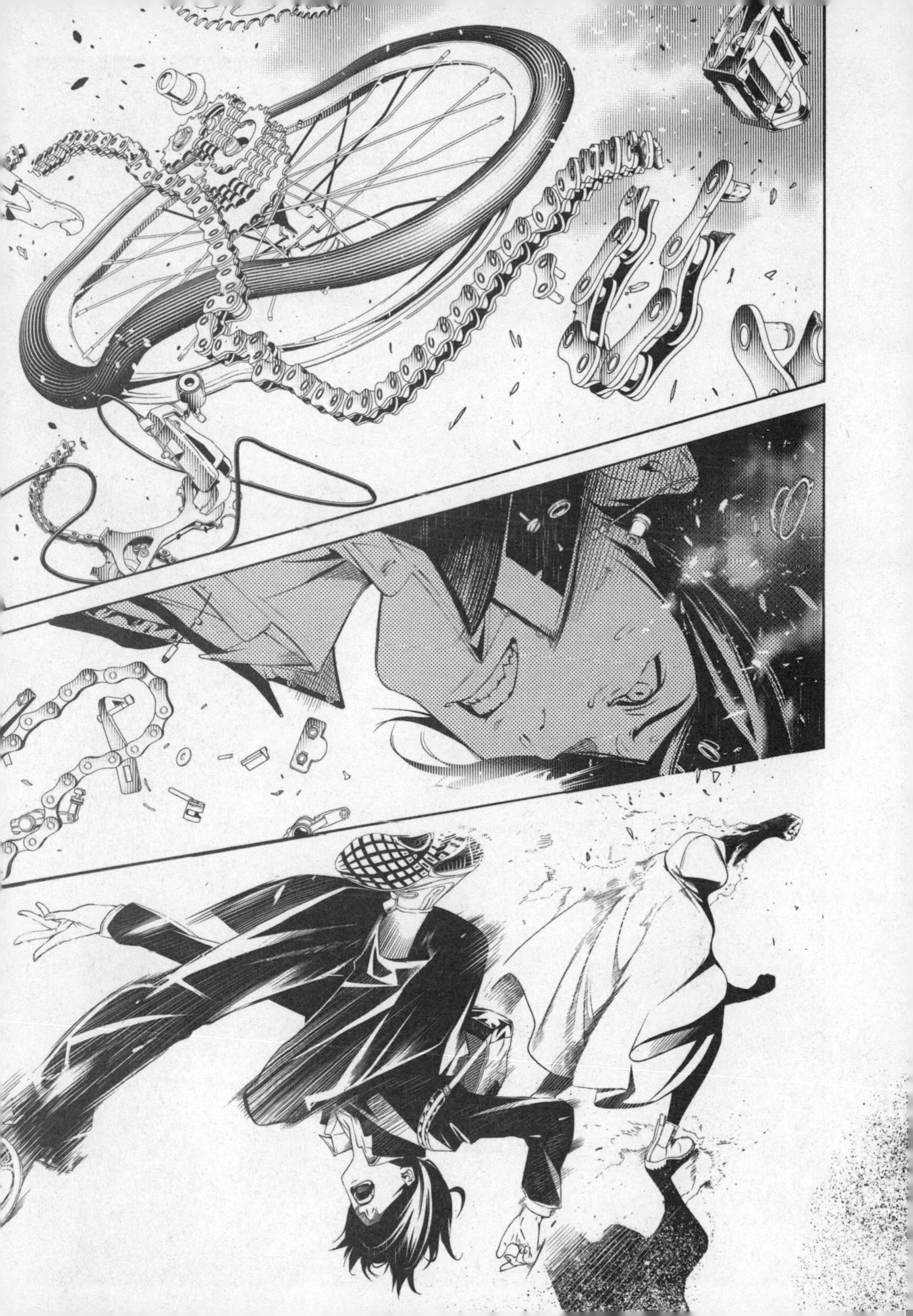

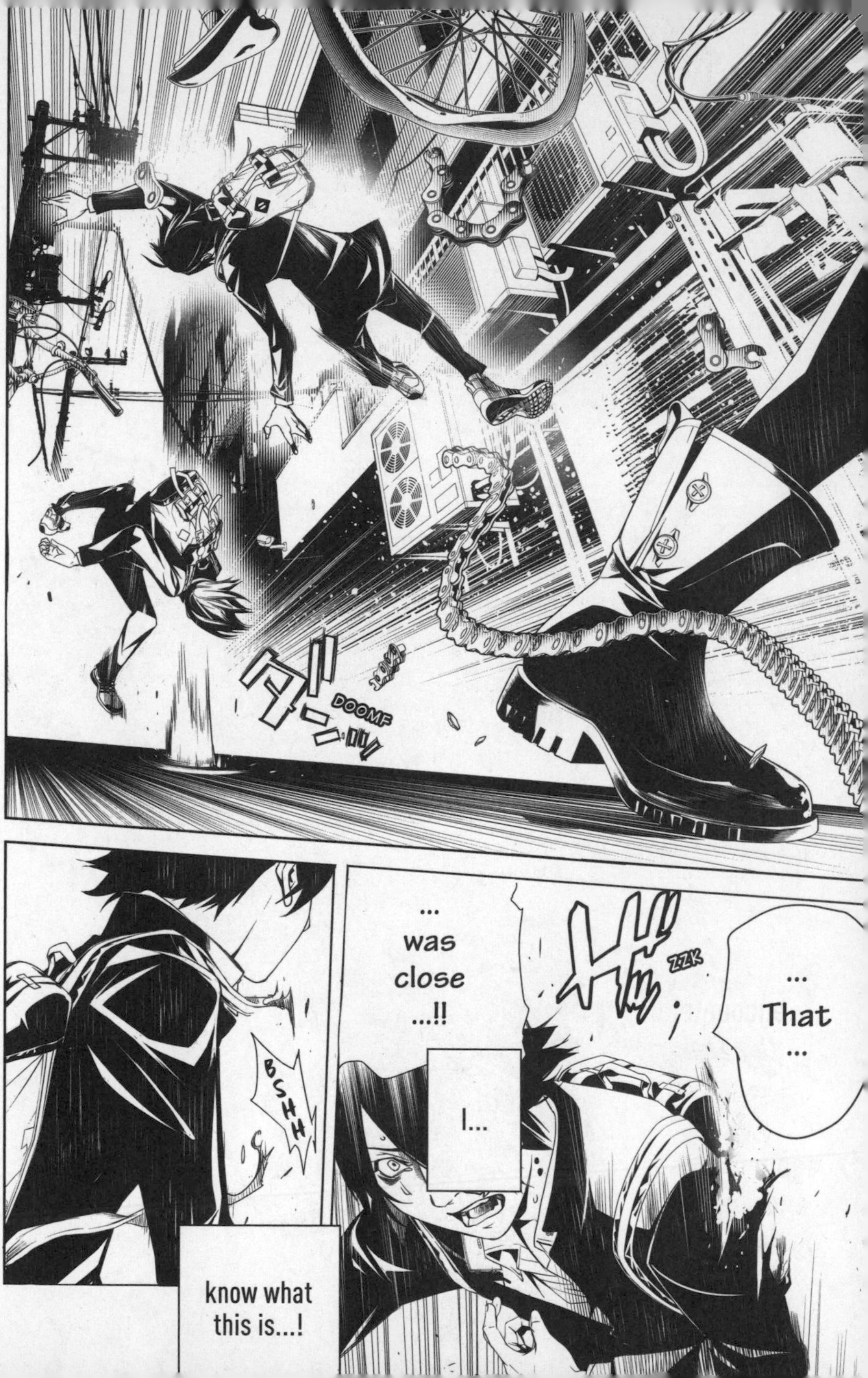
DOOMF
... That ...
ZZK
... was close ...!!
I...
BSHH
know what this is...!

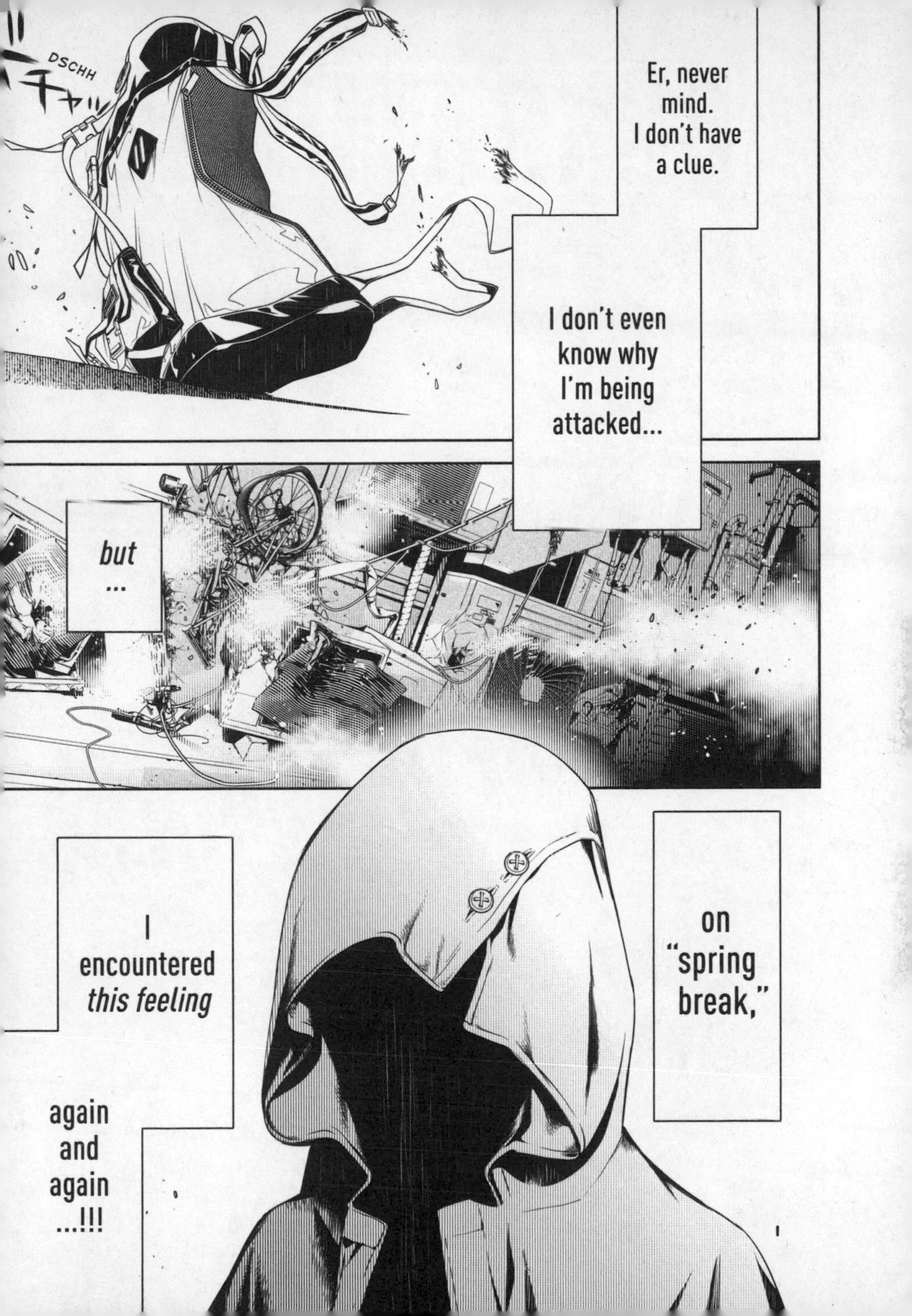
Er, never mind. I don't have a clue.
I don't even know why I'm being attacked...
DSCHH
but ...
on "spring break,"
I encountered *this feeling*
again and again ...!!!

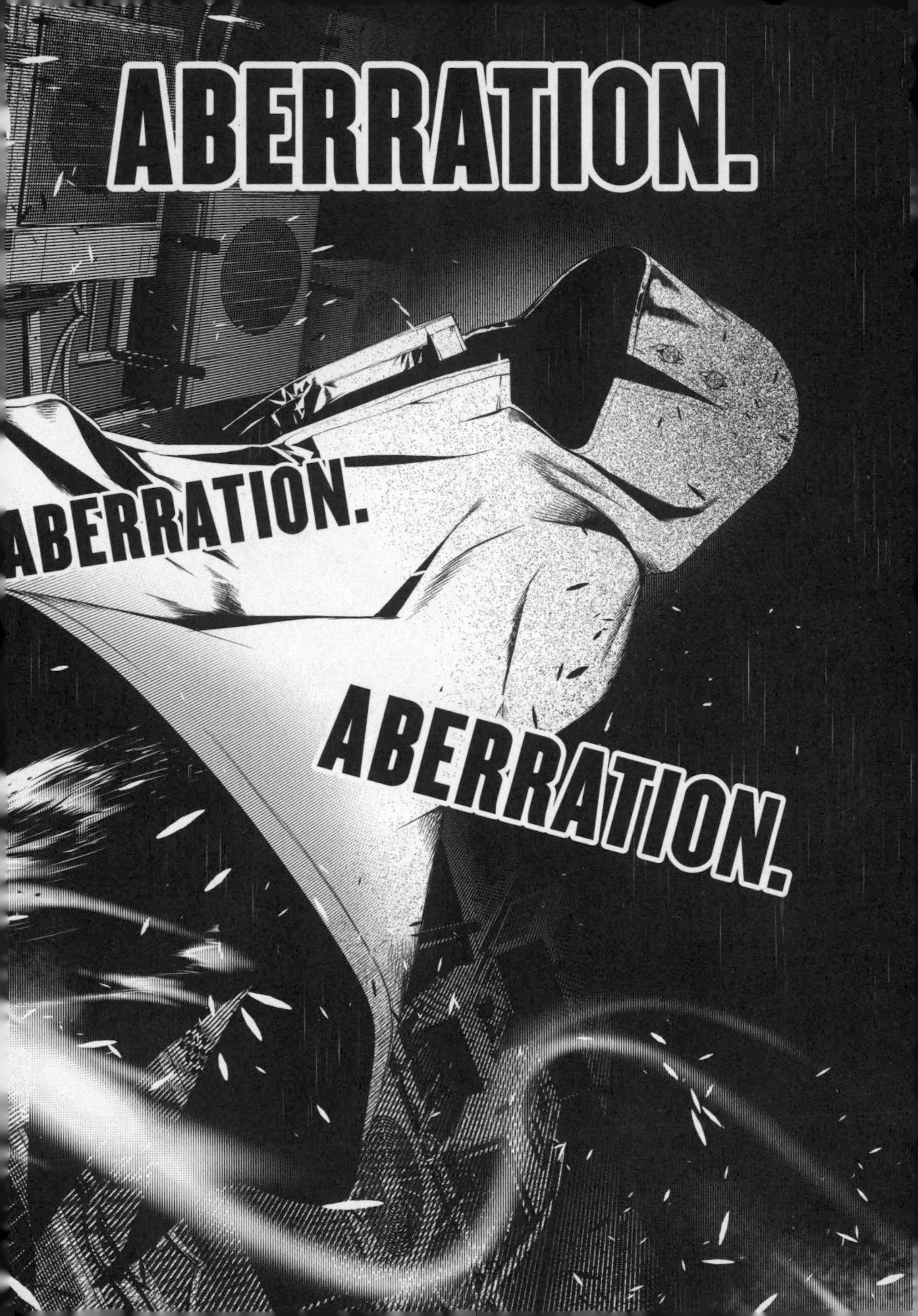
ABERRATION.
ABERRATION.
ABERRATION.

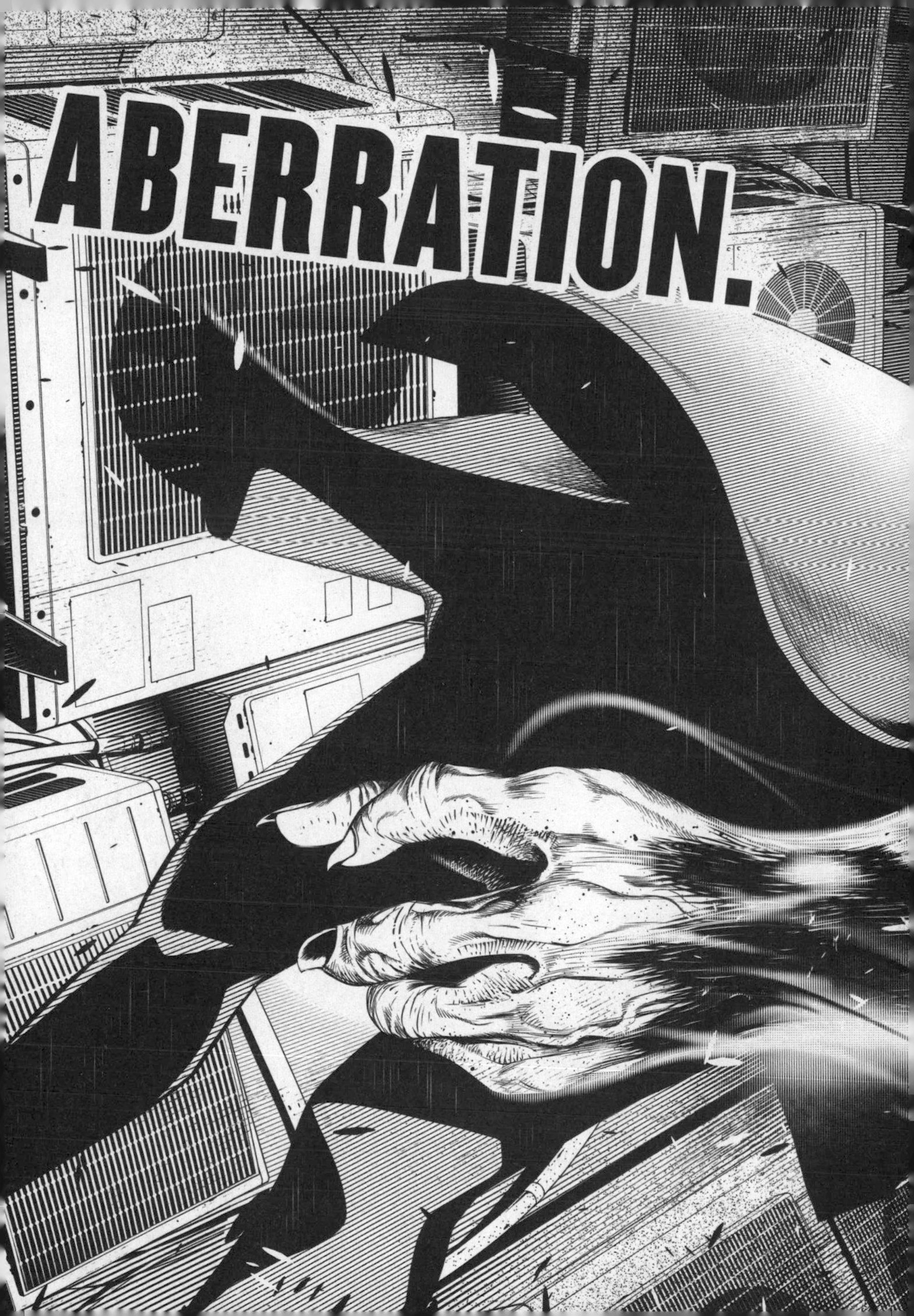
ABERRATION.

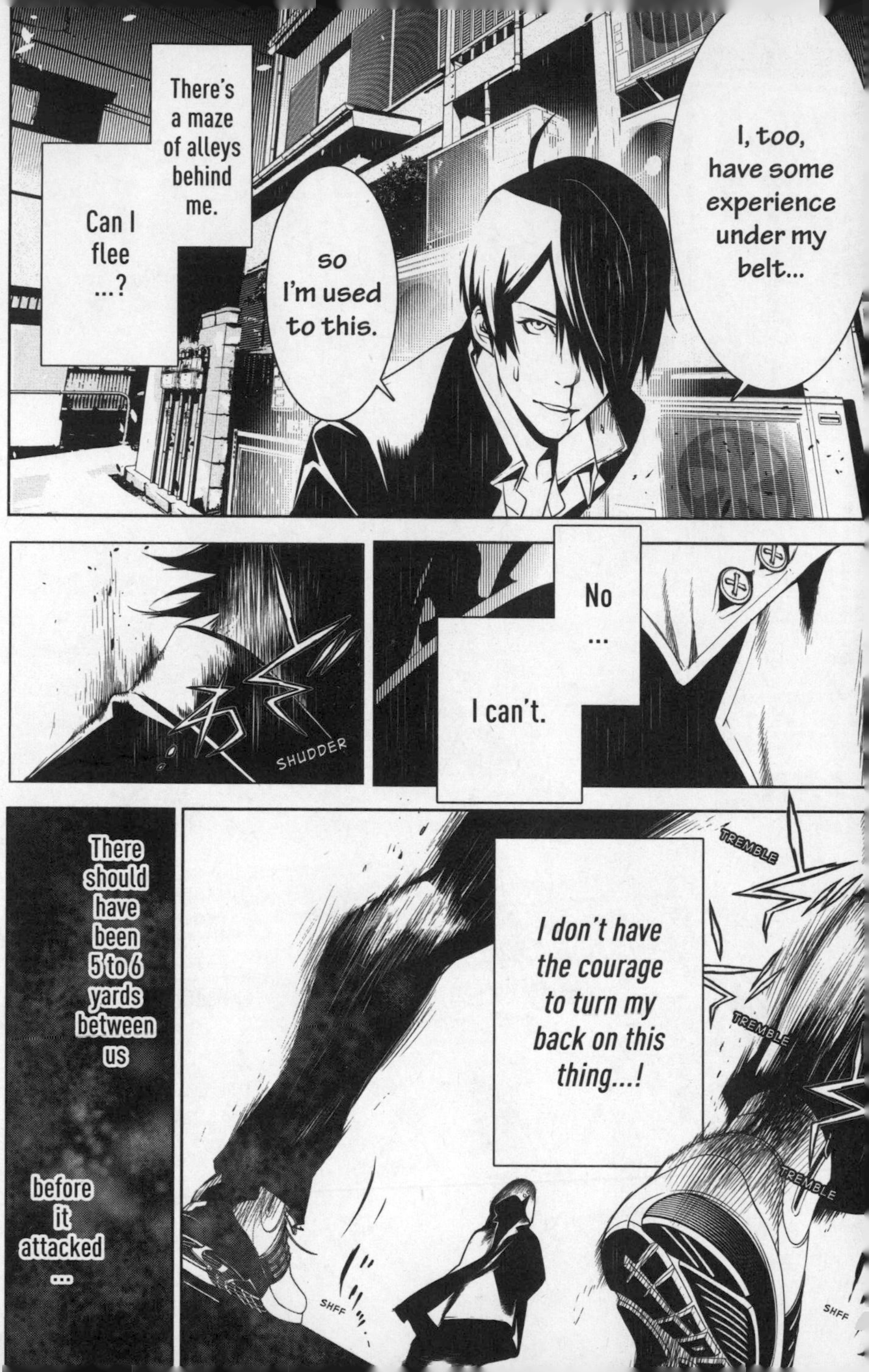
I, too, have some experience under my belt...
so I'm used to this.
There's a maze of alleys behind me.
Can I flee ...?
No ...
I can't.
SHUDDER
TREMBLE
I don't have the courage to turn my back on this thing...!
TREMBLE
TREMBLE
SHFF
SHFF
There should have been 5 to 6 yards between us
before it attacked ...

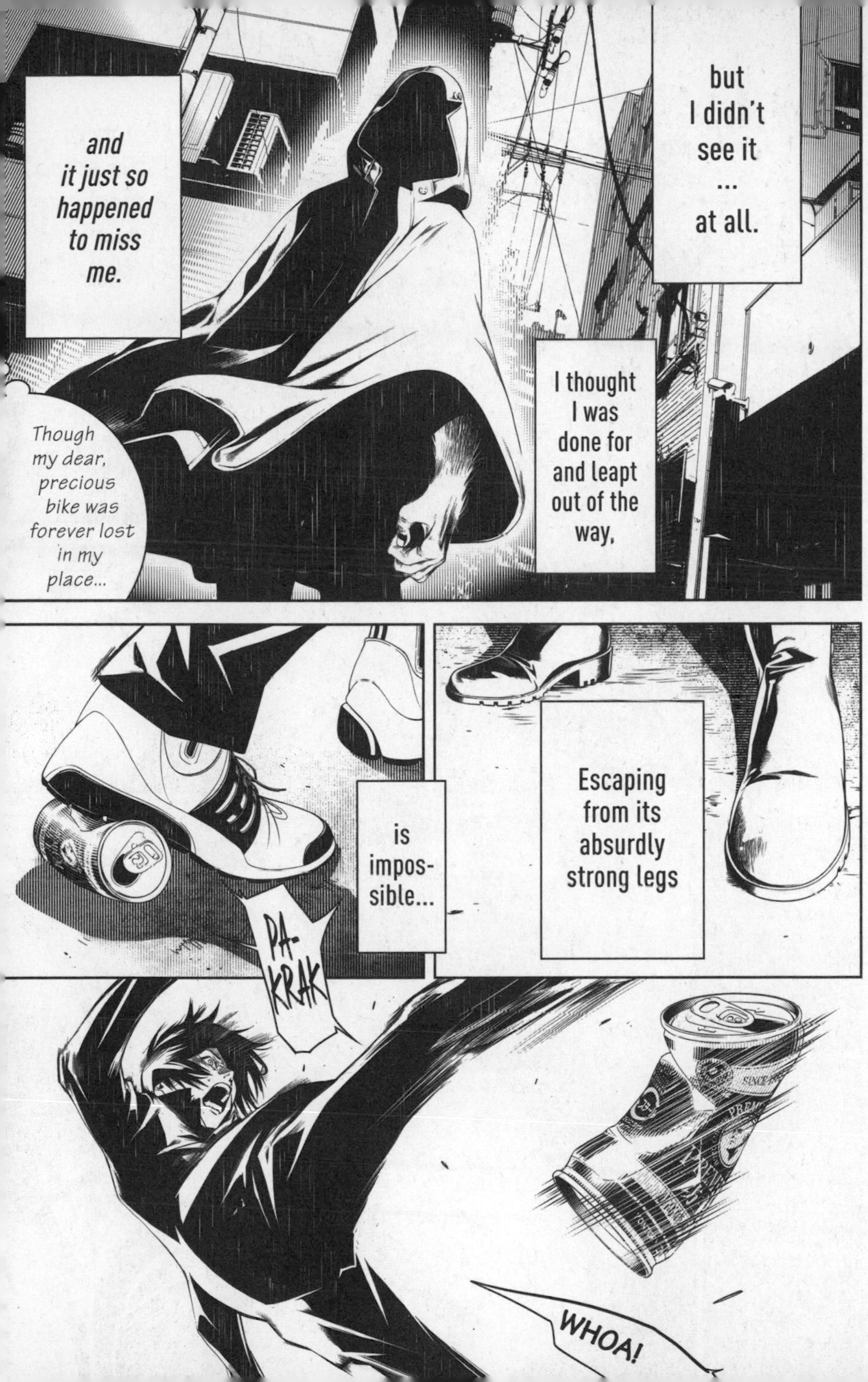
but I didn't see it ... at all.
I thought I was done for and leapt out of the way,
and it just so happened to miss me.
Though my dear, precious bike was forever lost in my place...
Escaping from its absurdly strong legs
is impos-sible...
PA-KRAK
WHOA!

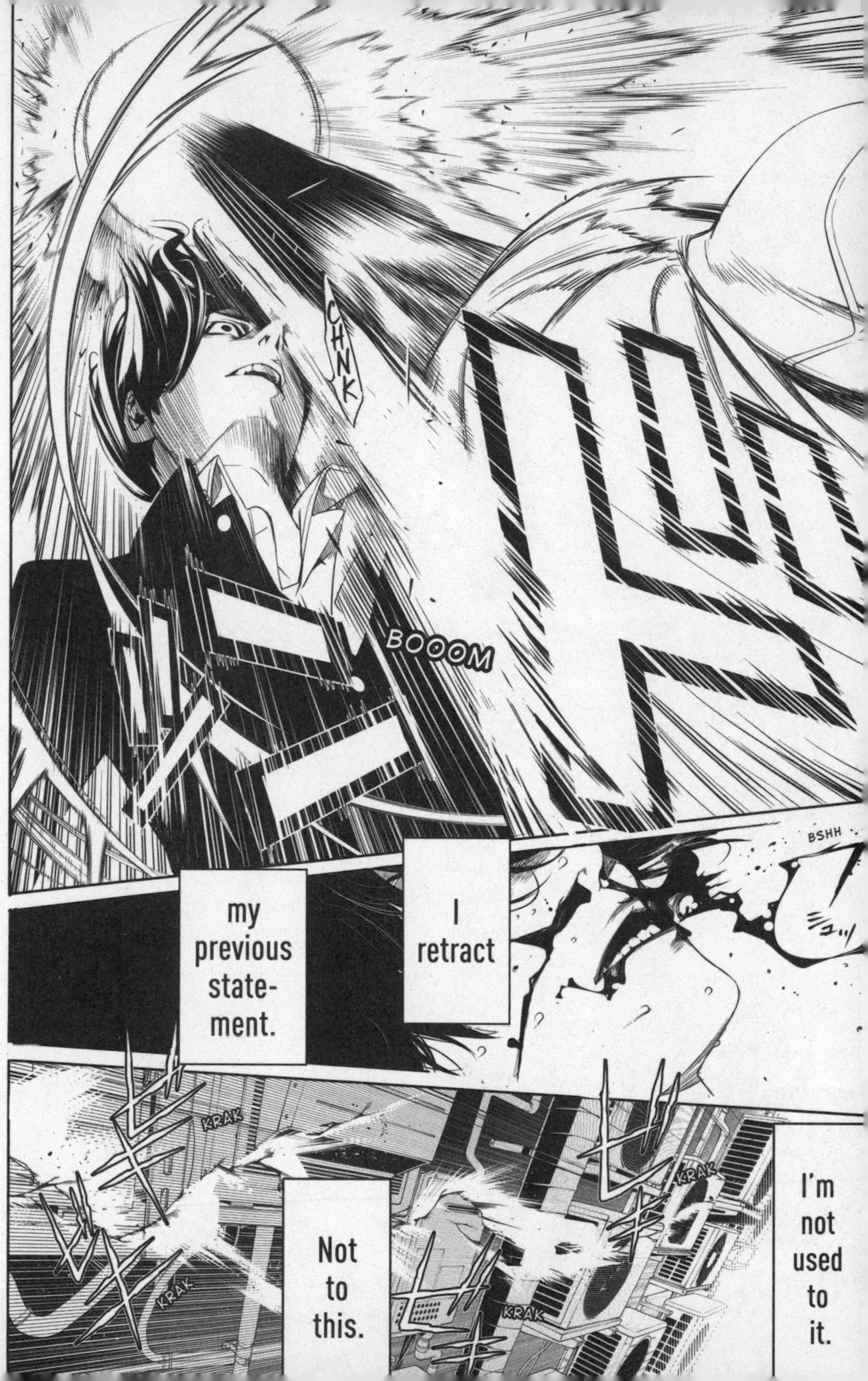
CHNK
BOOOM
BSHH
I retract
my previous state-ment.
I'm not used to it.
KRAK
Not to this.
KRAK
KRAK
KRAK

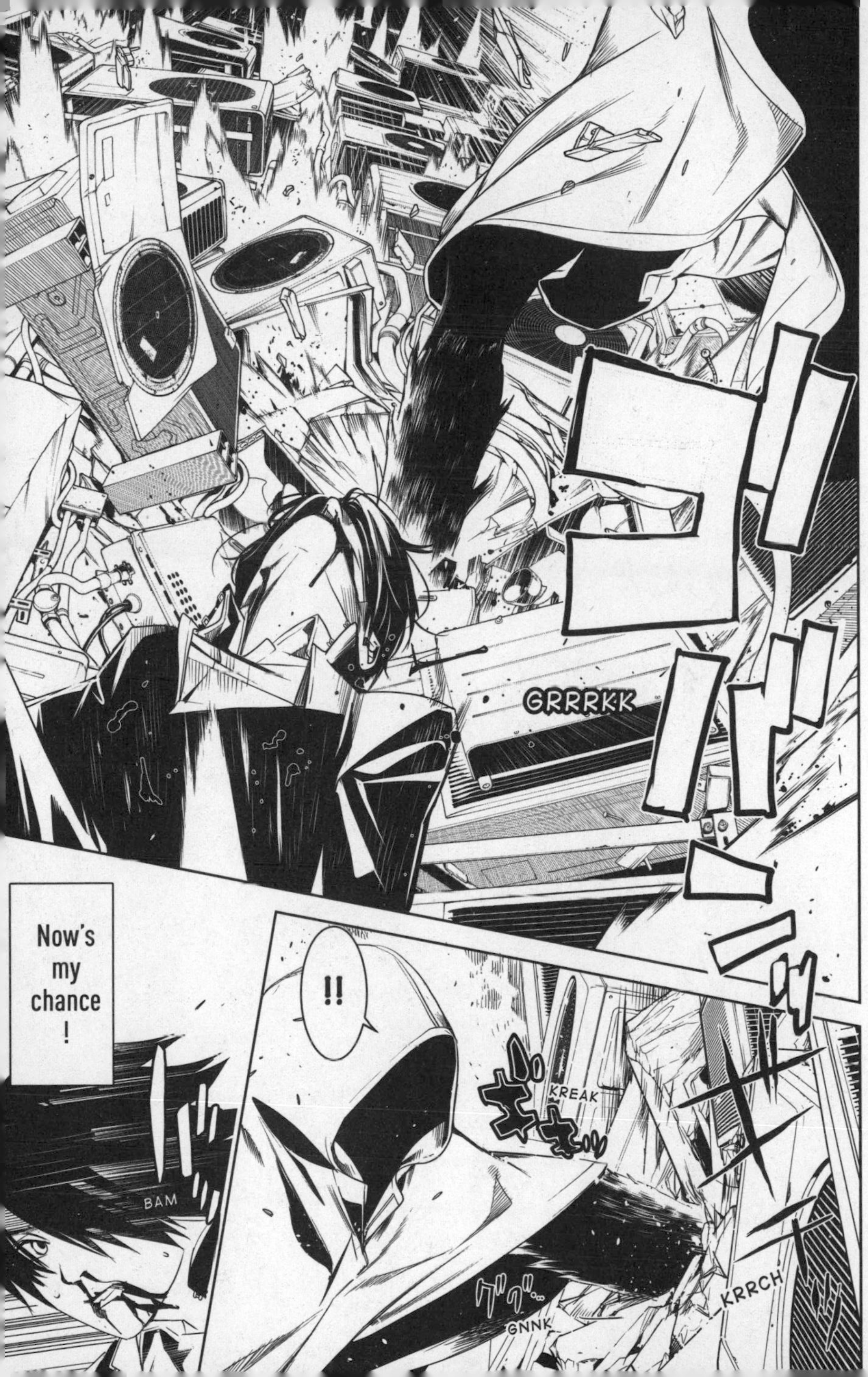
GRRRKK
KRRCH
KREAK
!!
GNNK
Now's my chance !
BAM

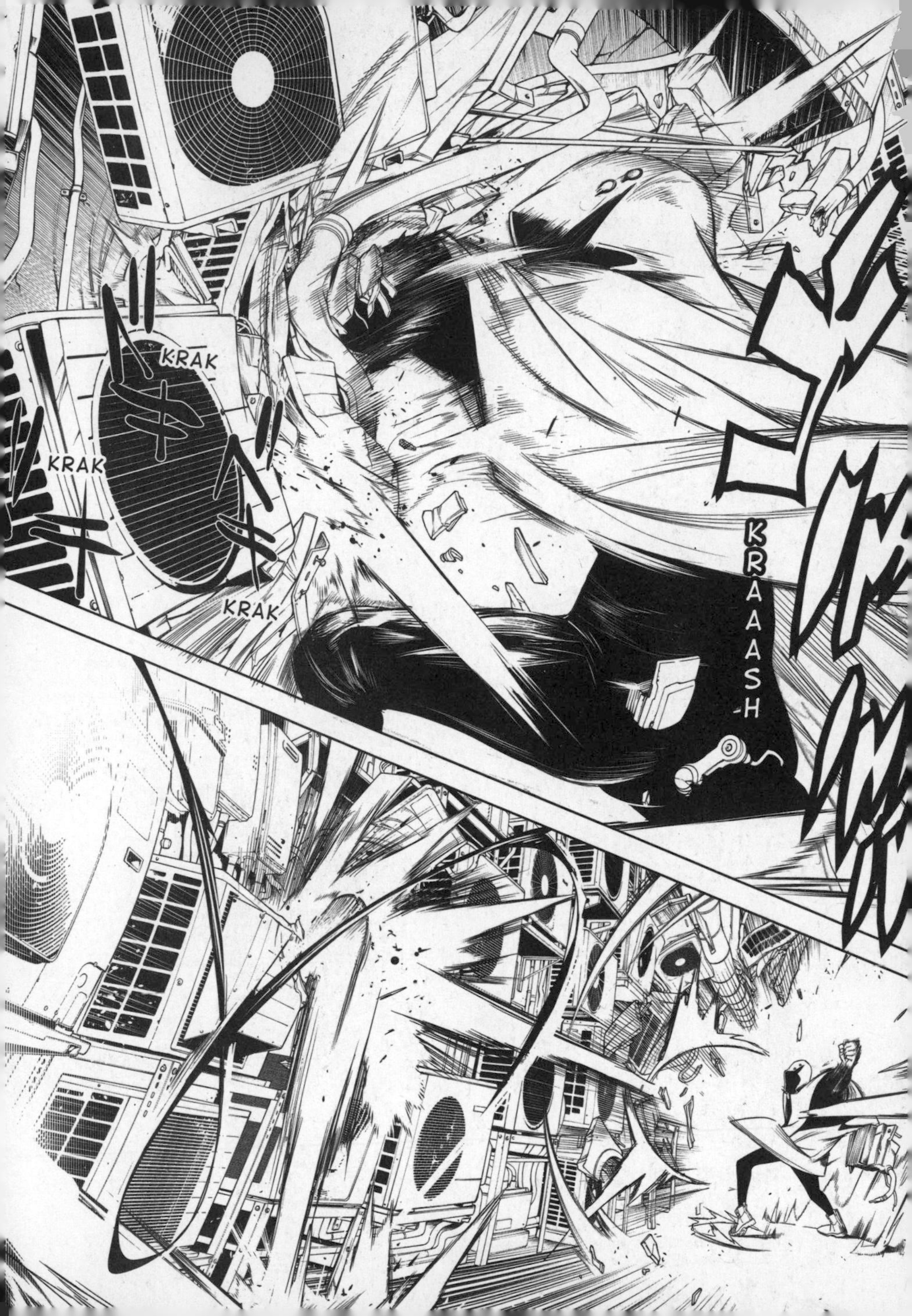
KRAAAASH
KRAK
KRAK
KRAK

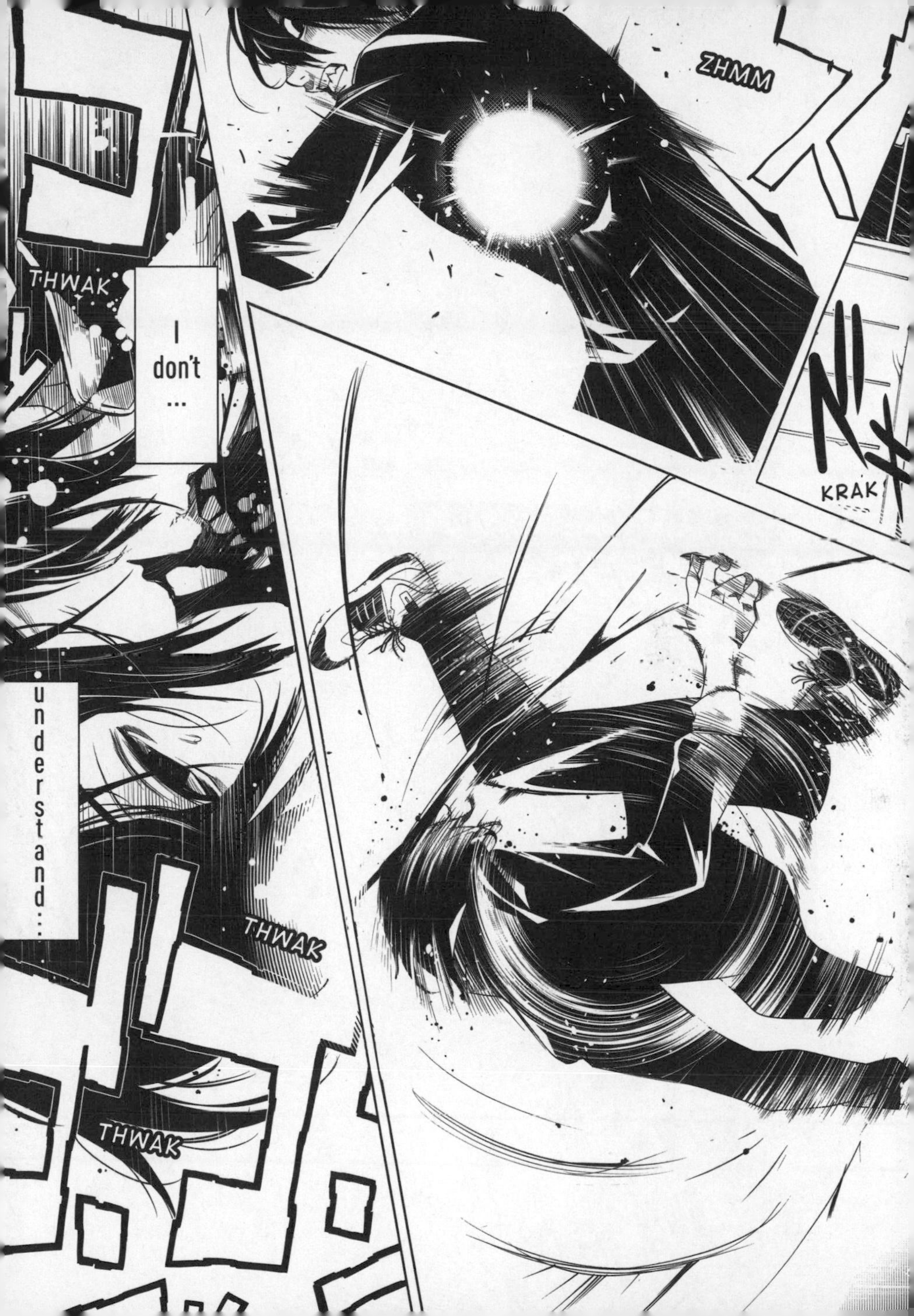
ZHMM
KRAK
THWAK
I don't ...
understand...
THWAK
THWAK

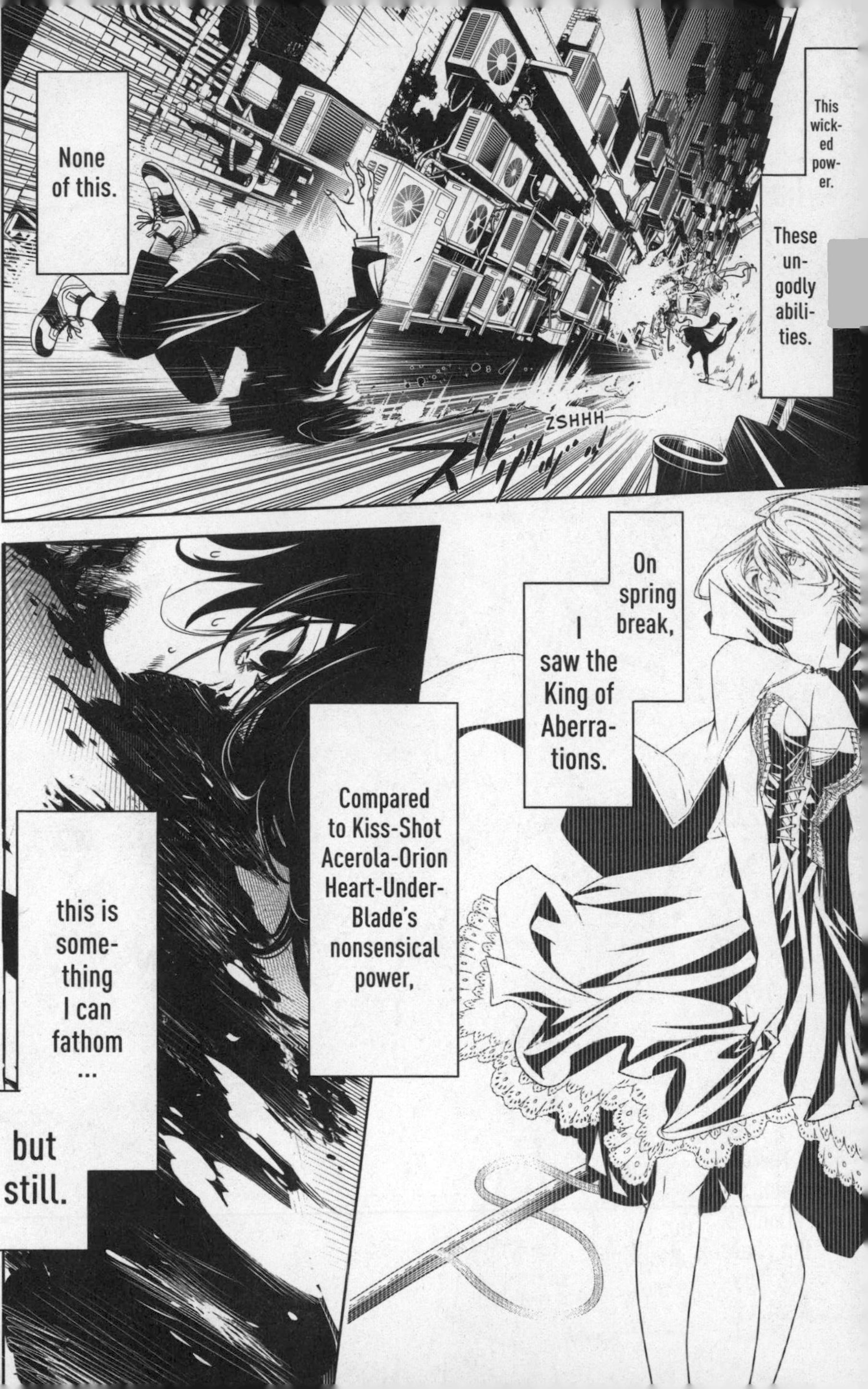
This wicked power.
These ungodly abilities.
None of this.
ZSHHH
On spring break, I saw the King of Aberrations.
Compared to Kiss-Shot Acerola-Orion Heart-Under-Blade's nonsensical power,
this is something I can fathom...
but still.

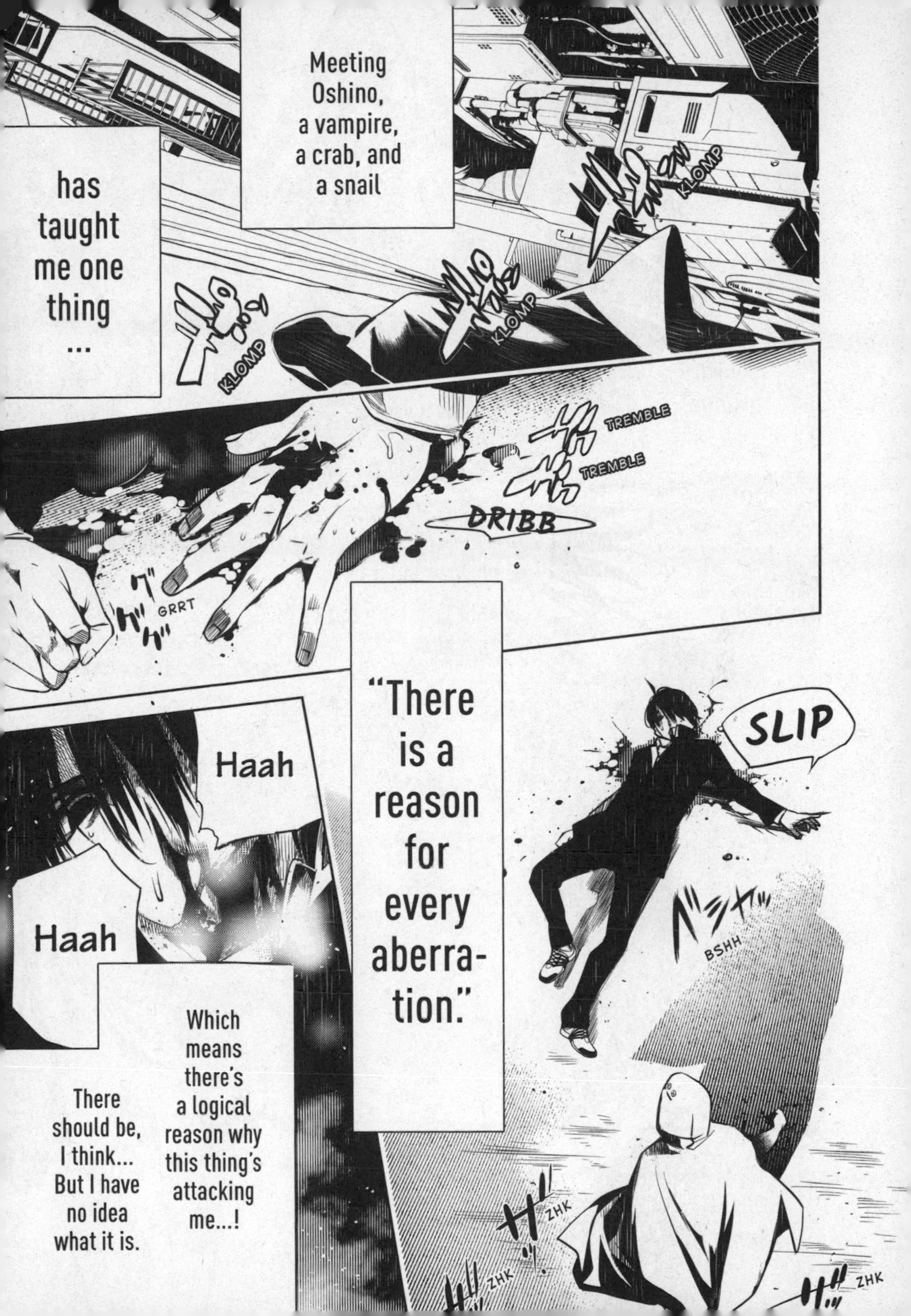
Meeting Oshino, a vampire, a crab, and a snail
KLOMP
KLOMP
has taught me one thing ...
KLOMP
TREMBLE
TREMBLE
DRIBB
GRRT
SLIP
"There is a reason for every aberration."
BSHH
ZHK
ZHK
ZHK
Haah
Haah
Which means there's a logical reason why this thing's attacking me...!
There should be, I think... But I have no idea what it is.

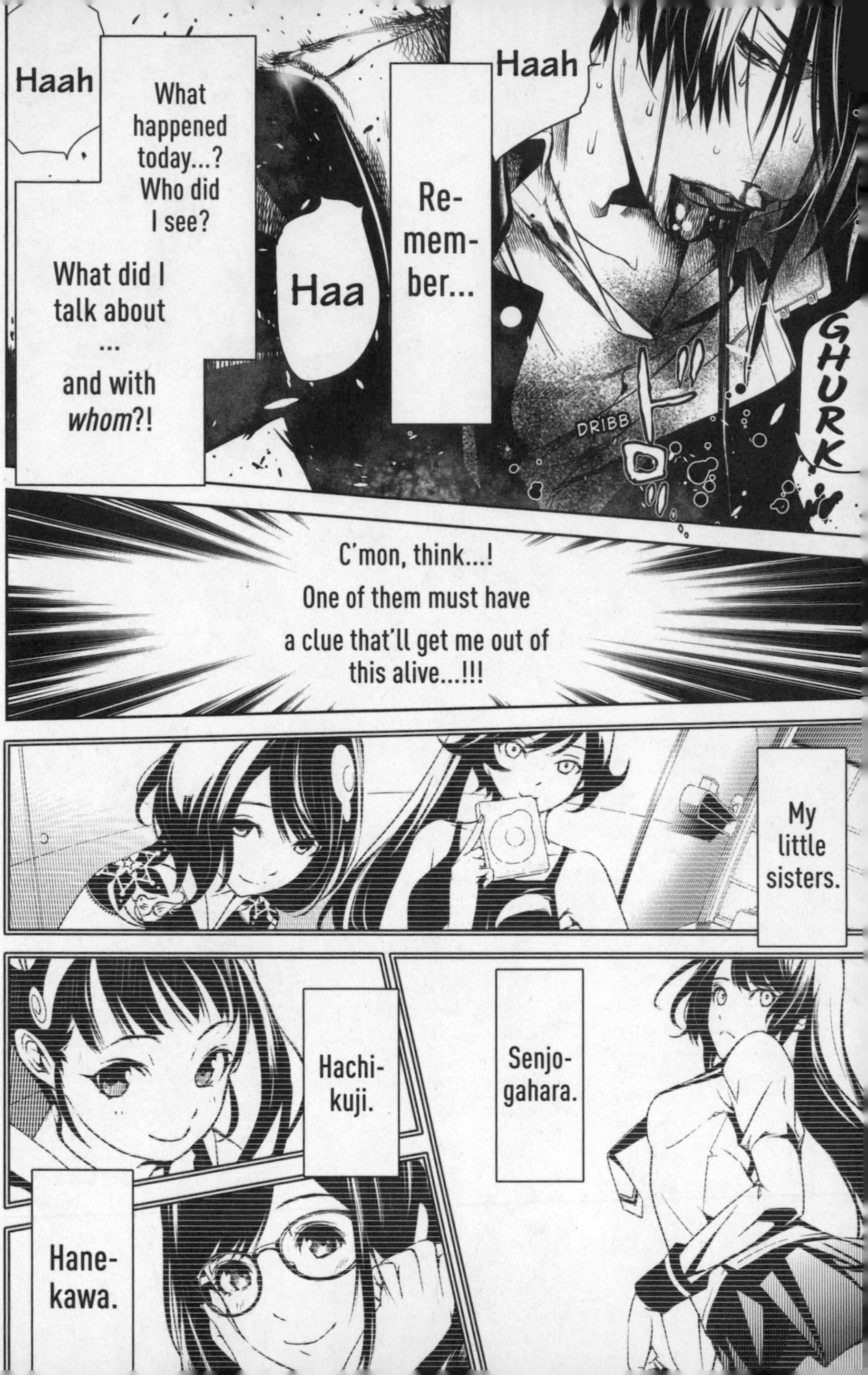

Haah
GHURK
Re-member...
DRIBB
Haa
What happened today...? Who did I see?
Haah
What did I talk about ... and with *whom*?!
C'mon, think...! One of them must have a clue that'll get me out of this alive...!!!
My little sisters.
Senjo-gahara.
Hachi-kuji.
Hane-kawa.

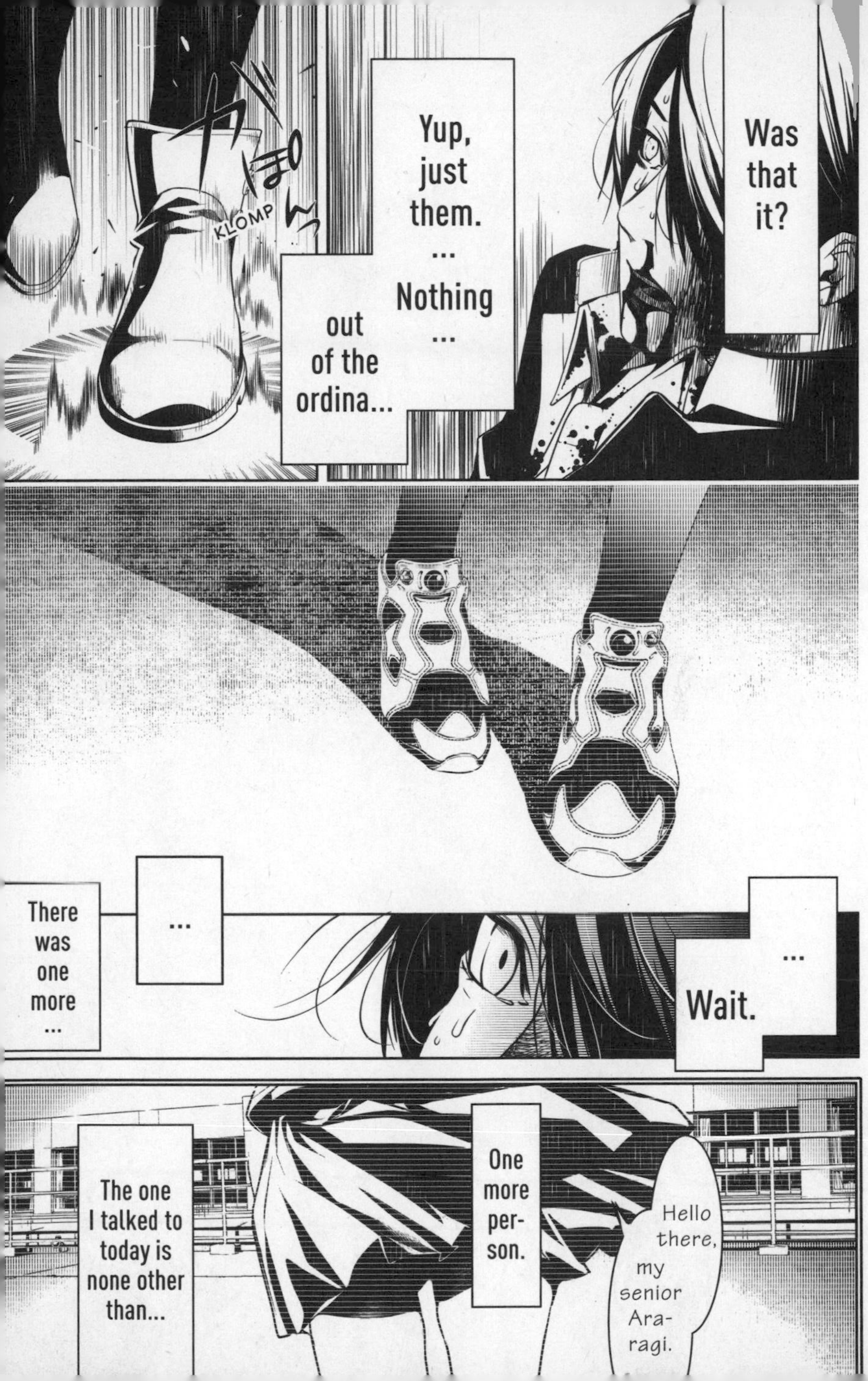
Was that it?
Yup, just them. ... Nothing ...
out of the ordina...
KLOMP
...
Wait.
...
There was one more ...
Hello there, my senior Araragi.
One more person.
The one I talked to today is none other than...

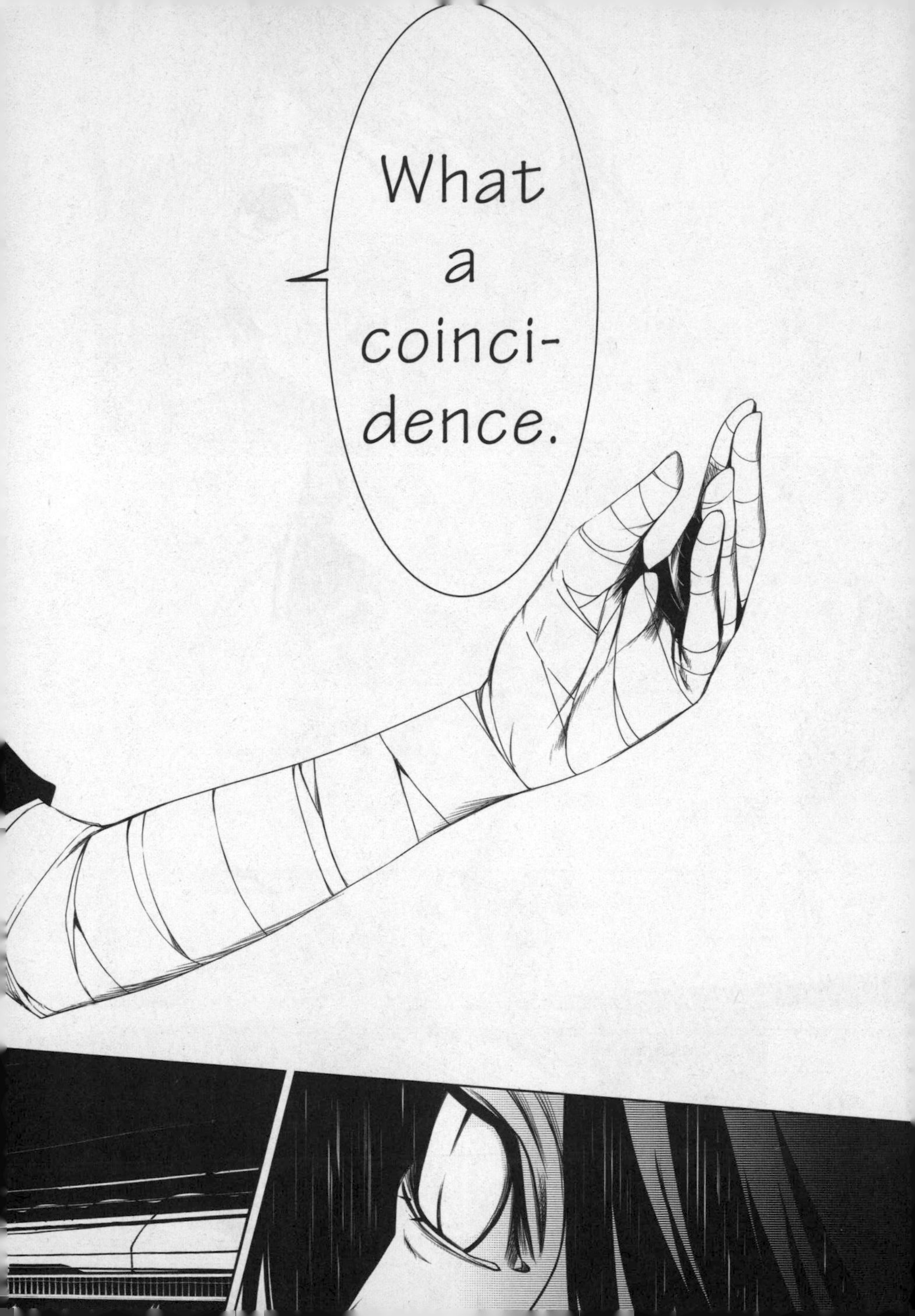
What a coinci-dence.

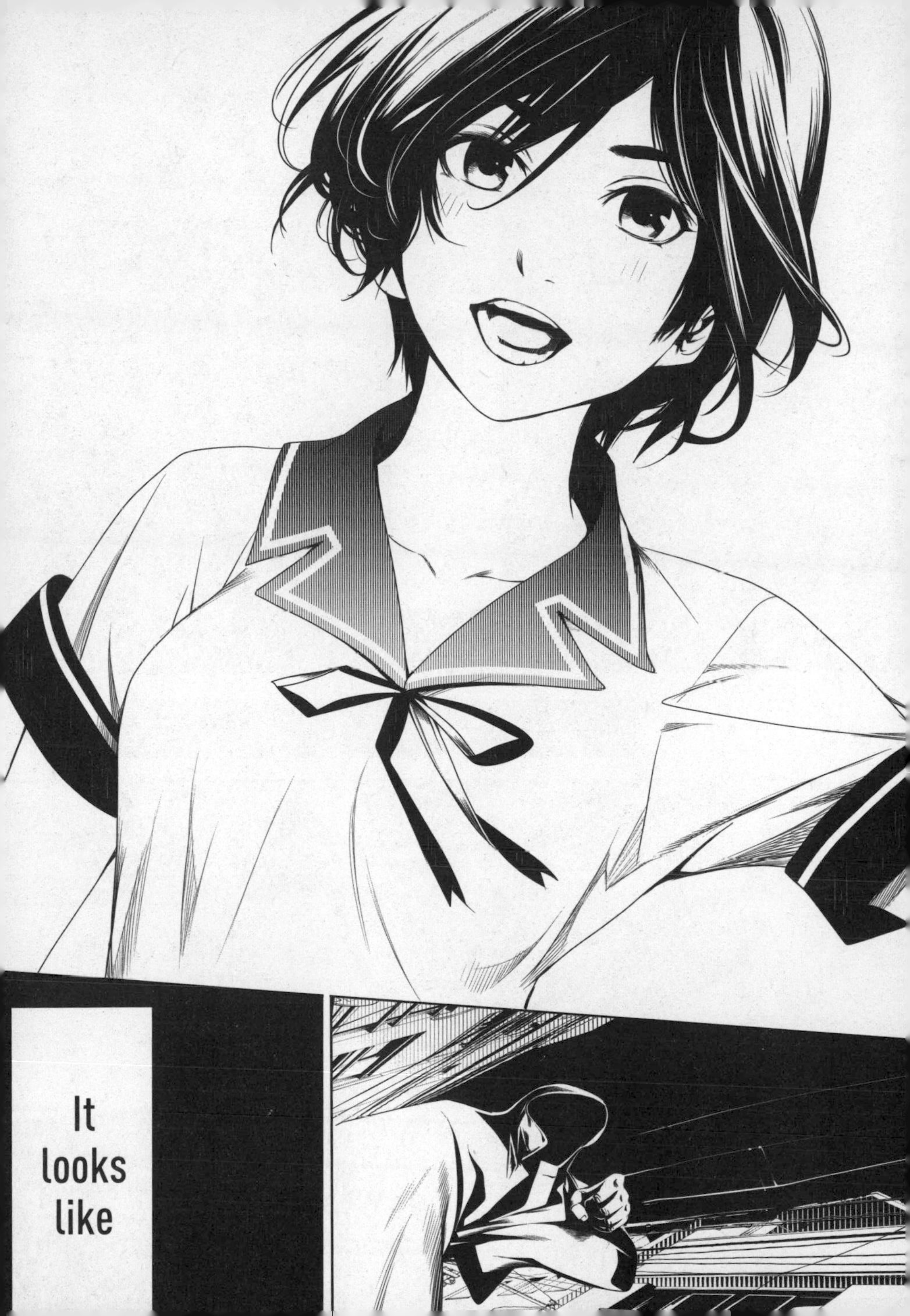
It looks like

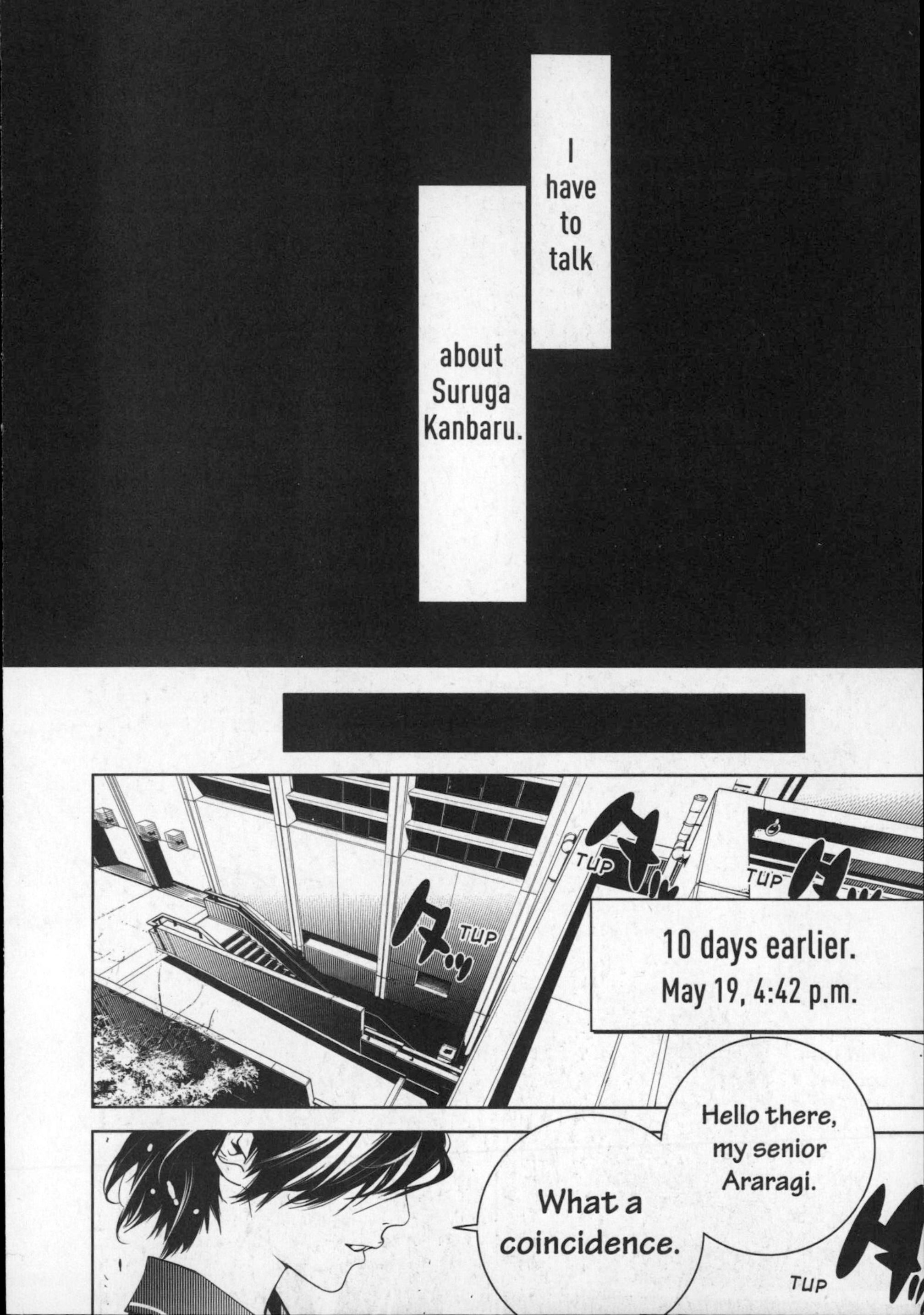
I have to talk
about Suruga Kanbaru.
TUP
TUP
TUP
10 days earlier.
May 19, 4:42 p.m.
Hello there, my senior Araragi.
What a coincidence.
TUP

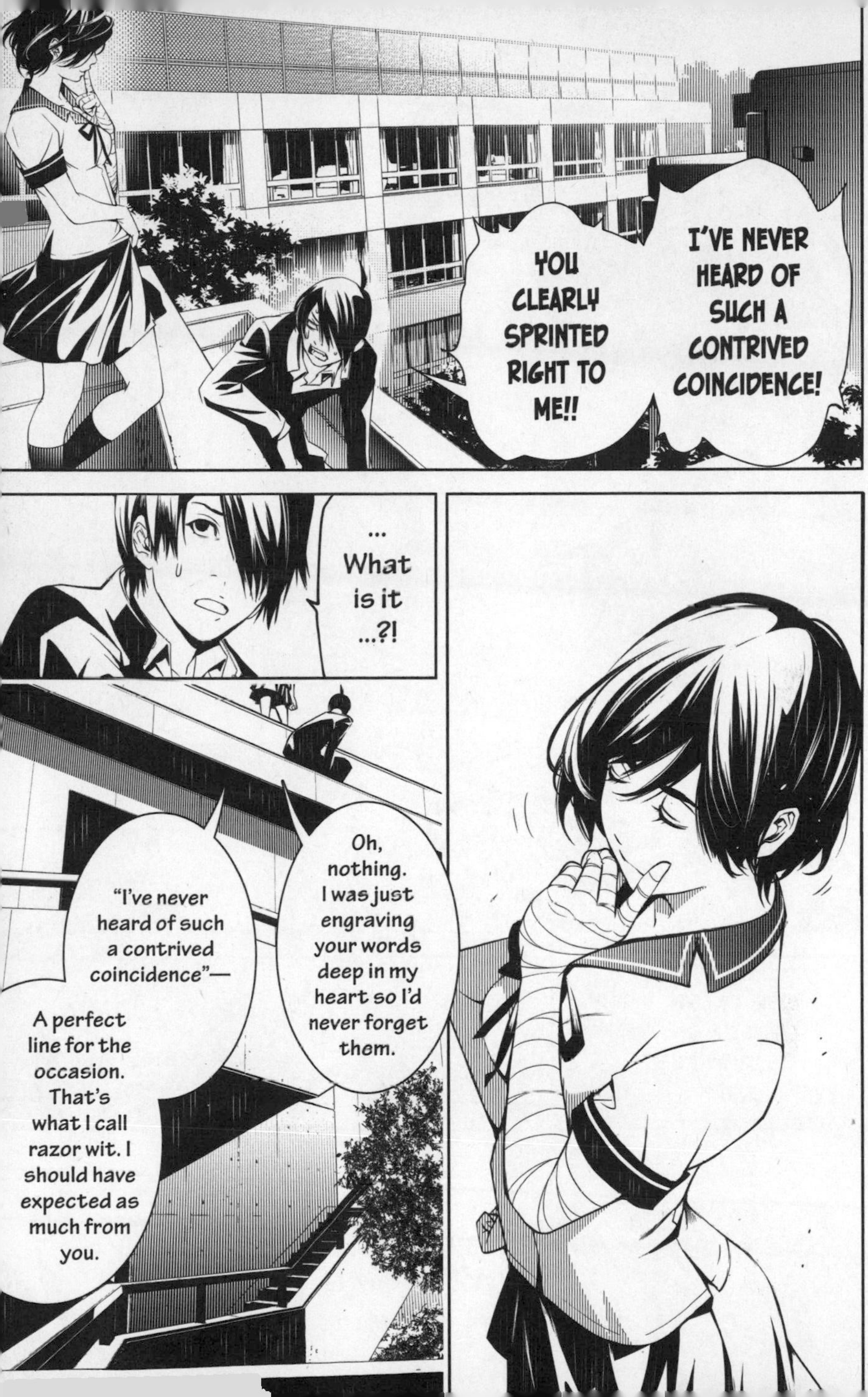
I'VE NEVER HEARD OF SUCH A CONTRIVED COINCIDENCE!
YOU CLEARLY SPRINTED RIGHT TO ME!!
... What is it ...?!
Oh, nothing. I was just engraving your words deep in my heart so I'd never forget them.
"I've never heard of such a contrived coincidence"—
A perfect line for the occasion. That's what I call razor wit. I should have expected as much from you.

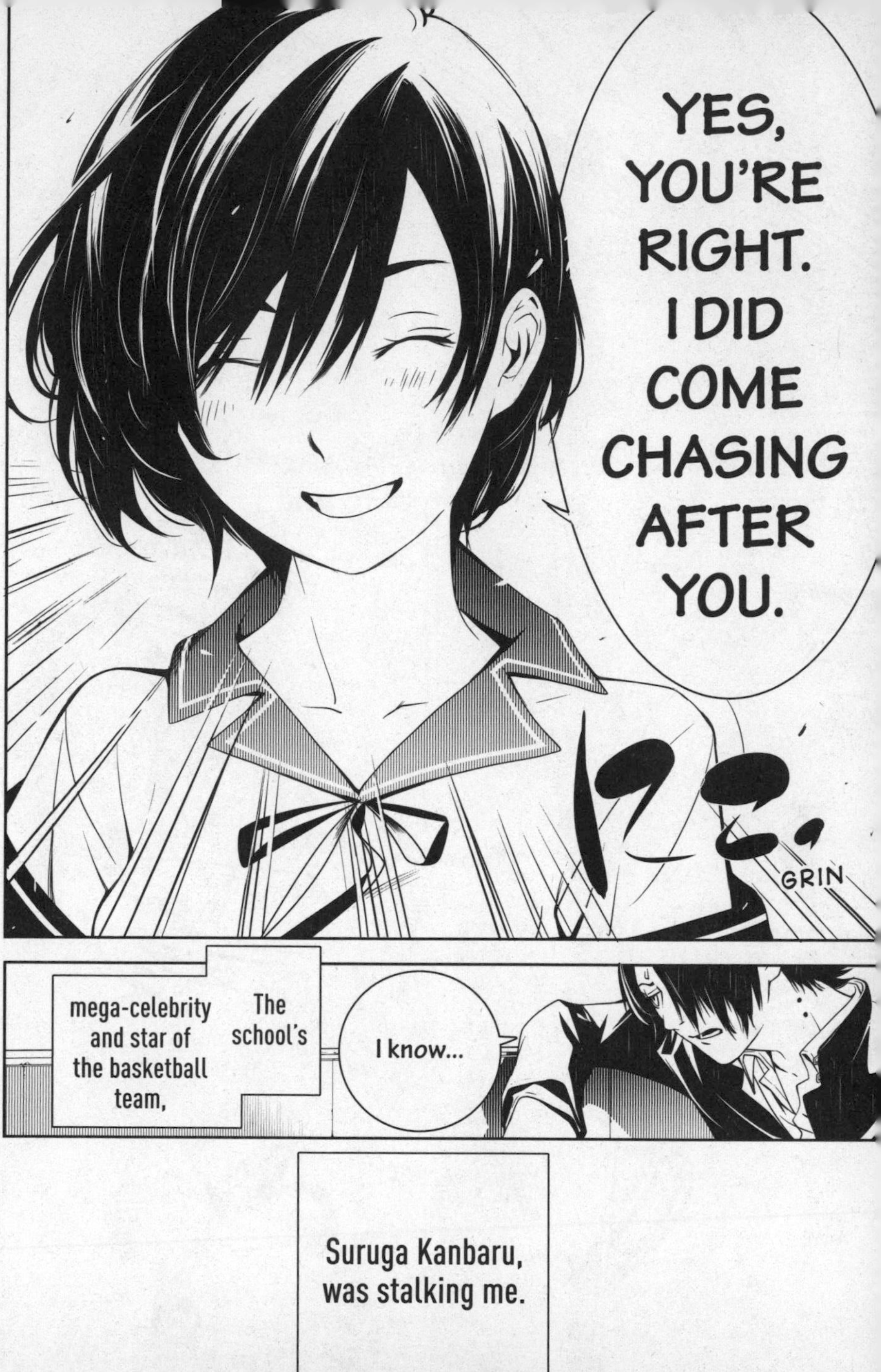
YES, YOU'RE RIGHT. I DID COME CHASING AFTER YOU.
にこ
GRIN
I know...
The school's mega-celebrity and star of the basketball team,
Suruga Kanbaru, was stalking me.

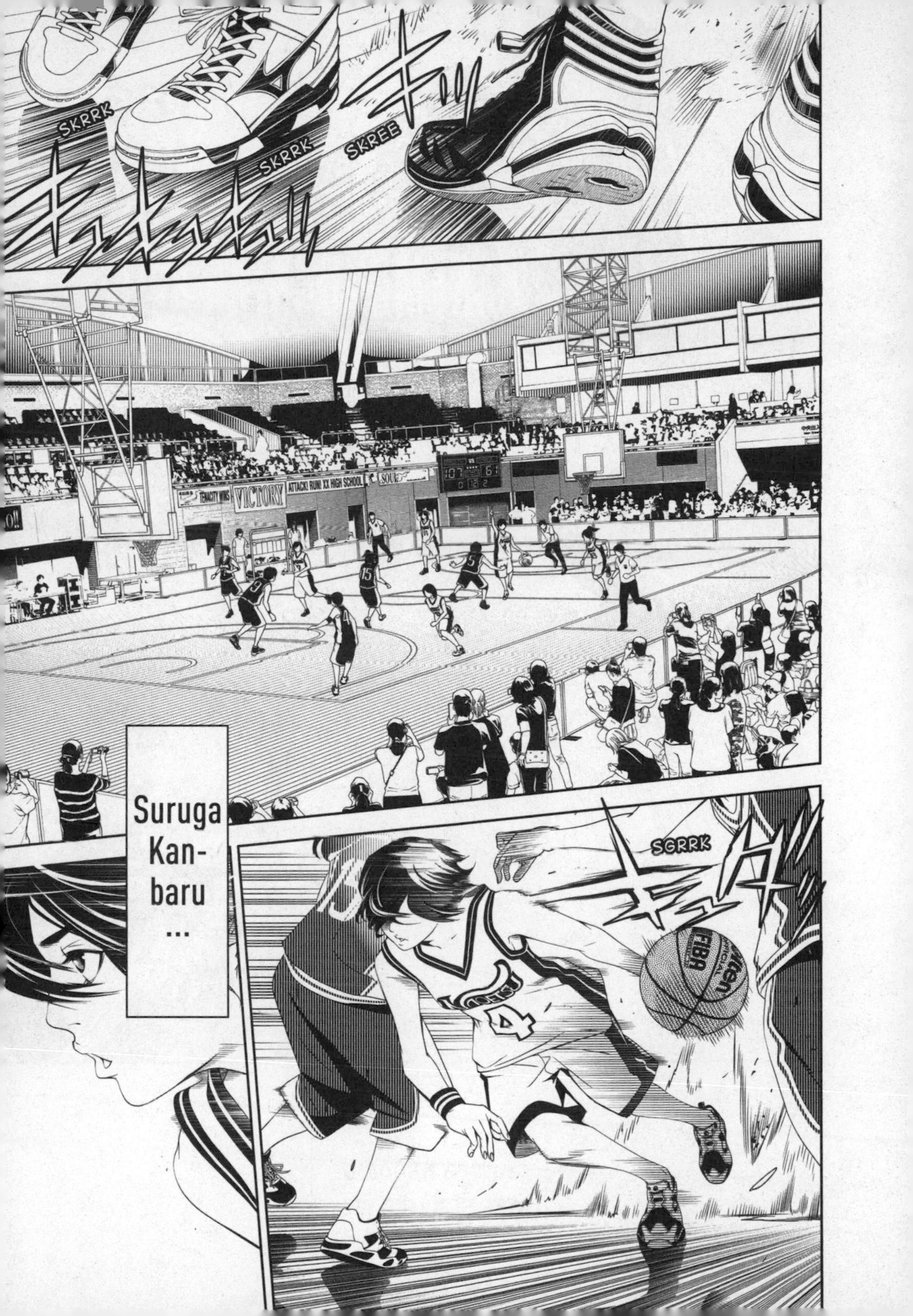
SKREE
SKRRK
SKRRK
VICTORY
ATTACK! RUN! XX HIGH SCHOOL
TENACITY WINS
SGRRK
Suruga Kan-baru ...

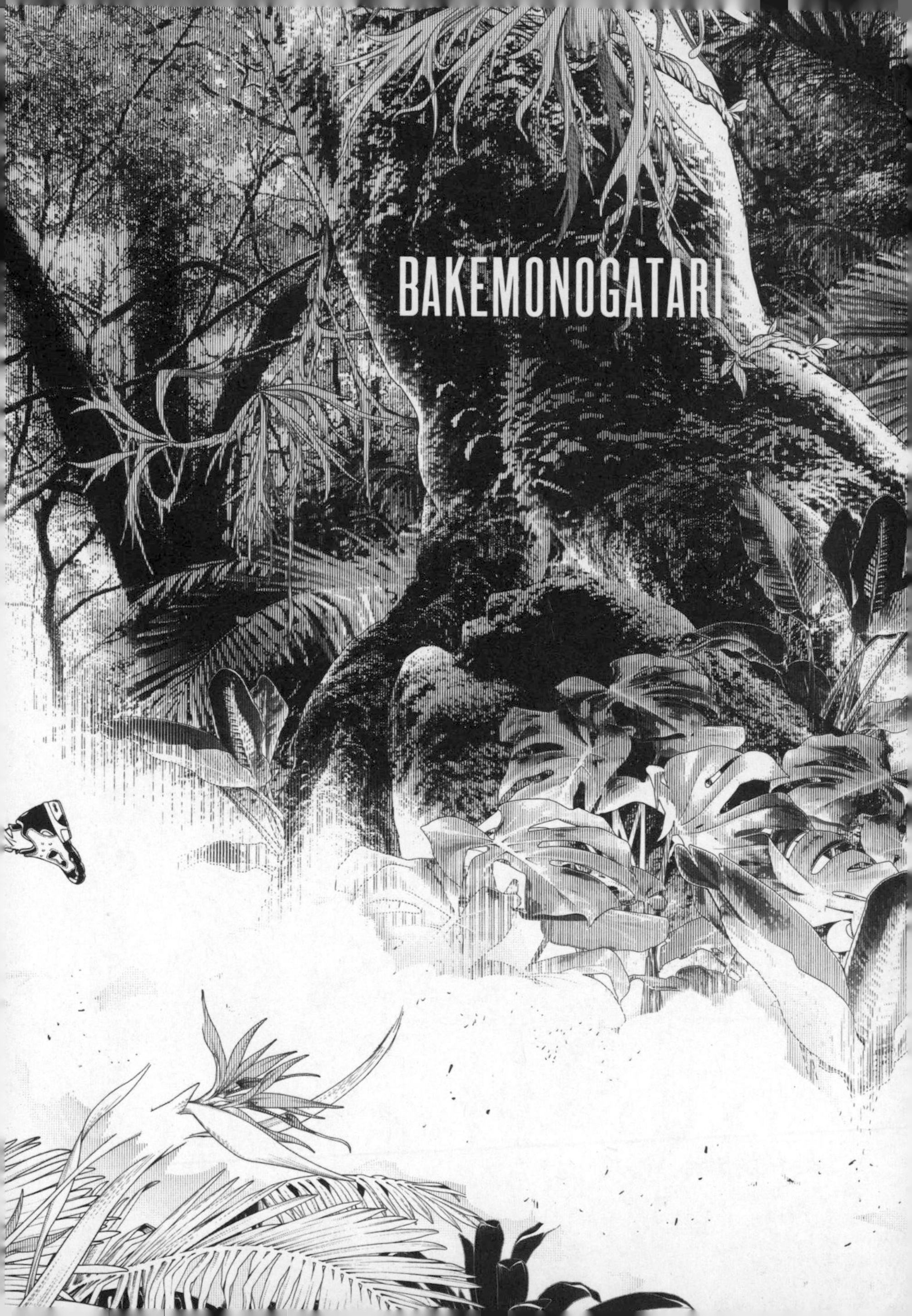
BAKEMONOGATARI

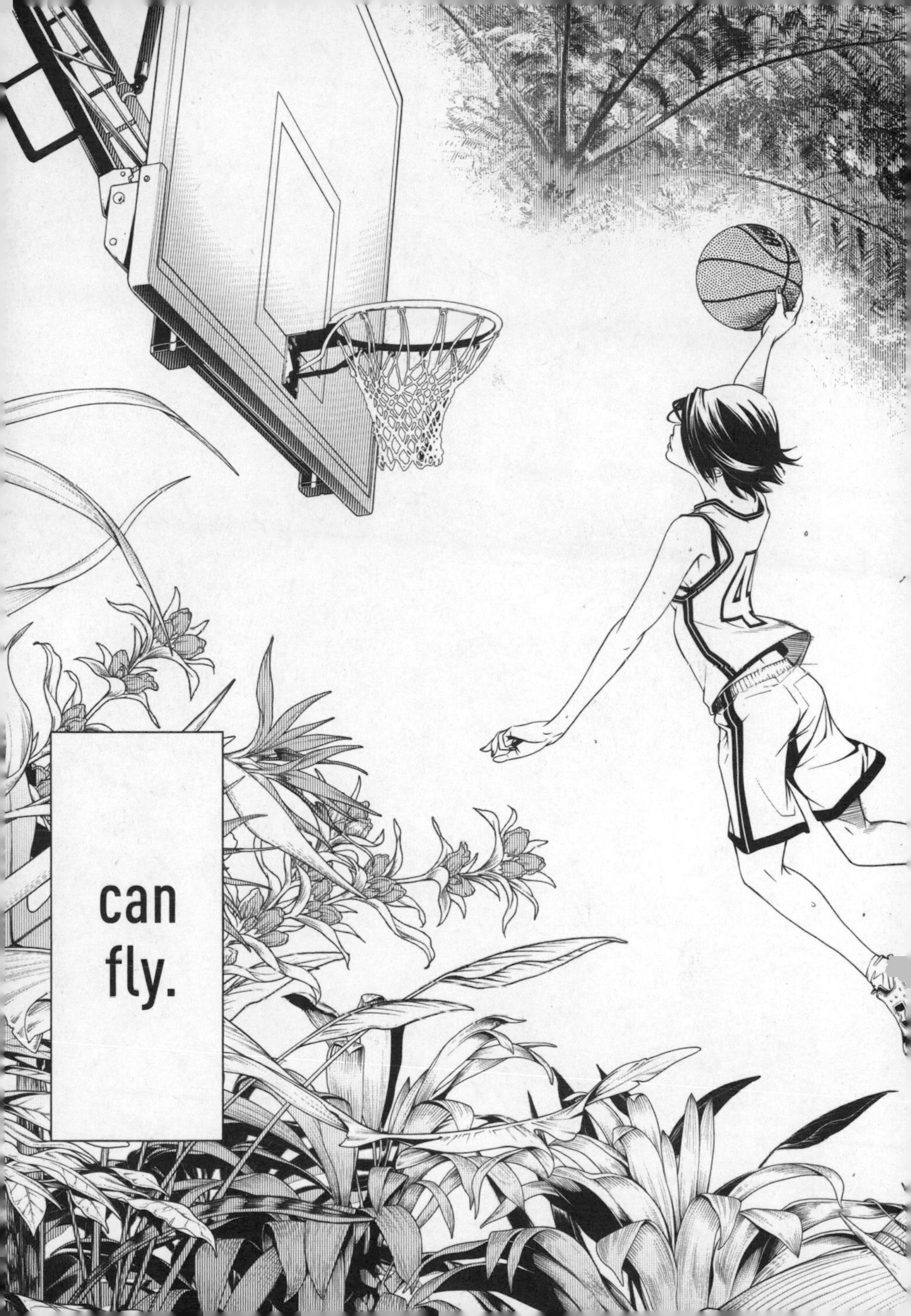
can
fly.

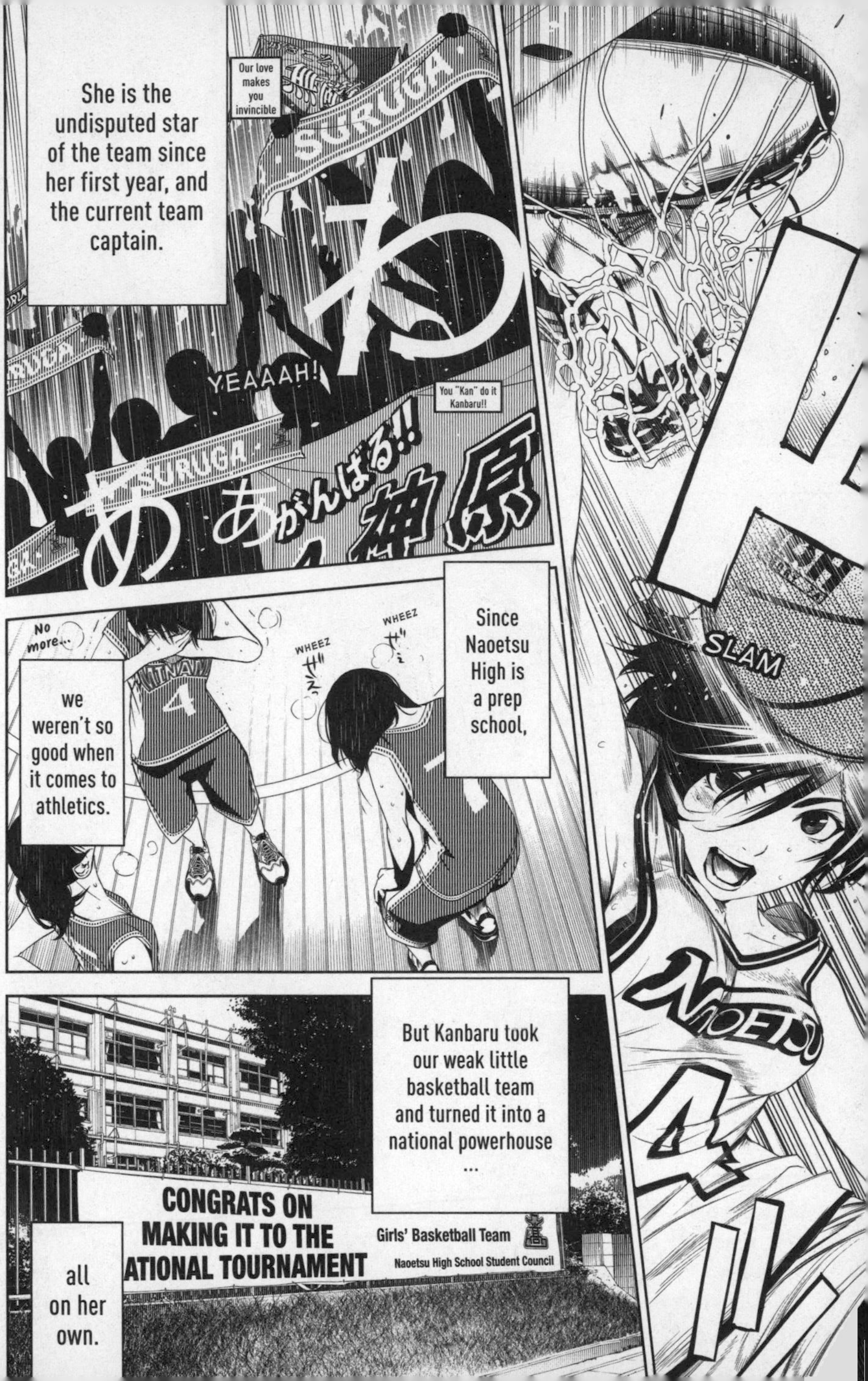
SLAM
NAOETSU
4
She is the undisputed star of the team since her first year, and the current team captain.
Our love makes you invincible
SURUGA
YEAAAH!
You "Kan" do it Kanbaru!!
SURUGA
がんばる!!
神原
Since Naoetsu High is a prep school,
WHEEZ
WHEEZ
No more...
we weren't so good when it comes to athletics.
But Kanbaru took our weak little basketball team and turned it into a national powerhouse ...
CONGRATS ON MAKING IT TO THE ATIONAL TOURNAMENT
Girls' Basketball Team
Naoetsu High School Student Council
all on her own.

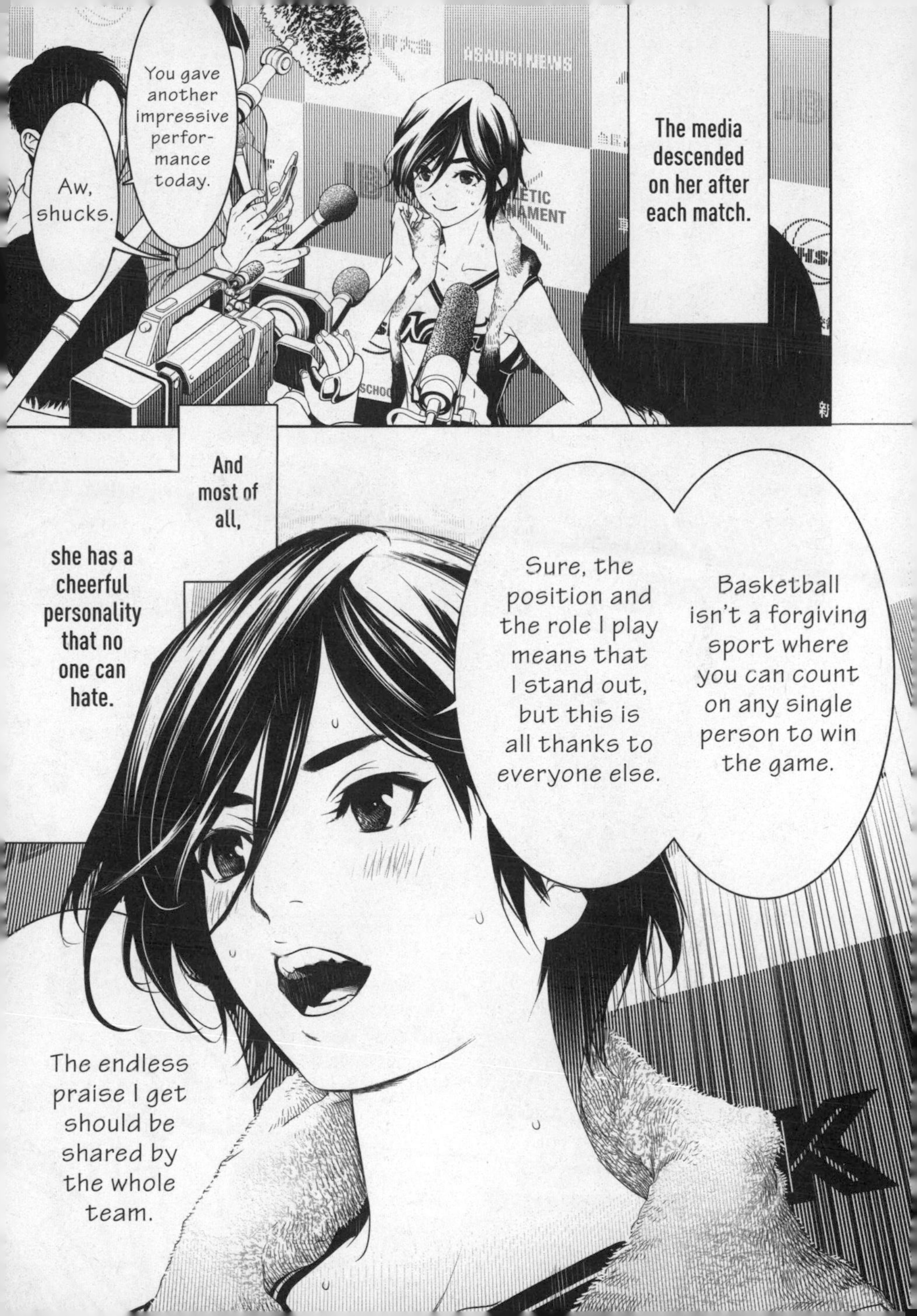
The media descended on her after each match.
You gave another impressive performance today.
Aw, shucks.
And most of all,
she has a cheerful personality that no one can hate.
Basketball isn't a forgiving sport where you can count on any single person to win the game.
Sure, the position and the role I play means that I stand out, but this is all thanks to everyone else.
The endless praise I get should be shared by the whole team.

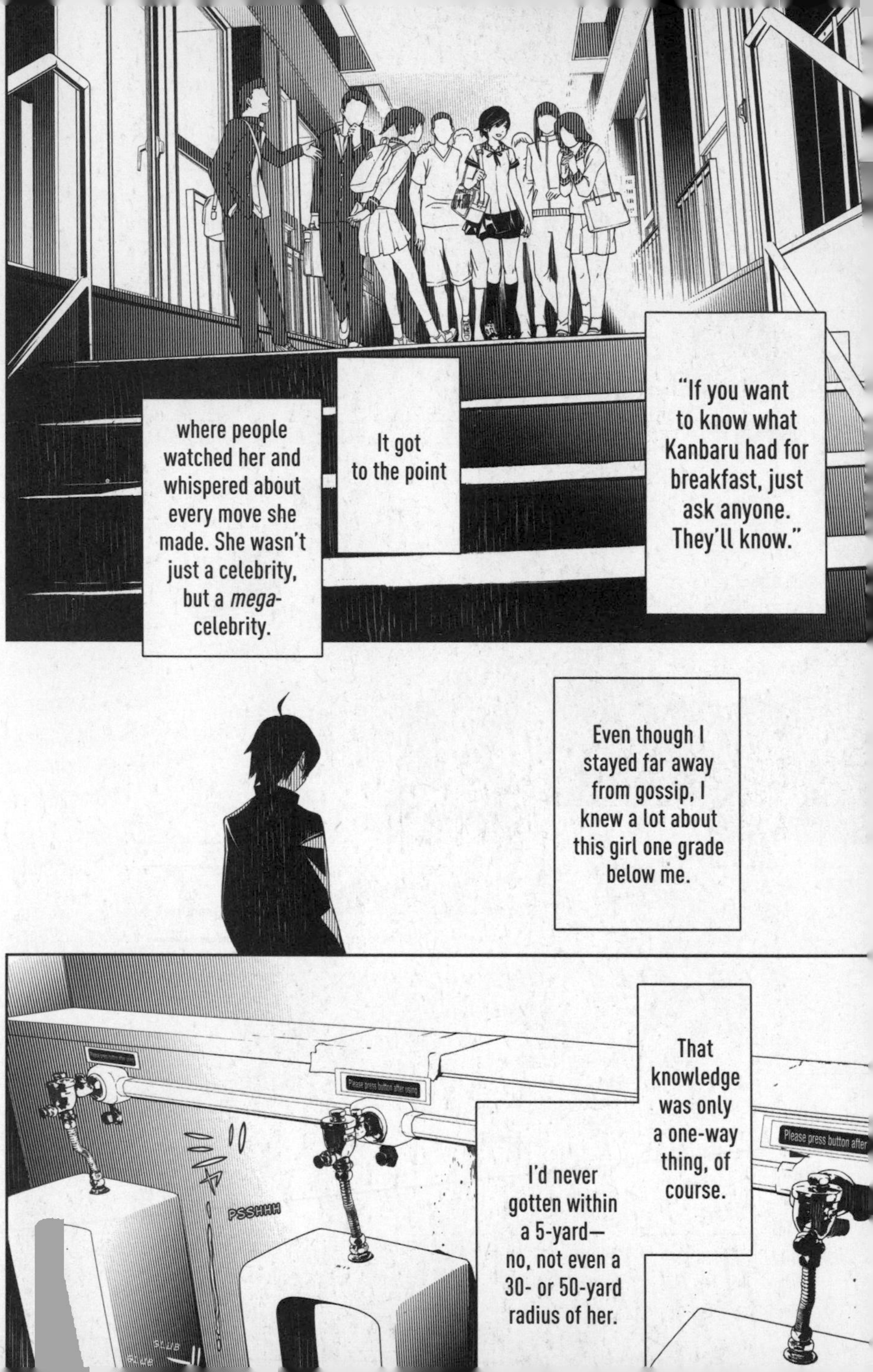
"If you want to know what Kanbaru had for breakfast, just ask anyone. They'll know."
It got to the point
where people watched her and whispered about every move she made. She wasn't just a celebrity, but a *mega*-celebrity.
Even though I stayed far away from gossip, I knew a lot about this girl one grade below me.
That knowledge was only a one-way thing, of course.
Please press button after
I'd never gotten within a 5-yard—no, not even a 30- or 50-yard radius of her.
Please press button after using
PSSHHH

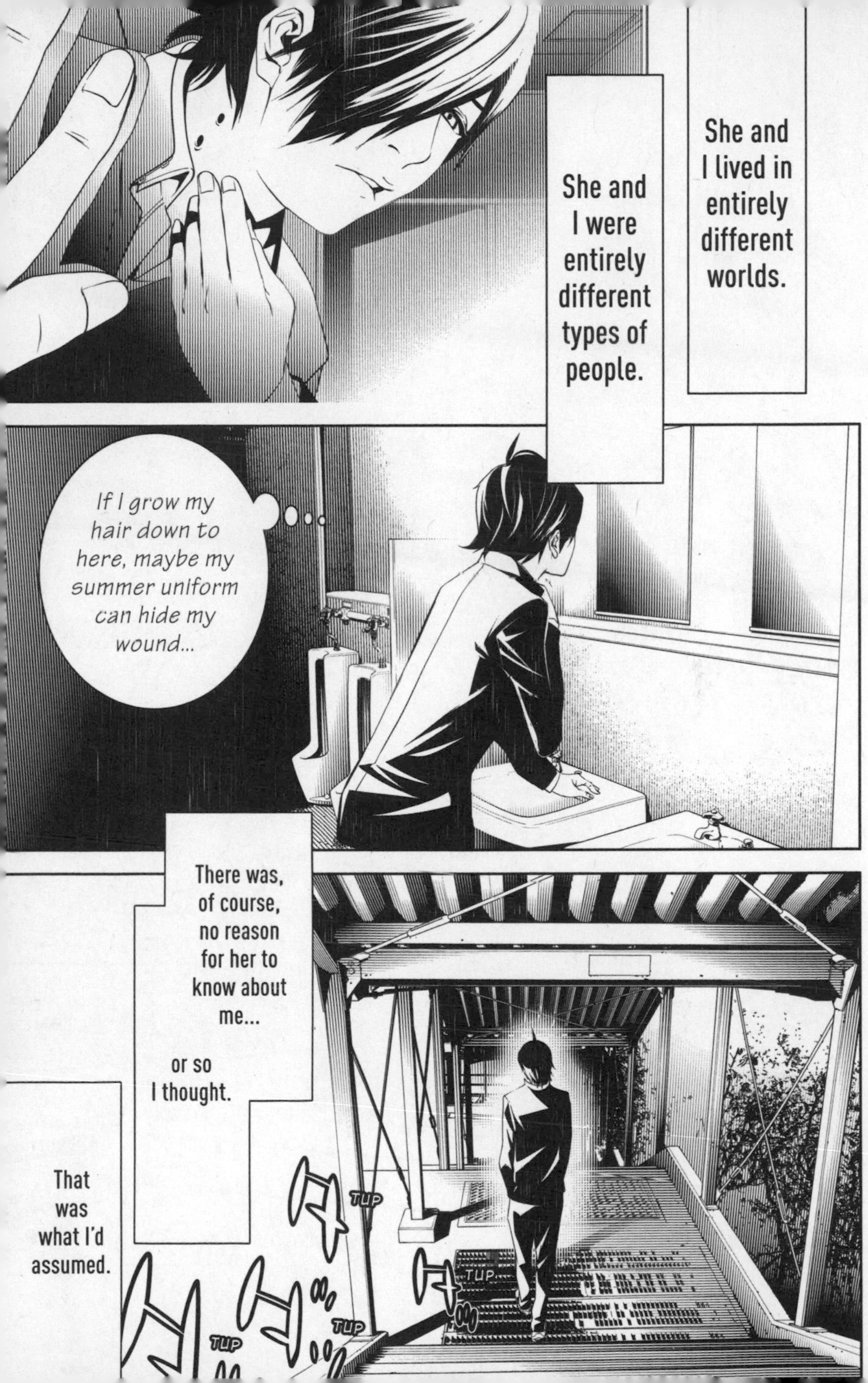
She and I lived in entirely different worlds.
She and I were entirely different types of people.
If I grow my hair down to here, maybe my summer uniform can hide my wound...
There was, of course, no reason for her to know about me...
or so I thought.
TUP
TUP
TUP
TUP
That was what I'd assumed.

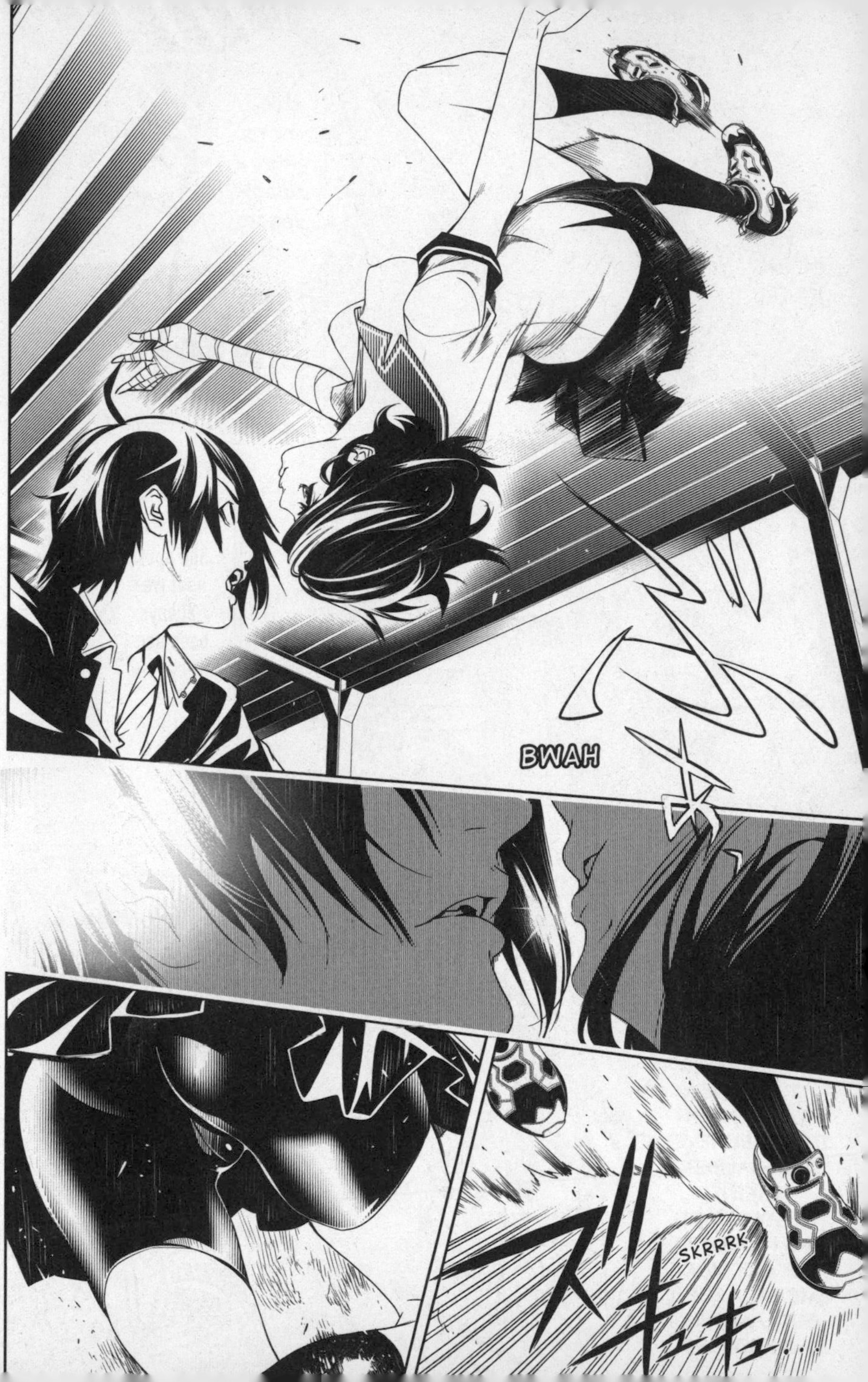
BWAH
SKRRRK

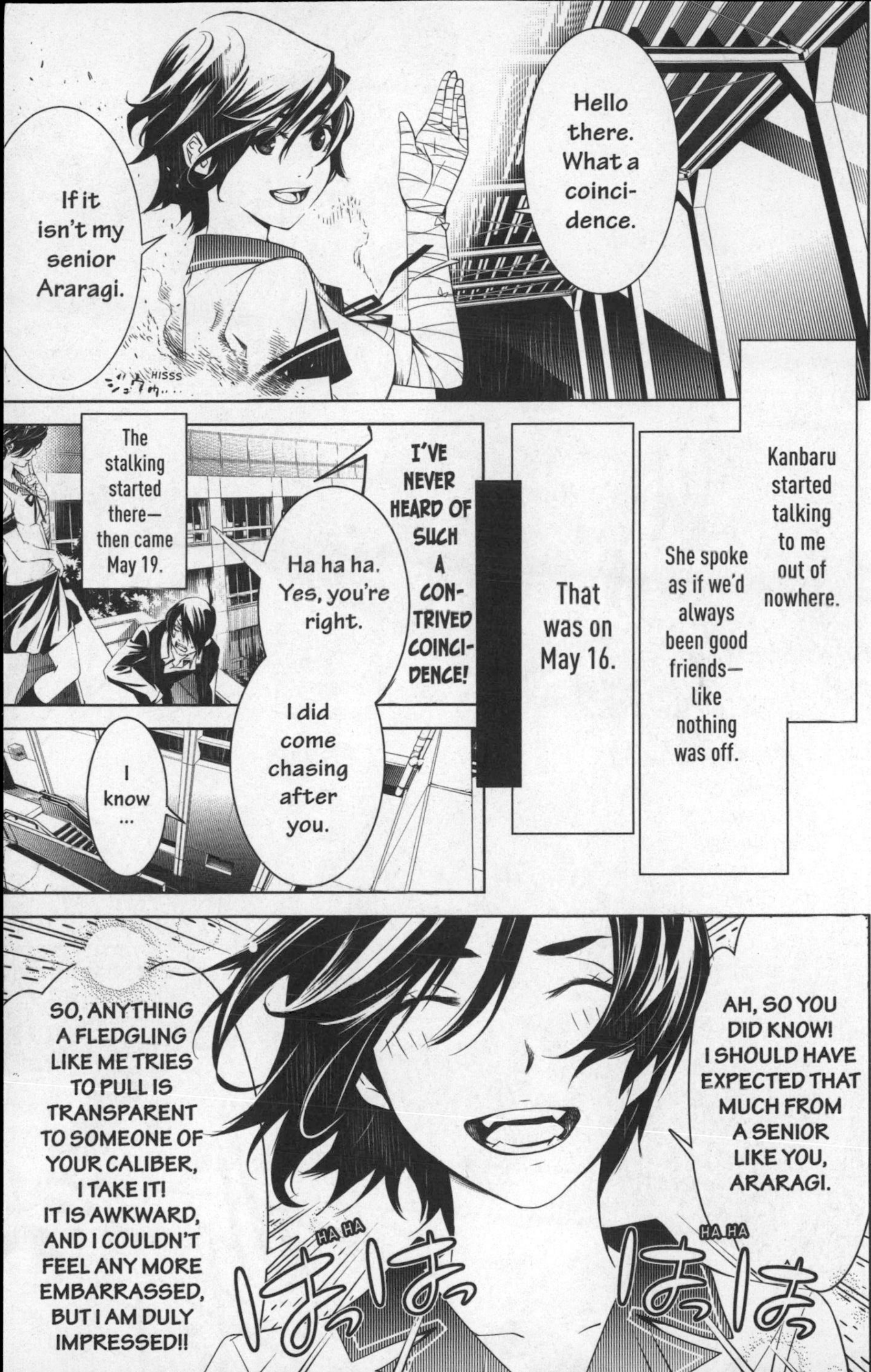
Hello there. What a coincidence.
If it isn't my senior Araragi.
HISSS
Kanbaru started talking to me out of nowhere.
She spoke as if we'd always been good friends—like nothing was off.
That was on May 16.
I'VE NEVER HEARD OF SUCH A CONTRIVED COINCIDENCE!
Ha ha ha. Yes, you're right.
The stalking started there—then came May 19.
I did come chasing after you.
I know ...
AH, SO YOU DID KNOW! I SHOULD HAVE EXPECTED THAT MUCH FROM A SENIOR LIKE YOU, ARARAGI.
HA HA
HA HA
SO, ANYTHING A FLEDGLING LIKE ME TRIES TO PULL IS TRANSPARENT TO SOMEONE OF YOUR CALIBER, I TAKE IT! IT IS AWKWARD, AND I COULDN'T FEEL ANY MORE EMBARRASSED, BUT I AM DULY IMPRESSED!!

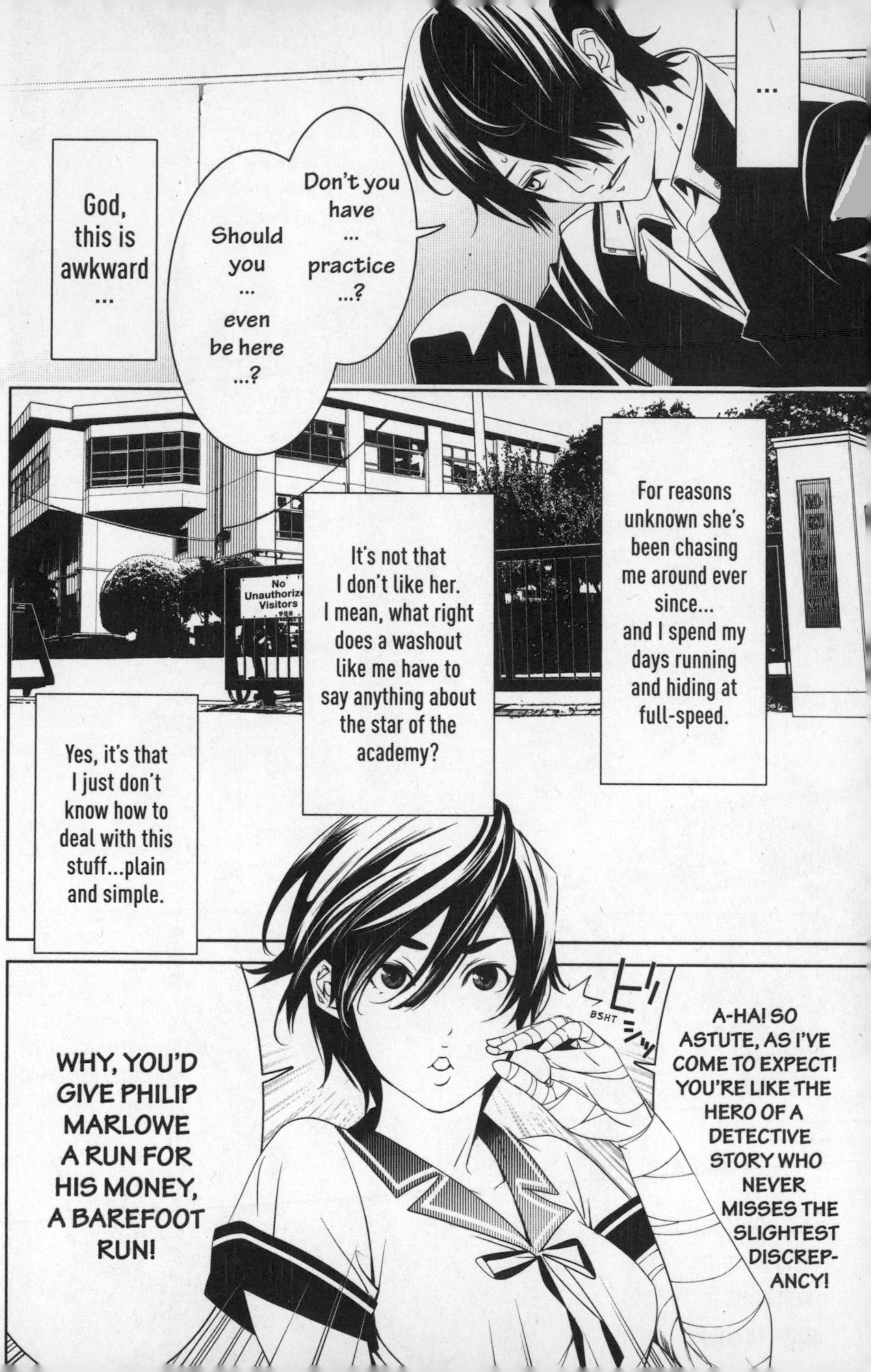
...
Don't you have ... practice ...?
Should you ... even be here ...?
God, this is awkward ...
For reasons unknown she's been chasing me around ever since... and I spend my days running and hiding at full-speed.
It's not that I don't like her. I mean, what right does a washout like me have to say anything about the star of the academy?
Yes, it's that I just don't know how to deal with this stuff...plain and simple.
A-HA! SO ASTUTE, AS I'VE COME TO EXPECT! YOU'RE LIKE THE HERO OF A DETECTIVE STORY WHO NEVER MISSES THE SLIGHTEST DISCREP-ANCY!
BSHT
WHY, YOU'D GIVE PHILIP MARLOWE A RUN FOR HIS MONEY, A BAREFOOT RUN!

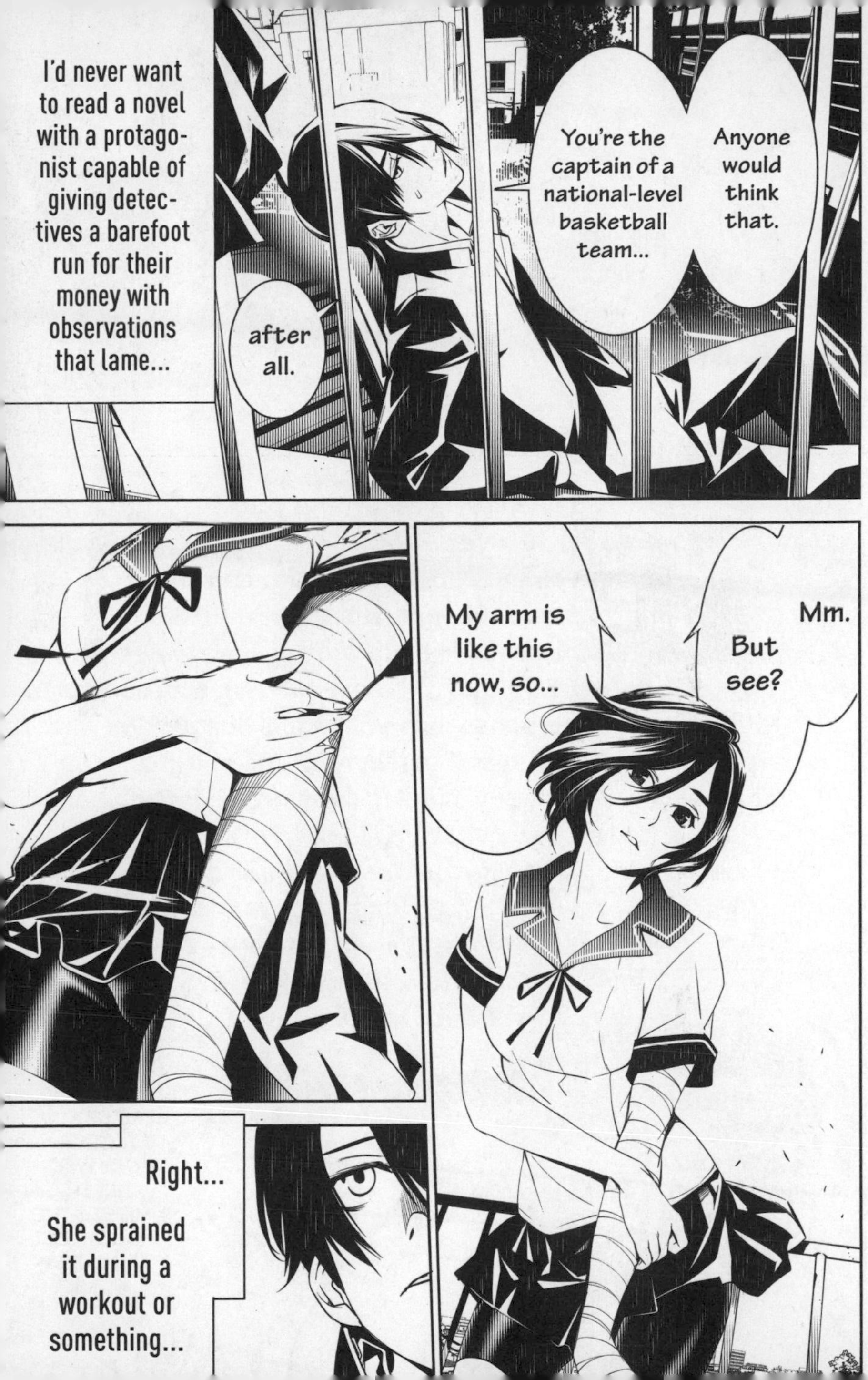
Anyone would think that.
You're the captain of a national-level basketball team...
after all.
I'd never want to read a novel with a protagonist capable of giving detectives a barefoot run for their money with observations that lame...
Mm. But see?
My arm is like this now, so...
Right...
She sprained it during a workout or something...

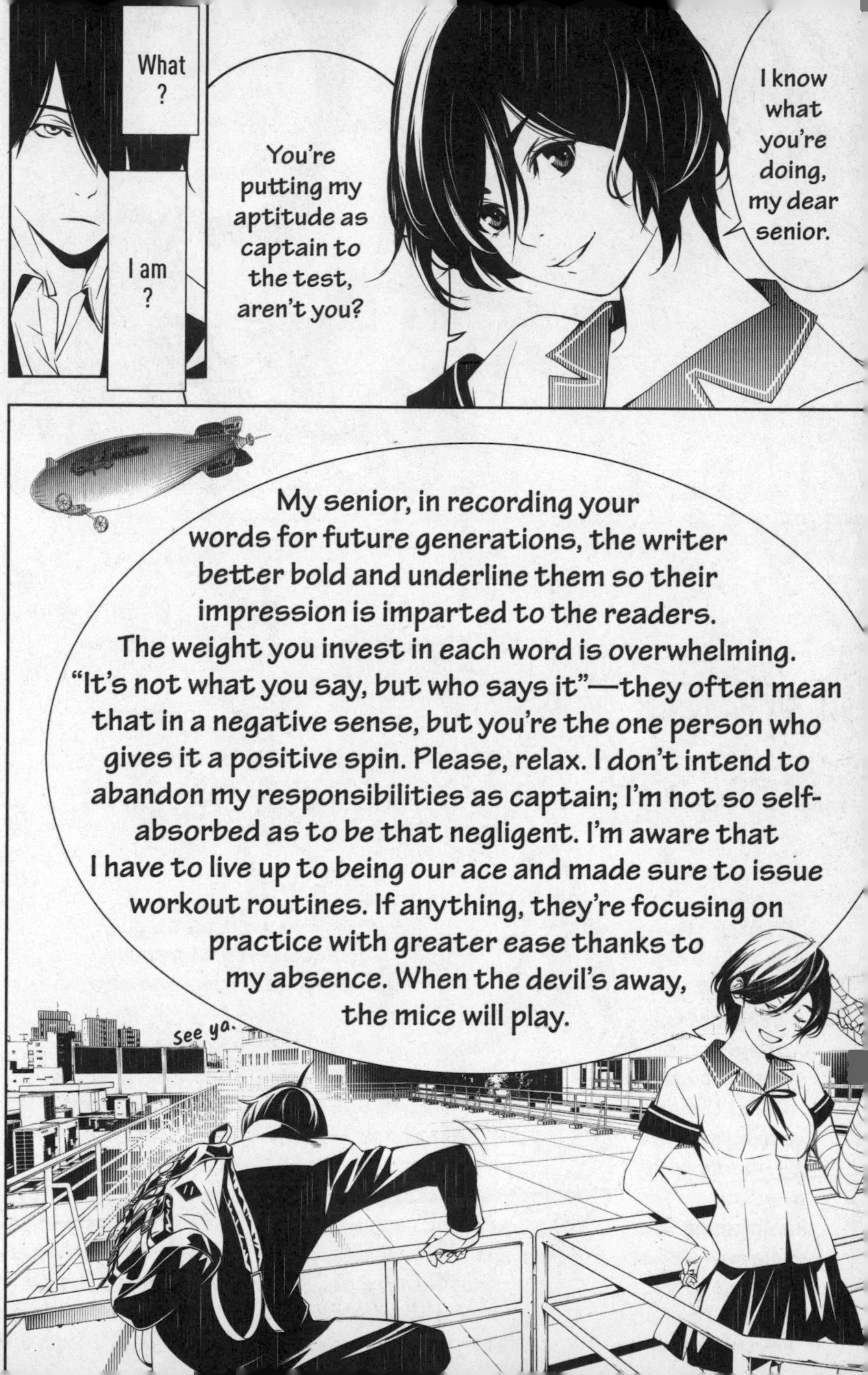
I know what you're doing, my dear senior.
You're putting my aptitude as captain to the test, aren't you?
What?
I am?
My senior, in recording your words for future generations, the writer better bold and underline them so their impression is imparted to the readers. The weight you invest in each word is overwhelming. "It's not what you say, but who says it"—they often mean that in a negative sense, but you're the one person who gives it a positive spin. Please, relax. I don't intend to abandon my responsibilities as captain; I'm not so self-absorbed as to be that negligent. I'm aware that I have to live up to being our ace and made sure to issue workout routines. If anything, they're focusing on practice with greater ease thanks to my absence. When the devil's away, the mice will play.
See ya.

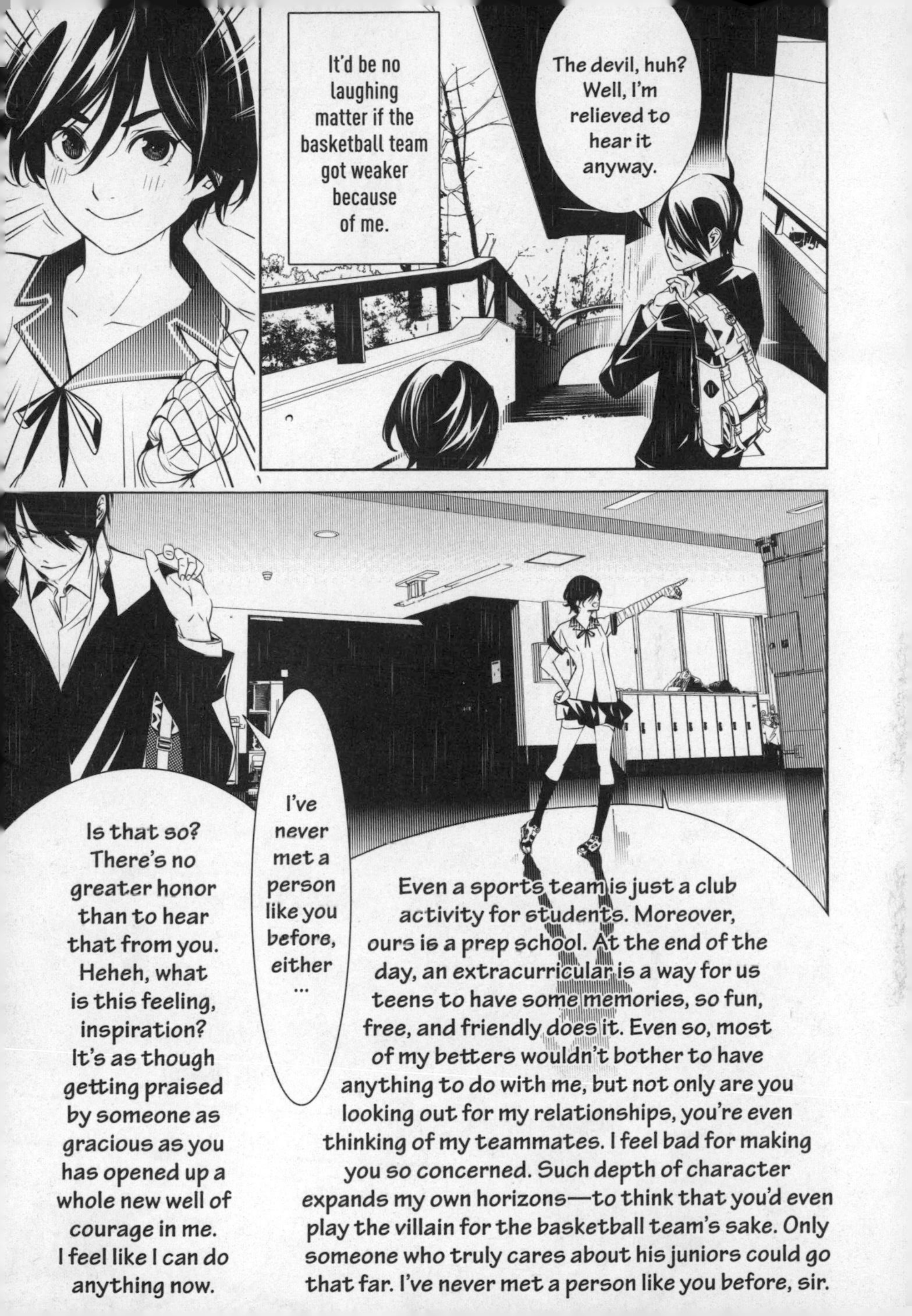
The devil, huh? Well, I'm relieved to hear it anyway.
It'd be no laughing matter if the basketball team got weaker because of me.
Even a sports team is just a club activity for students. Moreover, ours is a prep school. At the end of the day, an extracurricular is a way for us teens to have some memories, so fun, free, and friendly does it. Even so, most of my betters wouldn't bother to have anything to do with me, but not only are you looking out for my relationships, you're even thinking of my teammates. I feel bad for making you so concerned. Such depth of character expands my own horizons—to think that you'd even play the villain for the basketball team's sake. Only someone who truly cares about his juniors could go that far. I've never met a person like you before, sir.
I've never met a person like you before, either ...
Is that so? There's no greater honor than to hear that from you. Heheh, what is this feeling, inspiration? It's as though getting praised by someone as gracious as you has opened up a whole new well of courage in me. I feel like I can do anything now.

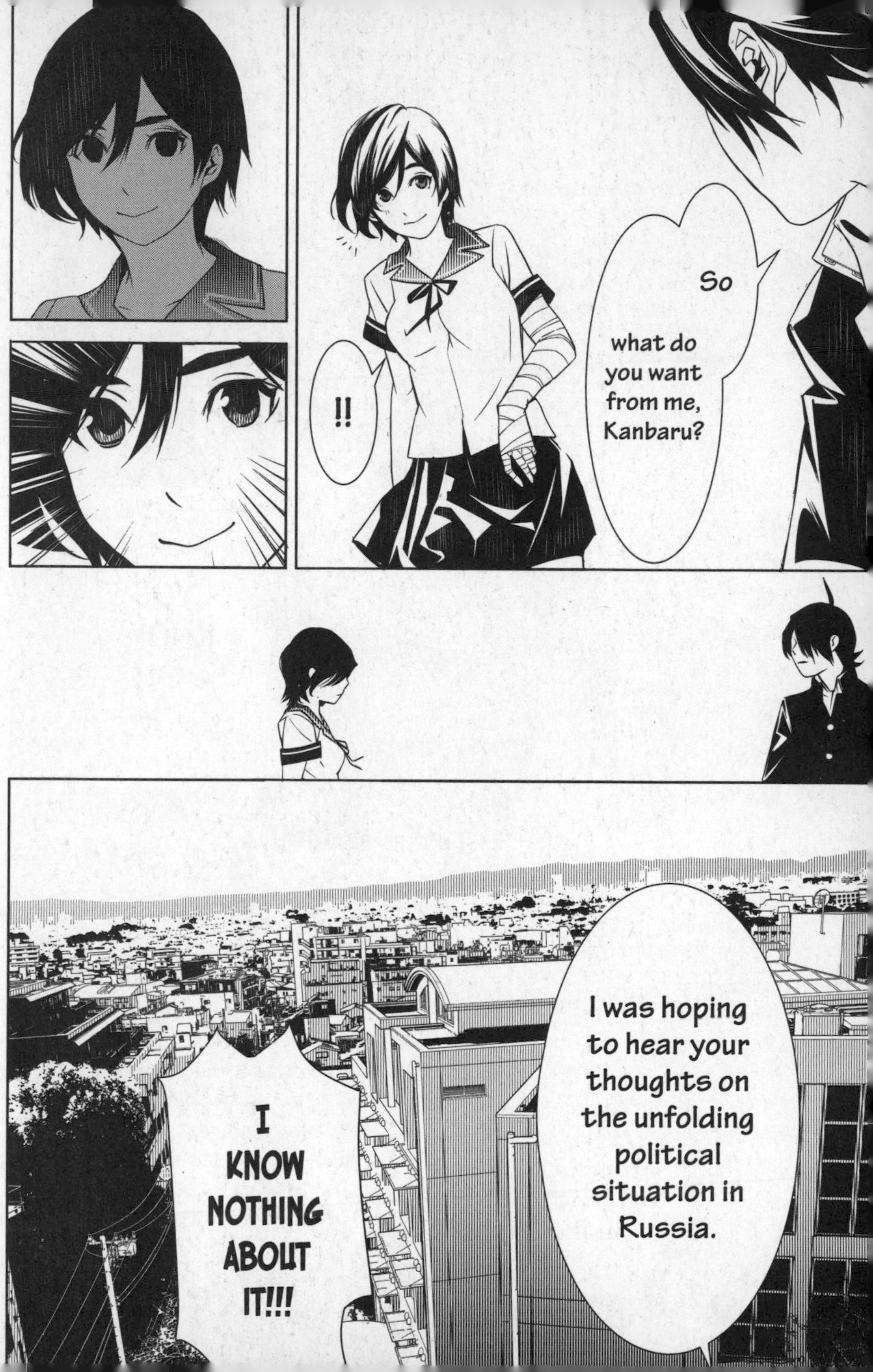
So what do you want from me, Kanbaru?
!!
I was hoping to hear your thoughts on the unfolding political situation in Russia.
I KNOW NOTHING ABOUT IT!!!

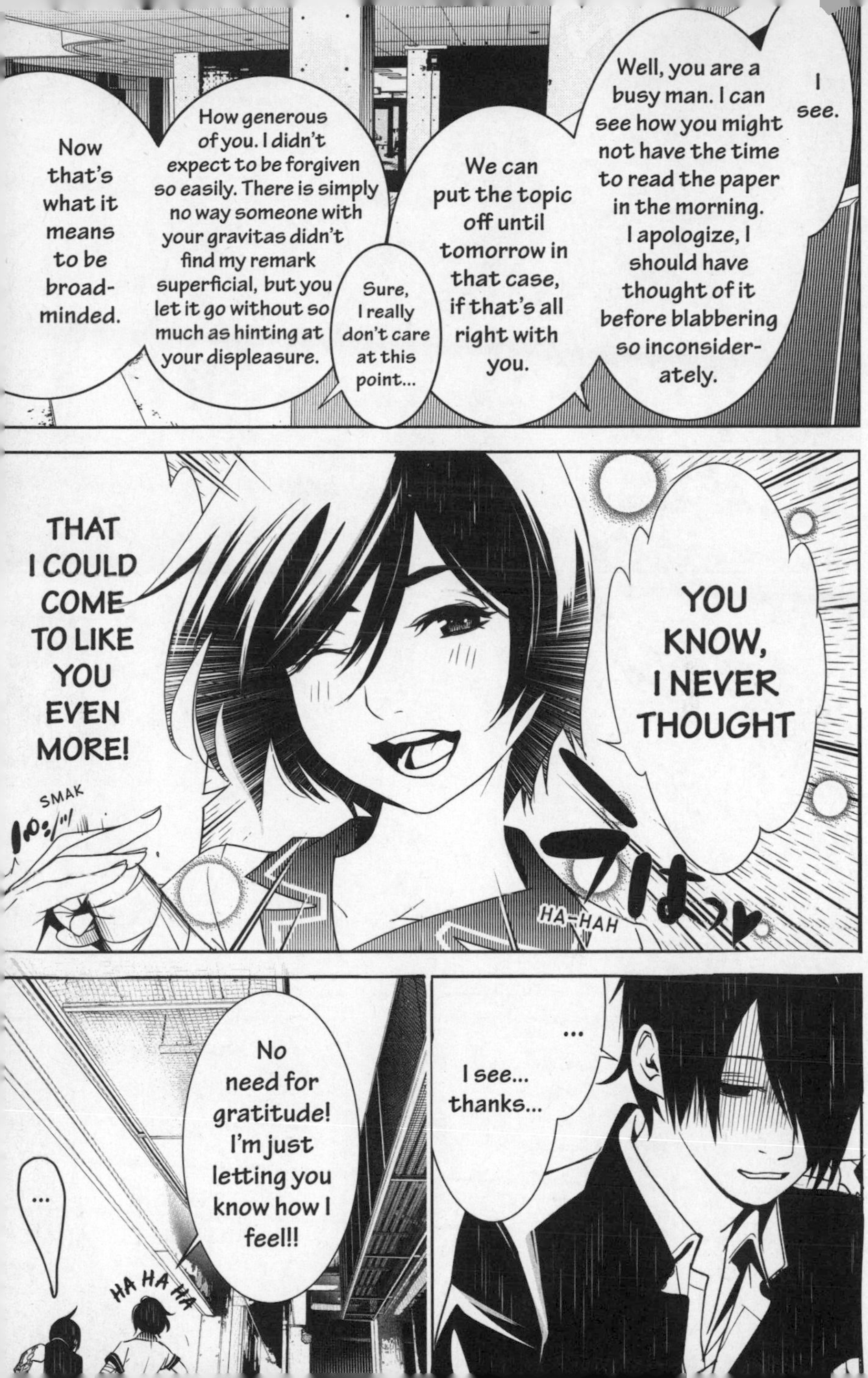
I see.
Well, you are a busy man. I can see how you might not have the time to read the paper in the morning. I apologize, I should have thought of it before blabbering so inconsiderately.
We can put the topic off until tomorrow in that case, if that's all right with you.
Sure, I really don't care at this point...
How generous of you. I didn't expect to be forgiven so easily. There is simply no way someone with your gravitas didn't find my remark superficial, but you let it go without so much as hinting at your displeasure.
Now that's what it means to be broad-minded.
YOU KNOW, I NEVER THOUGHT
HA-HAH
THAT I COULD COME TO LIKE YOU EVEN MORE!
SMAK
...
I see... thanks...
No need for gratitude! I'm just letting you know how I feel!!
...
HA HA HA

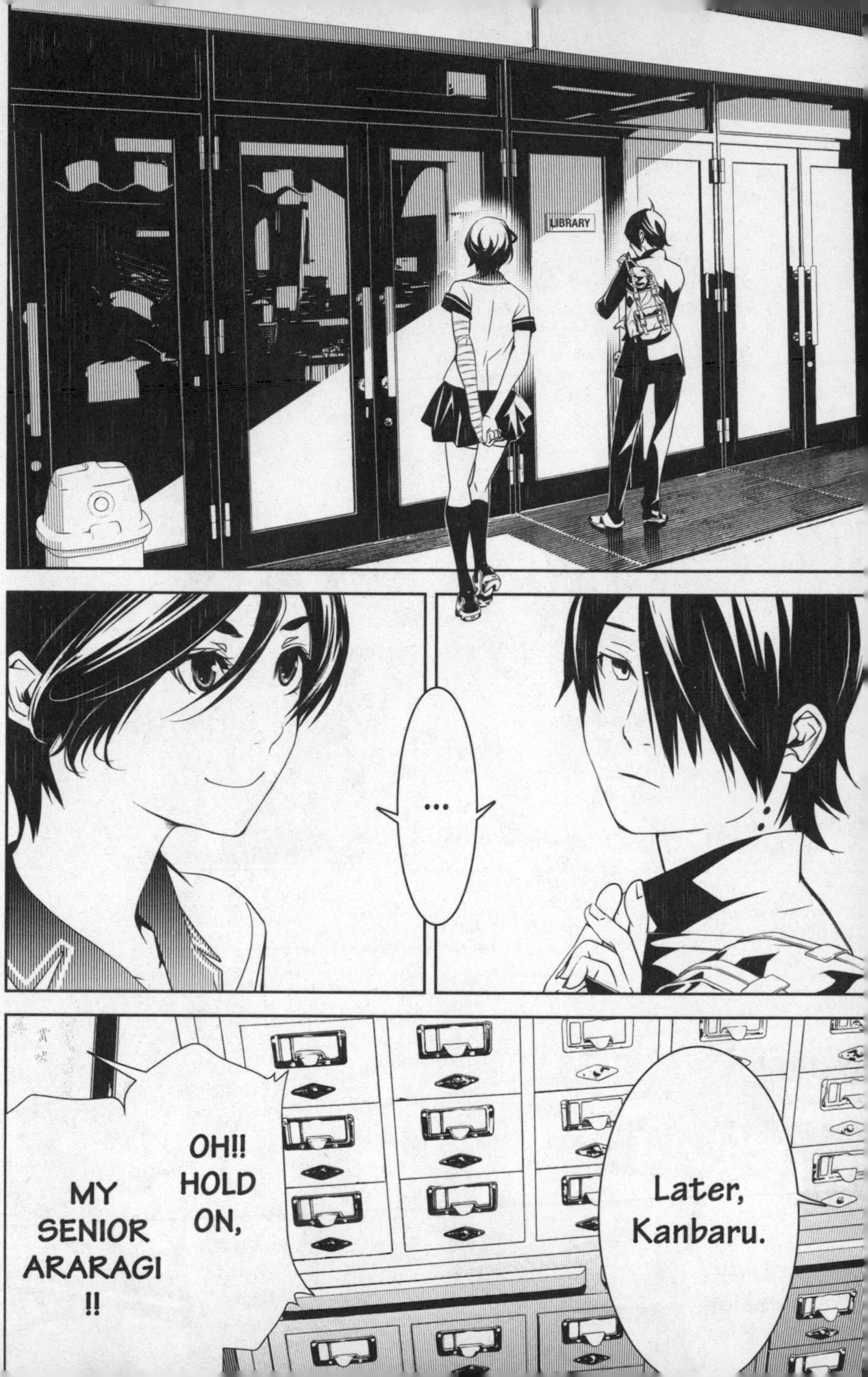
LIBRARY
...
Later, Kanbaru.
OH!! HOLD ON,
MY SENIOR ARARAGI !!

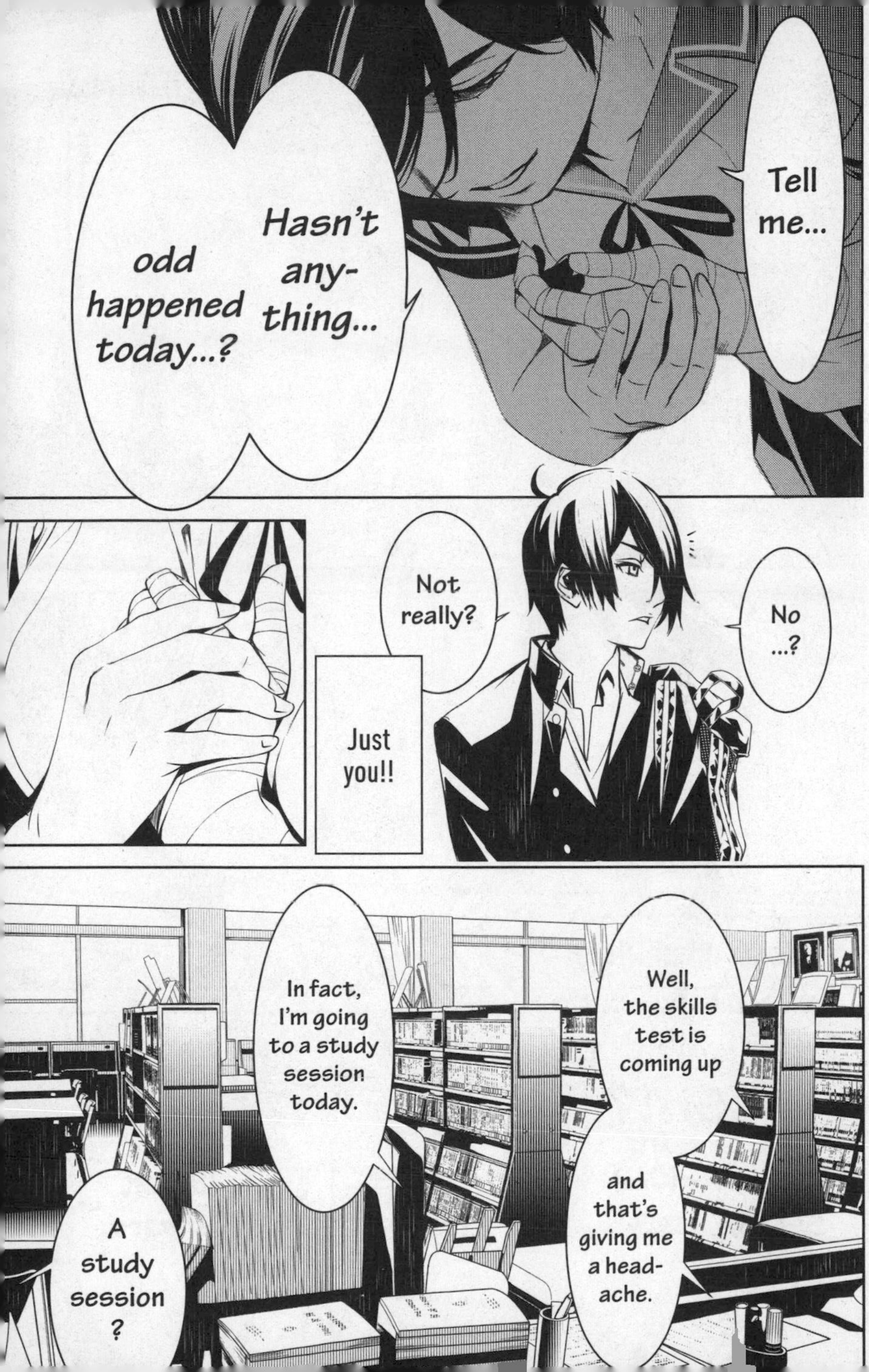
Tell me...
Hasn't anything... odd happened today...?
No ...?
Not really?
Just you!!
Well, the skills test is coming up
and that's giving me a headache.
In fact, I'm going to a study session today.
A study session ?

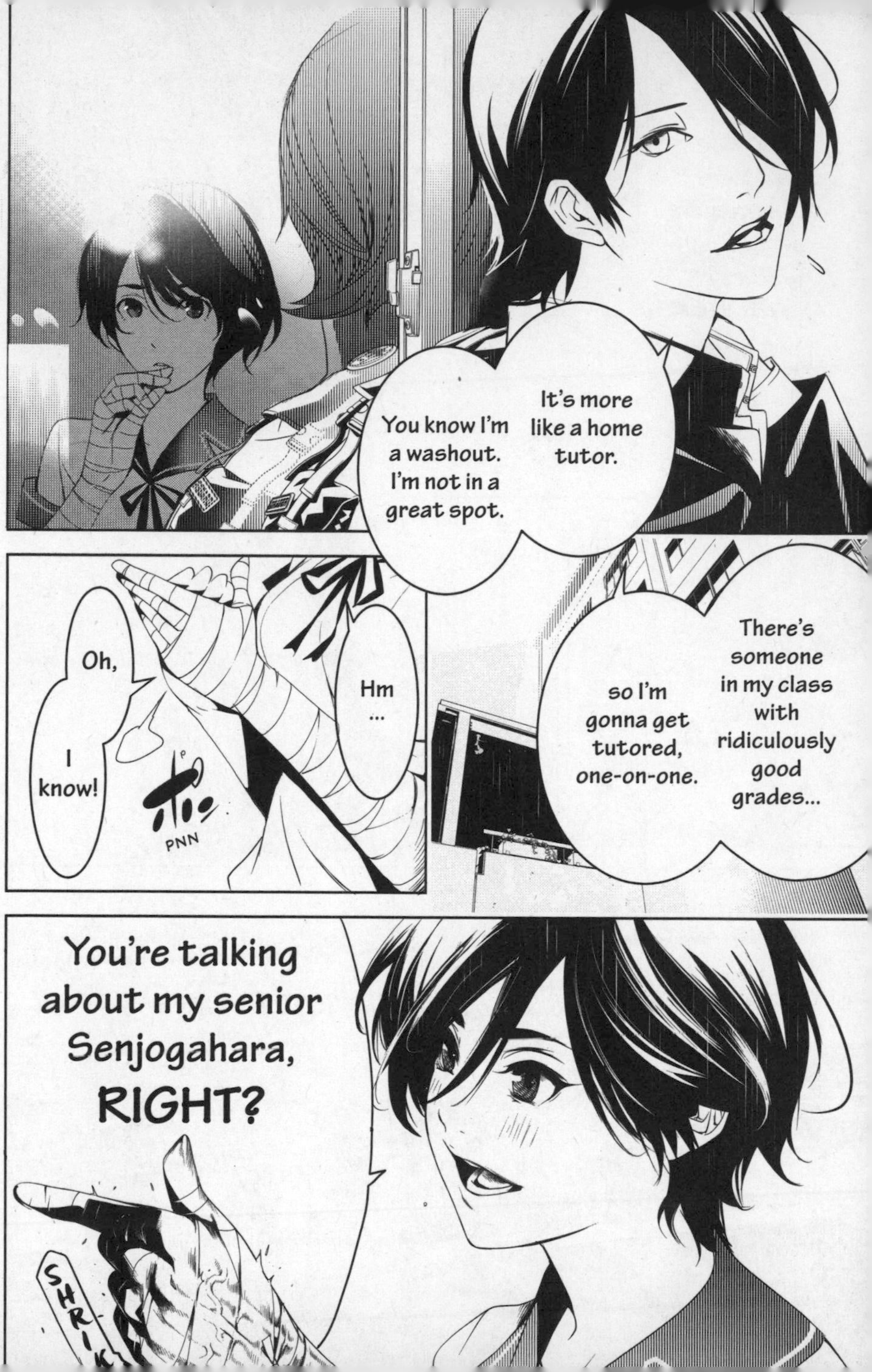
It's more like a home tutor.
You know I'm a washout. I'm not in a great spot.
There's someone in my class with ridiculously good grades...
so I'm gonna get tutored, one-on-one.
Hm ...
PNN
Oh, I know!
You're talking about my senior Senjogahara, RIGHT?
SHRIK

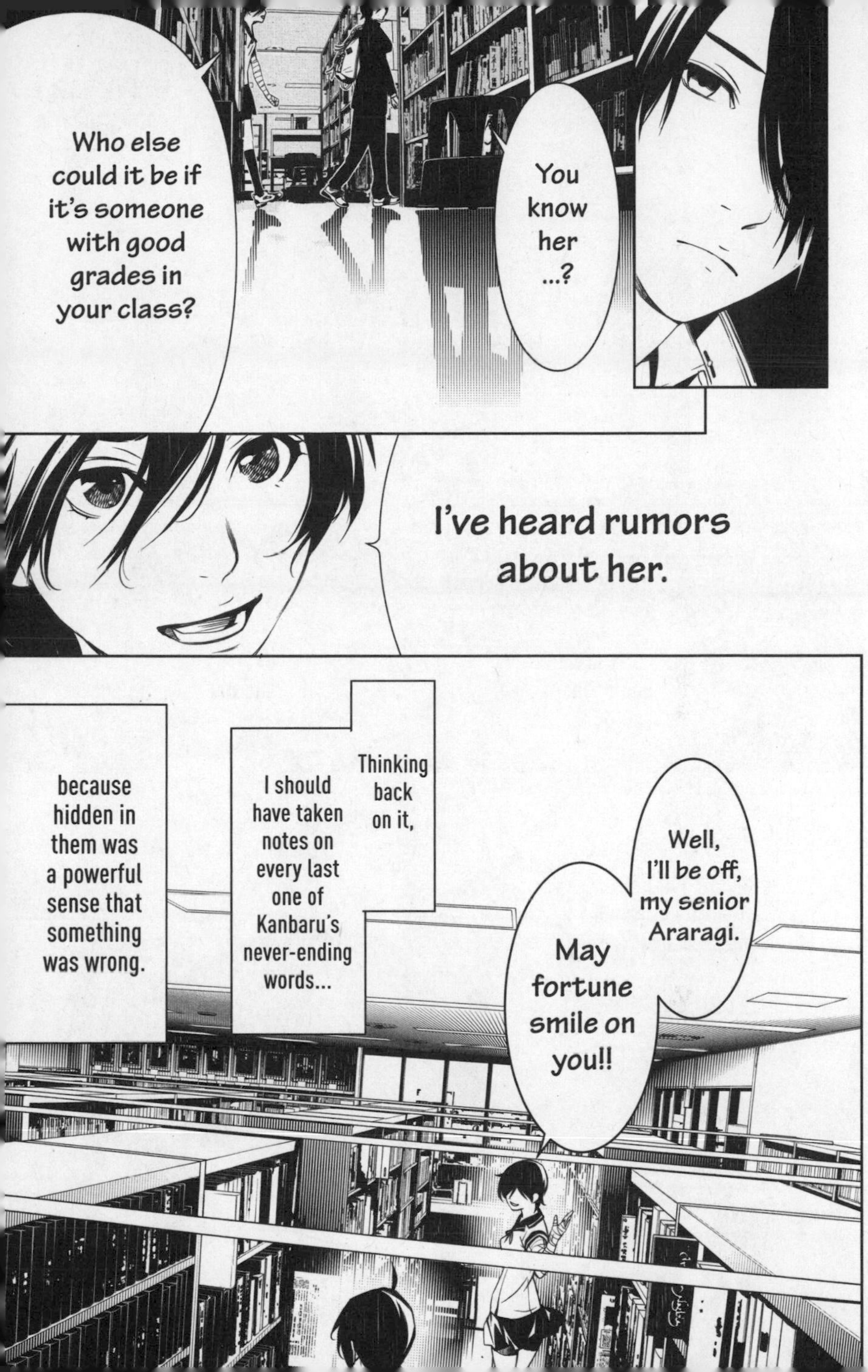
You know her ...?
Who else could it be if it's someone with good grades in your class?
I've heard rumors about her.
Well, I'll be off, my senior Araragi.
May fortune smile on you!!
Thinking back on it,
I should have taken notes on every last one of Kanbaru's never-ending words...
because hidden in them was a powerful sense that something was wrong.

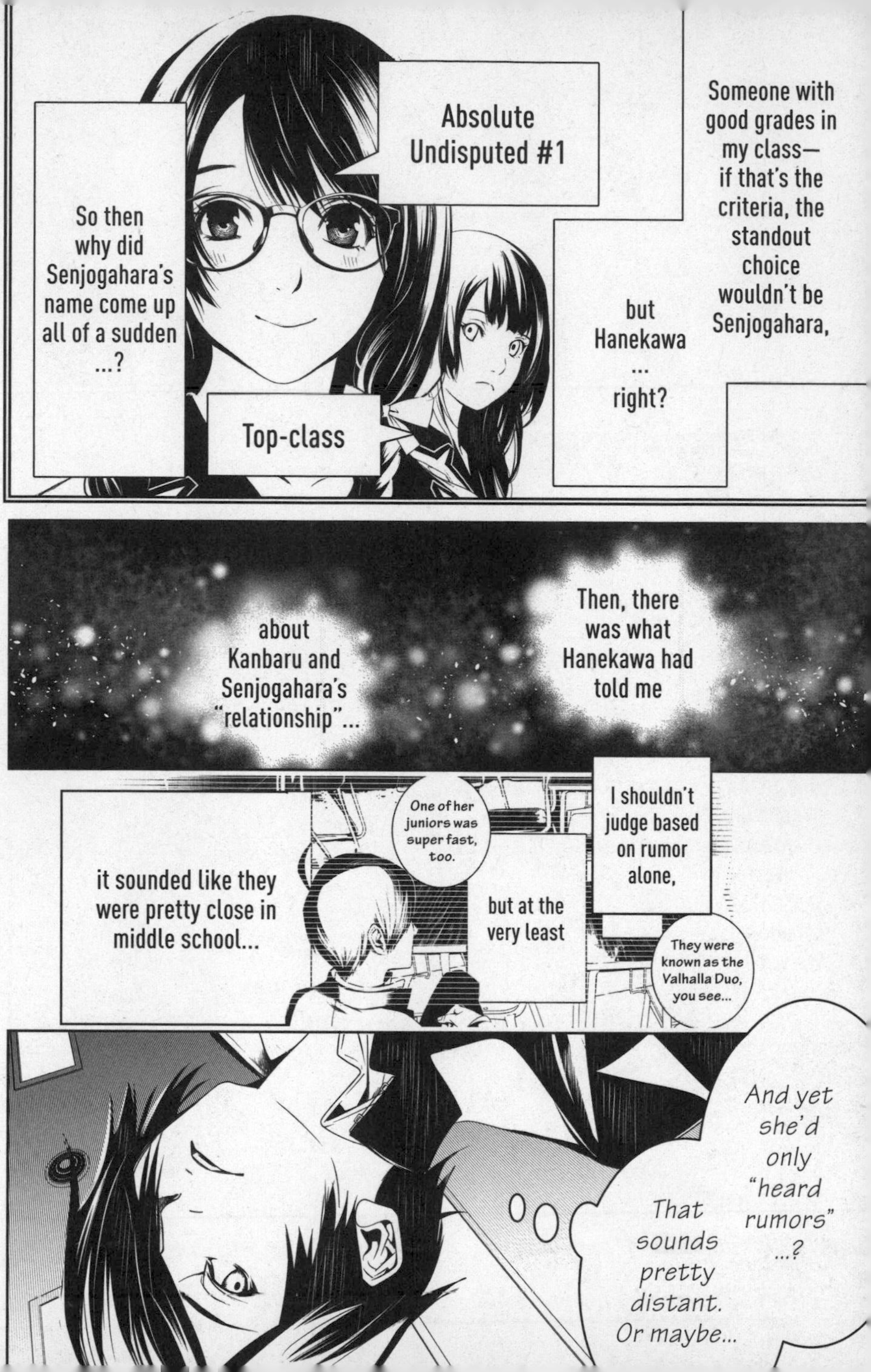
Someone with good grades in my class— if that's the criteria, the standout choice wouldn't be Senjogahara,
but Hanekawa ... right?
Absolute Undisputed #1
So then why did Senjogahara's name come up all of a sudden ...?
Top-class
Then, there was what Hanekawa had told me
about Kanbaru and Senjogahara's "relationship"...
I shouldn't judge based on rumor alone,
One of her juniors was super fast, too.
They were known as the Valhalla Duo, you see...
but at the very least
it sounded like they were pretty close in middle school...
And yet she'd only "heard rumors" ...?
That sounds pretty distant. Or maybe...

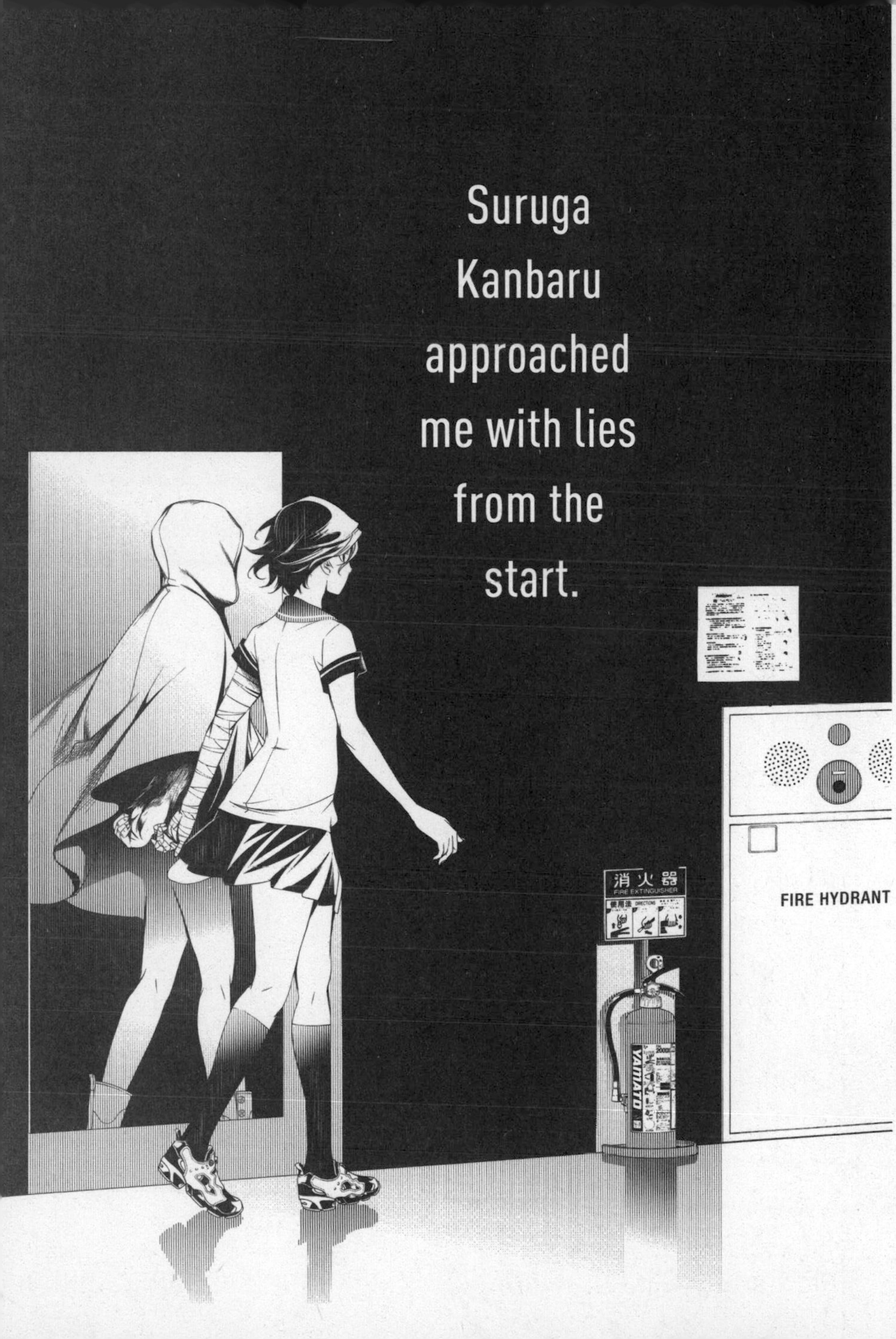
Suruga Kanbaru approached me with lies from the start.
消火器
FIRE EXTINGUISHER
FIRE HYDRANT

化 *bake*

牛勿 *mono*

<u>SURUGAmonkey</u>
4

語 *gatari*

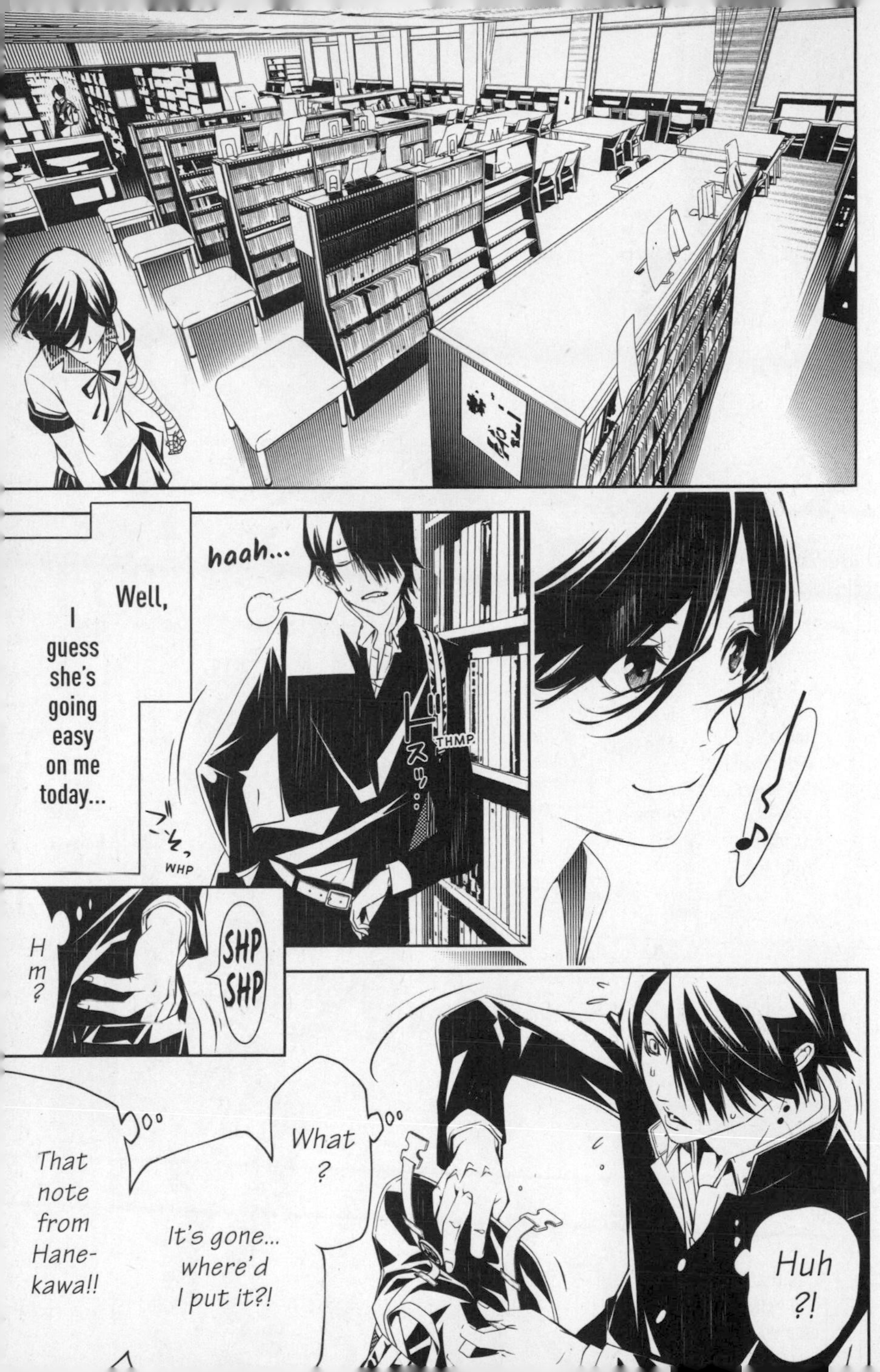
haah...
Well, I guess she's going easy on me today...
THMP
WHP
Hm?
SHP SHP
Huh?!
What?
It's gone... where'd I put it?!
That note from Hanekawa!!

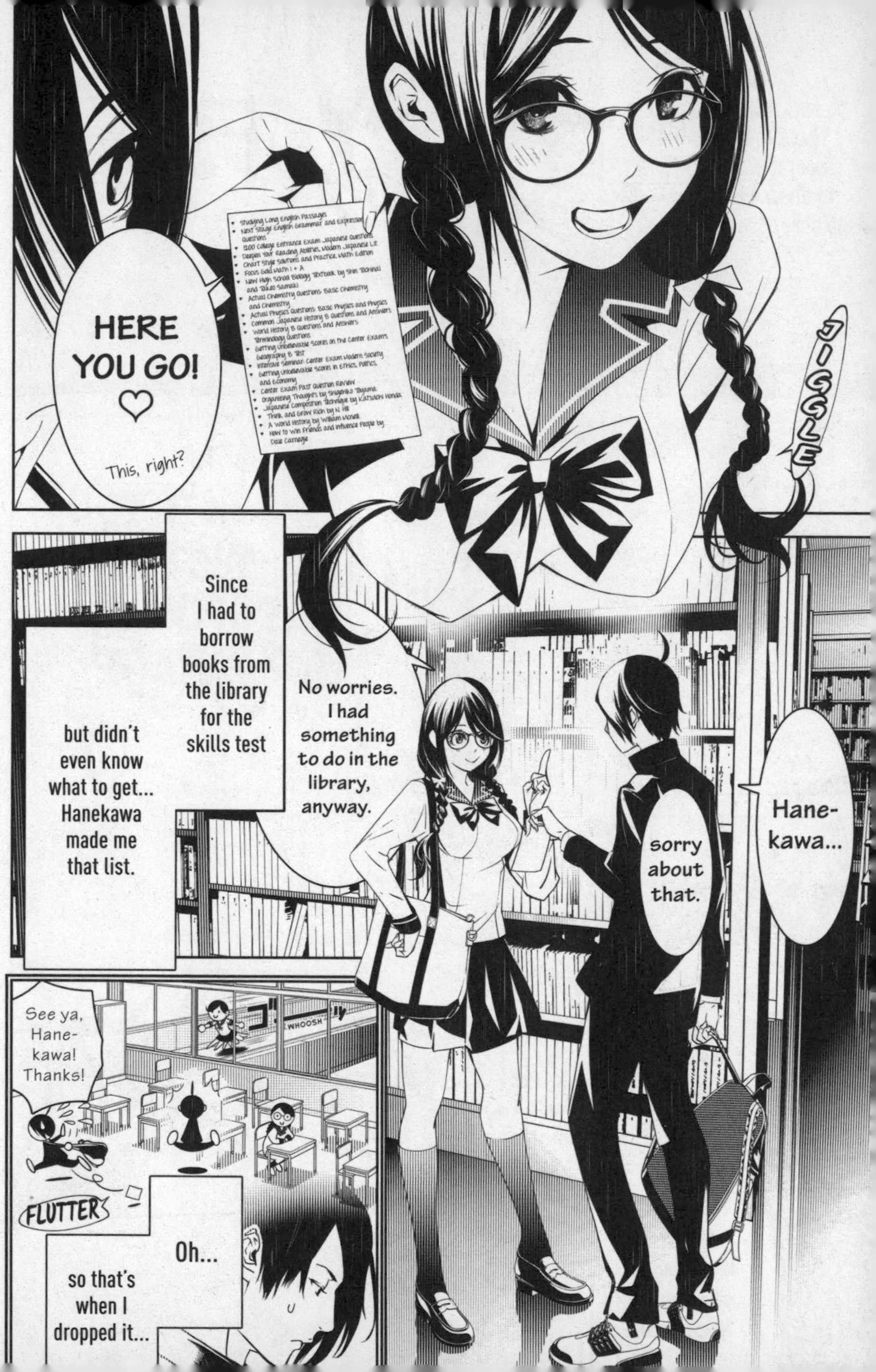
HERE YOU GO! ♡
This, right?
• Studying Long English Passages
• Next Stage English Grammar and Expression Questions
• 1200 College Entrance Exam Japanese Questions
• Deepen Your Reading Abilities, Modern Japanese Lit.
• Chart Style Solutions and Practice, Math Edition
• Focus Gold Math I + A
• New High School Biology Textbook by Shin Tochinai and Takeo Samaki
• Actual Chemistry Questions: Basic Chemistry and Chemistry
• Actual Physics Questions: Basic Physics and Physics
• Common Japanese History B Questions and Answers
• World History B Questions and Answers Terminology Questions
• Getting Unbelievable Scores on the Center Exam's Geography B Test
• Intensive Seminar: Center Exam Modern Society
• Getting Unbelievable Scores in Ethics, Politics, and Economy
• Center Exam Past Question Review
• Organizing Thoughts by Shigehiko Toyama
• Japanese Composition Technique by Katsuichi Honda
• Think and Grow Rich by N. Hill
• A World History by William McNeill
• How to Win Friends and Influence People by Dale Carnegie
JIGGLE
Hane-kawa...
sorry about that.
No worries. I had something to do in the library, anyway.
Since I had to borrow books from the library for the skills test
but didn't even know what to get... Hanekawa made me that list.
See ya, Hane-kawa! Thanks!
WHOOSH
FLUTTER
Oh...
so that's when I dropped it...

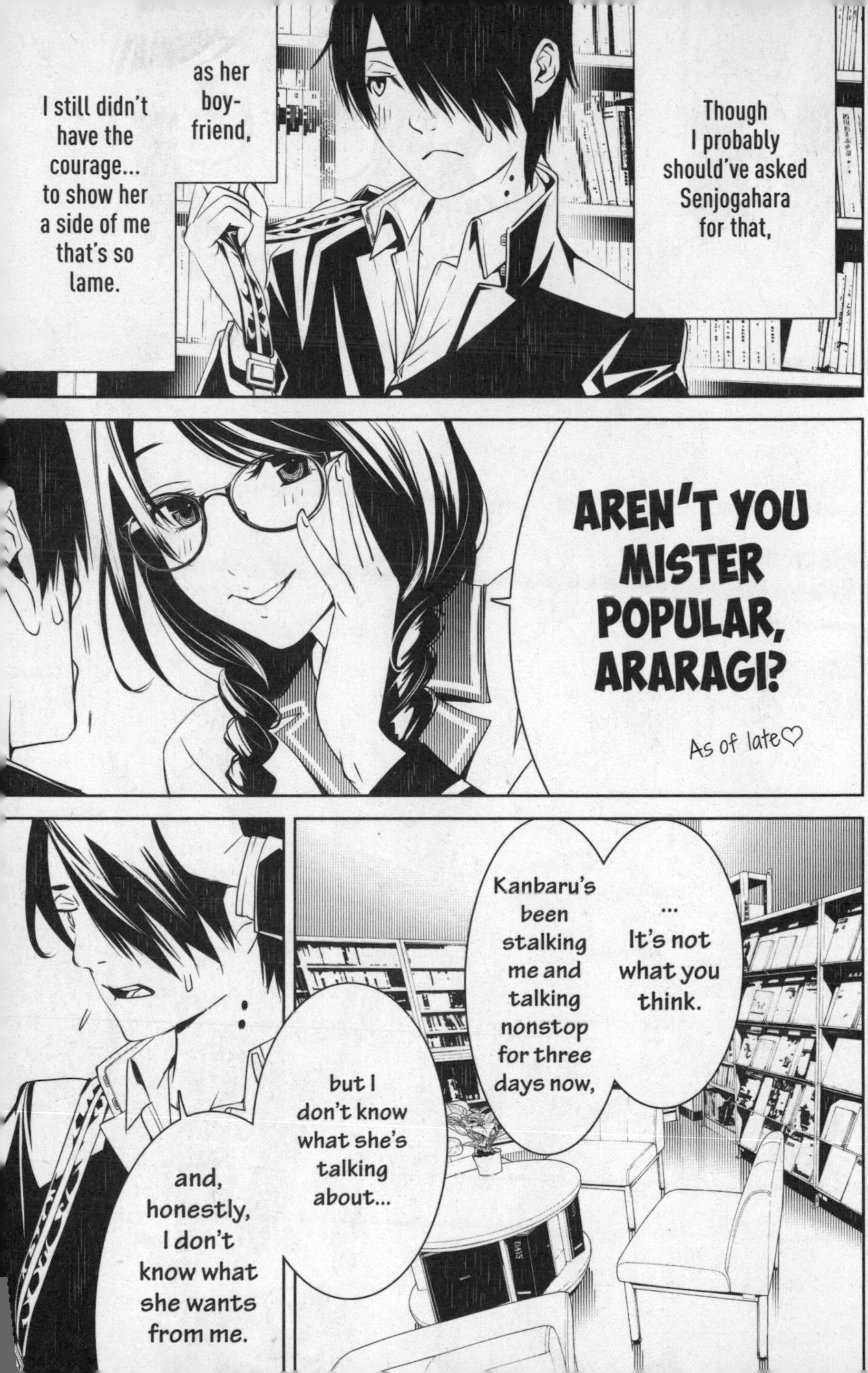
Though I probably should've asked Senjogahara for that,
as her boy-friend,
I still didn't have the courage... to show her a side of me that's so lame.
AREN'T YOU MISTER POPULAR, ARARAGI?
As of late♡
... It's not what you think.
Kanbaru's been stalking me and talking nonstop for three days now,
but I don't know what she's talking about...
and, honestly, I don't know what she wants from me.

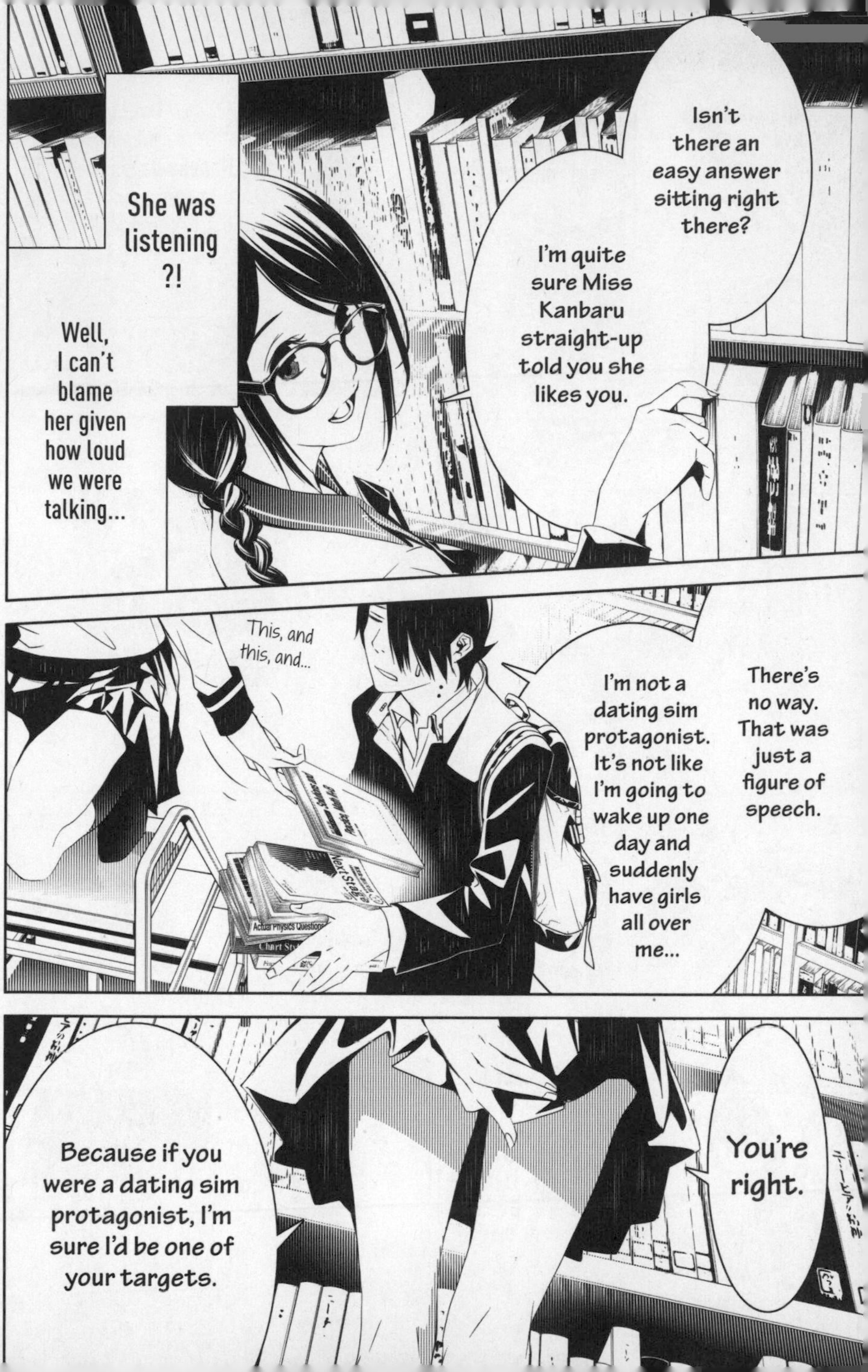
Isn't there an easy answer sitting right there?
I'm quite sure Miss Kanbaru straight-up told you she likes you.
She was listening?!
Well, I can't blame her given how loud we were talking...
There's no way. That was just a figure of speech.
I'm not a dating sim protagonist. It's not like I'm going to wake up one day and suddenly have girls all over me...
This, and this, and...
You're right.
Because if you were a dating sim protagonist, I'm sure I'd be one of your targets.

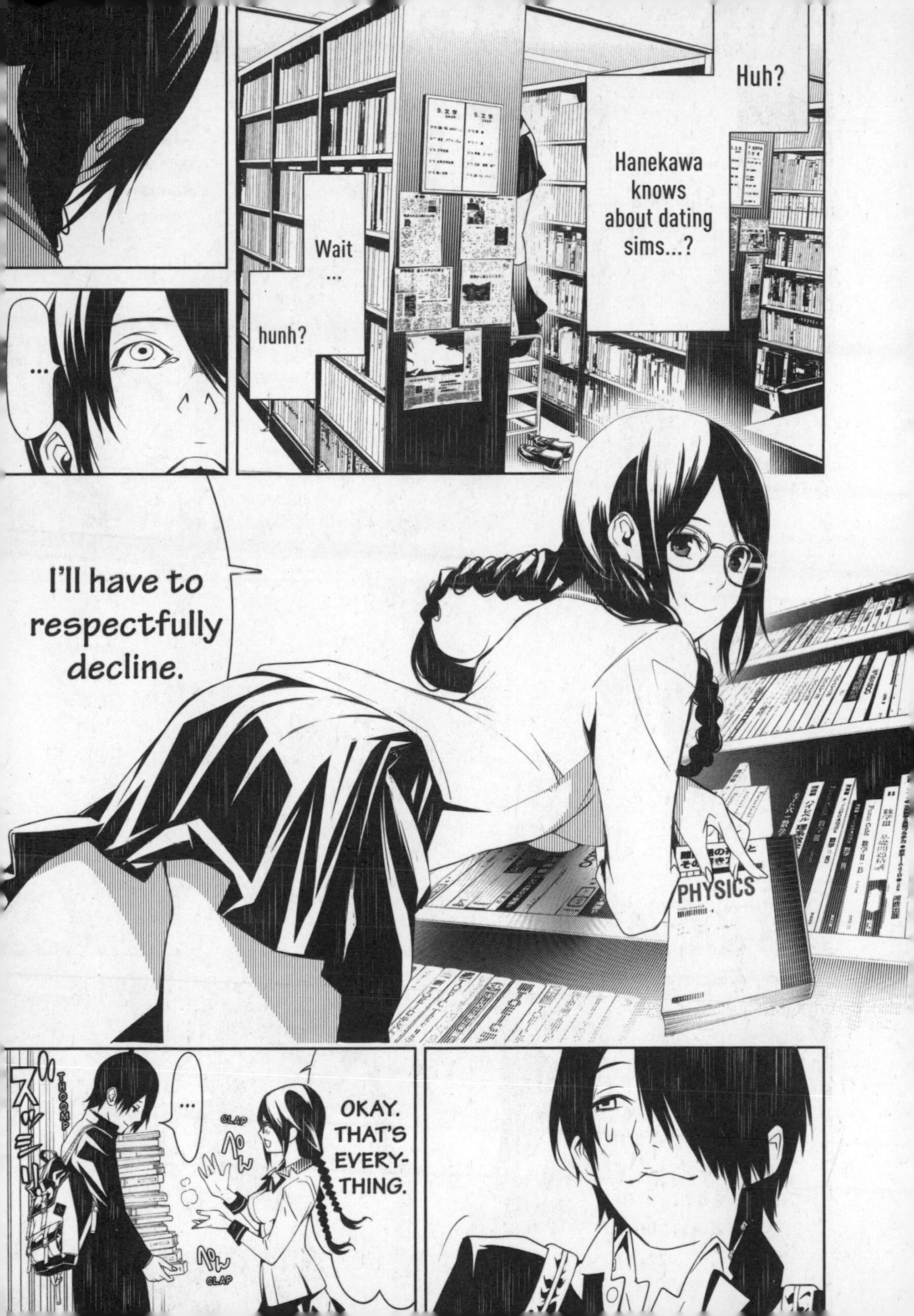
Huh?
Hanekawa knows about dating sims...?
Wait ... hunh?
...
I'll have to respectfully decline.
PHYSICS
OKAY. THAT'S EVERY-THING.
CLAP
CLAP
...
THOOOMP

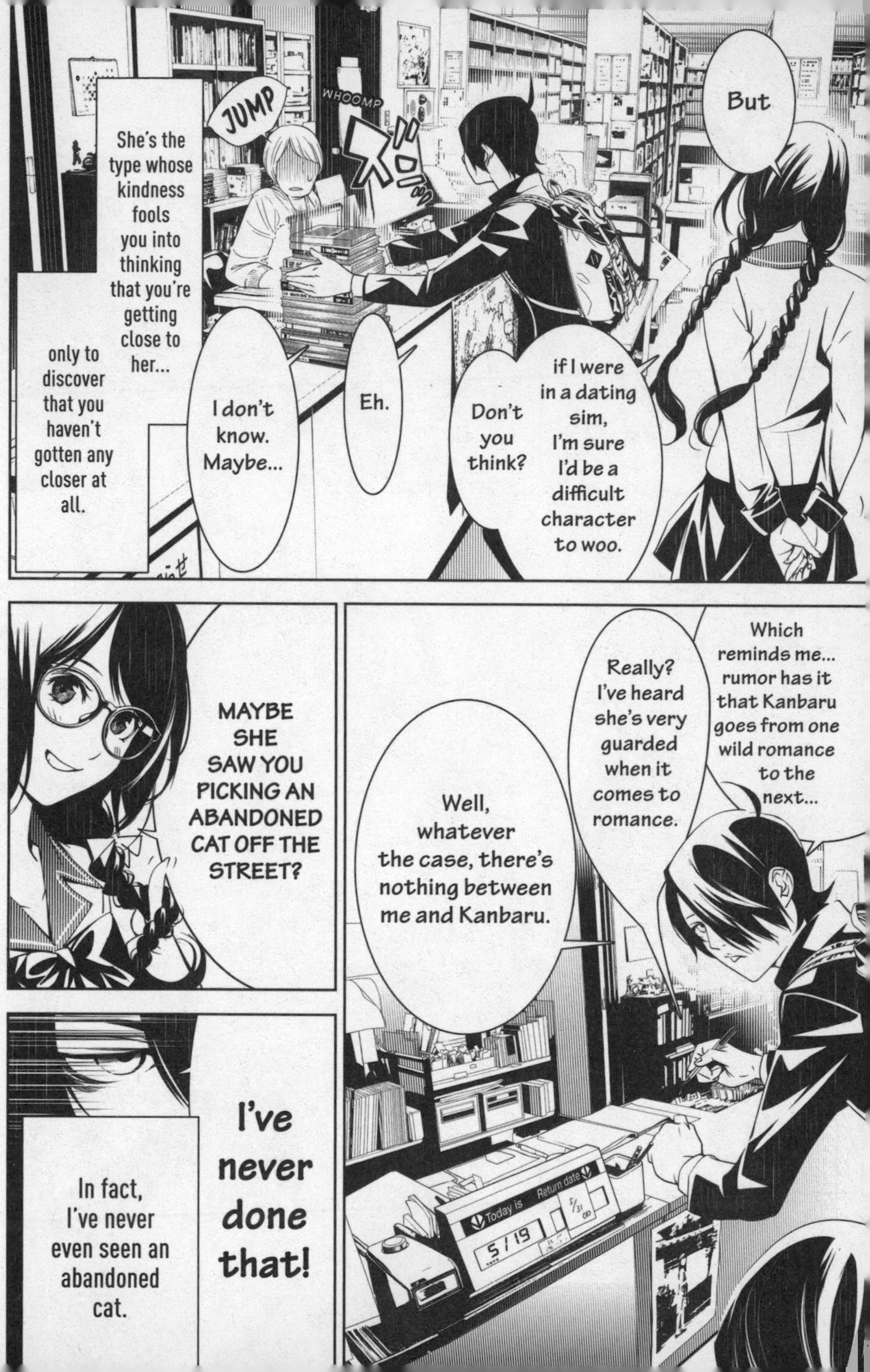
But
if I were in a dating sim, I'm sure I'd be a difficult character to woo.
Don't you think?
WHOOMP
JUMP
Eh.
I don't know. Maybe...
She's the type whose kindness fools you into thinking that you're getting close to her...
only to discover that you haven't gotten any closer at all.
Which reminds me... rumor has it that Kanbaru goes from one wild romance to the next...
Really? I've heard she's very guarded when it comes to romance.
Well, whatever the case, there's nothing between me and Kanbaru.
Today is
Return date
5/19
5/31
MAYBE SHE SAW YOU PICKING AN ABANDONED CAT OFF THE STREET?
I've never done that!
In fact, I've never even seen an abandoned cat.

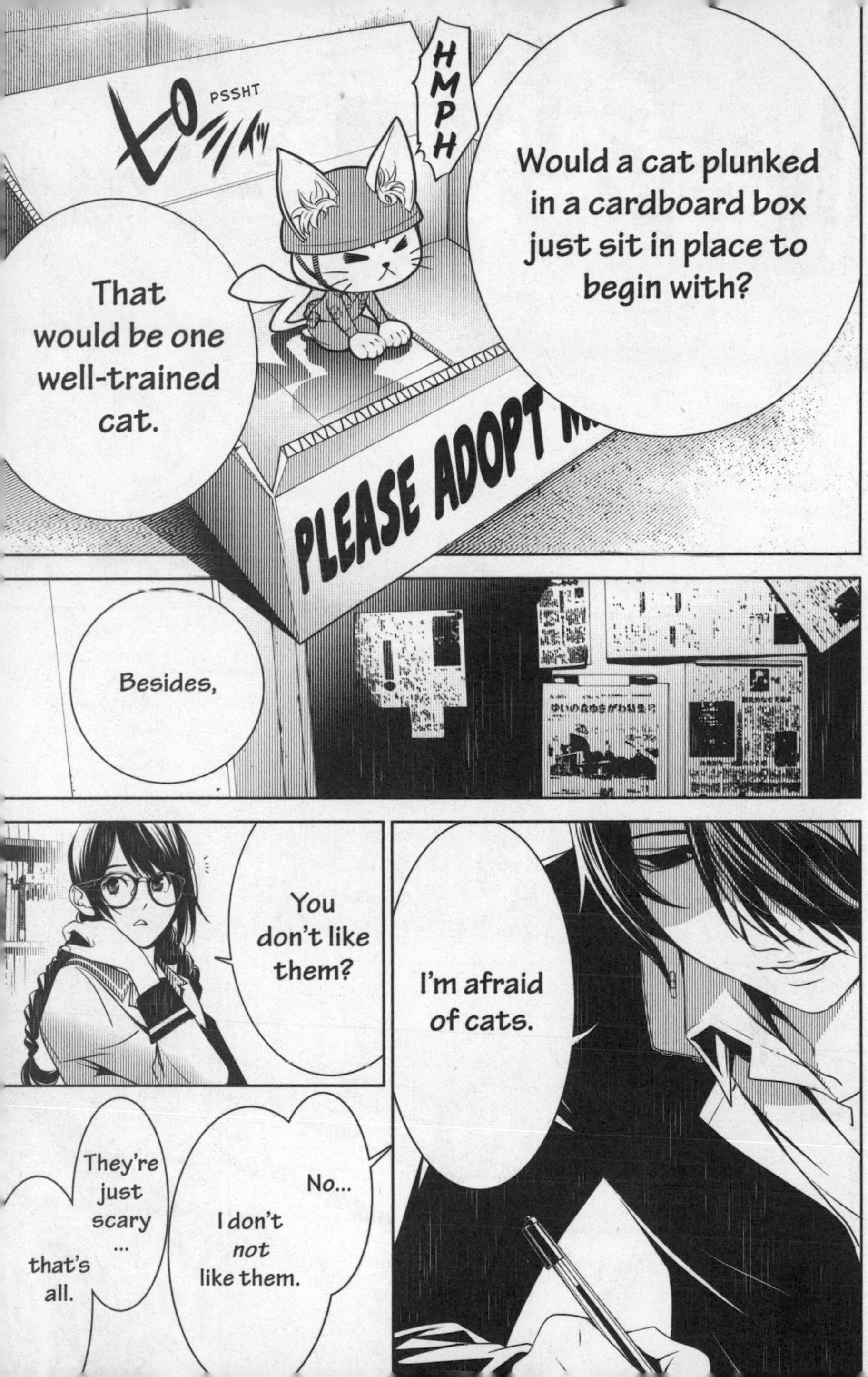
Would a cat plunked in a cardboard box just sit in place to begin with?
HMPH
PSSHT
That would be one well-trained cat.
PLEASE ADOPT
Besides,
I'm afraid of cats.
You don't like them?
No... I don't *not* like them.
They're just scary ... that's all.

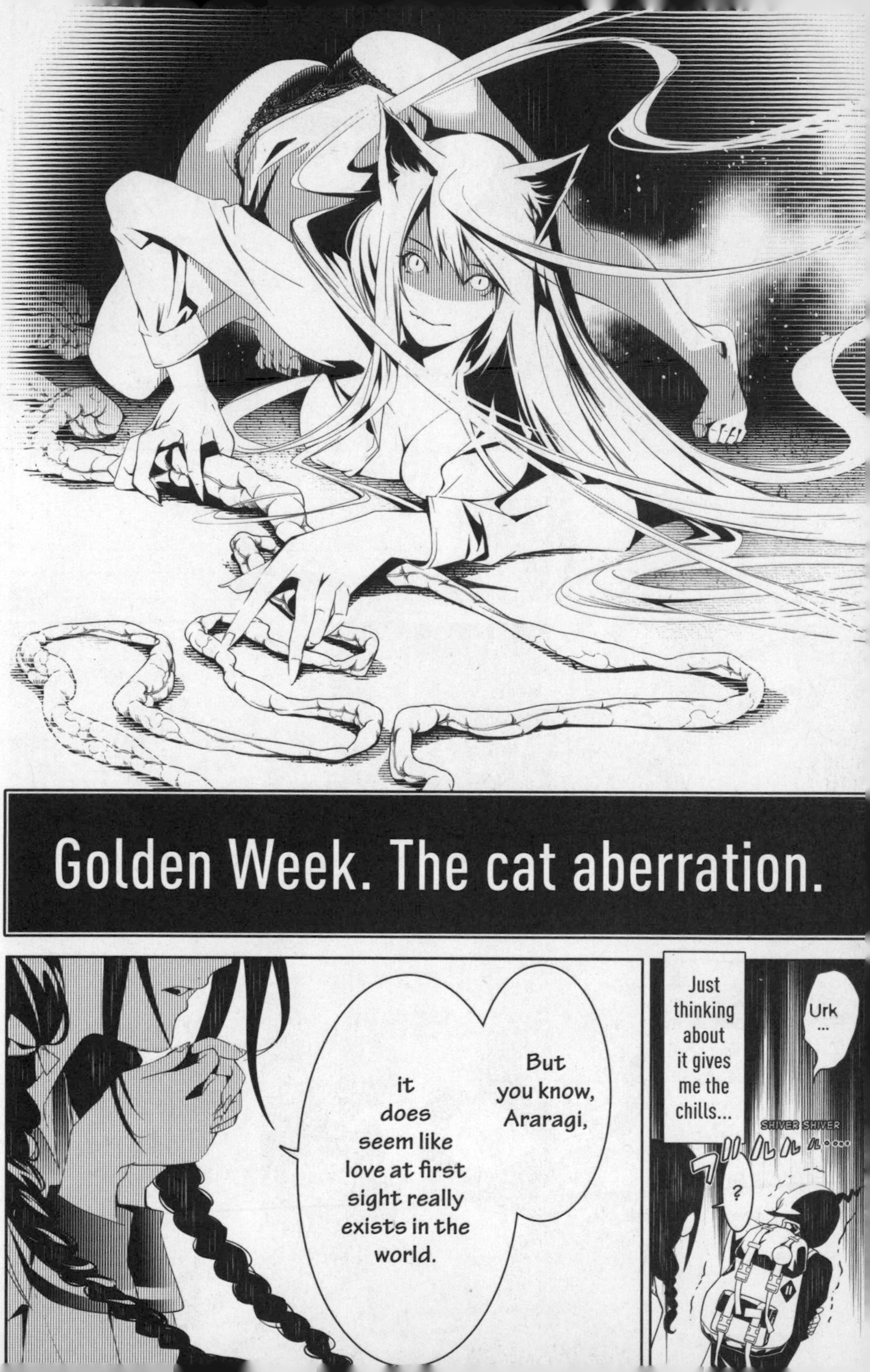
Golden Week. The cat aberration.
Just thinking about it gives me the chills...
Urk ...
SHIVER SHIVER
?
But you know, Araragi,
it does seem like love at first sight really exists in the world.

I mean, that's how you fell in love with Miss Senjogahara, RIIIIIIGHT? ♫

What're you, a grade schooler?

By the way, the fact that Senjogahara and I were going out

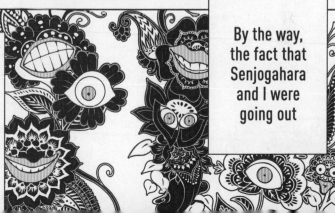

was public knowledge at that point.

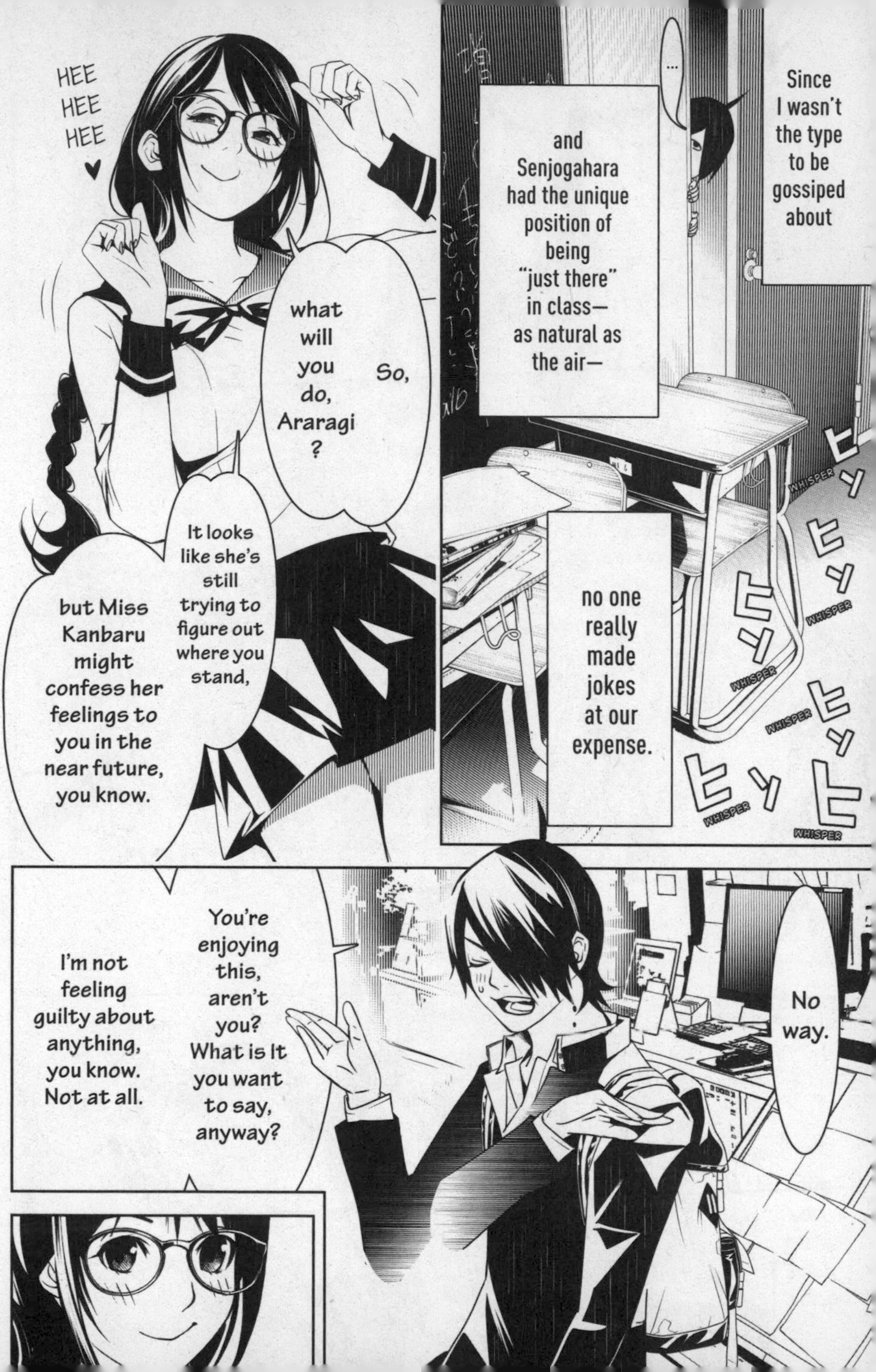

Since I wasn't the type to be gossiped about
...
and Senjogahara had the unique position of being "just there" in class— as natural as the air—
no one really made jokes at our expense.
WHISPER
WHISPER
WHISPER
WHISPER
WHISPER
WHISPER
HEE HEE HEE ♥
So, what will you do, Araragi?
It looks like she's still trying to figure out where you stand,
but Miss Kanbaru might confess her feelings to you in the near future, you know.
No way.
You're enjoying this, aren't you? What is It you want to say, anyway?
I'm not feeling guilty about anything, you know. Not at all.

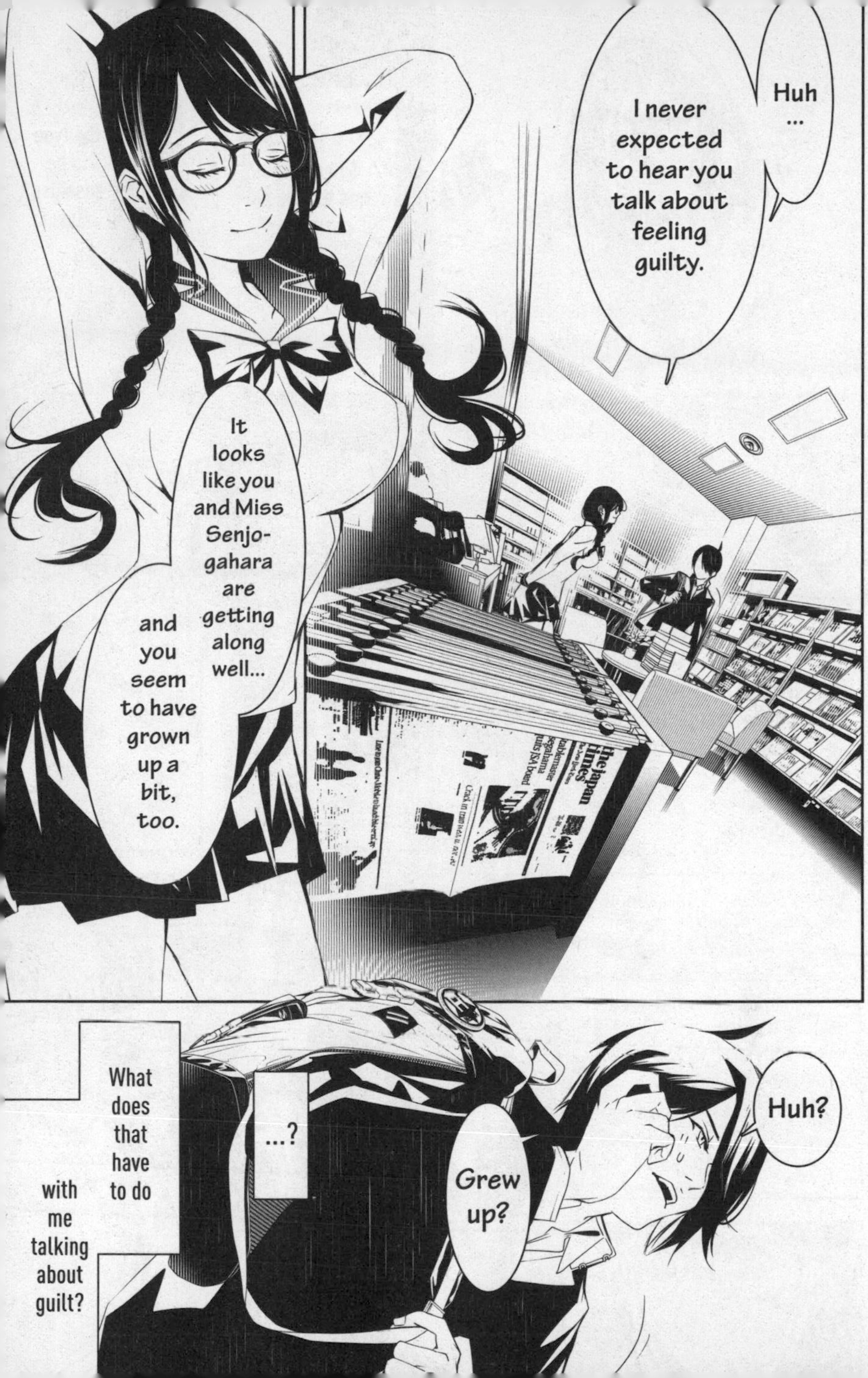
Huh ...
I never expected to hear you talk about feeling guilty.
It looks like you and Miss Senjo-gahara are getting along well...
and you seem to have grown up a bit, too.
the japan times
Huh?
Grew up?
...?
What does that have to do with me talking about guilt?

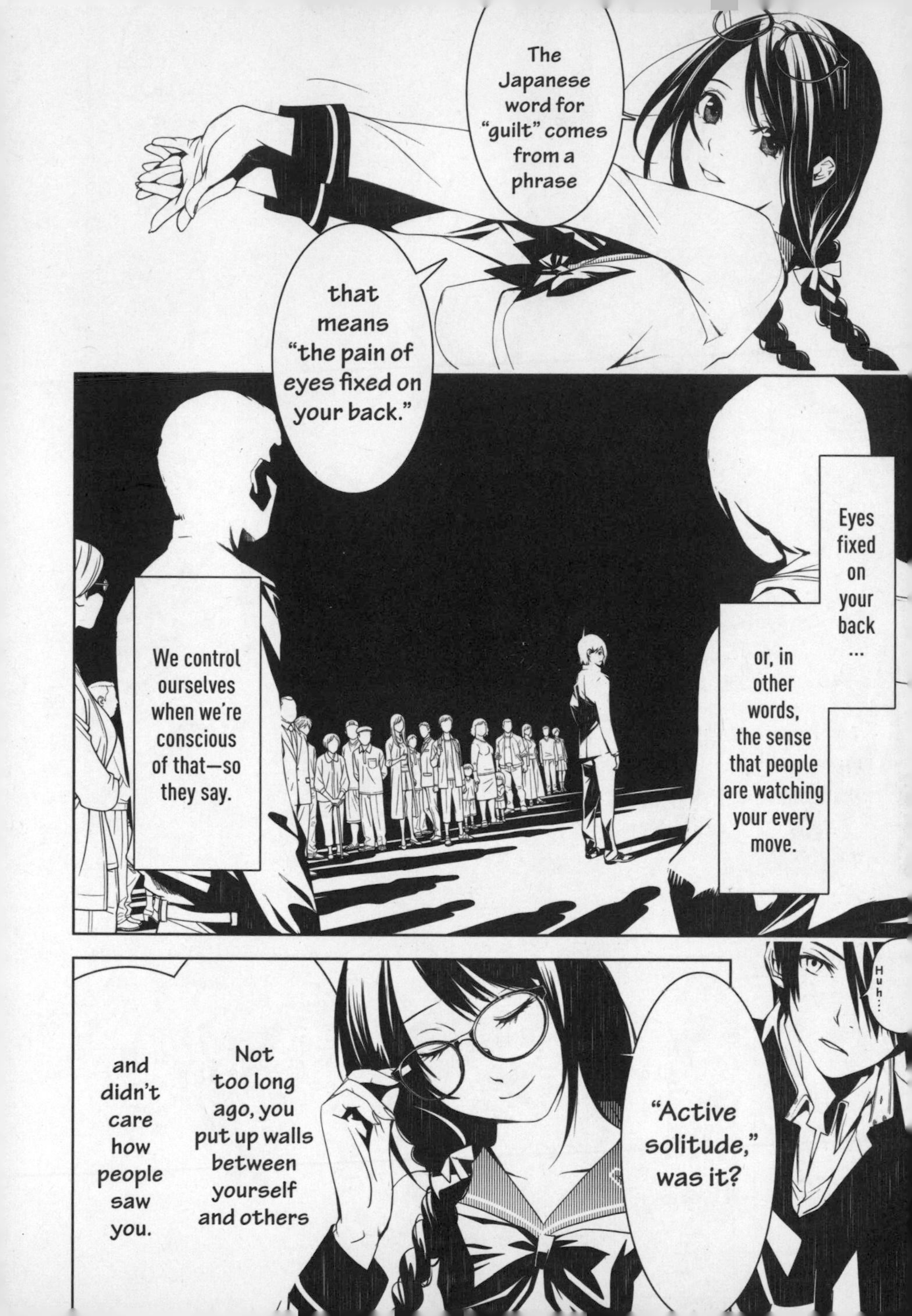
The Japanese word for "guilt" comes from a phrase
that means "the pain of eyes fixed on your back."
Eyes fixed on your back...
or, in other words, the sense that people are watching your every move.
We control ourselves when we're conscious of that—so they say.
Huh...
"Active solitude," was it?
Not too long ago, you put up walls between yourself and others
and didn't care how people saw you.

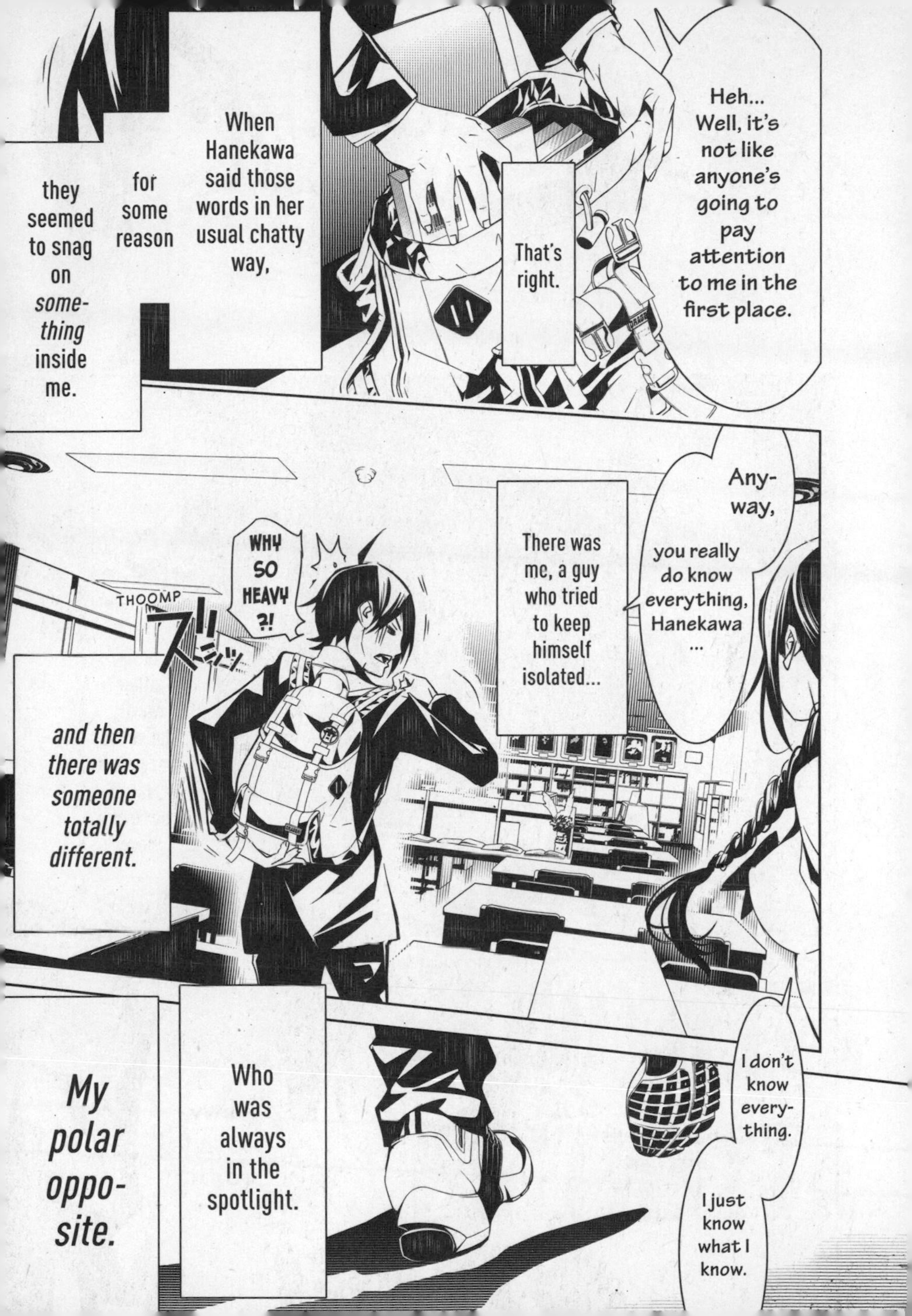
Heh... Well, it's not like anyone's going to pay attention to me in the first place.
That's right.
When Hanekawa said those words in her usual chatty way,
for some reason
they seemed to snag on *something* inside me.
Any-way,
you really do know everything, Hanekawa ...
There was me, a guy who tried to keep himself isolated...
WHY SO HEAVY ?!
THOOMP
and then there was someone totally different.
I don't know every-thing.
I just know what I know.
Who was always in the spotlight.
My polar oppo-site.

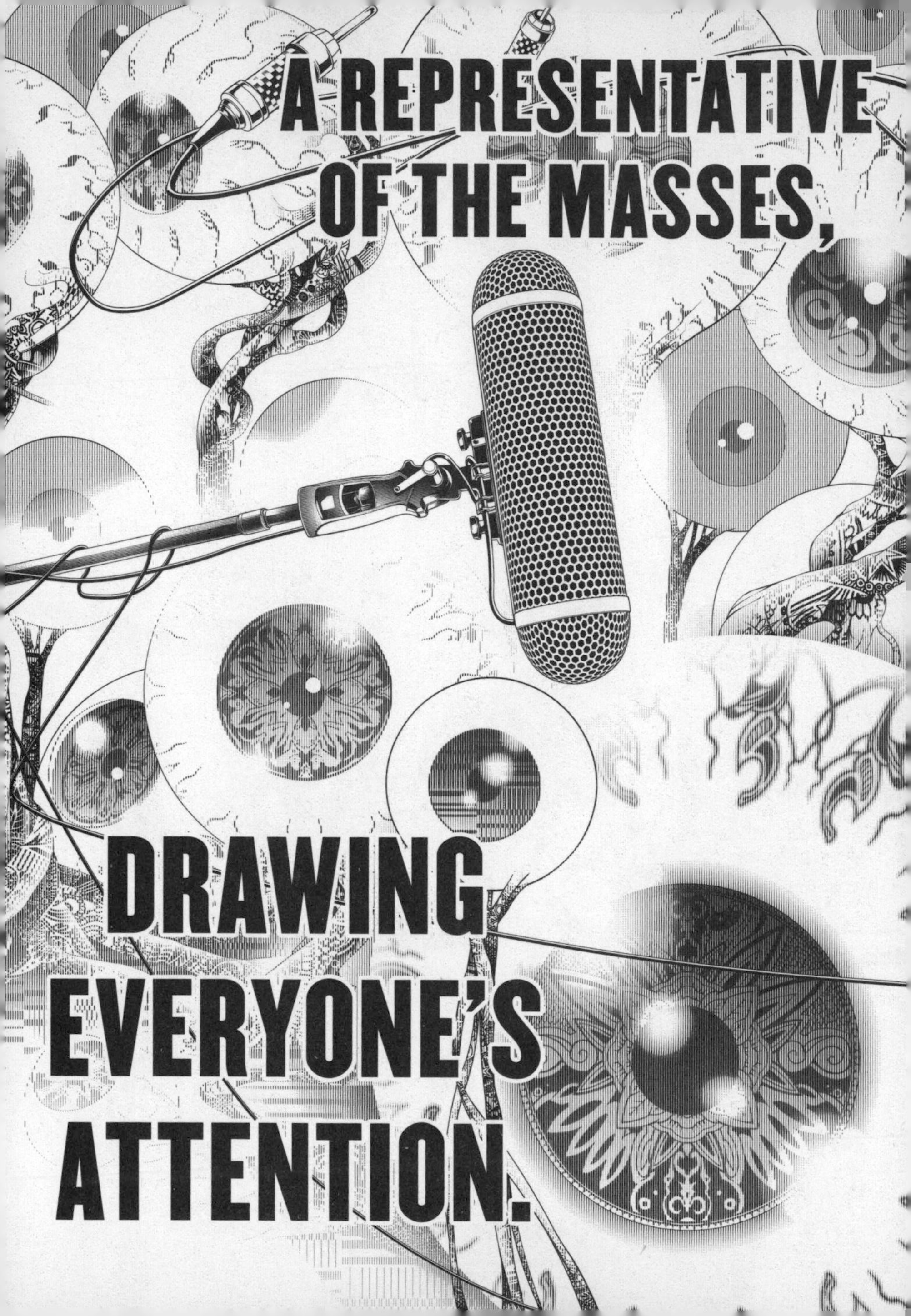
A REPRESENTATIVE OF THE MASSES,
DRAWING EVERYONE'S ATTENTION.

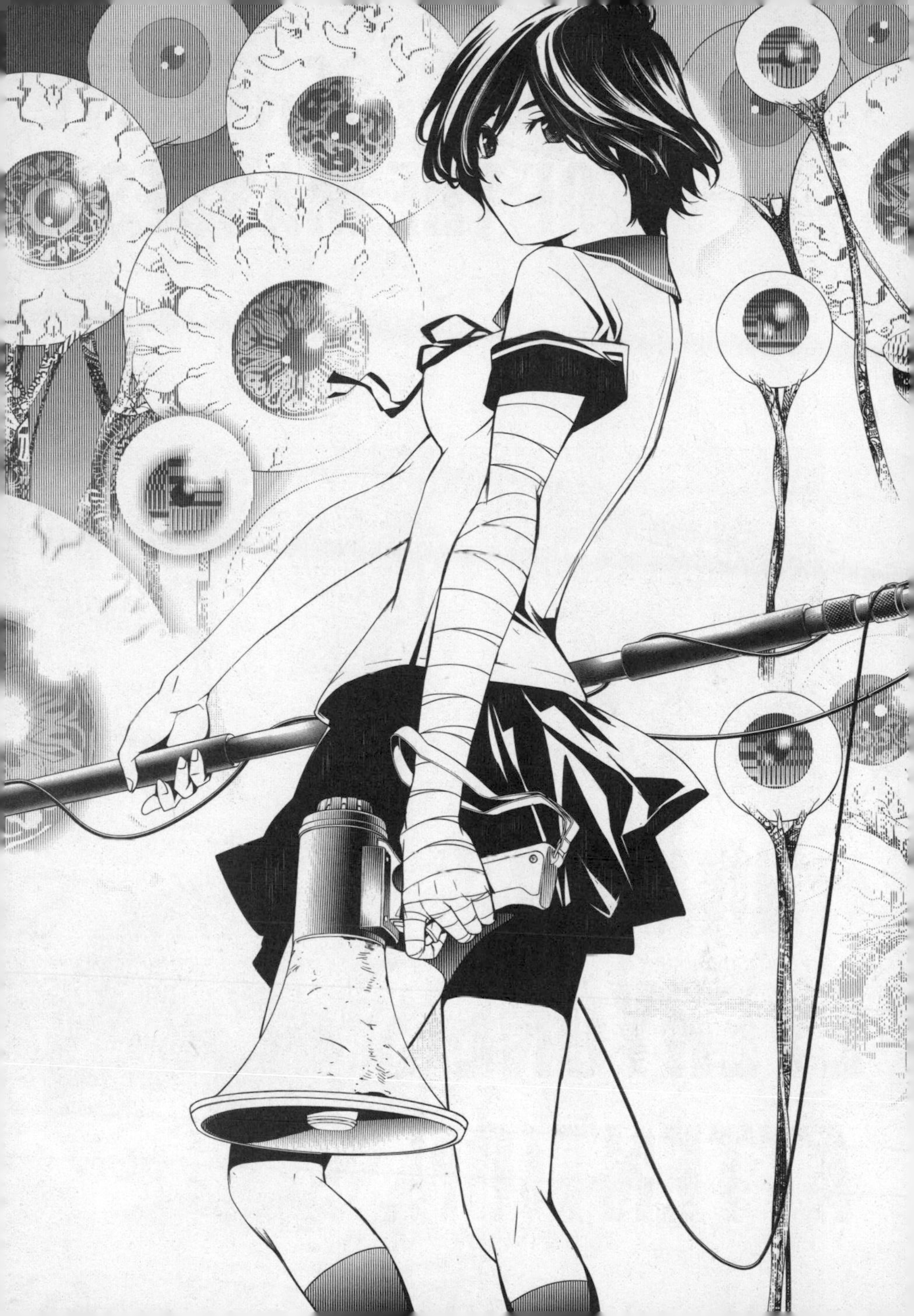

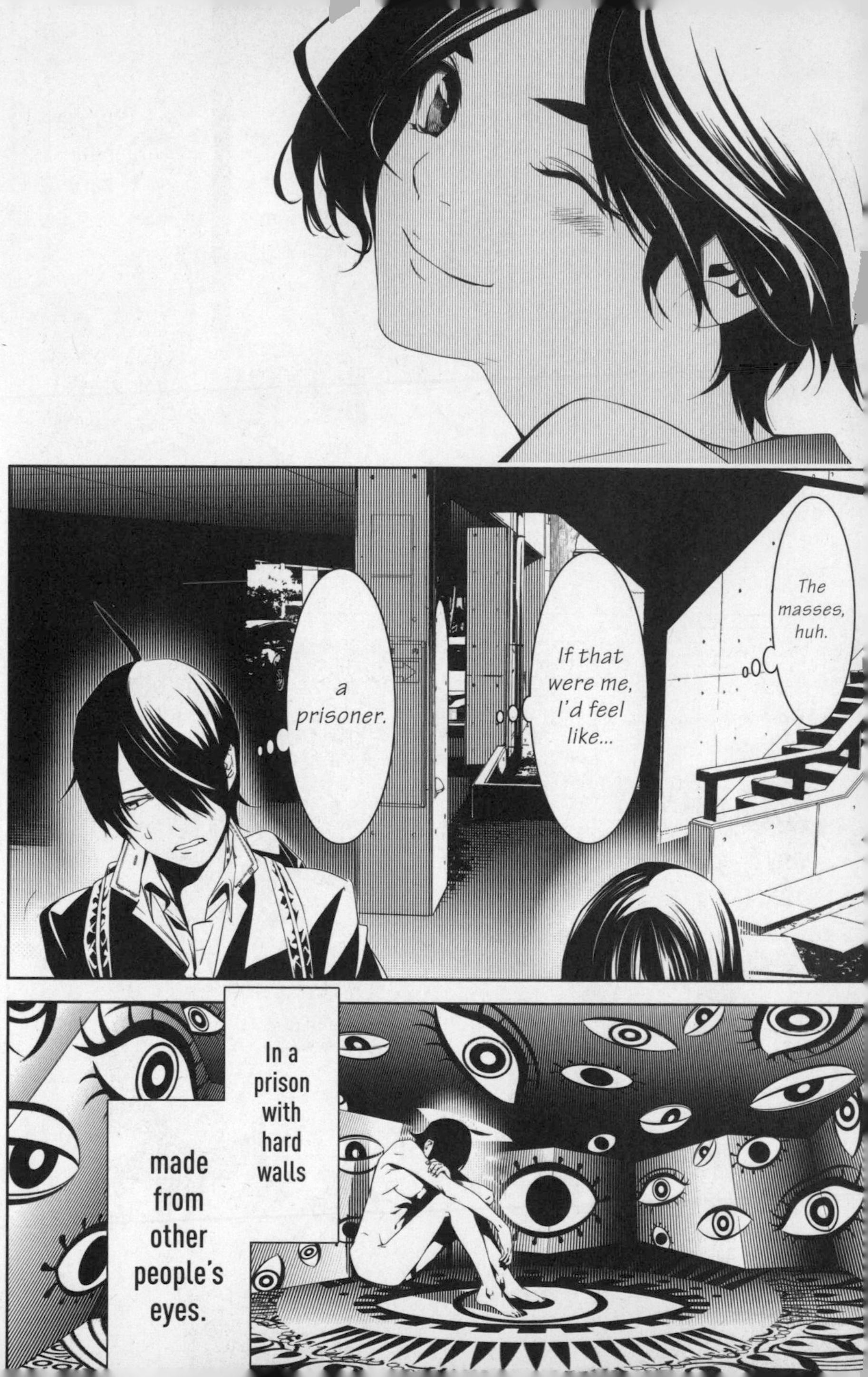
The masses, huh.
If that were me, I'd feel like...
a prisoner.
In a prison with hard walls
made from other people's eyes.

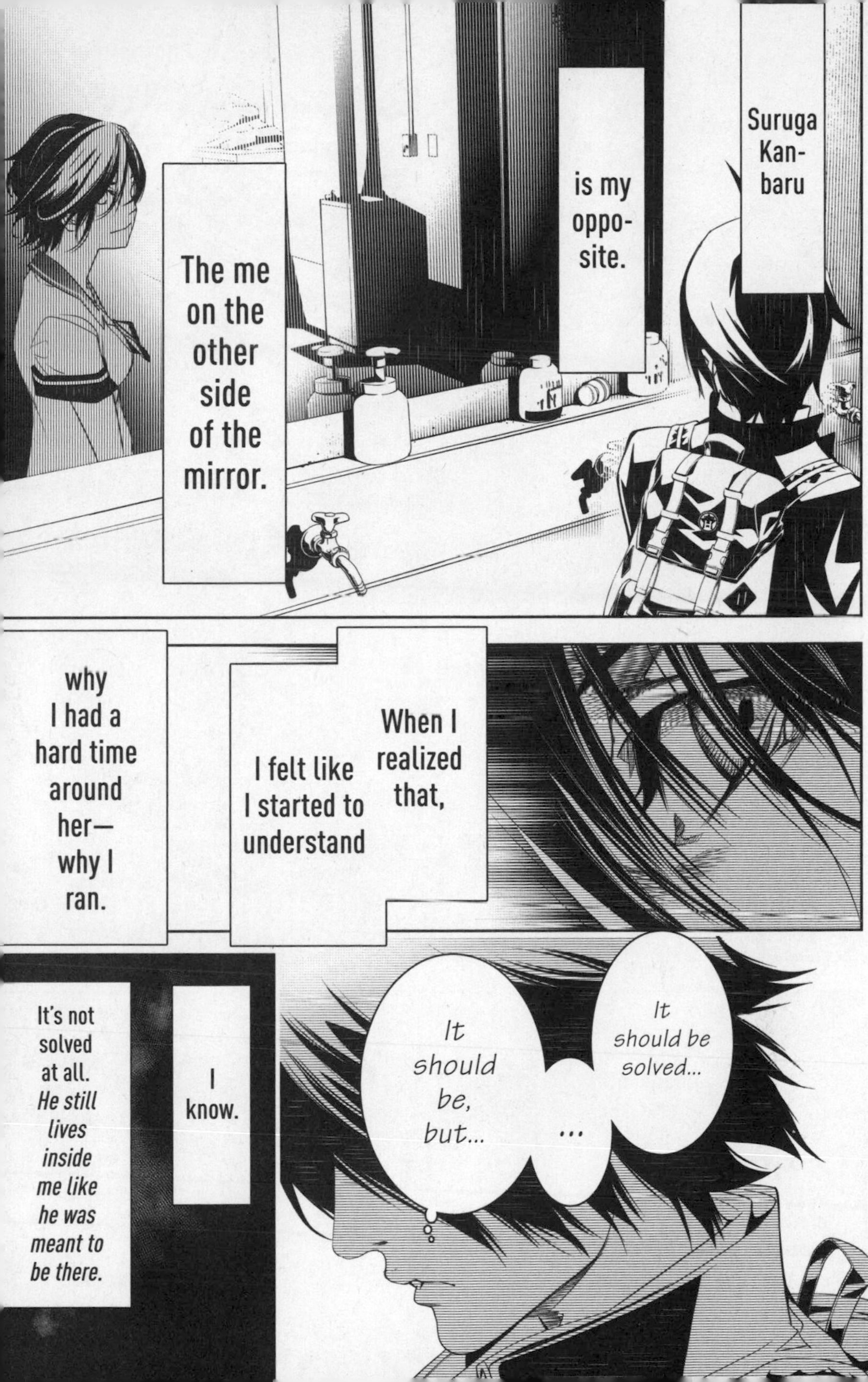
Suruga Kan-baru
is my oppo-site.
The me on the other side of the mirror.
When I realized that,
I felt like I started to understand
why I had a hard time around her—why I ran.
It should be solved...
...
It should be, but...
I know.
It's not solved at all. *He still lives inside me like he was meant to be there.*

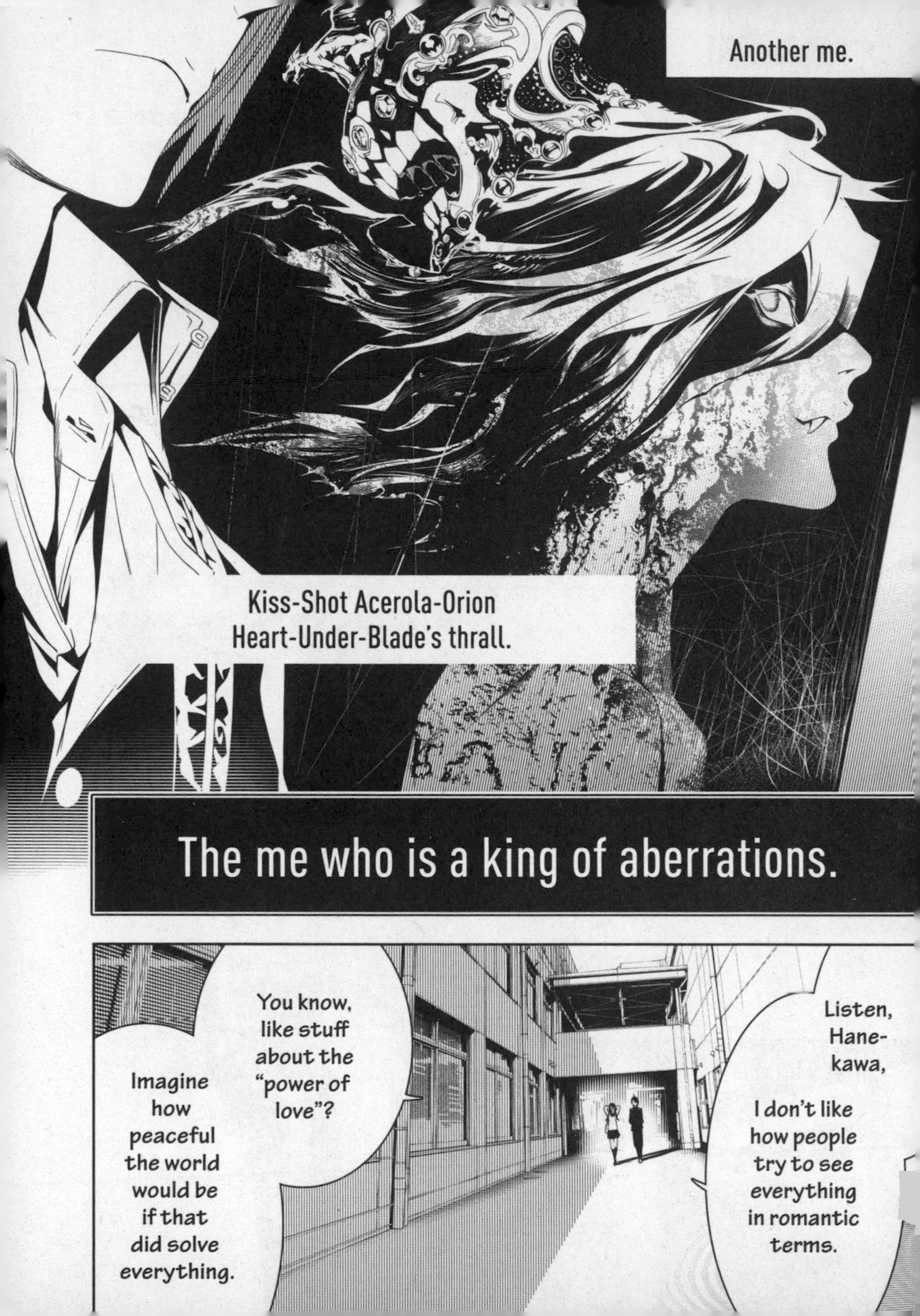
Another me.
Kiss-Shot Acerola-Orion Heart-Under-Blade's thrall.
The me who is a king of aberrations.
Listen, Hanekawa,
I don't like how people try to see everything in romantic terms.
You know, like stuff about the "power of love"?
Imagine how peaceful the world would be if that did solve everything.

It'd make a lot more sense to assume that Kanbaru has some kind of secondary, realistic goal.
And besides ...
... Besides?
TWING
I've already cleared the most difficult character of all.

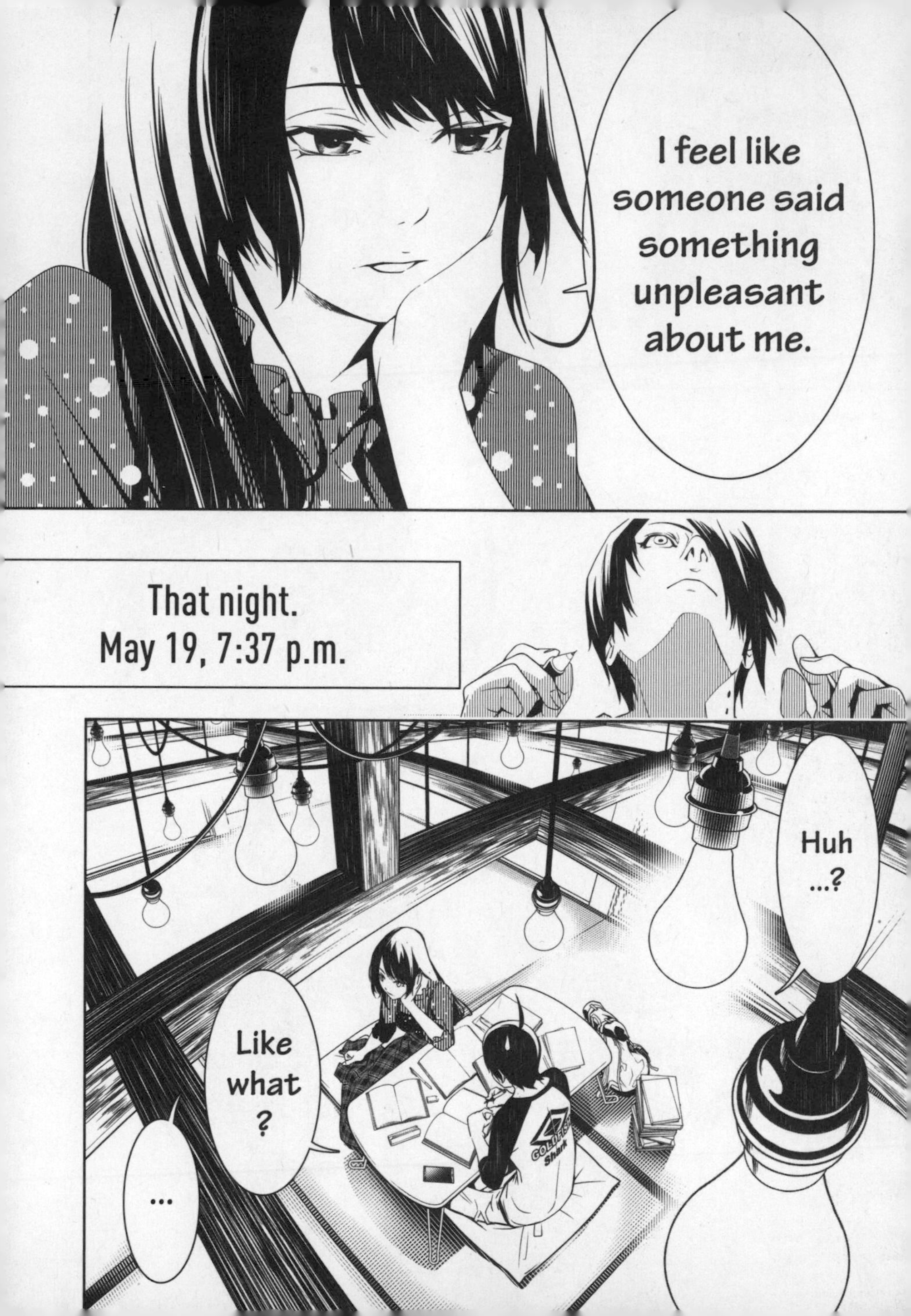
I feel like someone said something unpleasant about me.
That night. May 19, 7:37 p.m.
Huh ...?
Like what ?
...

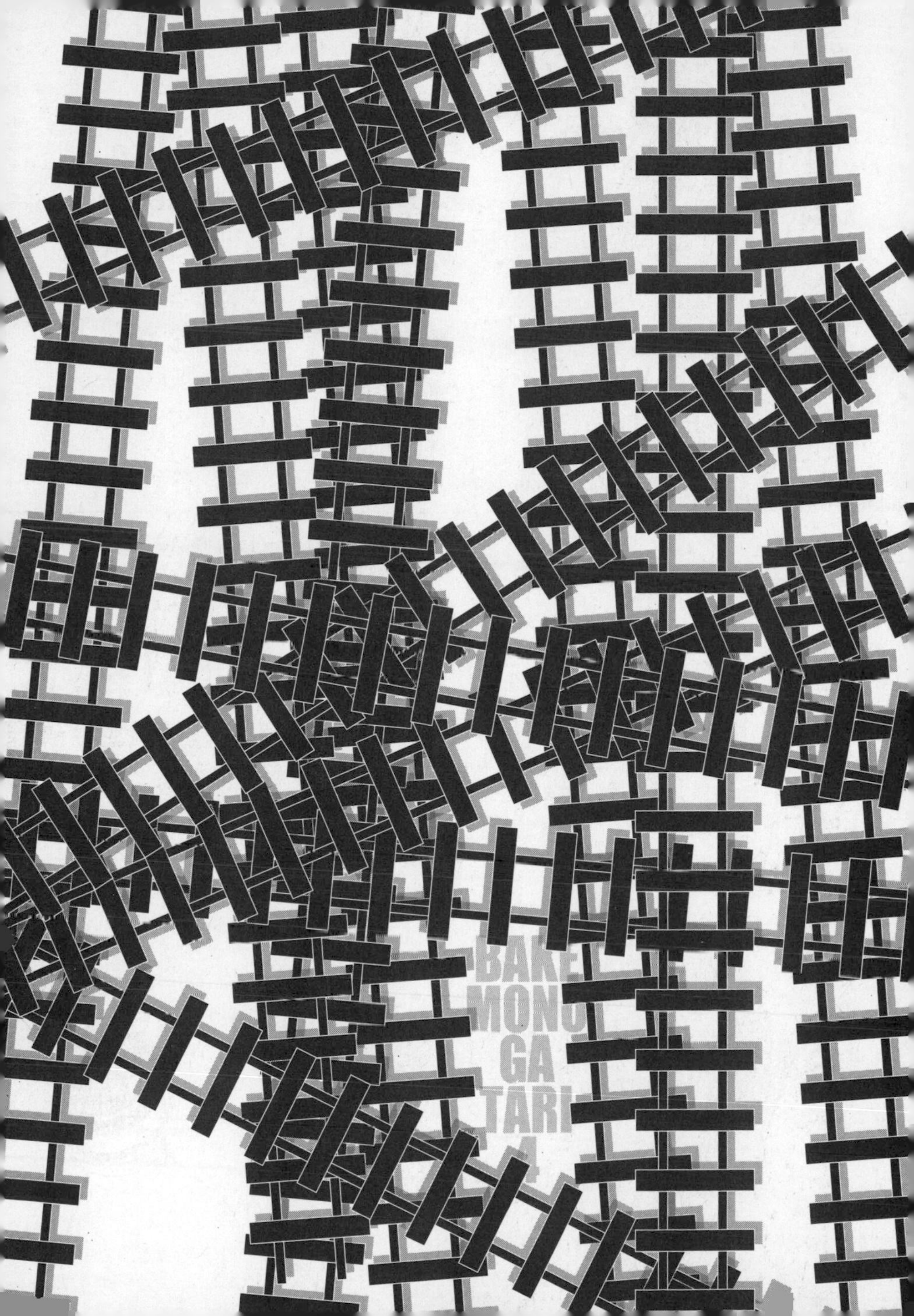
BAKE
MONO
GA
TARI
4

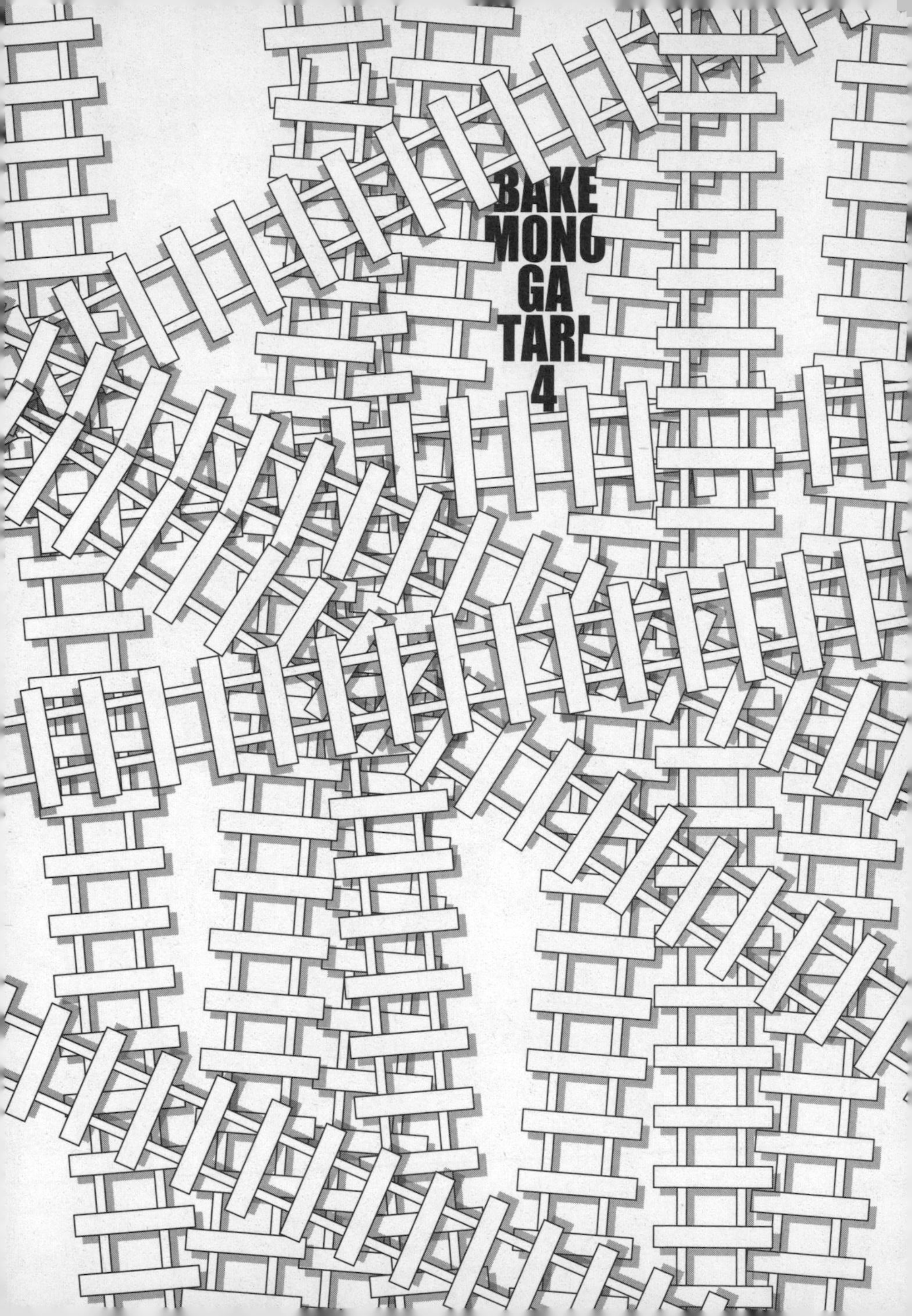
BAKE
MONO
GA
TARI
4

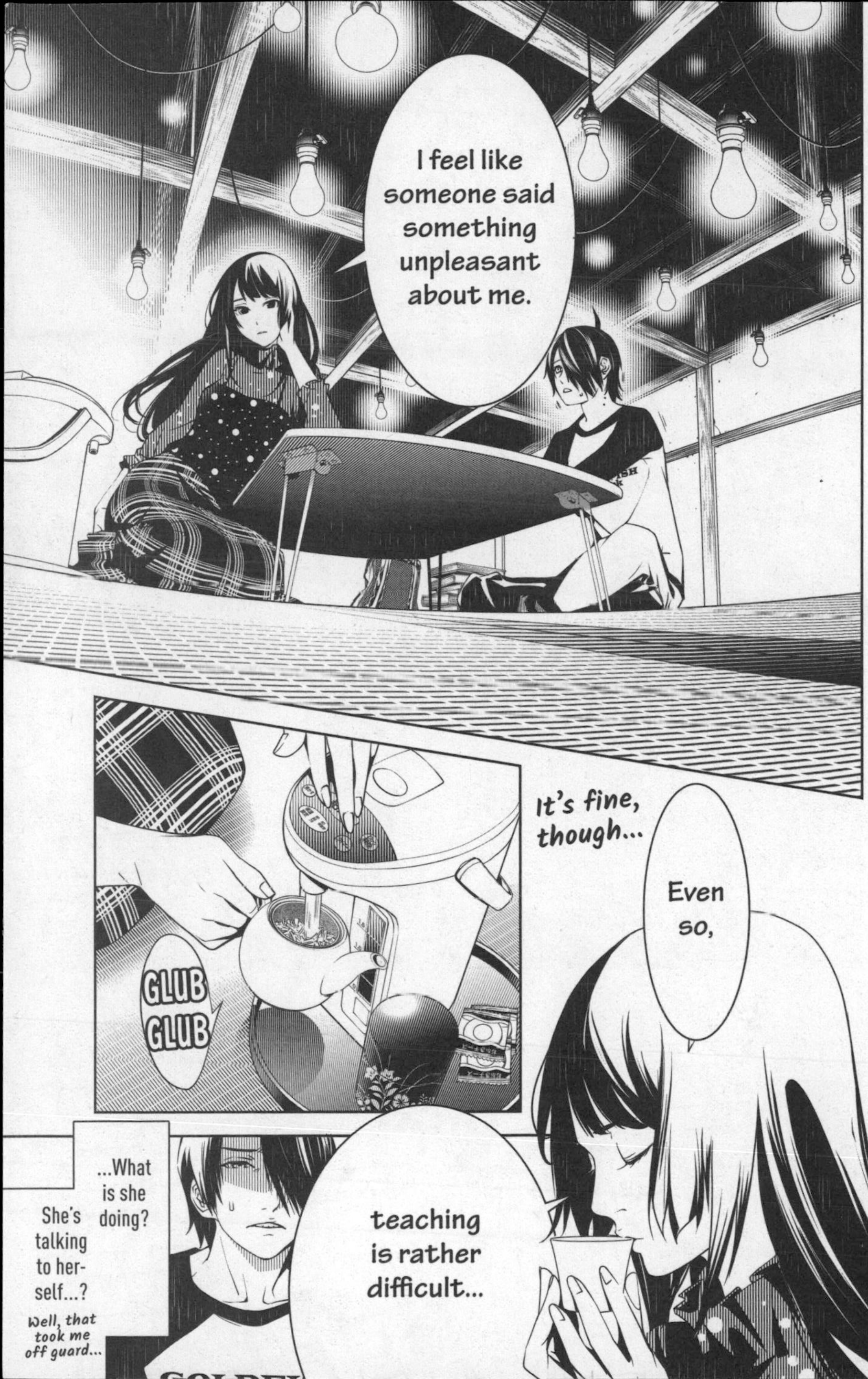
I feel like someone said something unpleasant about me.
It's fine, though...
Even so,
teaching is rather difficult...
GLUB GLUB
...What is she doing?
She's talking to her-self...?
Well, that took me off guard...

Apt. 201 of the Tamikura Apartments.

Alone with Senjogahara, studying at her place.

Yes... just the two of us.

All alone.

Senjogahara is what you'd call the only child of a single-father household...

and her father's always so busy with work...

that he doesn't get home until late...!

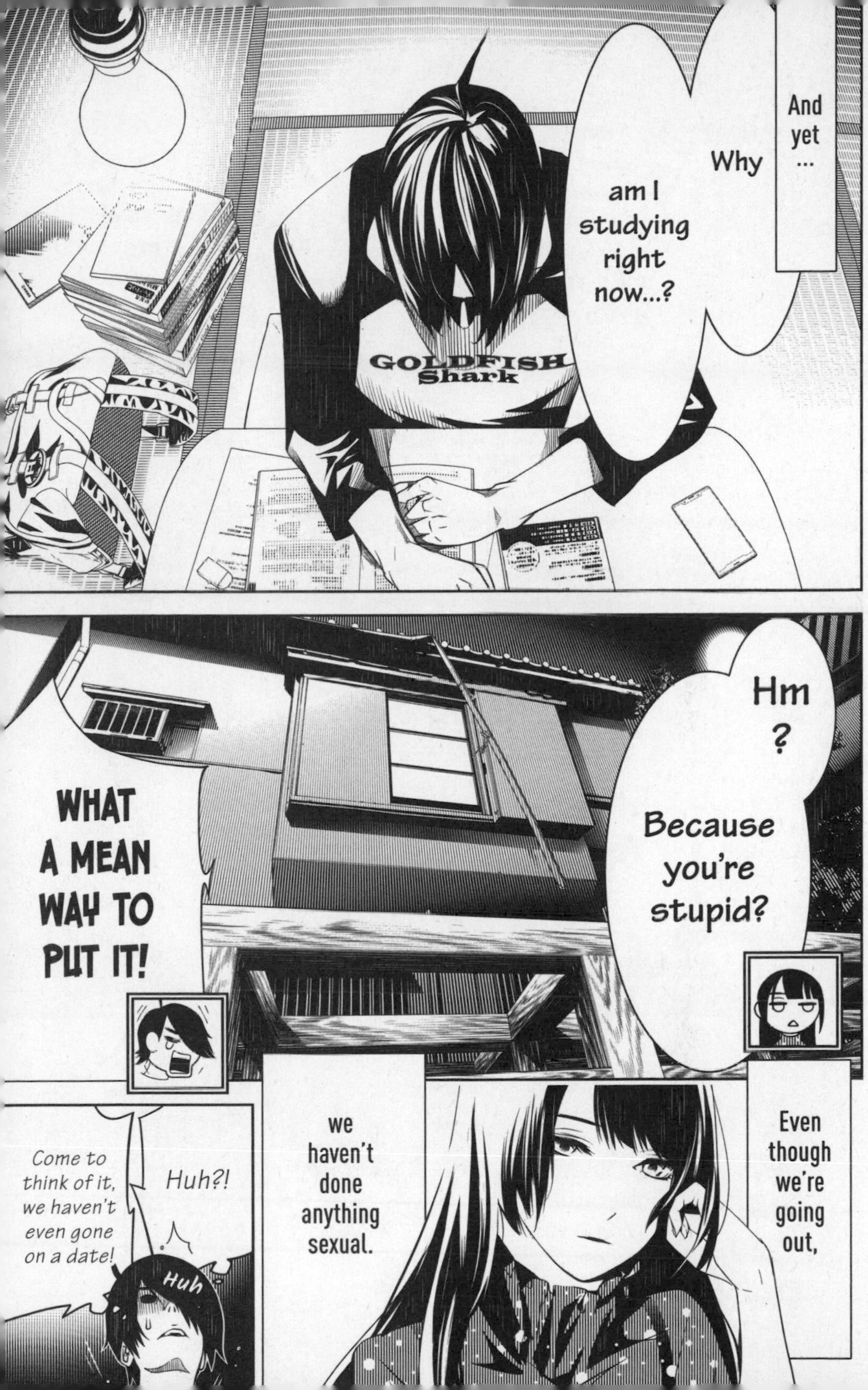
And yet ...
Why am I studying right now...?
GOLDFISH Shark
Hm? Because you're stupid?
WHAT A MEAN WAY TO PUT IT!
Even though we're going out,
we haven't done anything sexual.
Huh?!
Come to think of it, we haven't even gone on a date!
Huh

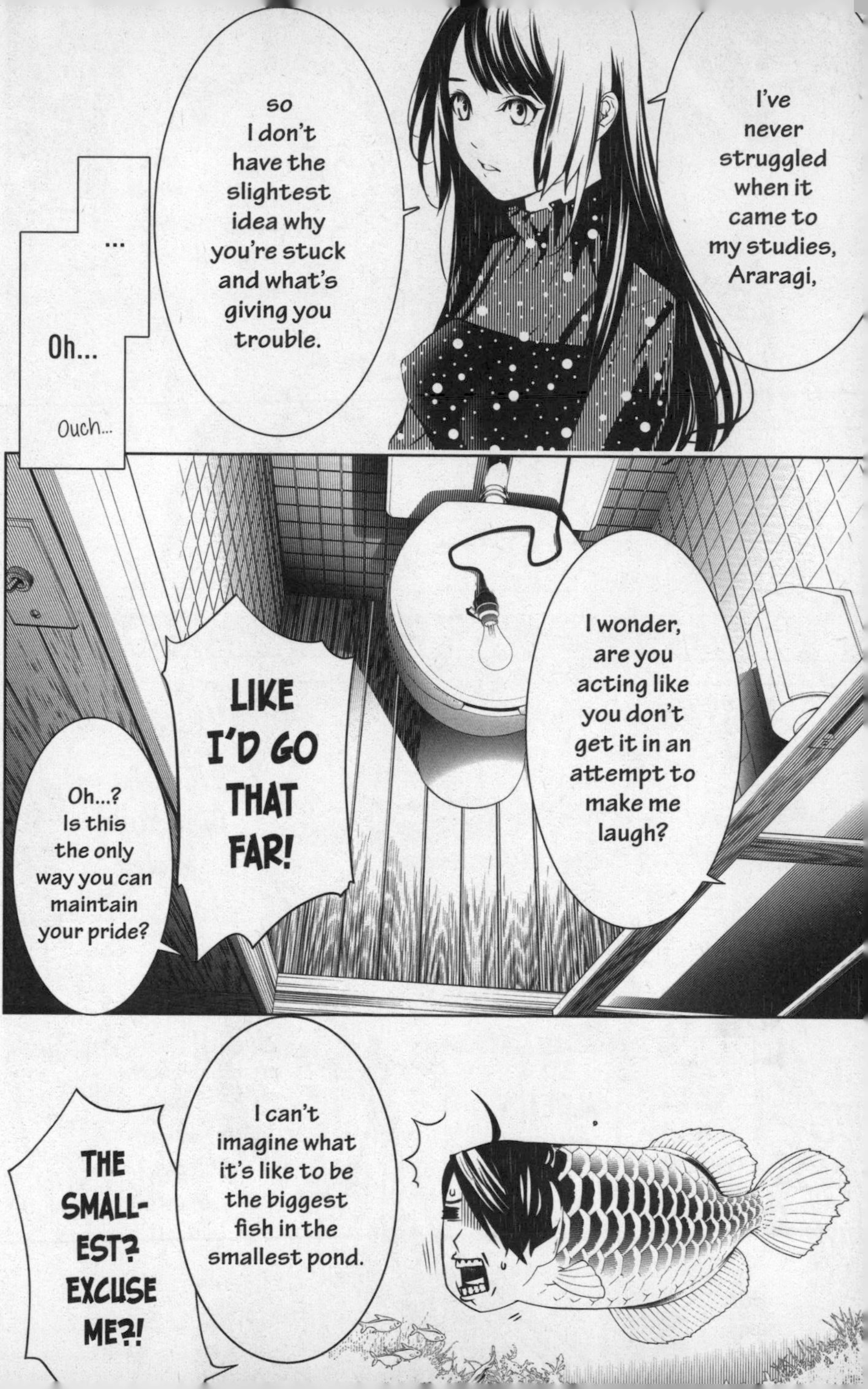
I've never struggled when it came to my studies, Araragi,
so I don't have the slightest idea why you're stuck and what's giving you trouble.
...
Oh...
Ouch...
I wonder, are you acting like you don't get it in an attempt to make me laugh?
LIKE I'D GO THAT FAR!
Oh...? Is this the only way you can maintain your pride?
I can't imagine what it's like to be the biggest fish in the smallest pond.
THE SMALL-EST? EXCUSE ME?!

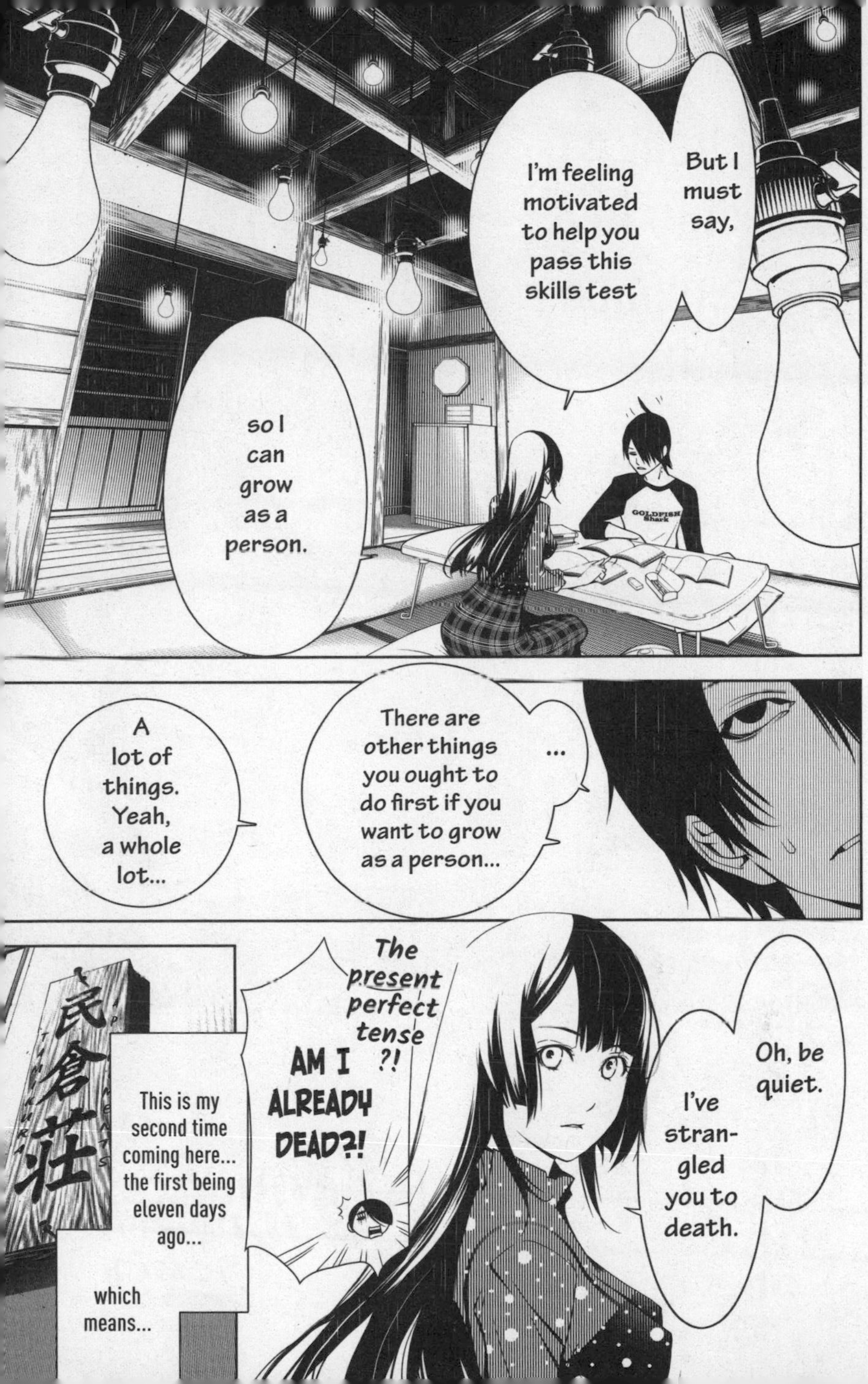
But I must say,
I'm feeling motivated to help you pass this skills test
so I can grow as a person.
GOLDFISH Shark
...
There are other things you ought to do first if you want to grow as a person...
A lot of things. Yeah, a whole lot...
Oh, be quiet.
I've stran-gled you to death.
The present perfect tense ?!
AM I ALREADY DEAD?!
民倉荘
This is my second time coming here... the first being eleven days ago...
which means...

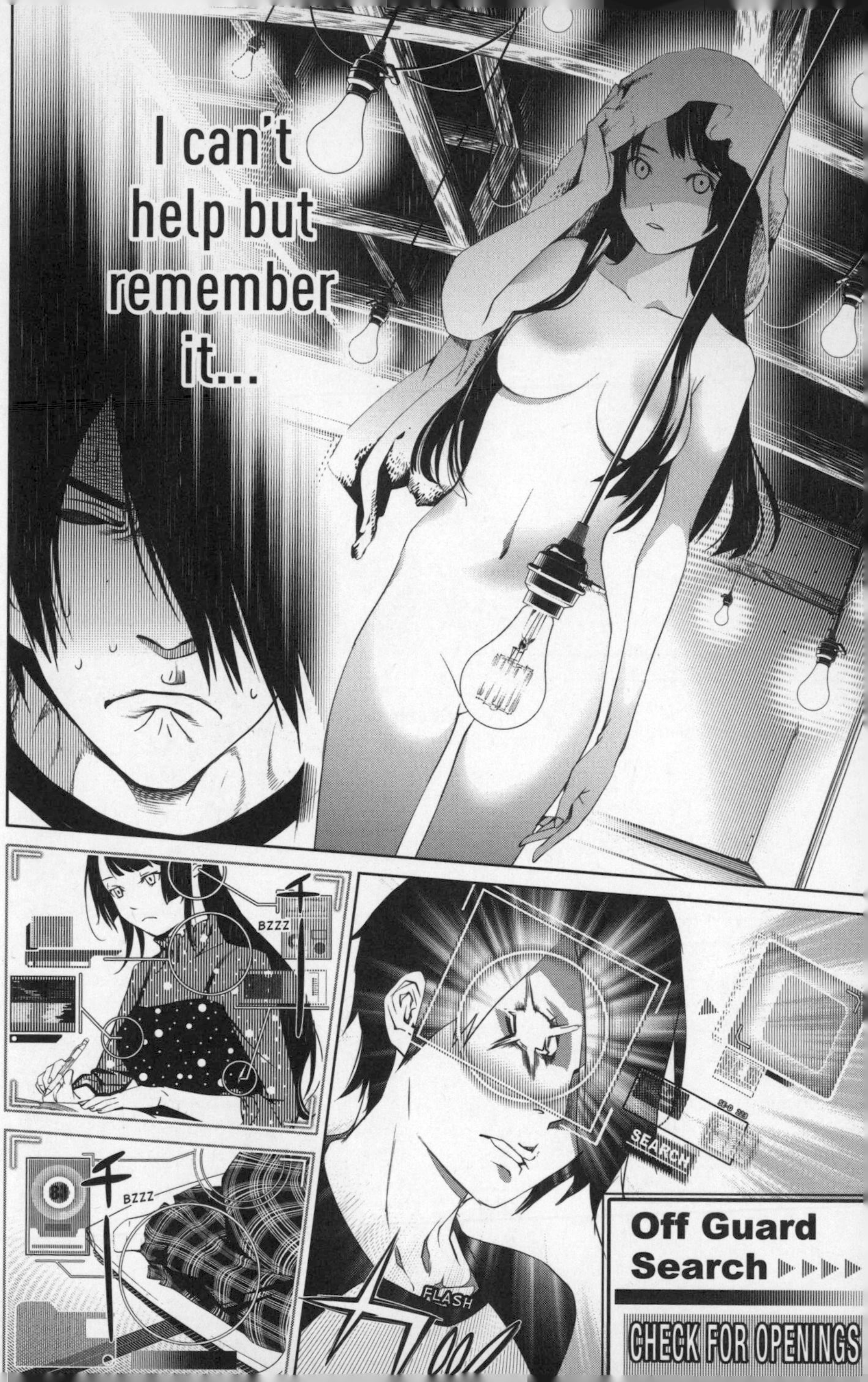
I can't help but remember it...
SEARCH
Off Guard Search
CHECK FOR OPENINGS
FLASH
チ
BZZZ
チ
BZZZ

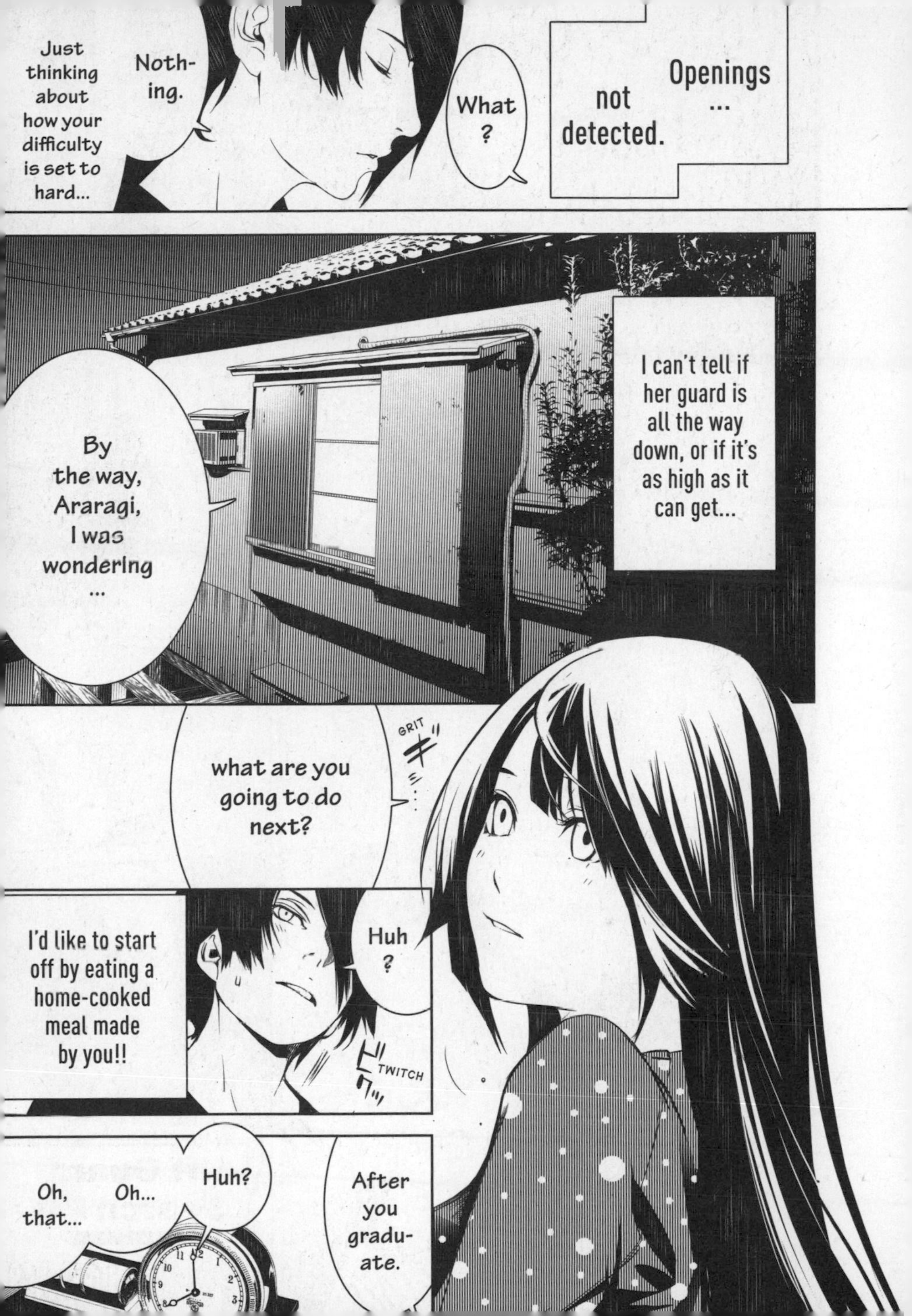
Openings ... not detected.
What?
Noth-ing.
Just thinking about how your difficulty is set to hard...
I can't tell if her guard is all the way down, or if it's as high as it can get...
By the way, Araragi, I was wondering ...
what are you going to do next?
GRIT
I'd like to start off by eating a home-cooked meal made by you!!
Huh?
TWITCH
After you graduate.
Huh?
Oh...
Oh, that...

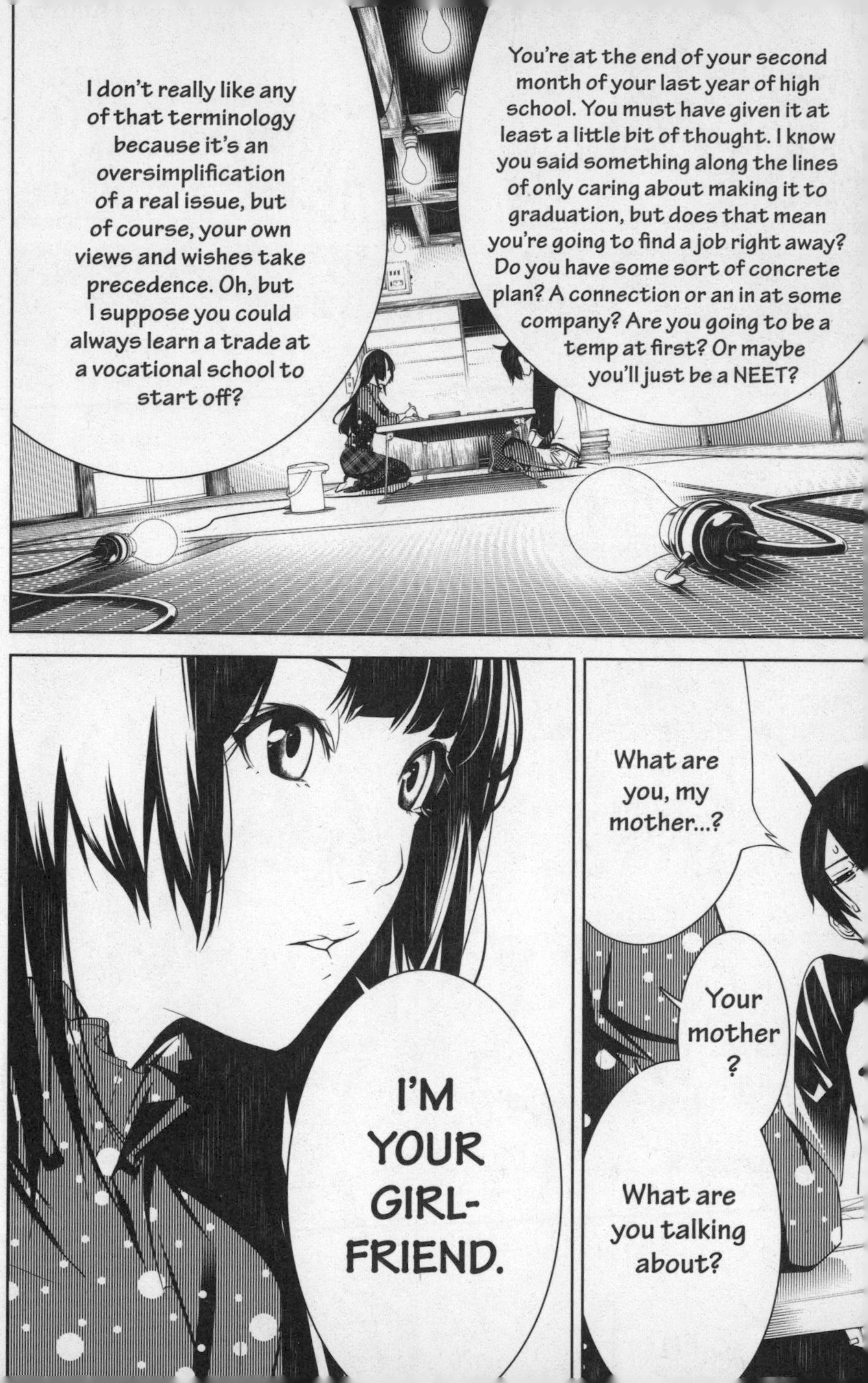
You're at the end of your second month of your last year of high school. You must have given it at least a little bit of thought. I know you said something along the lines of only caring about making it to graduation, but does that mean you're going to find a job right away? Do you have some sort of concrete plan? A connection or an in at some company? Are you going to be a temp at first? Or maybe you'll just be a NEET?
I don't really like any of that terminology because it's an oversimplification of a real issue, but of course, your own views and wishes take precedence. Oh, but I suppose you could always learn a trade at a vocational school to start off?
What are you, my mother...?
Your mother ?
What are you talking about?
I'M YOUR GIRL-FRIEND.

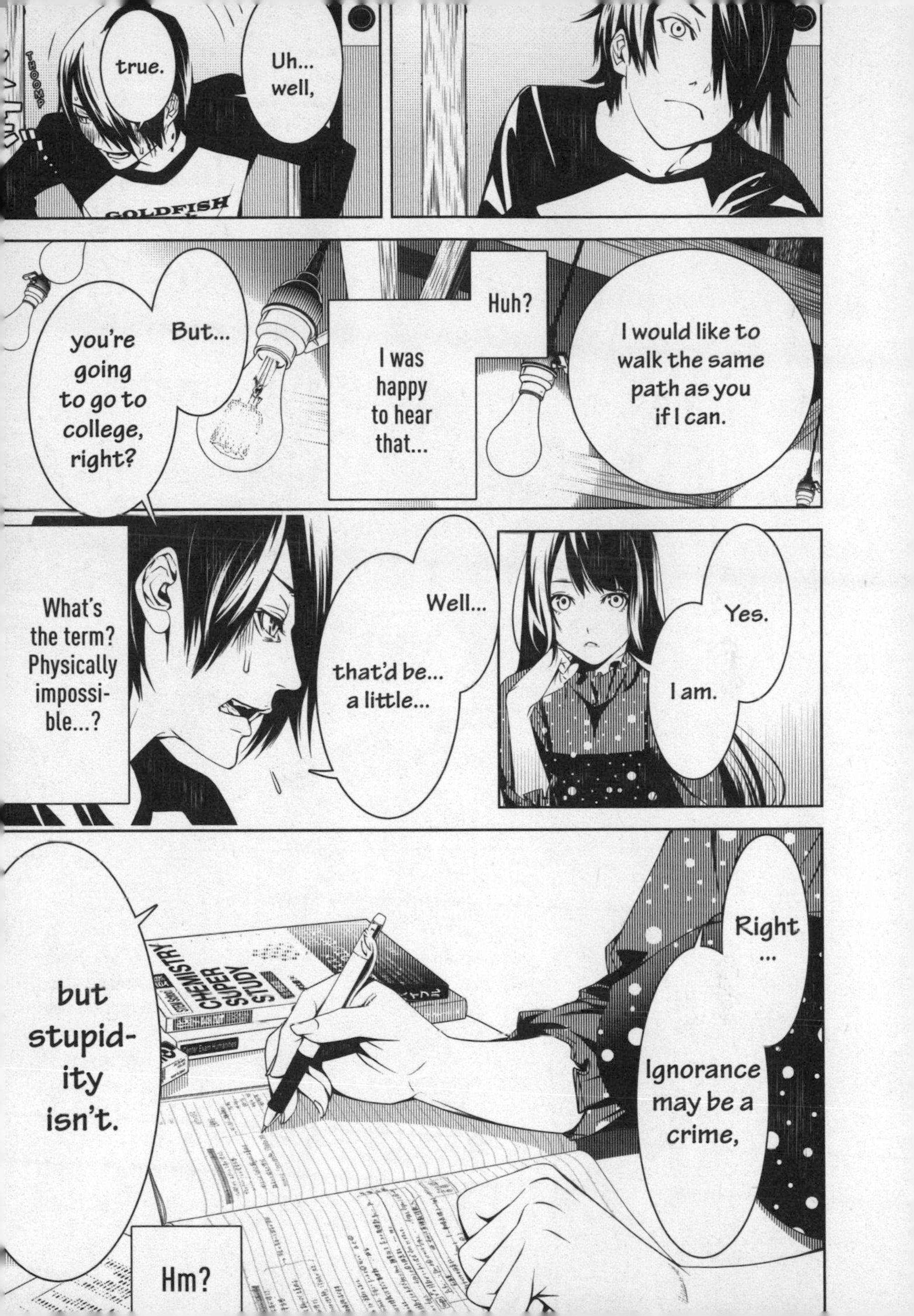
Uh... well,
true.
THOOMP
GOLDFISH
I would like to walk the same path as you if I can.
Huh?
I was happy to hear that...
But...
you're going to go to college, right?
Yes.
I am.
Well...
that'd be... a little...
What's the term? Physically impossible...?
Right...
Ignorance may be a crime,
but stupidity isn't.
Hm?
CHEMISTRY SUPER STUDY

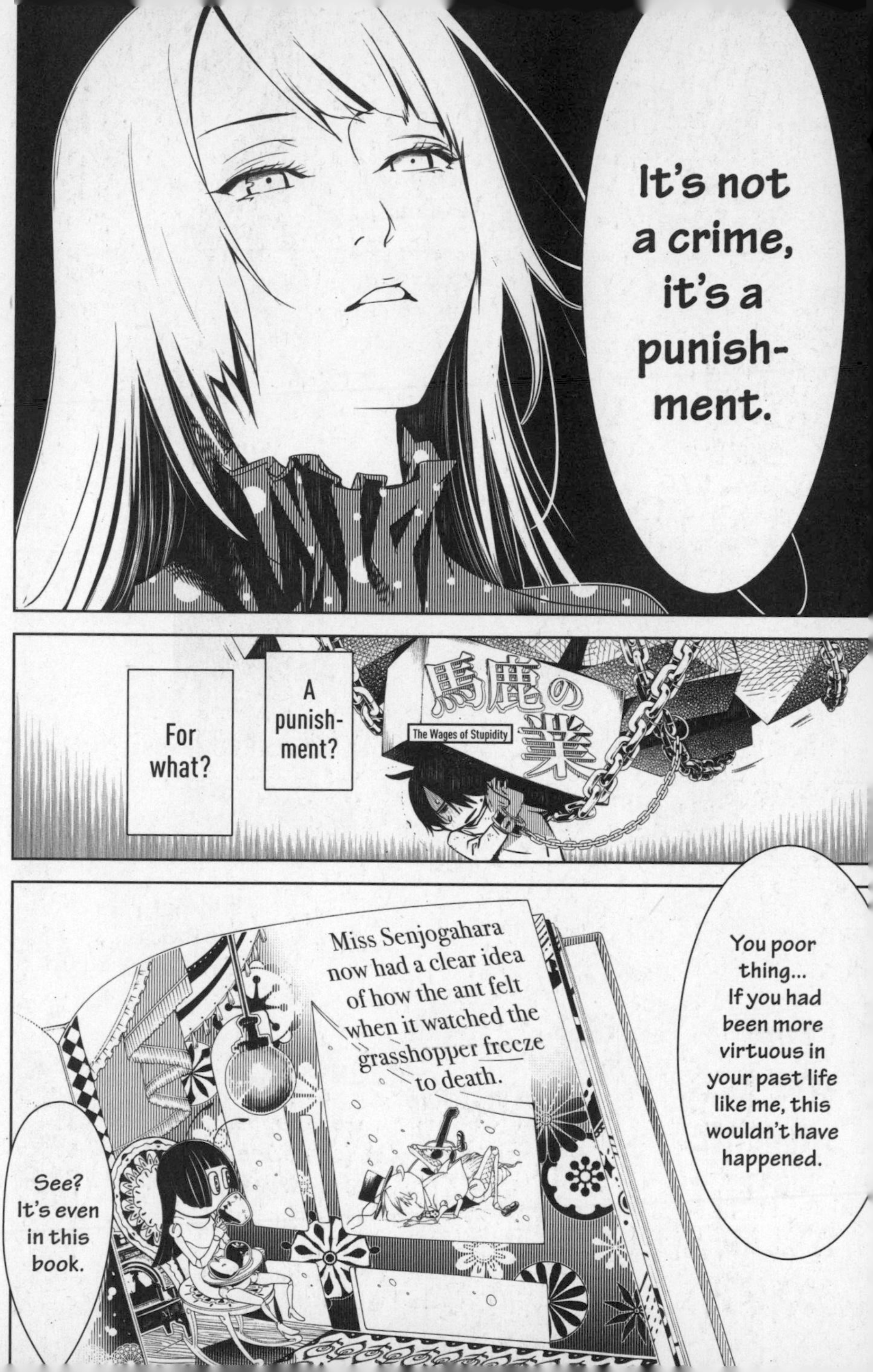

It's not a crime, it's a punish-ment.
馬鹿の業
The Wages of Stupidity
A punish-ment?
For what?
You poor thing... If you had been more virtuous in your past life like me, this wouldn't have happened.
Miss Senjogahara now had a clear idea of how the ant felt when it watched the grasshopper freeze to death.
See? It's even in this book.

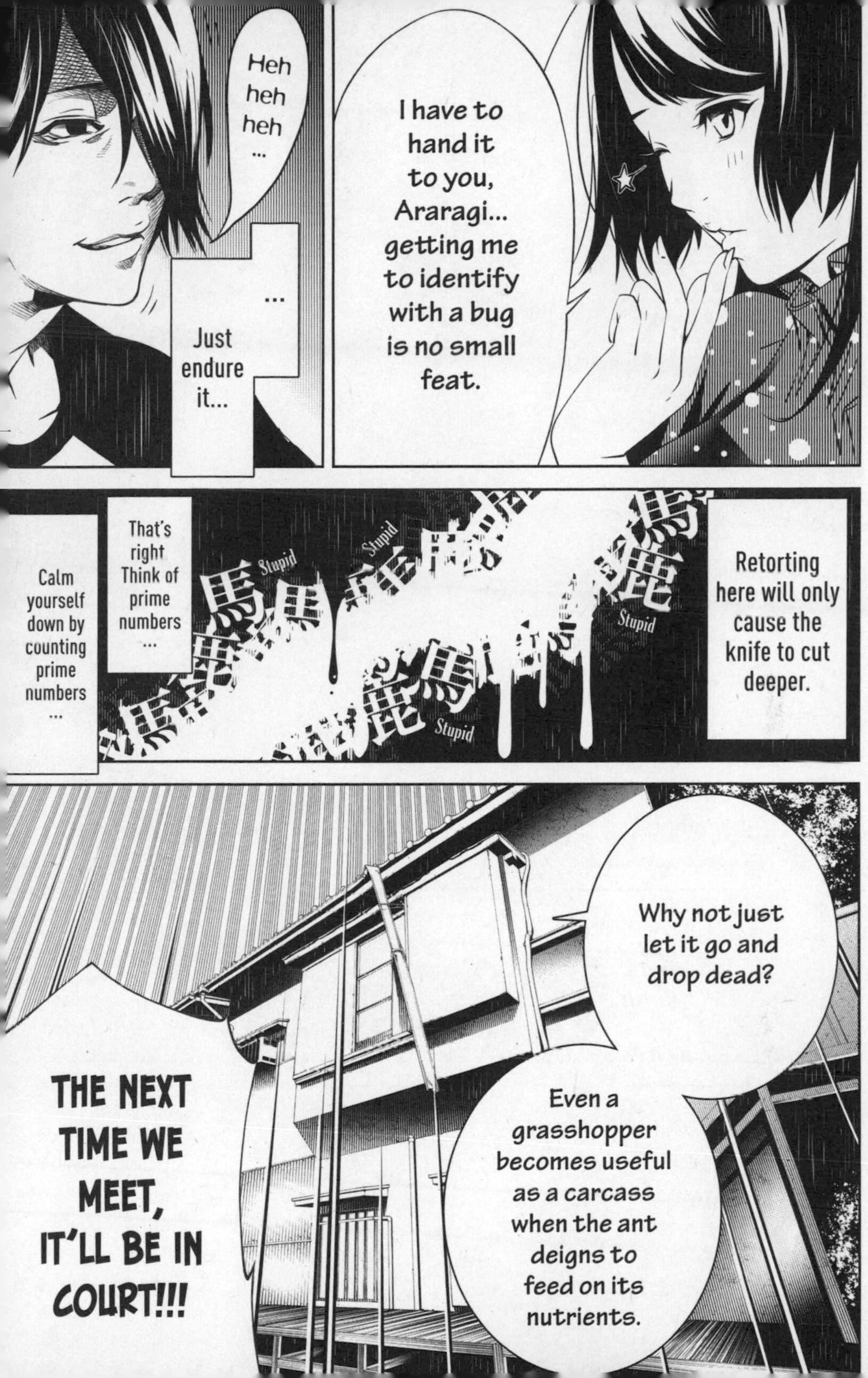
I have to hand it to you, Araragi... getting me to identify with a bug is no small feat.
Heh heh heh ...
... Just endure it...
Retorting here will only cause the knife to cut deeper.
Stupid
Stupid
Stupid
Stupid
That's right Think of prime numbers ...
Calm yourself down by counting prime numbers ...
Why not just let it go and drop dead?
Even a grasshopper becomes useful as a carcass when the ant deigns to feed on its nutrients.
THE NEXT TIME WE MEET, IT'LL BE IN COURT!!!

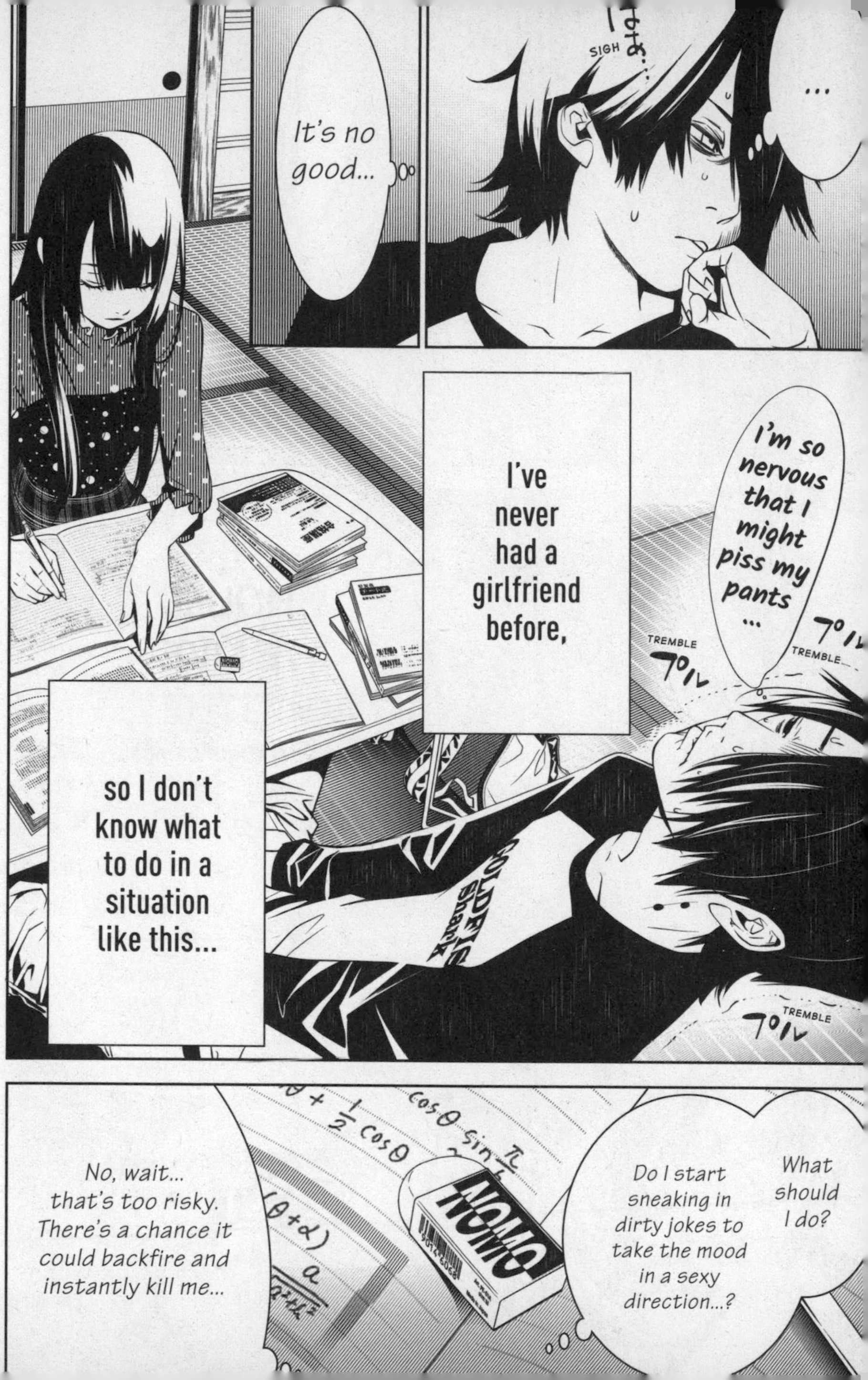

はぁ…
SIGH
...
It's no good...
I'm so nervous that I might piss my pants...
プル
TREMBLE
プル
TREMBLE
I've never had a girlfriend before,
so I don't know what to do in a situation like this...
プル
TREMBLE
What should I do?
Do I start sneaking in dirty jokes to take the mood in a sexy direction...?
No, wait... that's too risky. There's a chance it could backfire and instantly kill me...

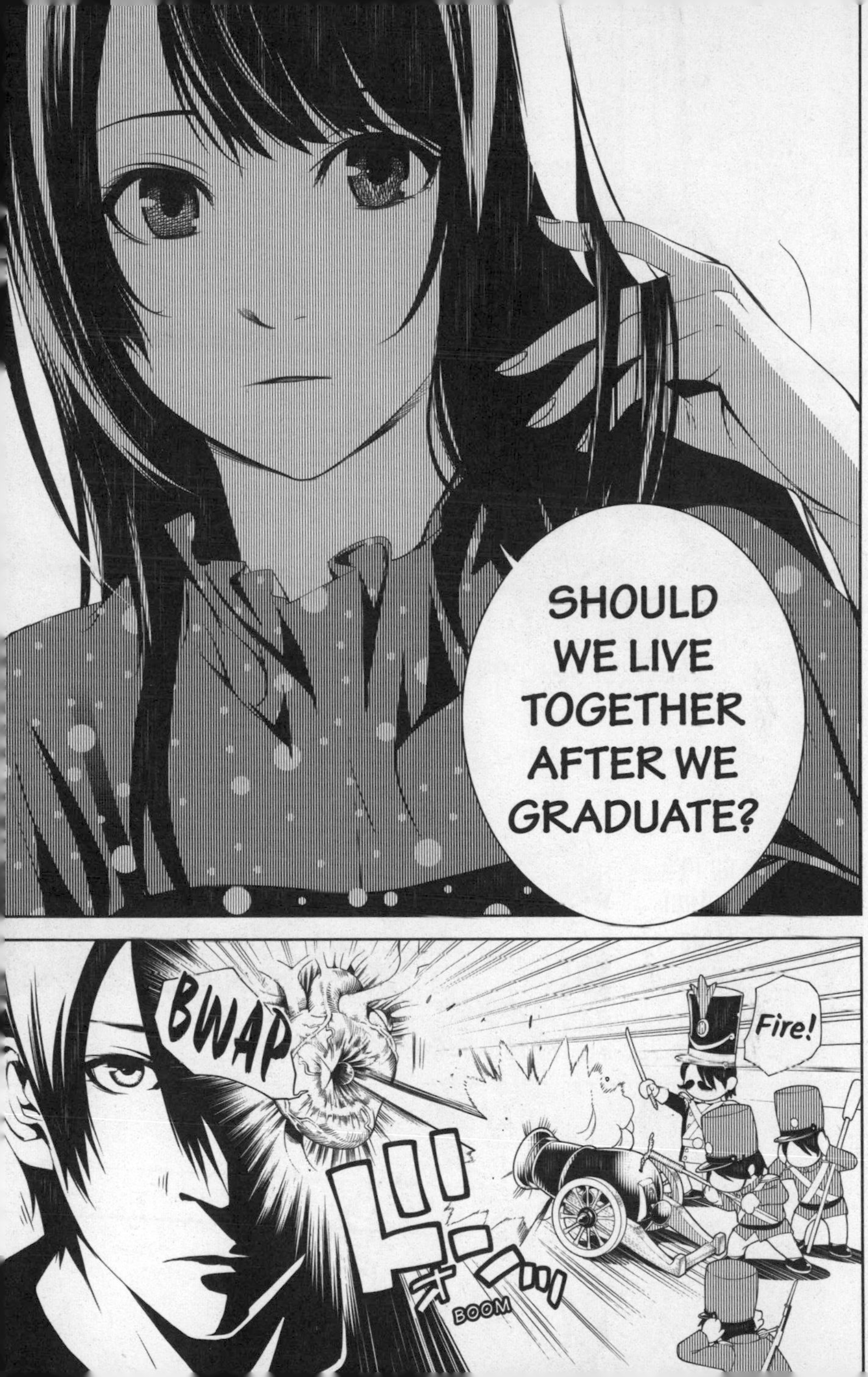
SHOULD WE LIVE TOGETHER AFTER WE GRADUATE?
Fire!
BWAP
BOOM

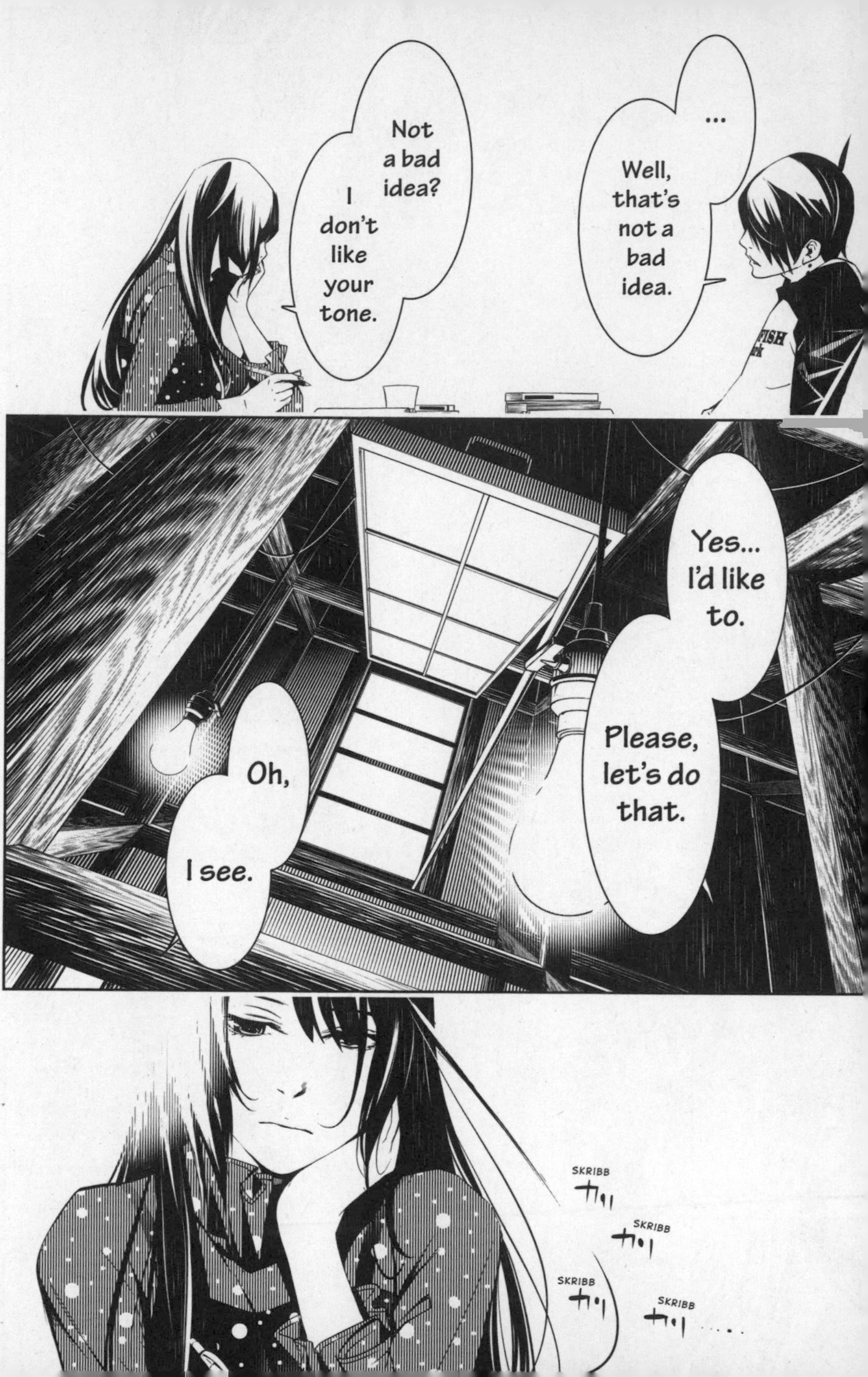
...
Well, that's not a bad idea.
Not a bad idea?
I don't like your tone.
Yes... I'd like to.
Please, let's do that.
Oh,
I see.
SKRIBB
SKRIBB
SKRIBB
SKRIBB

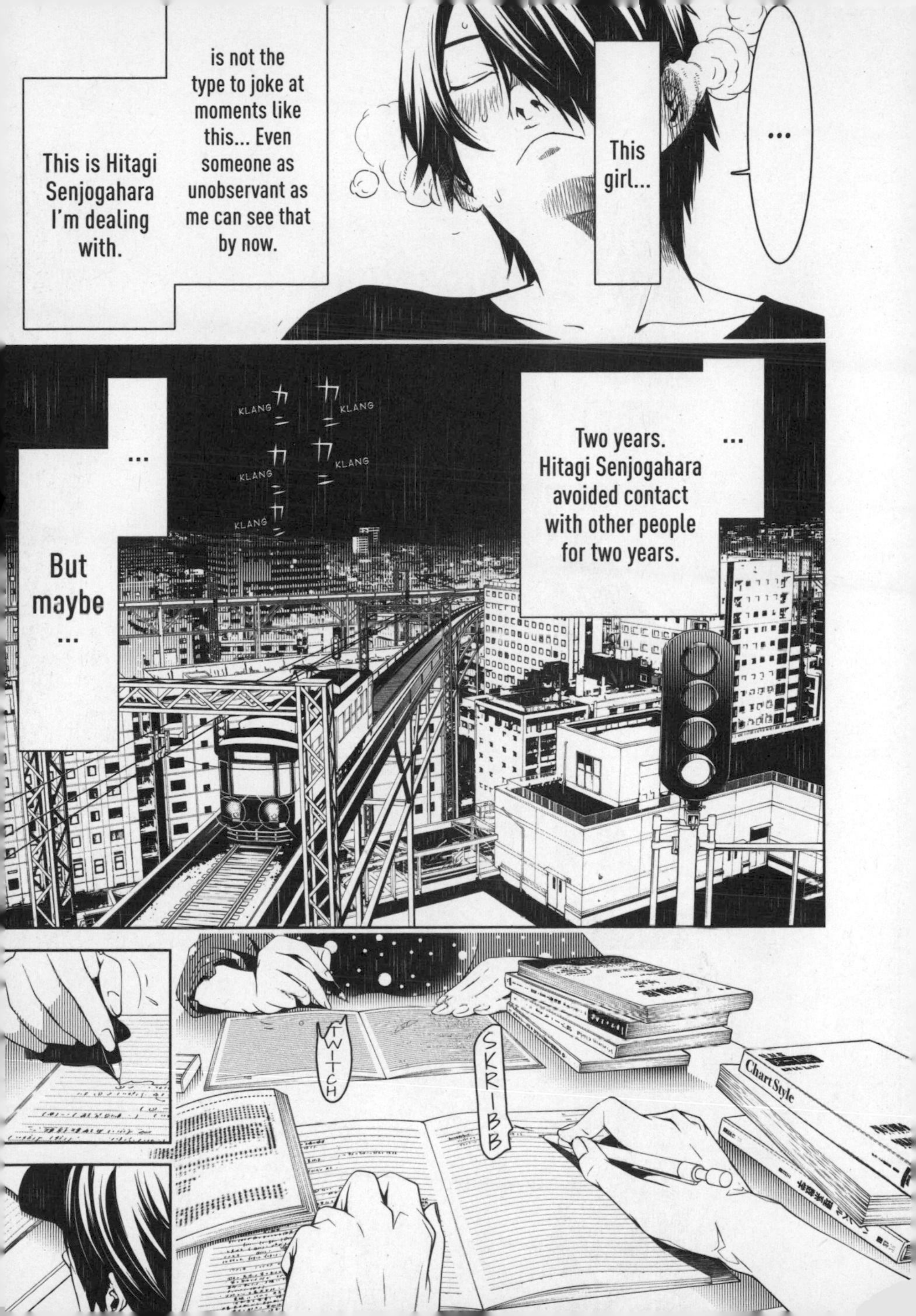
...
This girl...
is not the type to joke at moments like this... Even someone as unobservant as me can see that by now.
This is Hitagi Senjogahara I'm dealing with.
...
Two years. Hitagi Senjogahara avoided contact with other people for two years.
KLANG
KLANG
KLANG
KLANG
KLANG
...
But maybe ...
SKRIBB
TWITCH
Chart Style

Maybe Senjogahara is
just as clueless as I am
about what to do in
a moment like this.

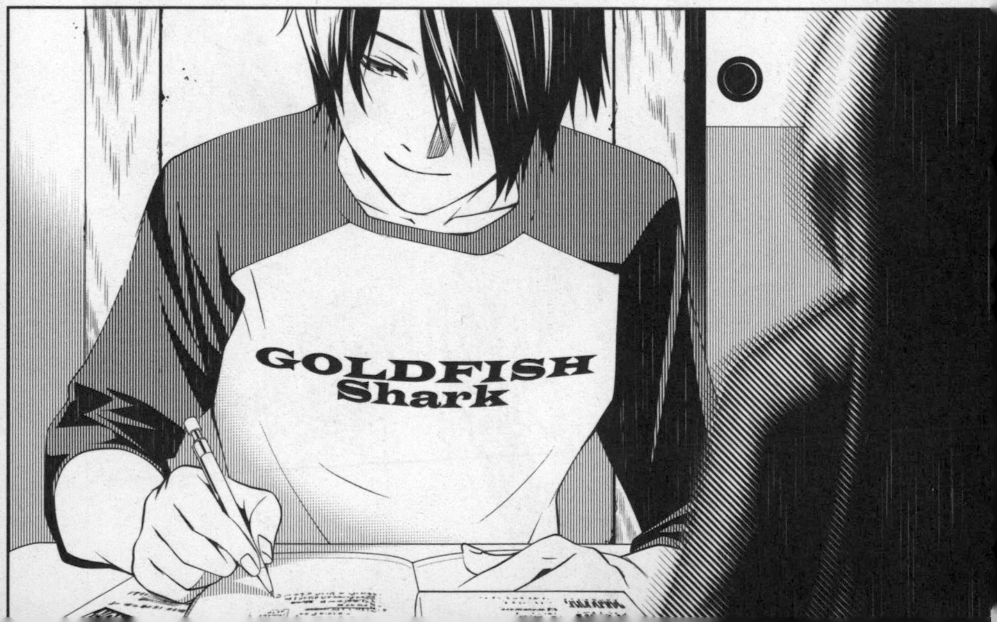
GOLDFISH
Shark

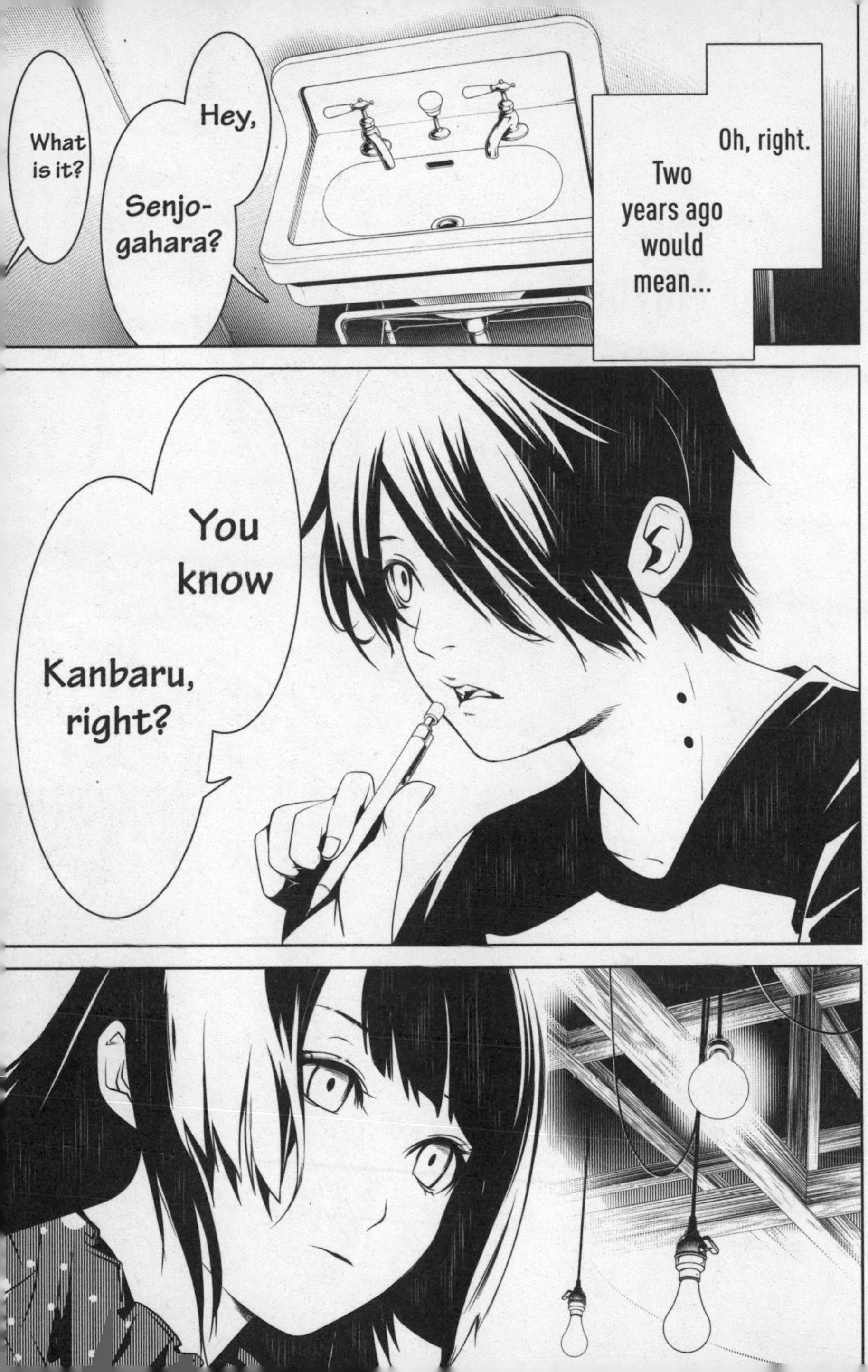
Oh, right. Two years ago would mean...
Hey, Senjo-gahara?
What is it?
You know Kanbaru, right?

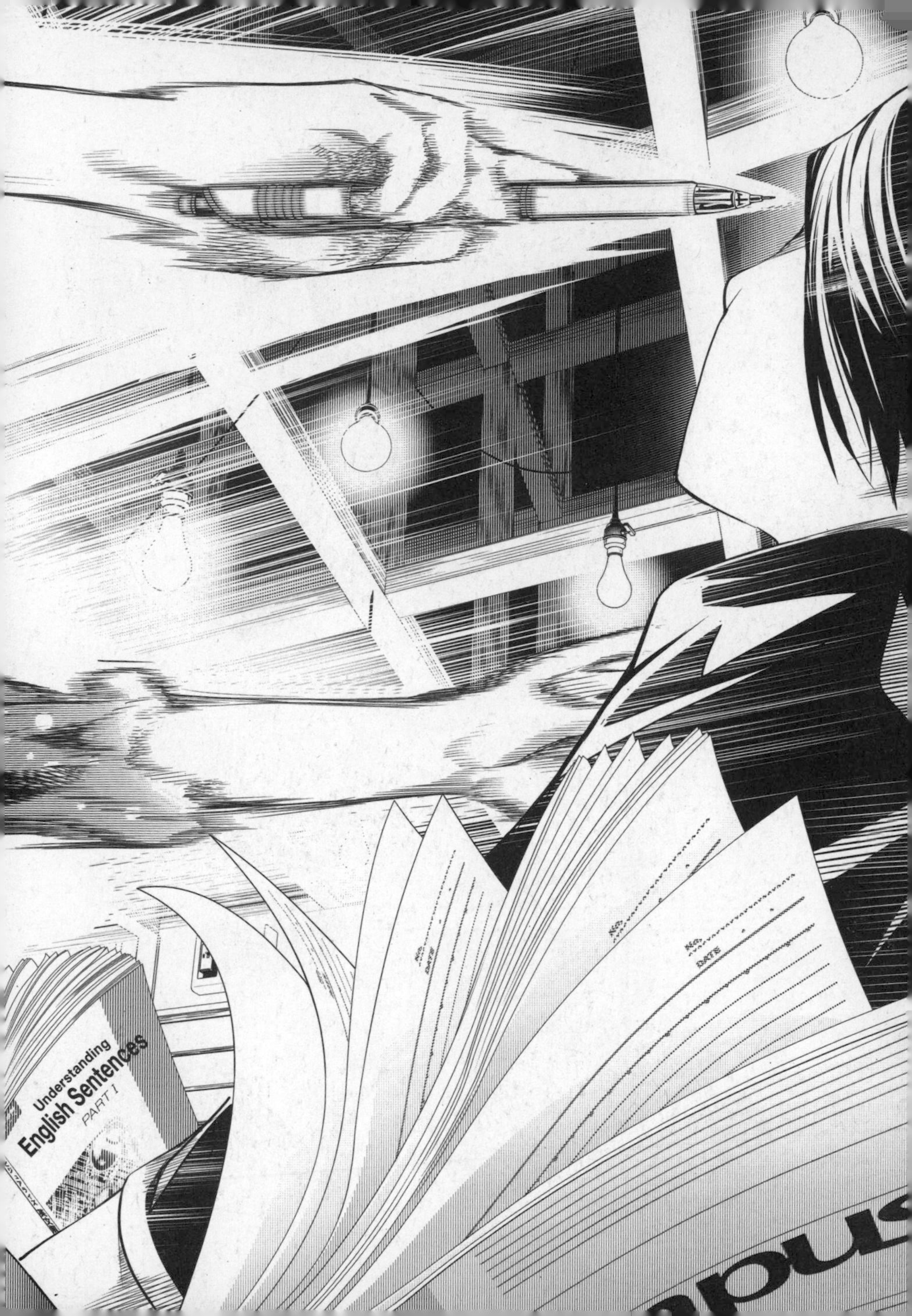
Understanding
English Sentences
PART I

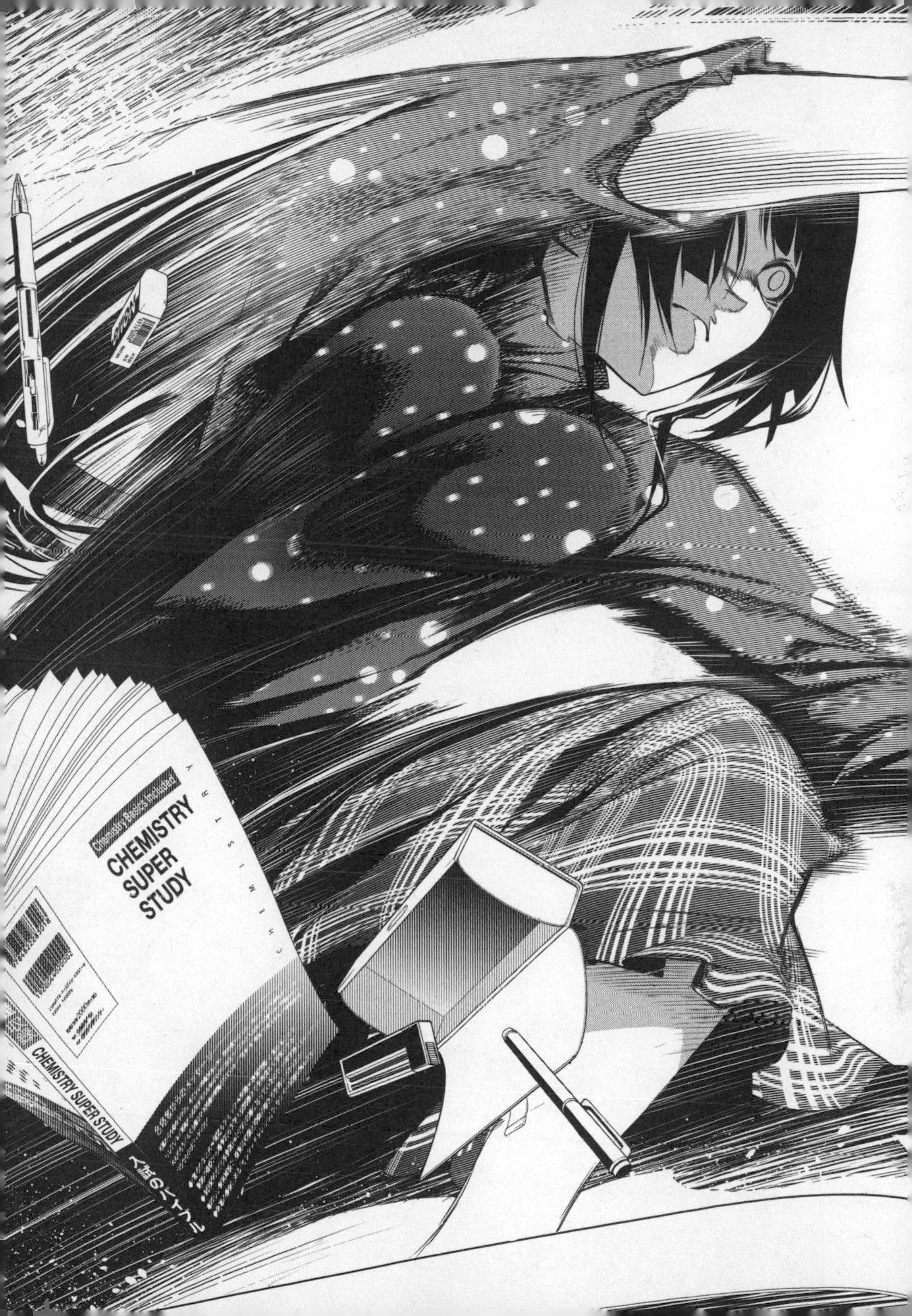
Chemistry Basics Included
CHEMISTRY SUPER STUDY
CHEMISTRY
CHEMISTRY SUPER STUDY

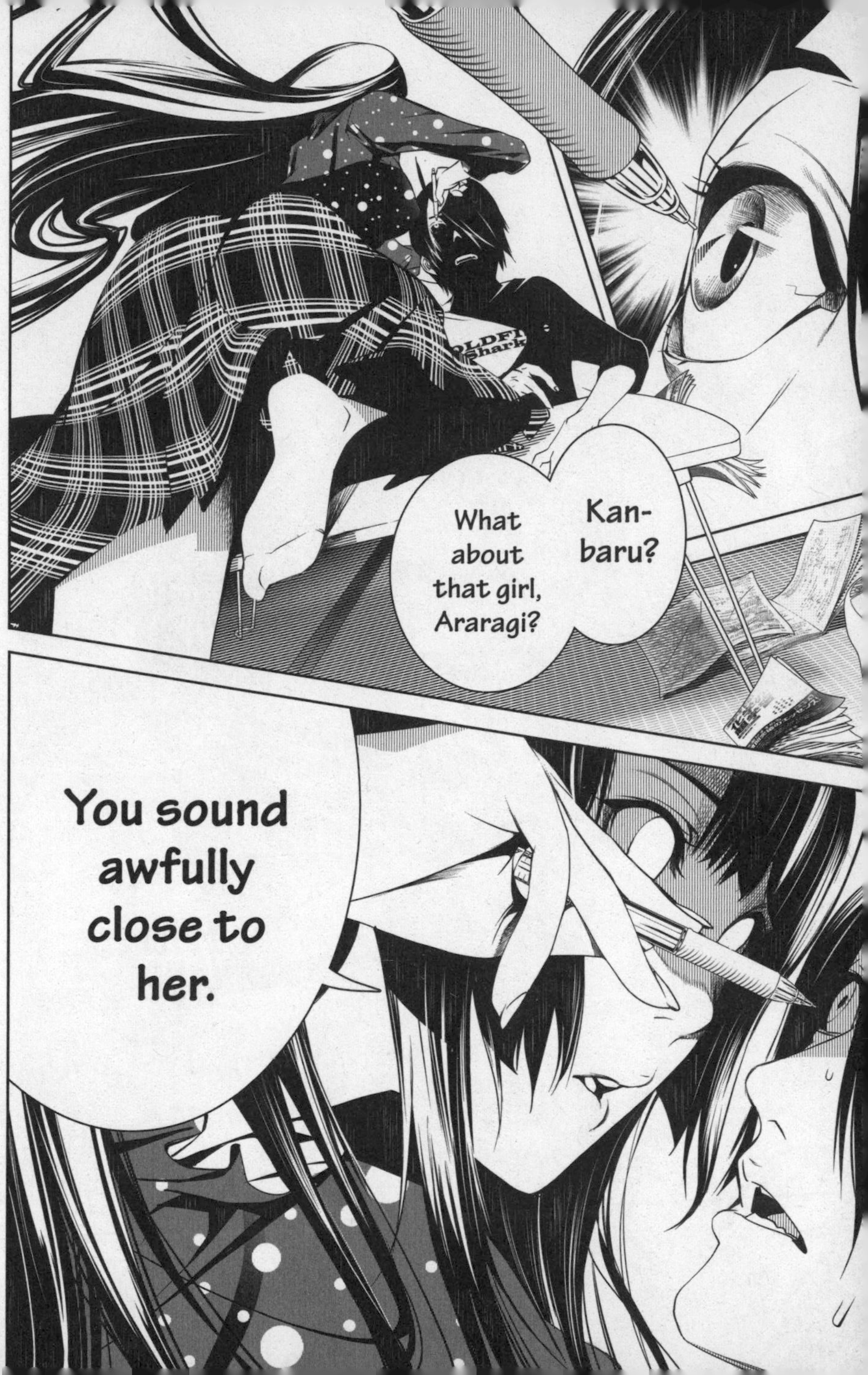
Kan-baru?
What about that girl, Araragi?
You sound awfully close to her.

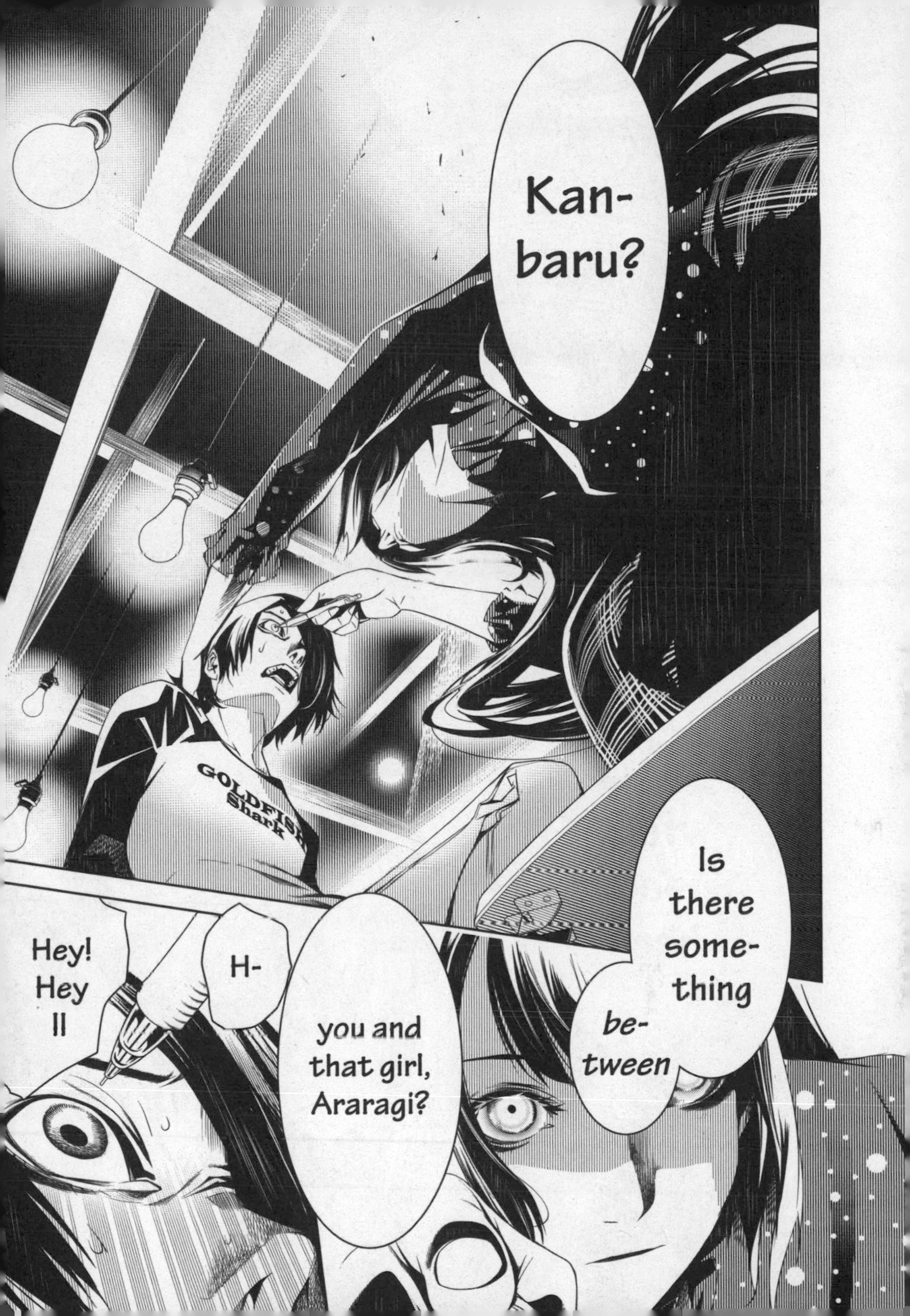
Kan-baru?
Is there some-thing be-tween
you and that girl, Araragi?
H-
Hey! Hey!!

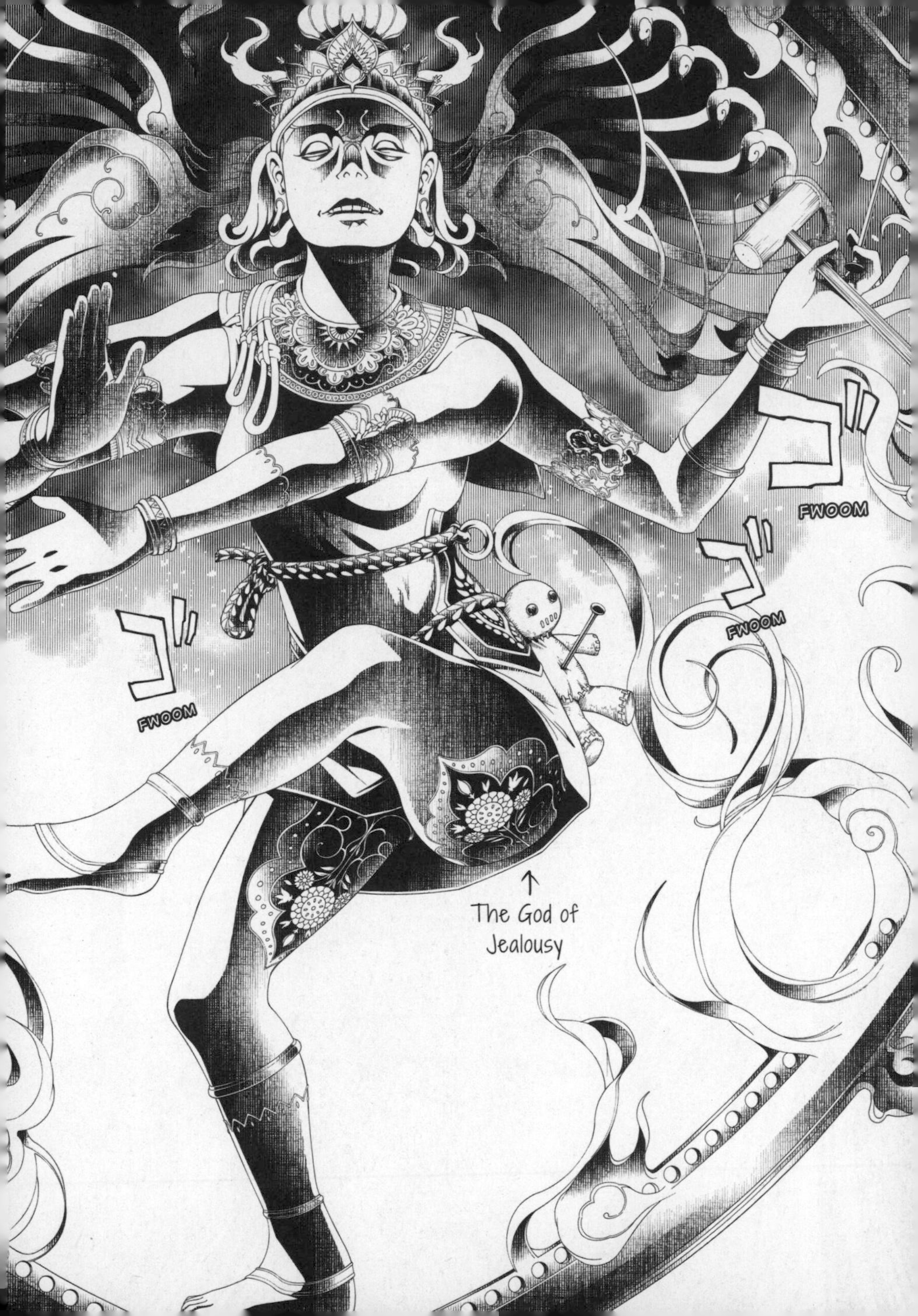
ゴ
FWOOM
ゴ
FWOOM
ゴ
FWOOM
The God of Jealousy

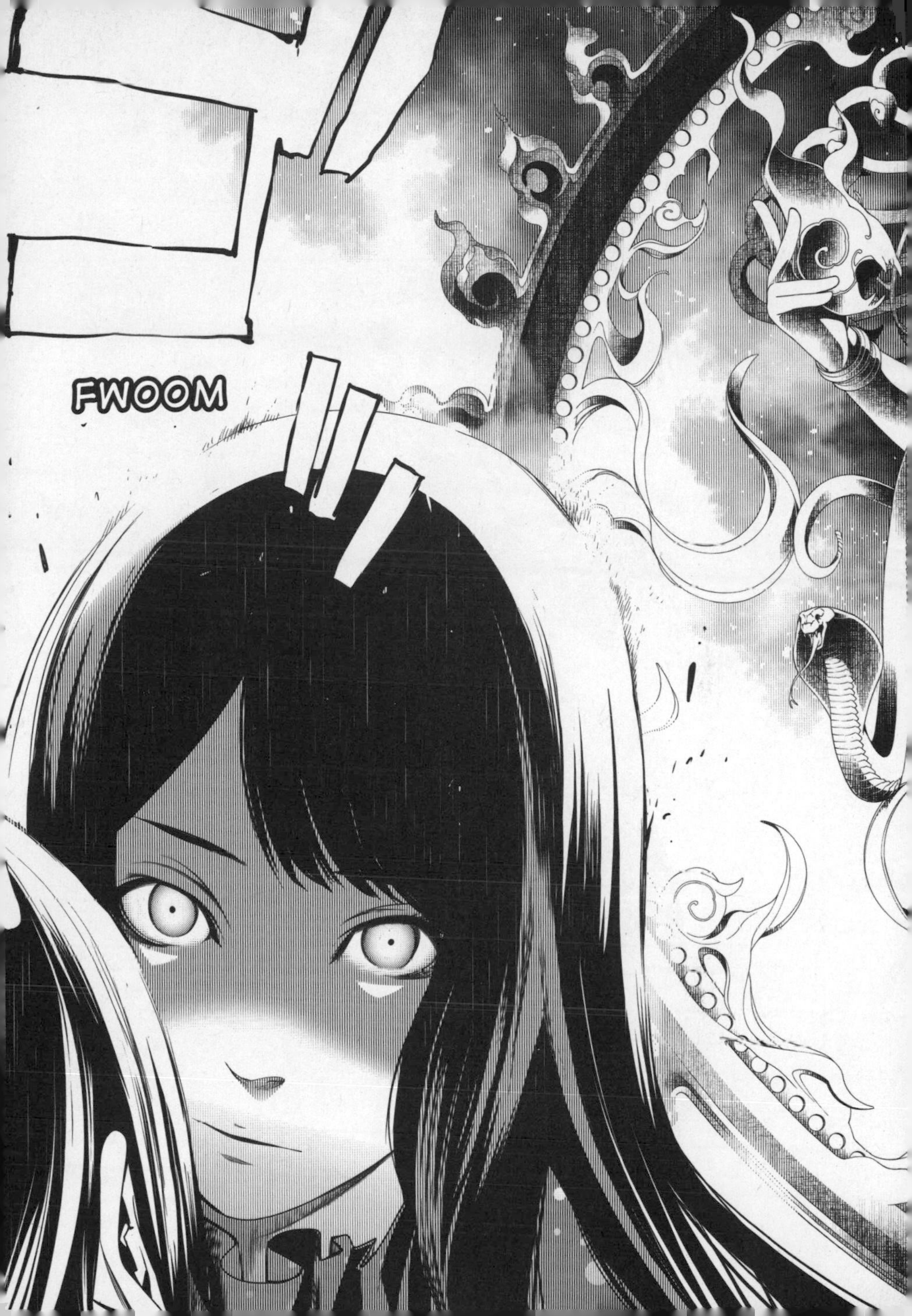
FWOOM

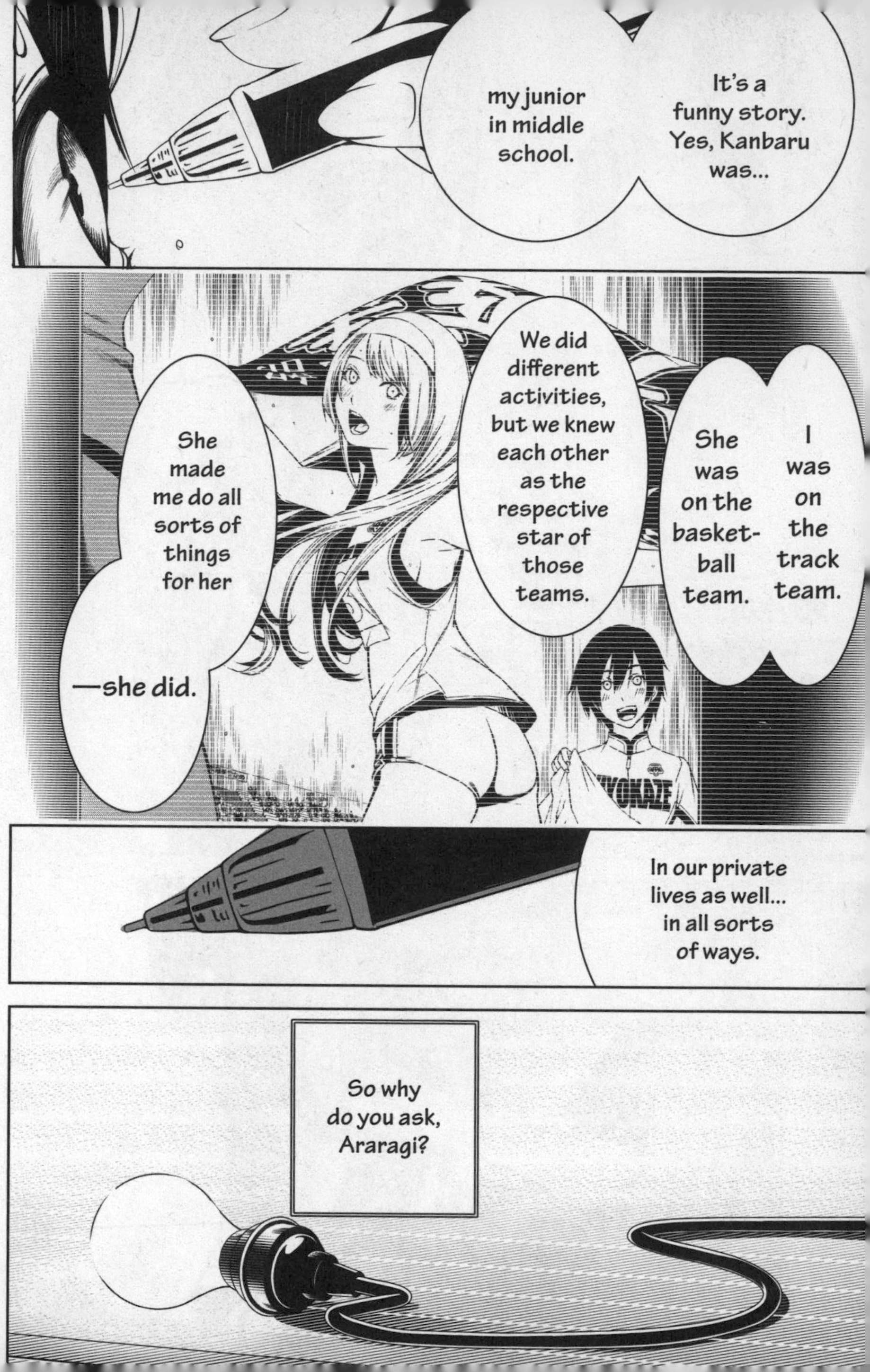
It's a funny story. Yes, Kanbaru was...
my junior in middle school.
I was on the track team.
She was on the basket-ball team.
We did different activities, but we knew each other as the respective star of those teams.
She made me do all sorts of things for her
—she did.
In our private lives as well... in all sorts of ways.
So why do you ask, Araragi?

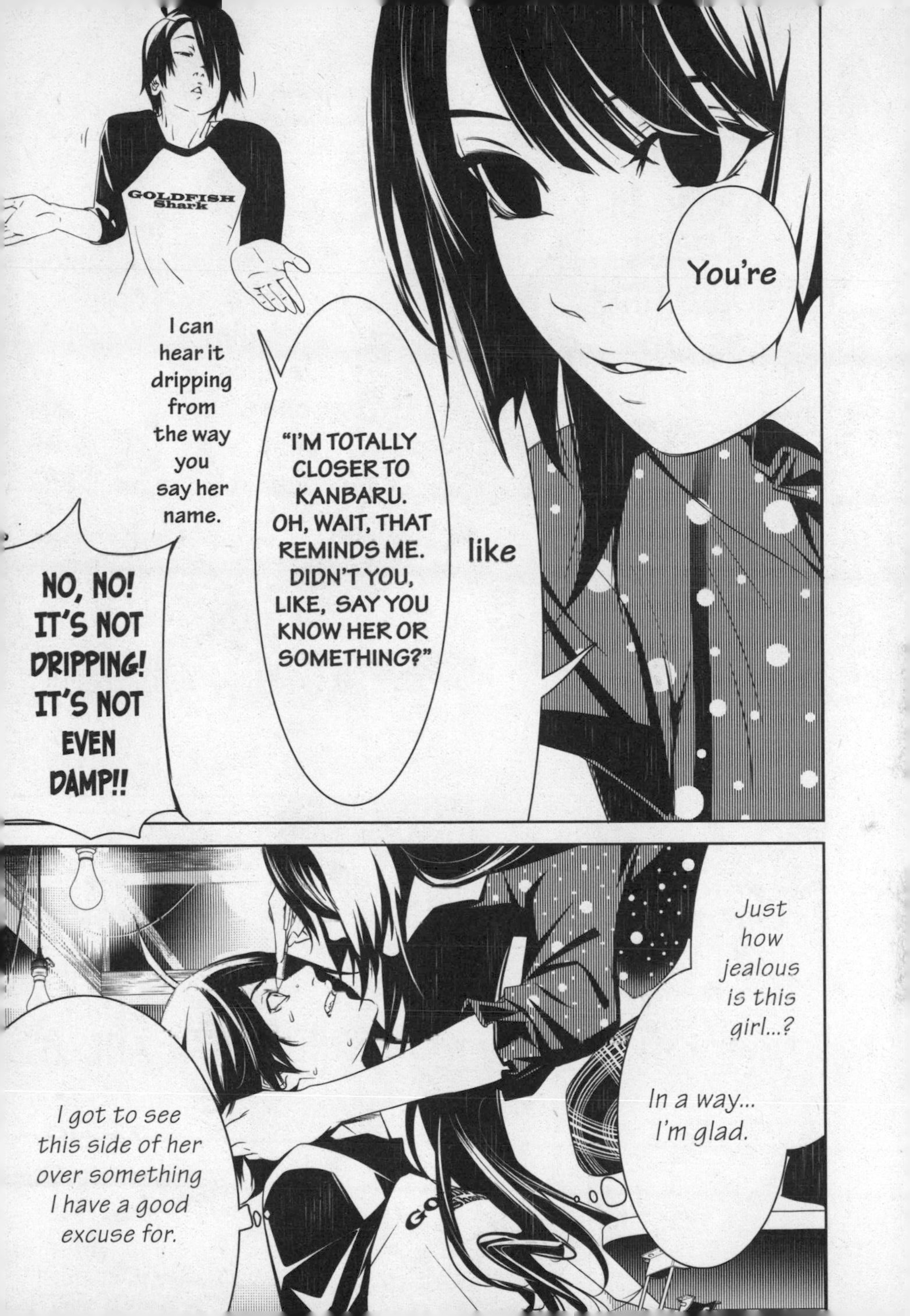
You're
like
"I'M TOTALLY CLOSER TO KANBARU. OH, WAIT, THAT REMINDS ME. DIDN'T YOU, LIKE, SAY YOU KNOW HER OR SOMETHING?"
I can hear it dripping from the way you say her name.
GOLDFISH Shark
NO, NO! IT'S NOT DRIPPING! IT'S NOT EVEN DAMP!!
Just how jealous is this girl...?
In a way... I'm glad.
I got to see this side of her over something I have a good excuse for.

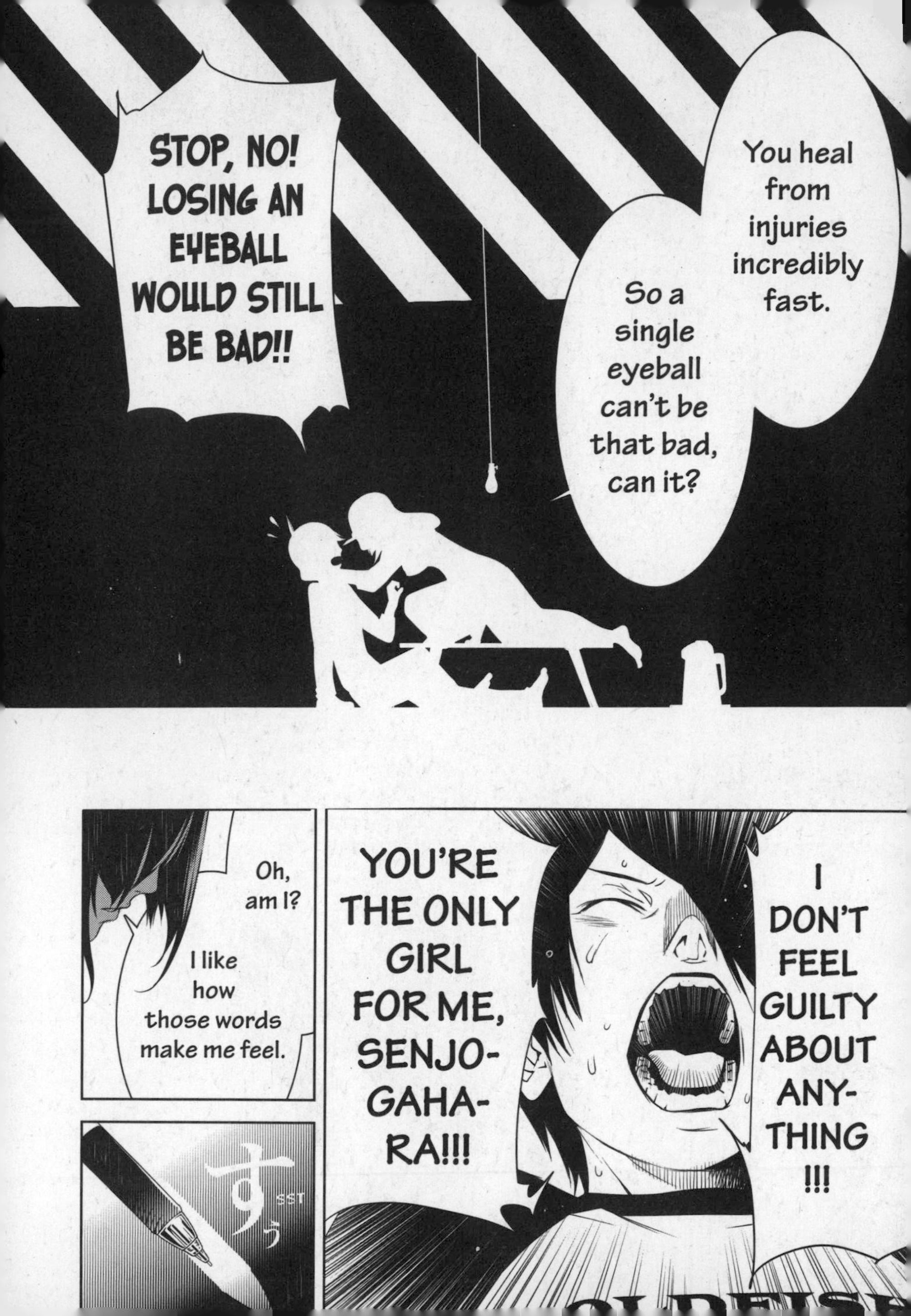
You heal from injuries incredibly fast.
So a single eyeball can't be that bad, can it?
STOP, NO! LOSING AN EYEBALL WOULD STILL BE BAD!!
I DON'T FEEL GUILTY ABOUT ANY-THING!!!
YOU'RE THE ONLY GIRL FOR ME, SENJO-GAHA-RA!!!
Oh, am I?
I like how those words make me feel.
すぅ
SST

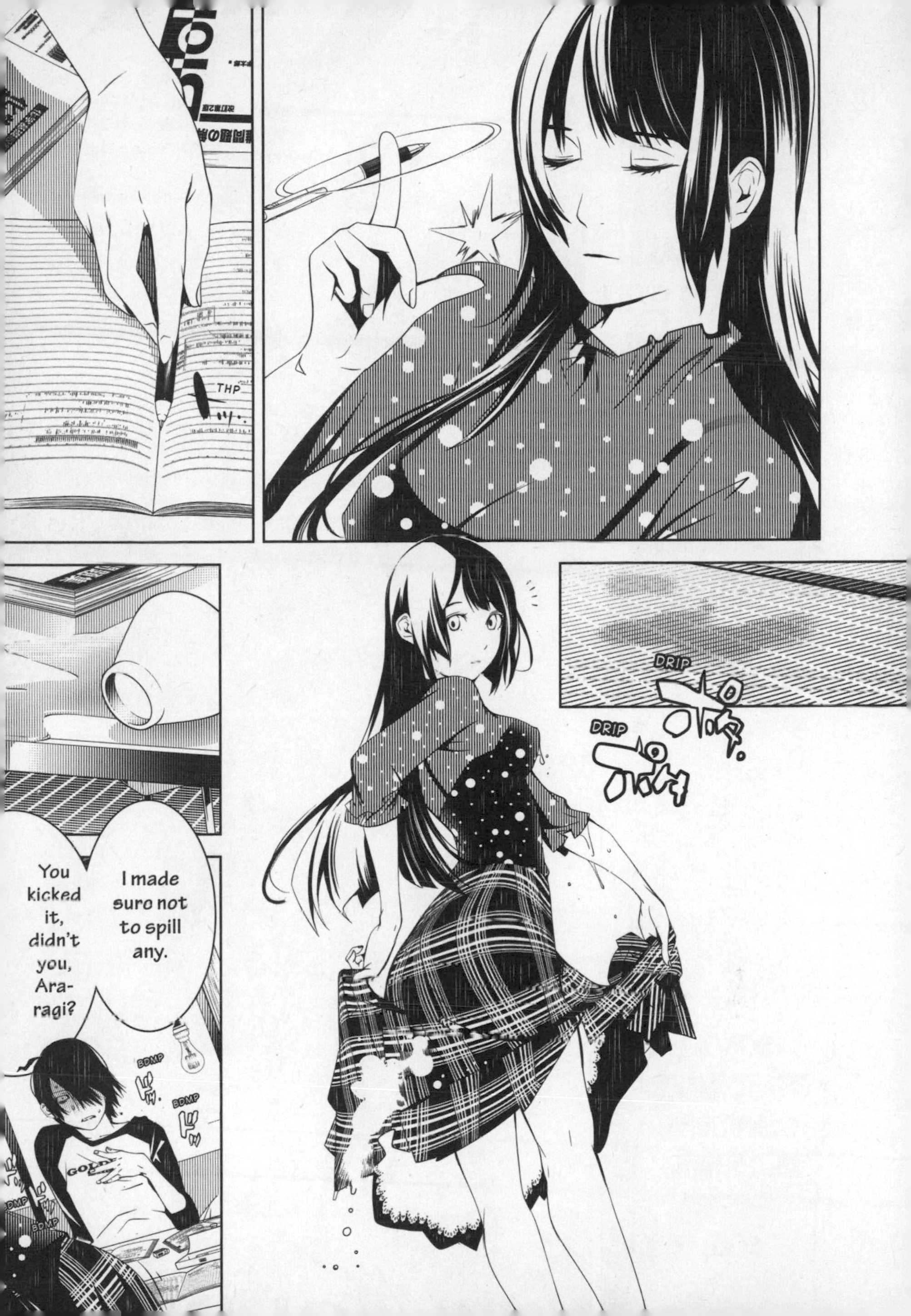
THP
DRIP
DRIP
I made sure not to spill any.
You kicked it, didn't you, Ara-ragi?
BDMP
BDMP
BDMP
BDMP

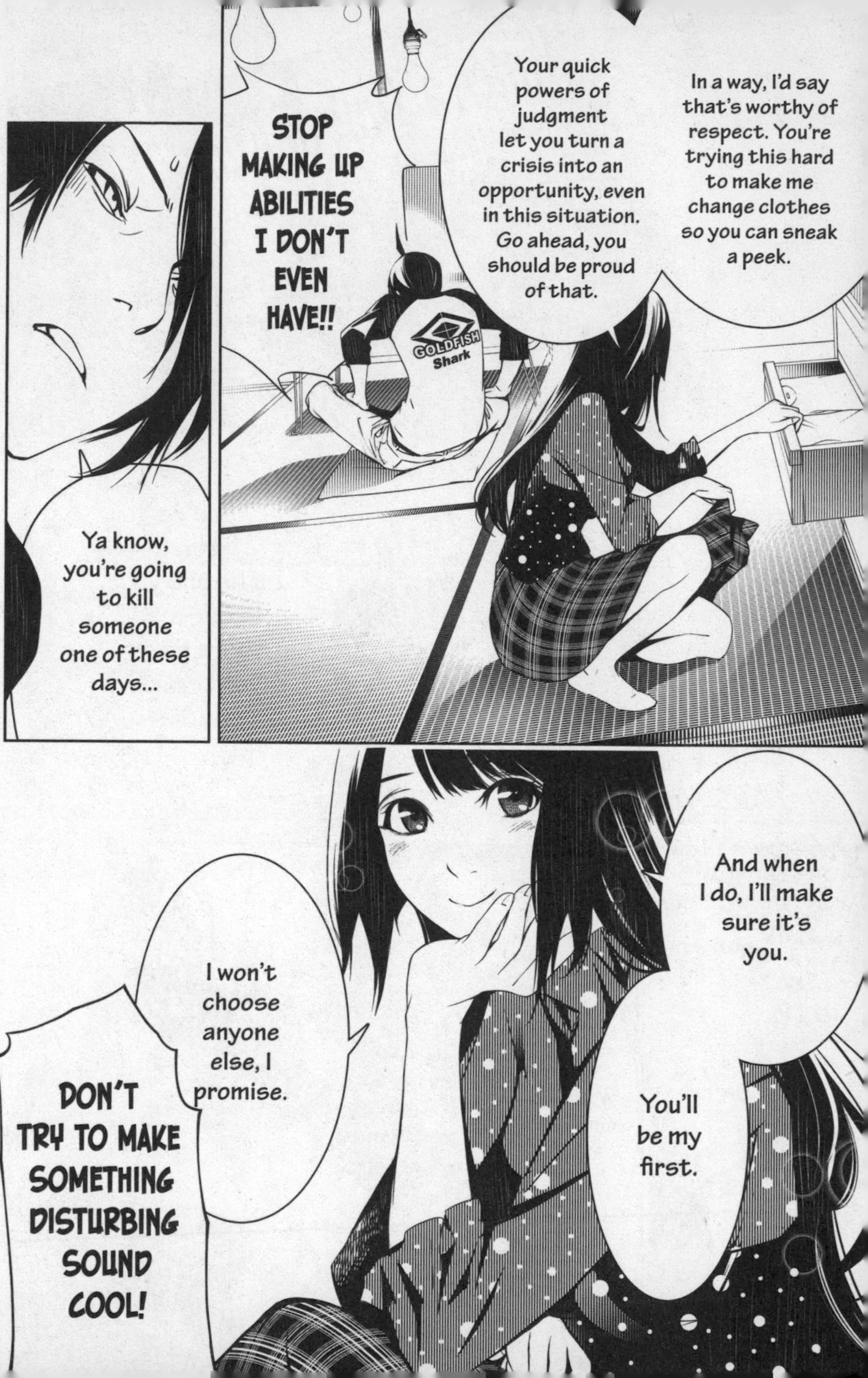
In a way, I'd say that's worthy of respect. You're trying this hard to make me change clothes so you can sneak a peek.
Your quick powers of judgment let you turn a crisis into an opportunity, even in this situation. Go ahead, you should be proud of that.
STOP MAKING UP ABILITIES I DON'T EVEN HAVE!!
GOLDFISH Shark
Ya know, you're going to kill someone one of these days...
And when I do, I'll make sure it's you.
You'll be my first.
I won't choose anyone else, I promise.
DON'T TRY TO MAKE SOMETHING DISTURBING SOUND COOL!

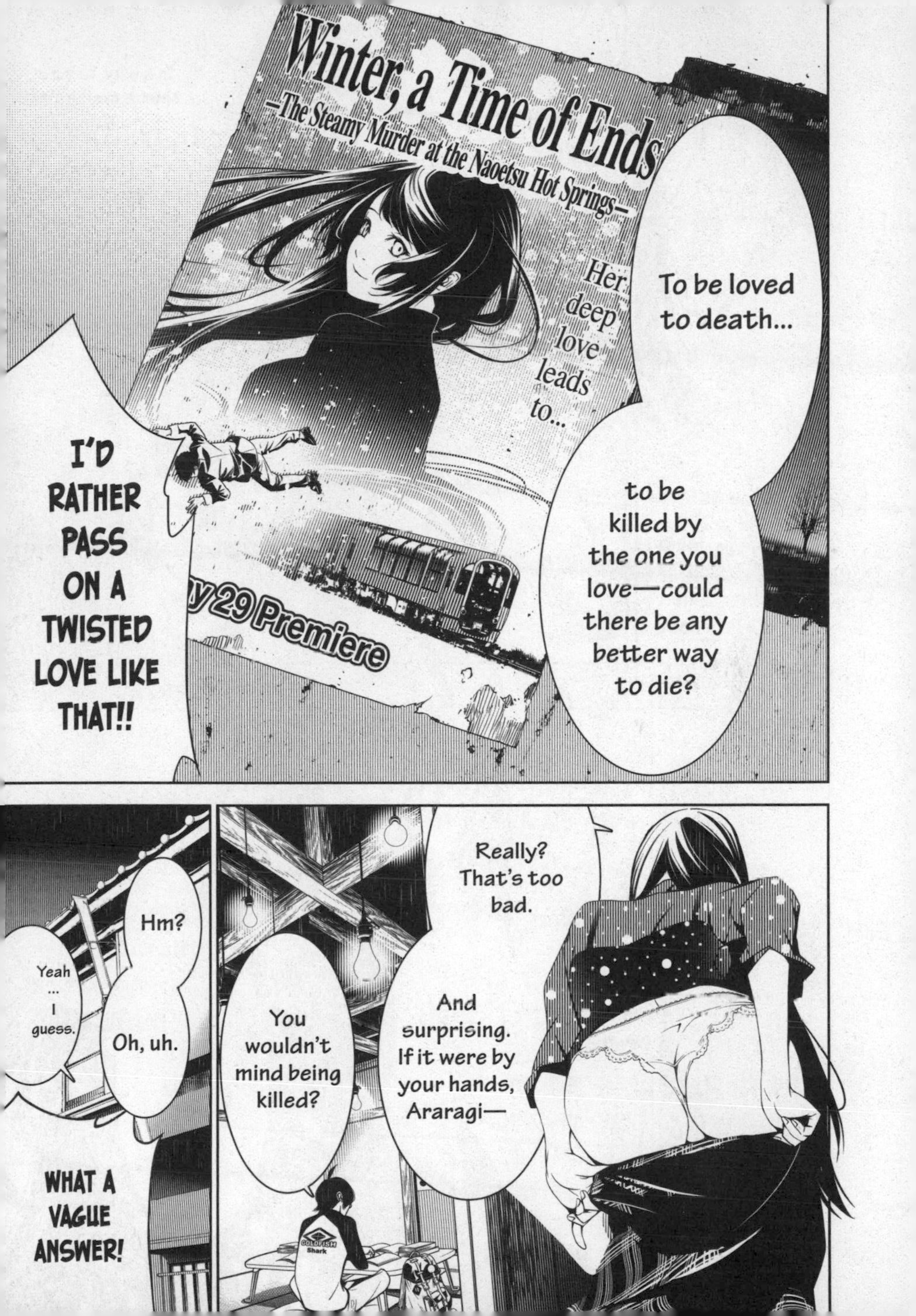
Winter, a Time of Ends
—The Steamy Murder at the Naoetsu Hot Springs—
Her deep love leads to...
29 Premiere
To be loved to death...
to be killed by the one you love—could there be any better way to die?
I'D RATHER PASS ON A TWISTED LOVE LIKE THAT!!
Really? That's too bad.
And surprising. If it were by your hands, Araragi—
You wouldn't mind being killed?
Hm?
Oh, uh.
Yeah... I guess.
GOLDFISH Shark
WHAT A VAGUE ANSWER!

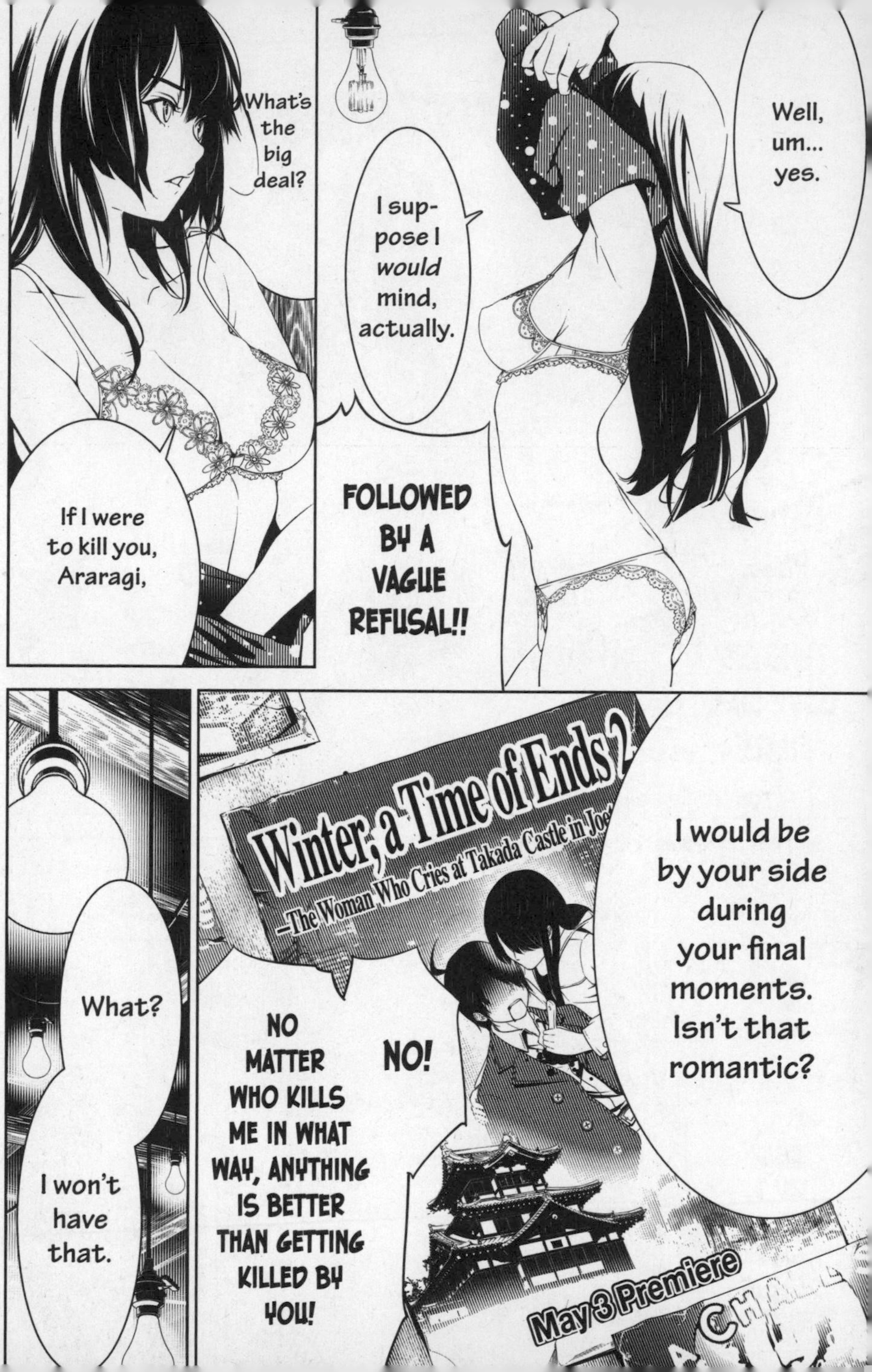
Well, um... yes.
I sup-pose I would mind, actually.
FOLLOWED BY A VAGUE REFUSAL!!
What's the big deal?
If I were to kill you, Araragi,
I would be by your side during your final moments. Isn't that romantic?
Winter, a Time of Ends 2
—The Woman Who Cries at Takada Castle in
May 3 Premiere
NO!
NO MATTER WHO KILLS ME IN WHAT WAY, ANYTHING IS BETTER THAN GETTING KILLED BY YOU!
What?
I won't have that.

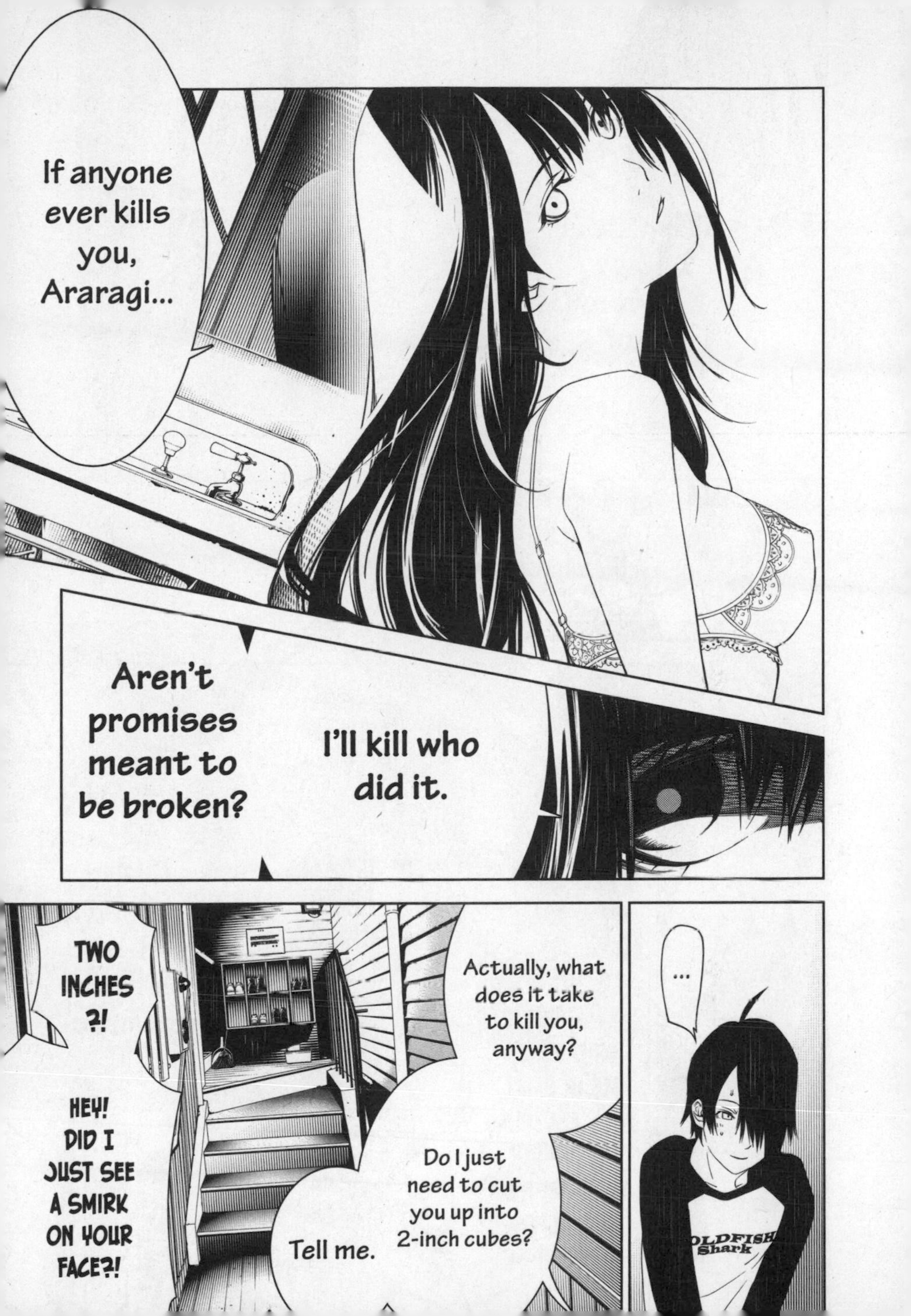
If anyone ever kills you, Araragi...
I'll kill who did it.
Aren't promises meant to be broken?
...
Actually, what does it take to kill you, anyway?
Do I just need to cut you up into 2-inch cubes?
Tell me.
TWO INCHES ?!
HEY! DID I JUST SEE A SMIRK ON YOUR FACE?!
OLDFISH Shark

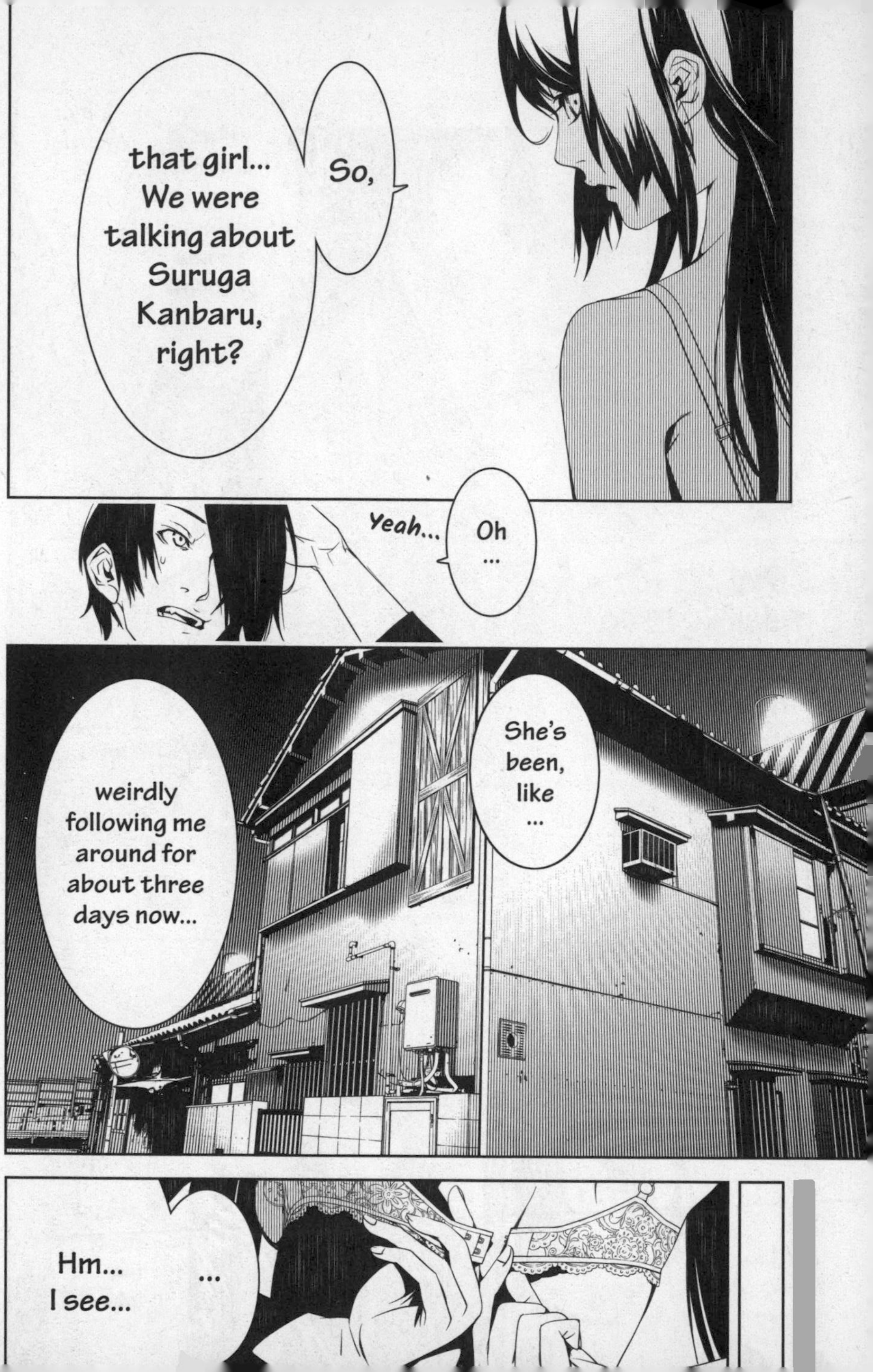
So,
that girl... We were talking about Suruga Kanbaru, right?
Oh ...
Yeah...
She's been, like ...
weirdly following me around for about three days now...
...
Hm... I see...

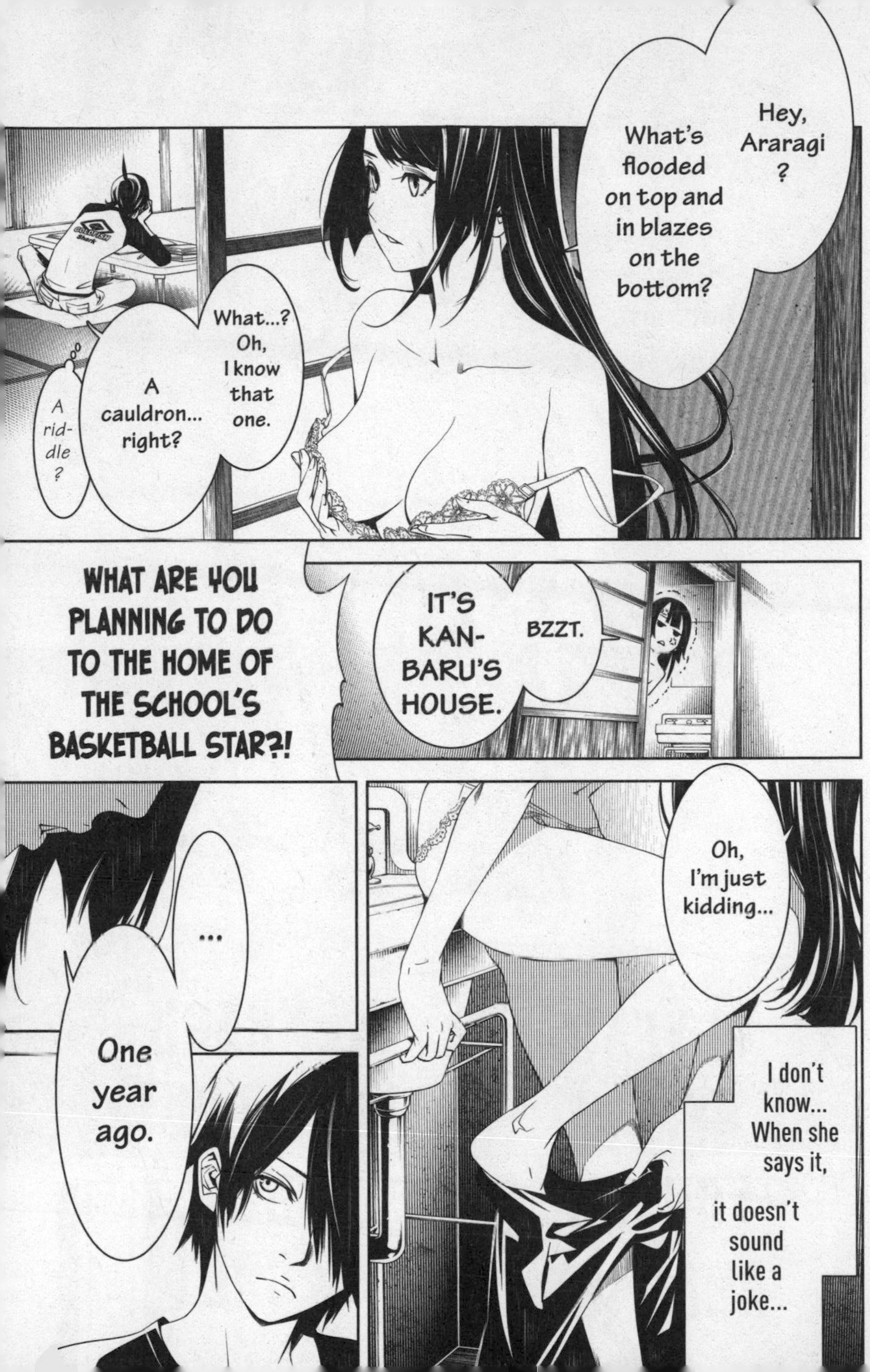
Hey, Araragi?
What's flooded on top and in blazes on the bottom?
What...? Oh, I know that one.
A cauldron... right?
A riddle?
BZZT.
IT'S KAN-BARU'S HOUSE.
WHAT ARE YOU PLANNING TO DO TO THE HOME OF THE SCHOOL'S BASKETBALL STAR?!
Oh, I'm just kidding...
I don't know... When she says it,
it doesn't sound like a joke...
...
One year ago.

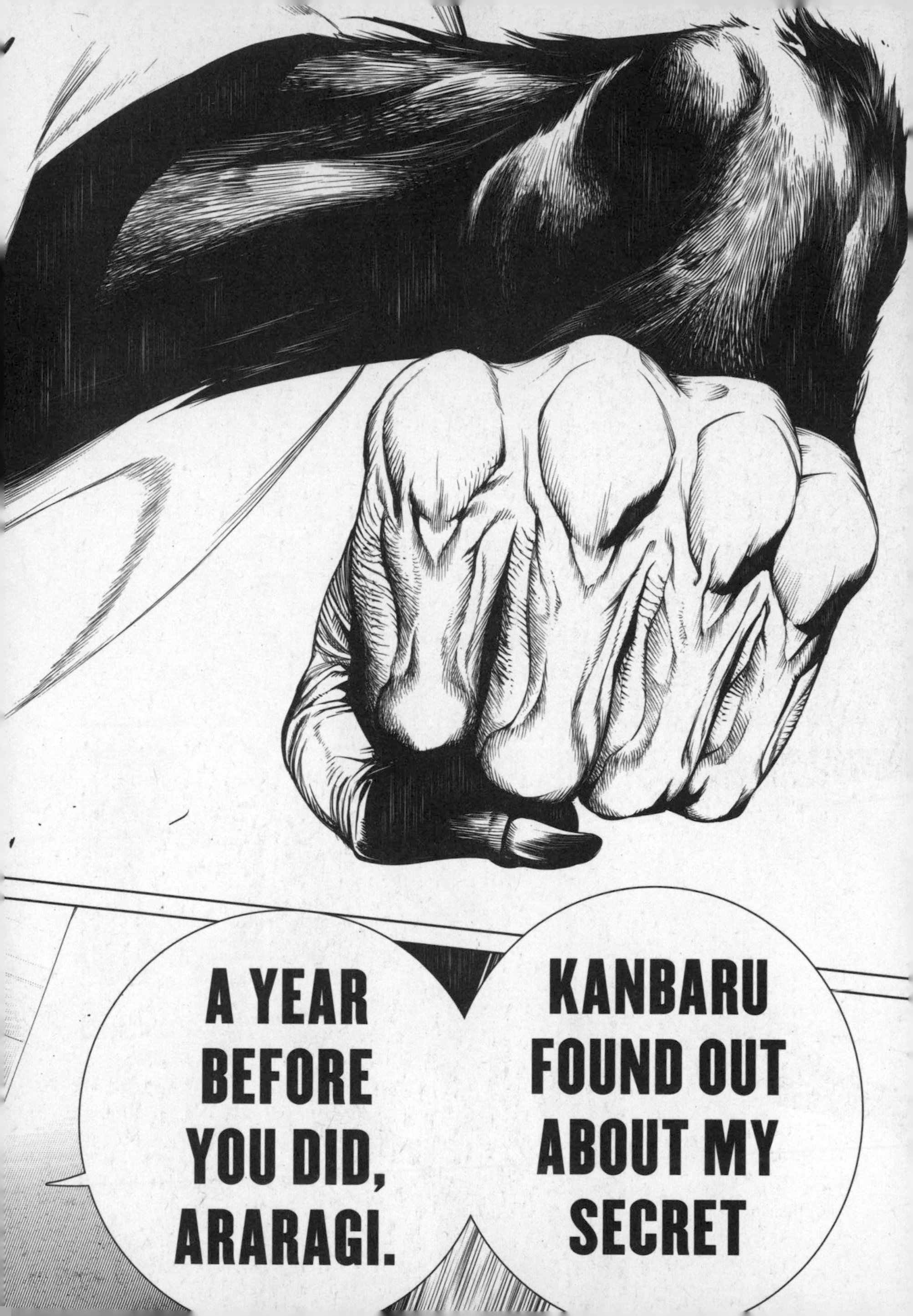
KANBARU FOUND OUT ABOUT MY SECRET
A YEAR BEFORE YOU DID, ARARAGI.

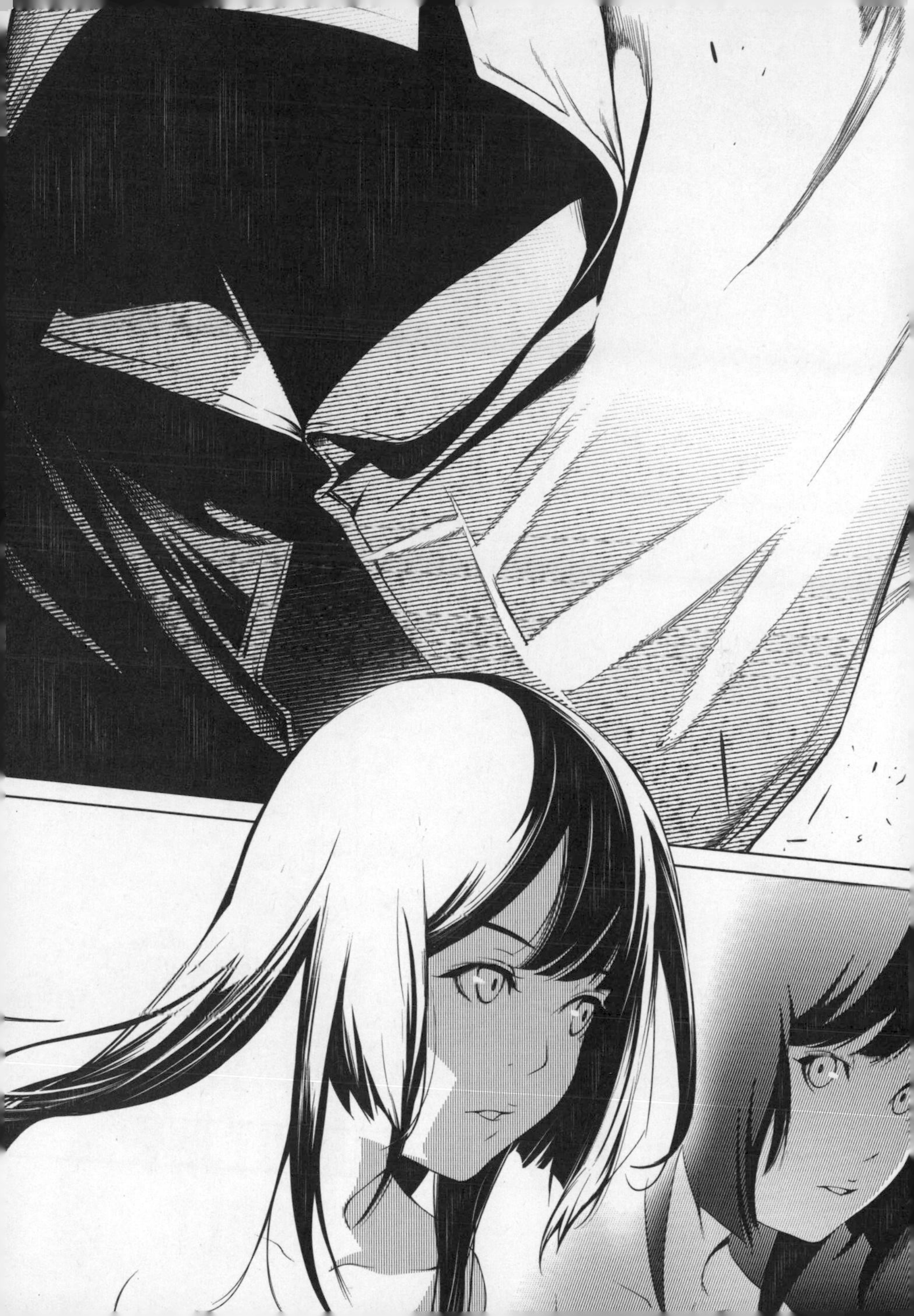

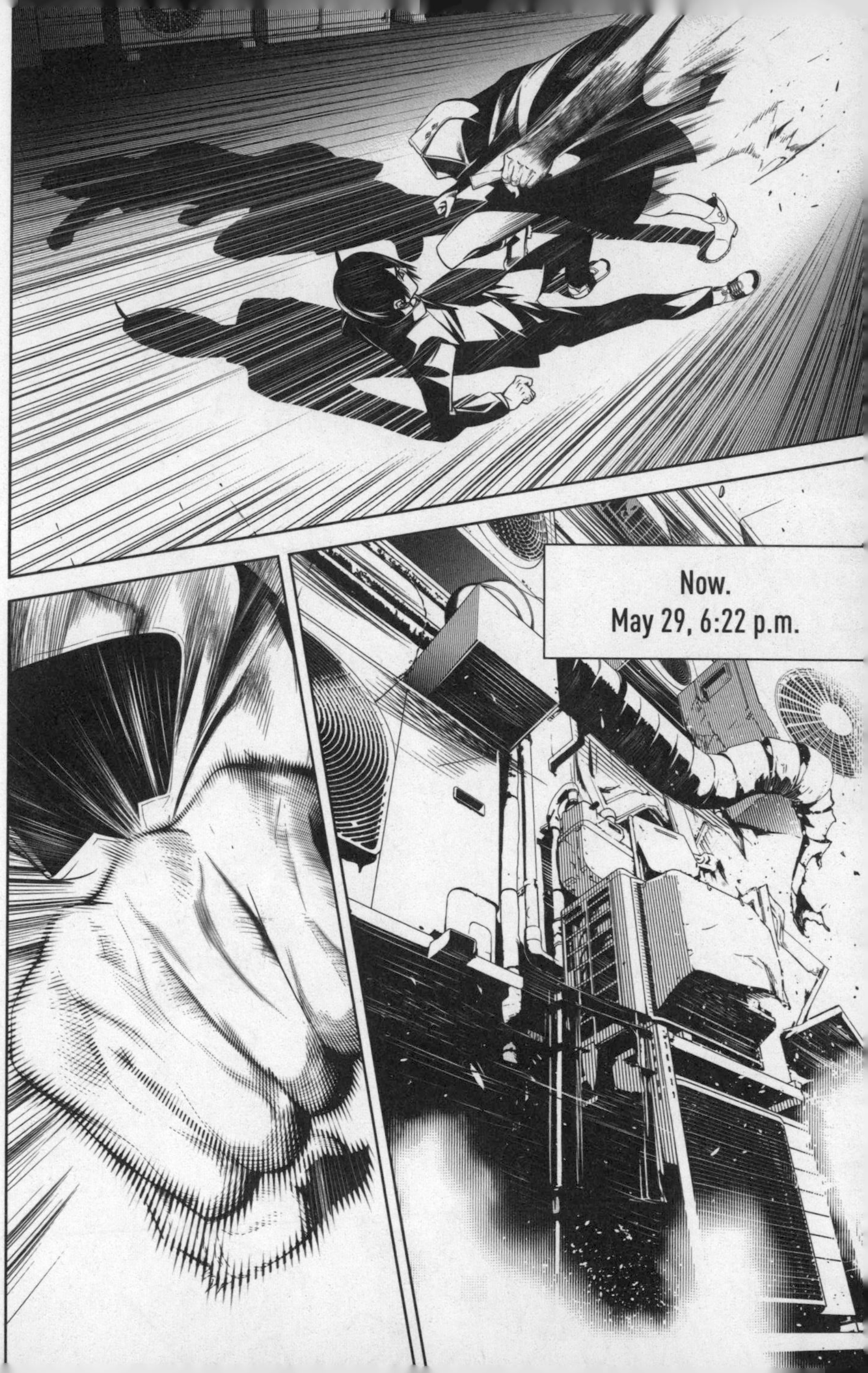
Now.
May 29, 6:22 p.m.

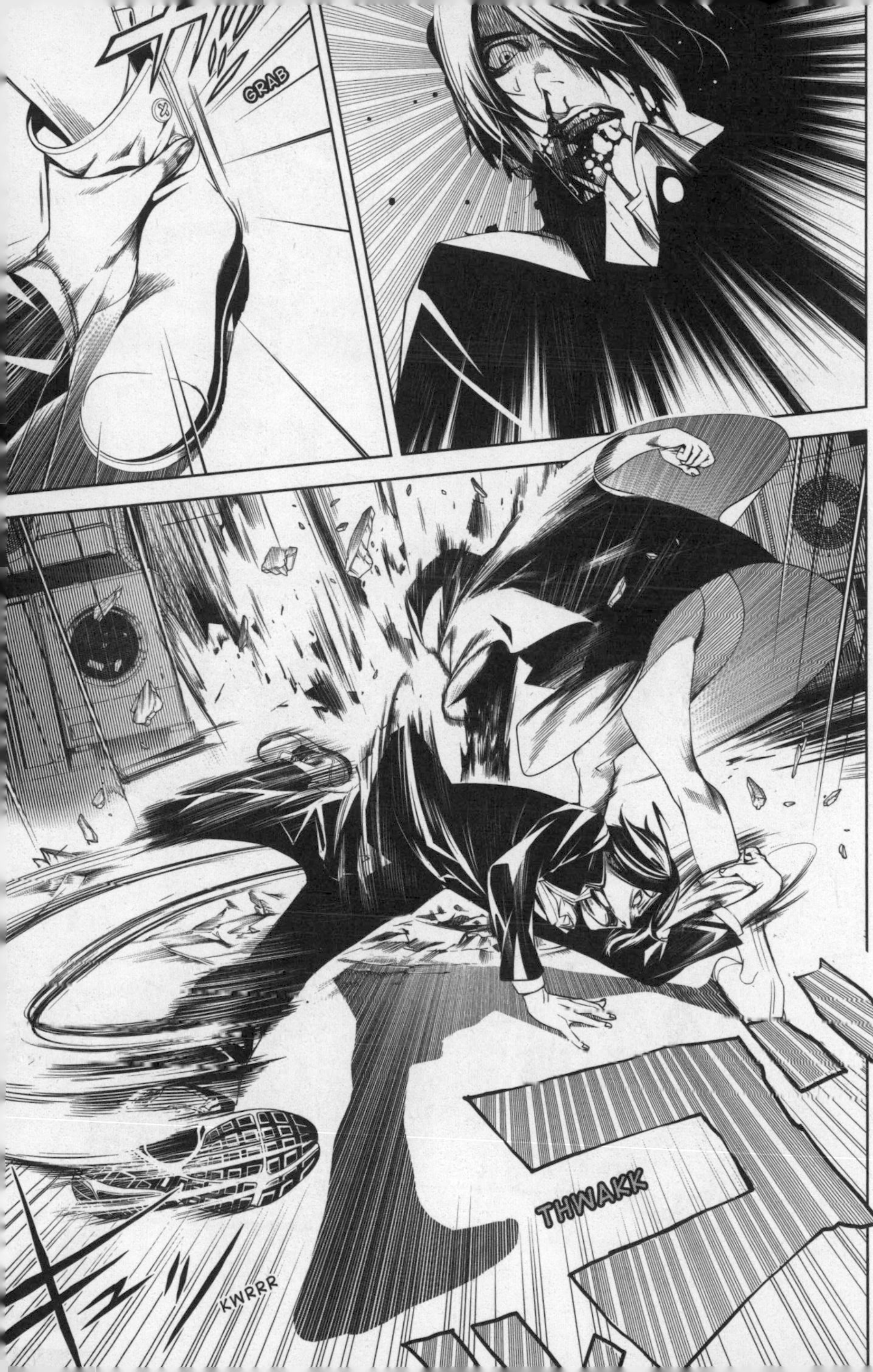
GRAB
THWAKK
KWRRR

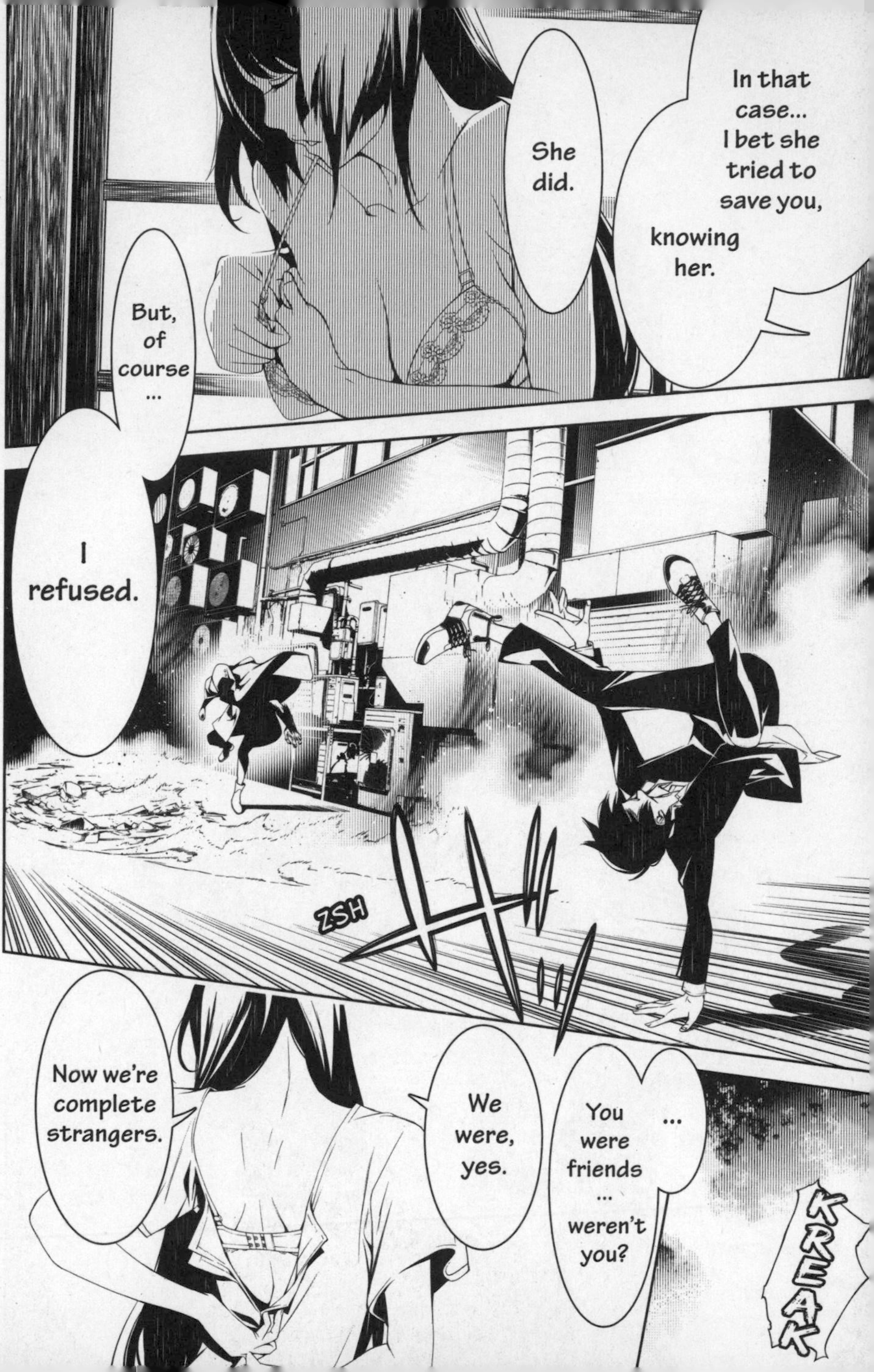
In that case... I bet she tried to save you, knowing her.
She did.
But, of course ...
I refused.
ZSH
KREAK
...
You were friends ... weren't you?
We were, yes.
Now we're complete strangers.

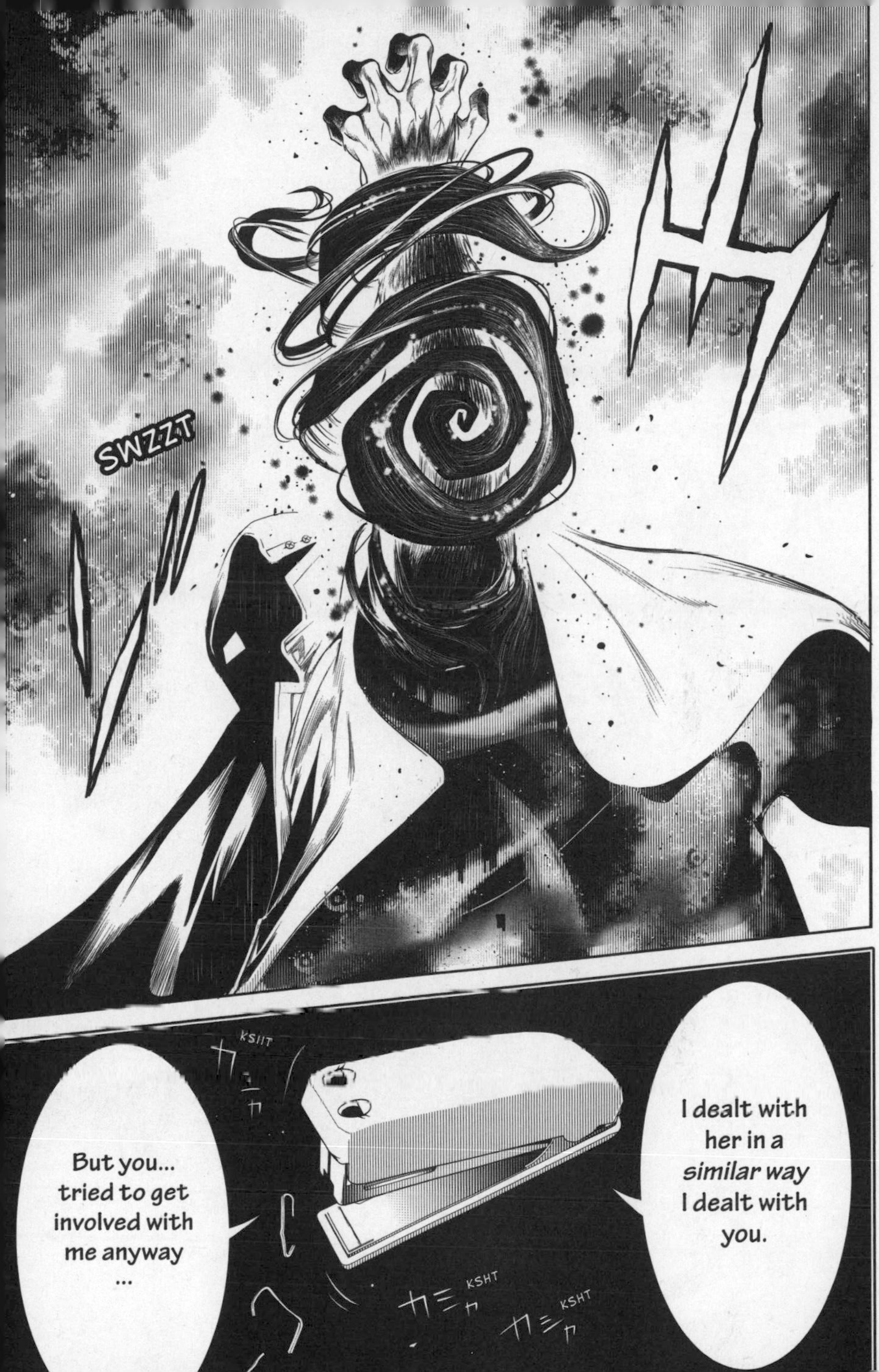
SWZZT
I dealt with her in a *similar way* I dealt with you.
KSIIT
But you... tried to get involved with me anyway ...
KSHT
KSHT

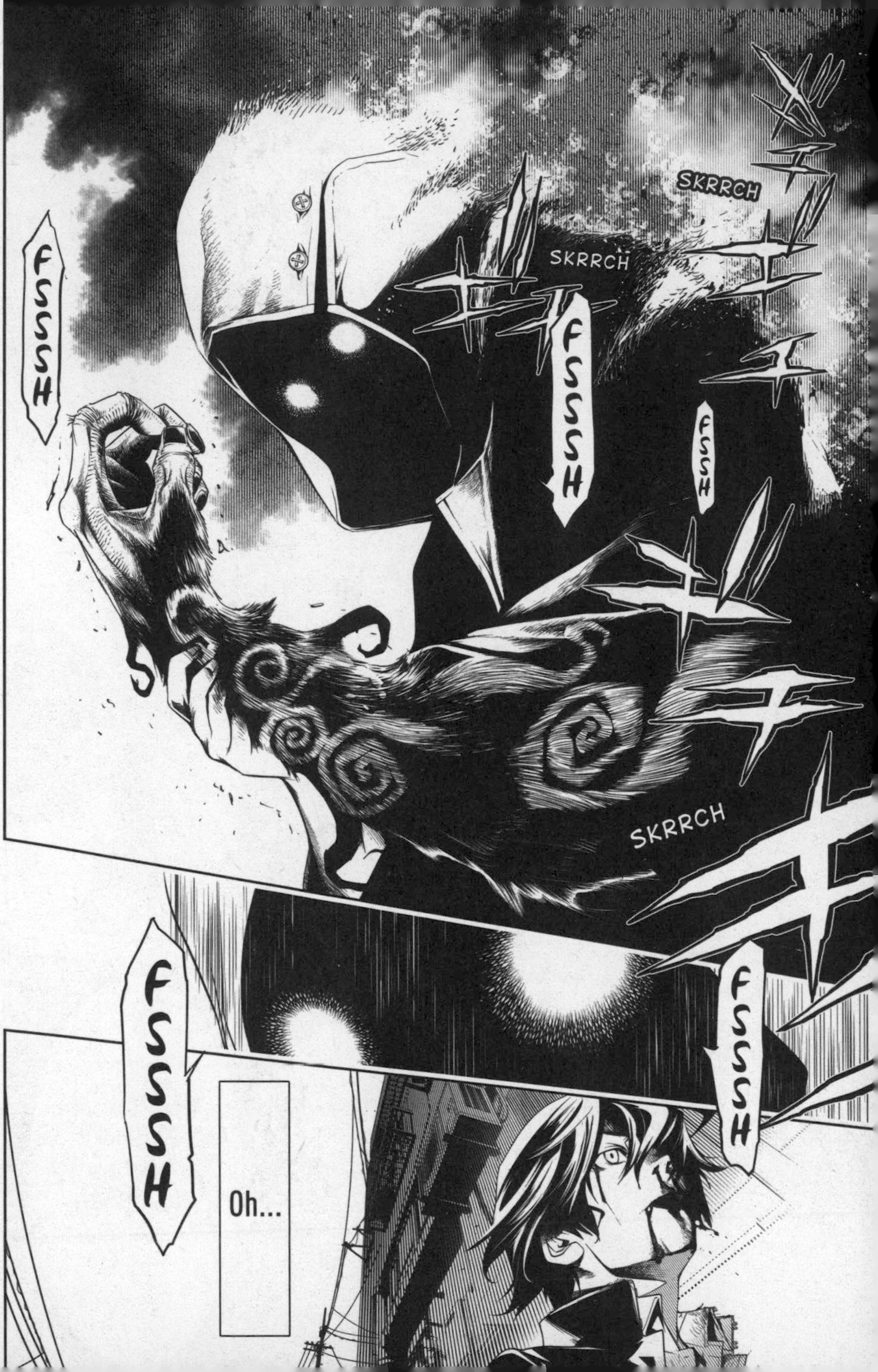

SKRRCH
SKRRCH
FSSH
FSSSH
FSSSH
SKRRCH
FSSSH
FSSSH
Oh...

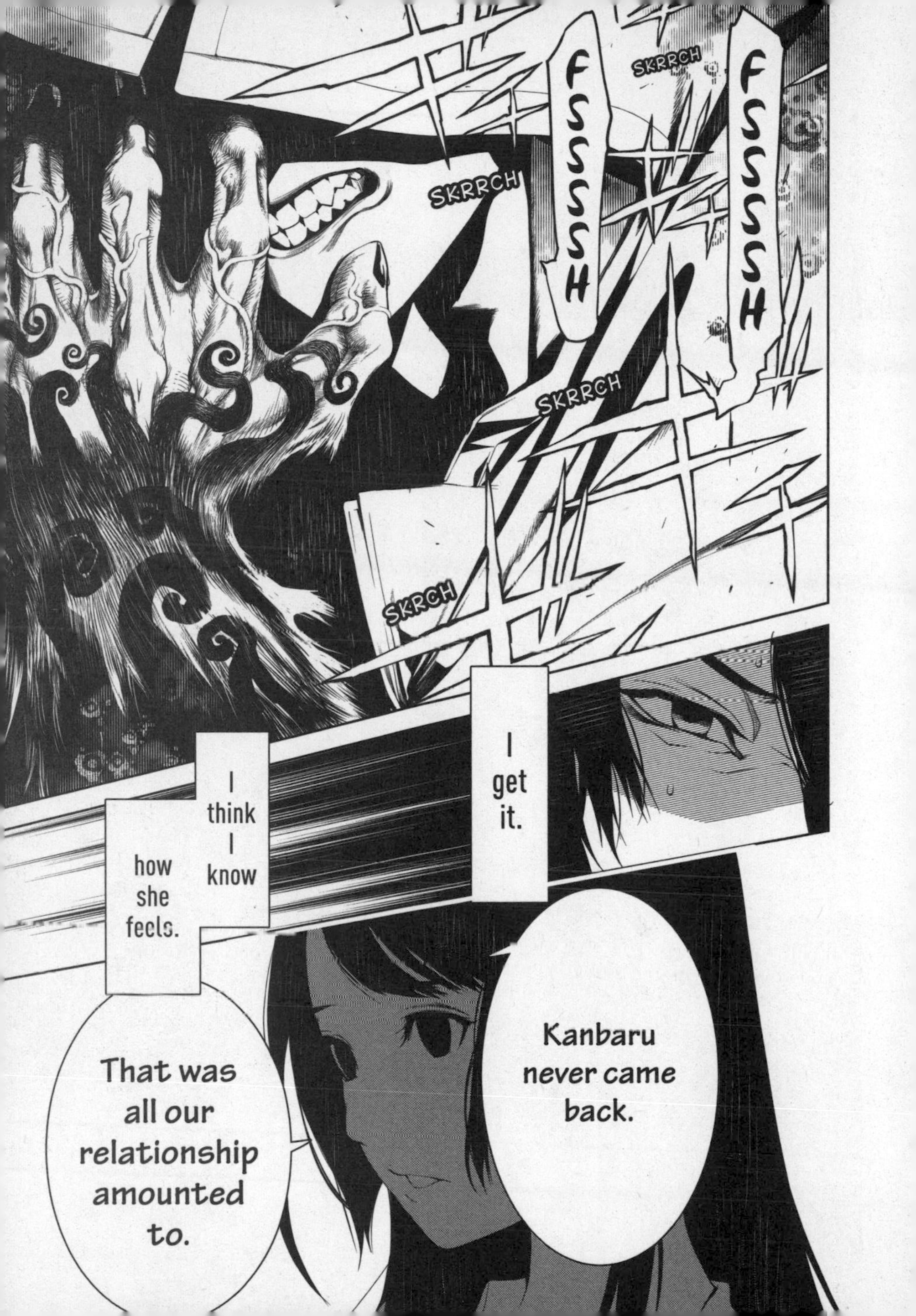
FSSSSH
SKRRCH
FSSSSH
SKRRCH
SKRRCH
SKRCH
I get it.
I think I know how she feels.
Kanbaru never came back.
That was all our relationship amounted to.

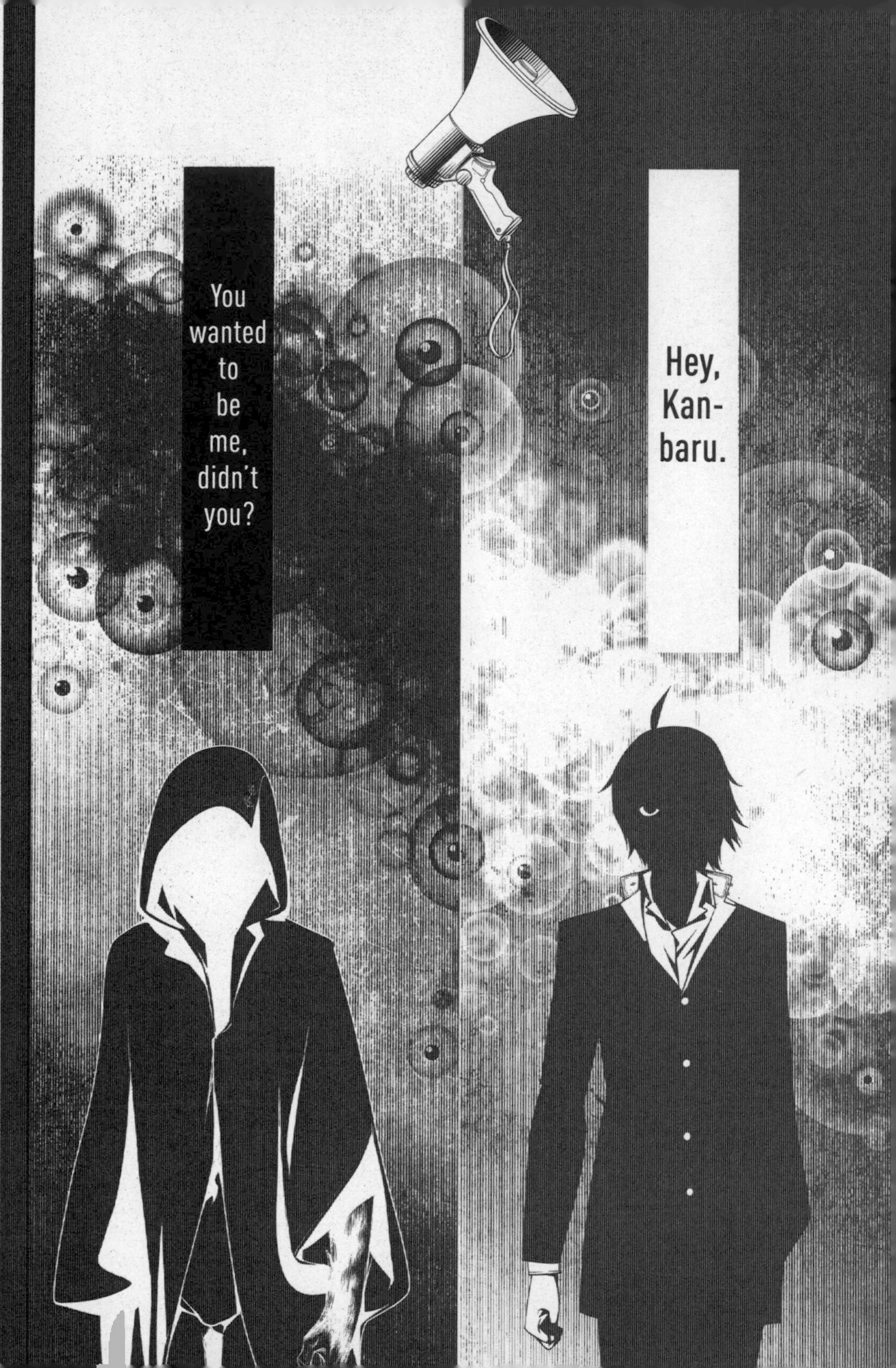
Hey, Kan-
baru.
You wanted to be me, didn't you?

化 bake

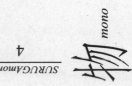
mono

SURUGAmonkey
4

語 gatari

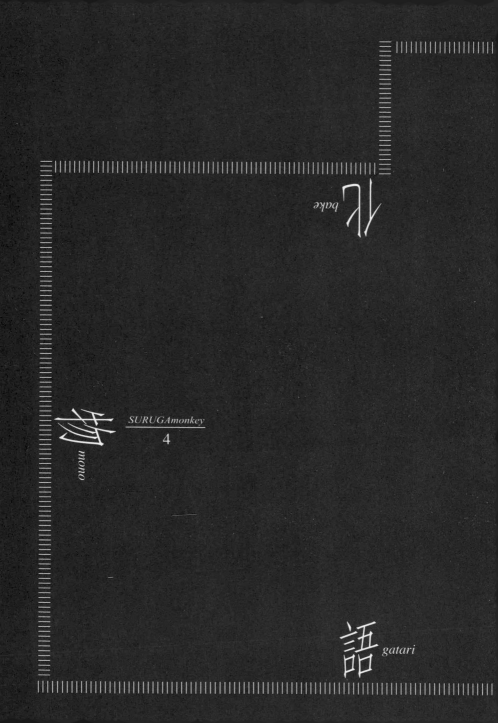

化 *bake*

怪 *mono*

SURUGAmonkey
4

語 *gatari*

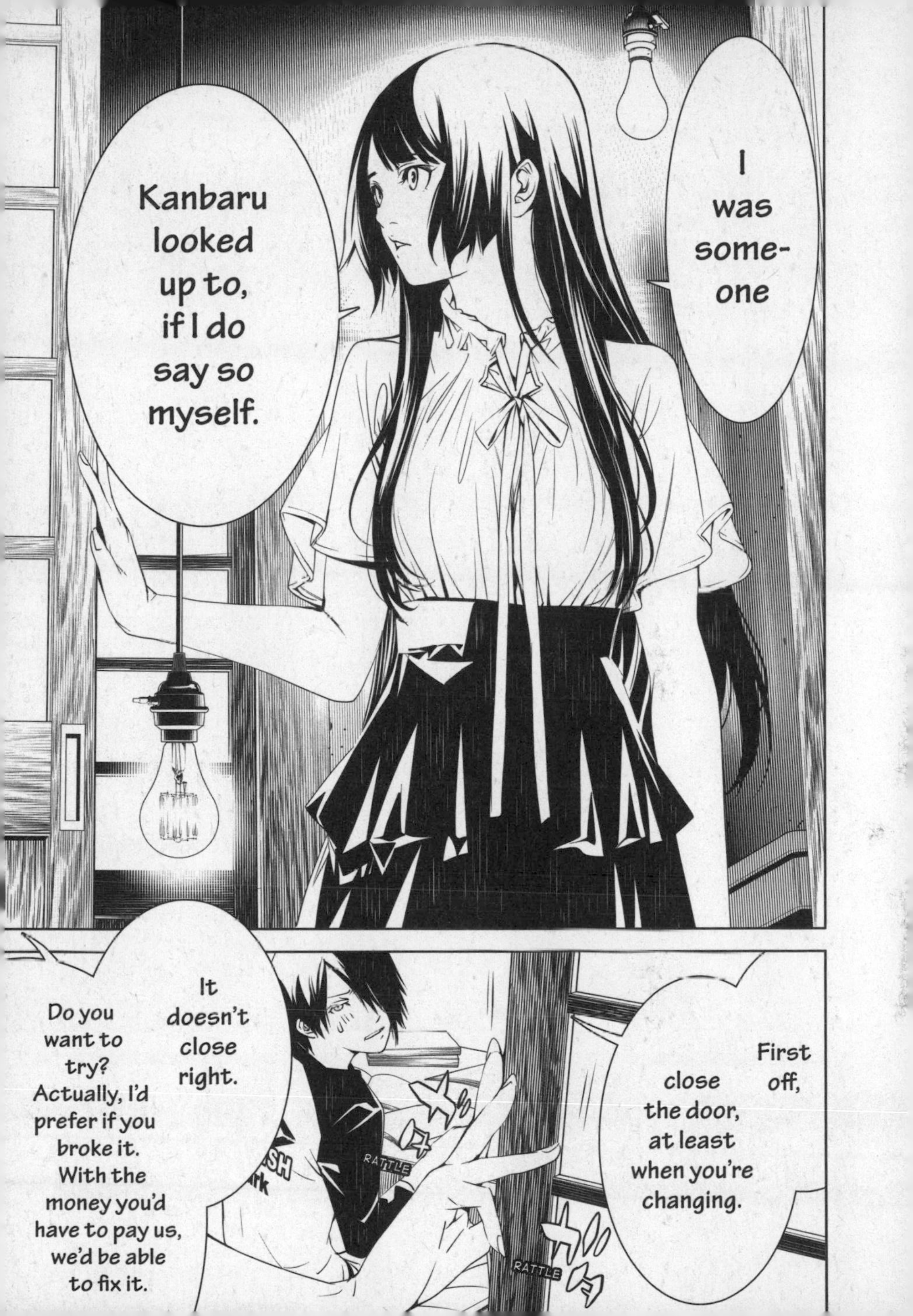
I was someone
Kanbaru looked up to, if I do say so myself.
First off, close the door, at least when you're changing.
It doesn't close right.
RATTLE
RATTLE
Do you want to try? Actually, I'd prefer if you broke it. With the money you'd have to pay us, we'd be able to fix it.

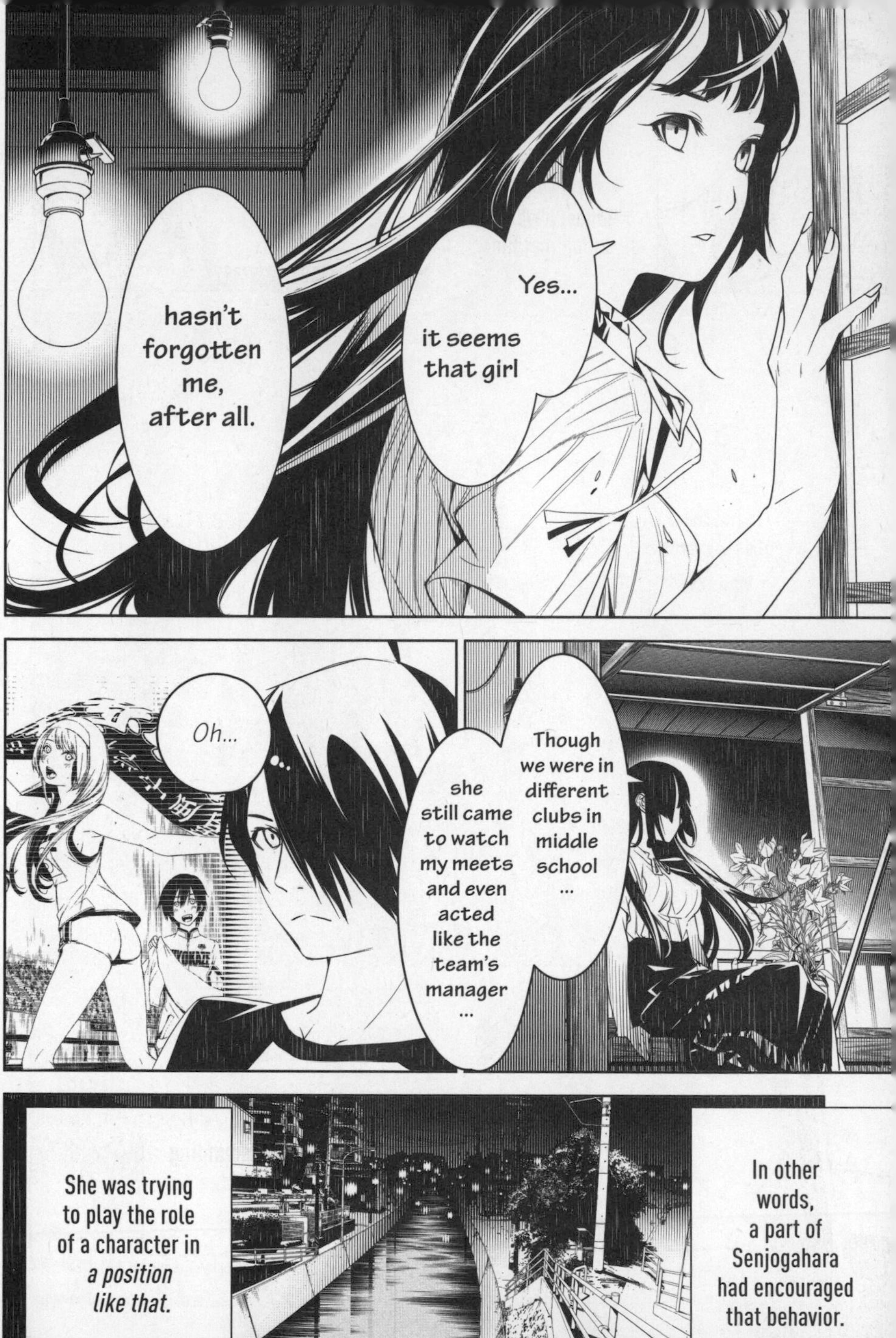
Yes...
it seems that girl
hasn't forgotten me, after all.
Though we were in different clubs in middle school ...
she still came to watch my meets and even acted like the team's manager ...
Oh...
In other words, a part of Senjogahara had encouraged that behavior.
She was trying to play the role of a character in *a position like that.*

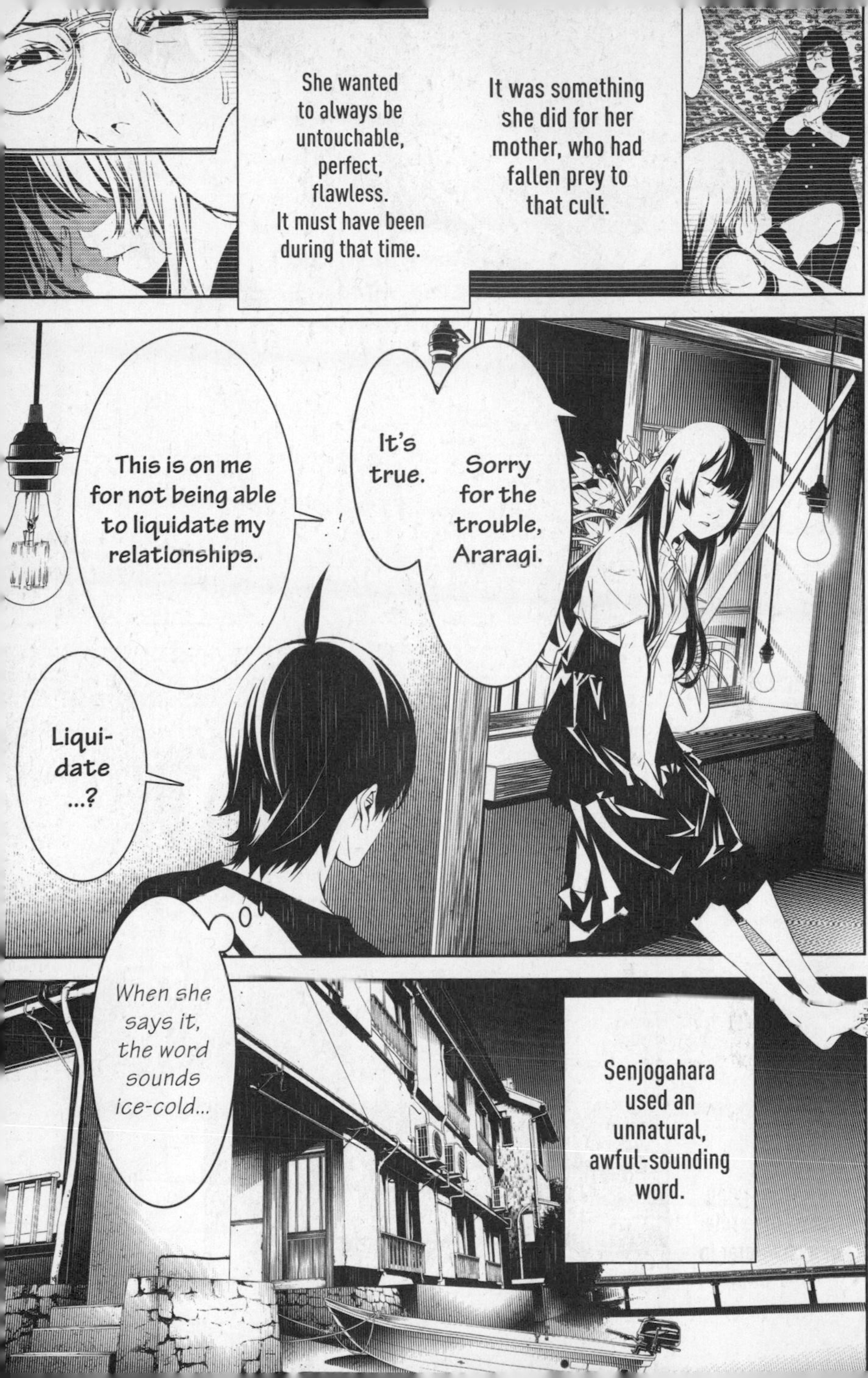
It was something she did for her mother, who had fallen prey to that cult.
She wanted to always be untouchable, perfect, flawless. It must have been during that time.
It's true.
Sorry for the trouble, Araragi.
This is on me for not being able to liquidate my relationships.
Liqui-date ...?
Senjogahara used an unnatural, awful-sounding word.
When she says it, the word sounds ice-cold...

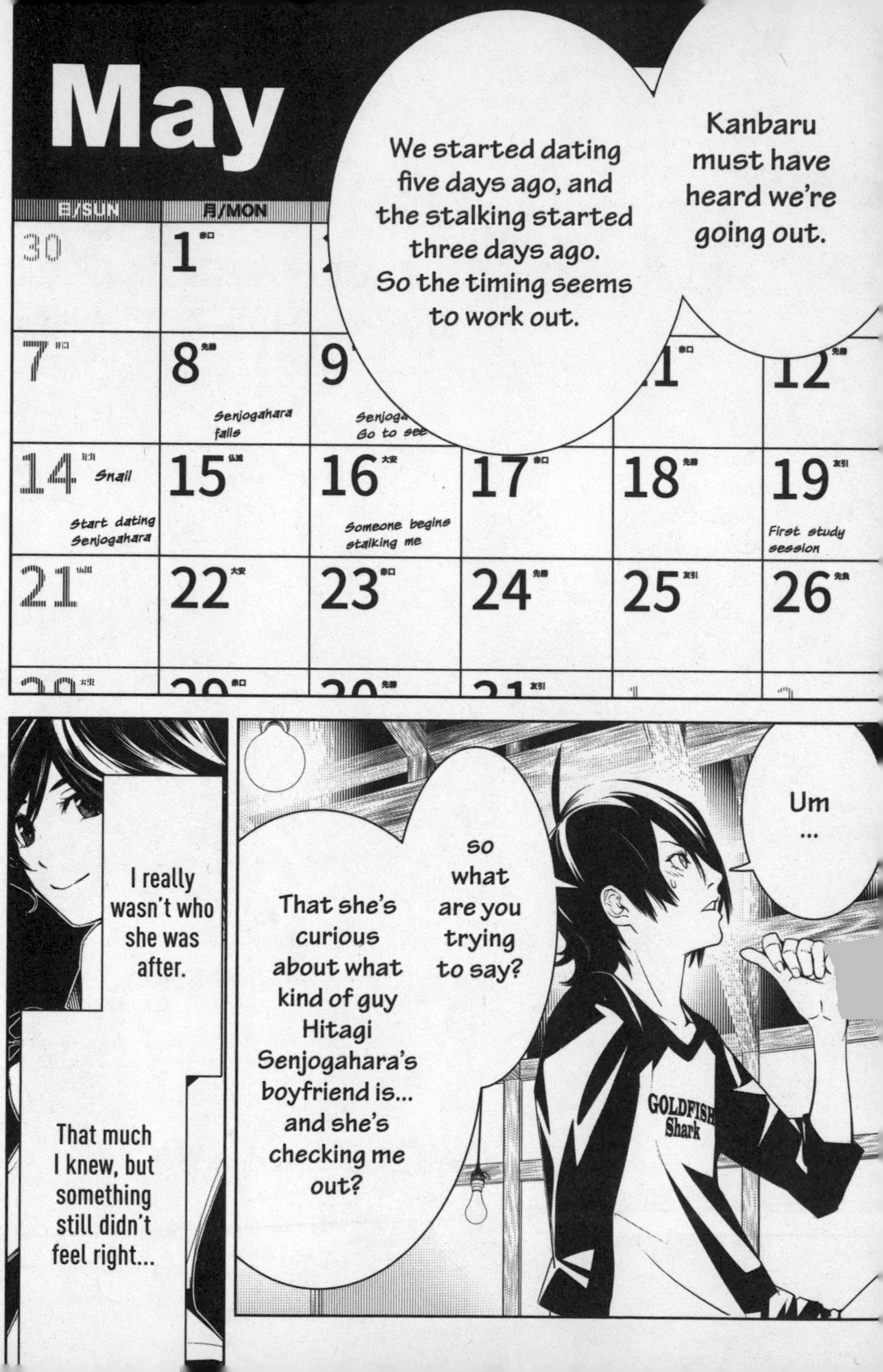
Kanbaru must have heard we're going out.
We started dating five days ago, and the stalking started three days ago. So the timing seems to work out.
May
SUN
MON
Senjogahara falls
Snail
Start dating Senjogahara
Someone begins stalking me
First study session
Um ...
so what are you trying to say?
That she's curious about what kind of guy Hitagi Senjogahara's boyfriend is... and she's checking me out?
GOLDFISH Shark
I really wasn't who she was after.
That much I knew, but something still didn't feel right...

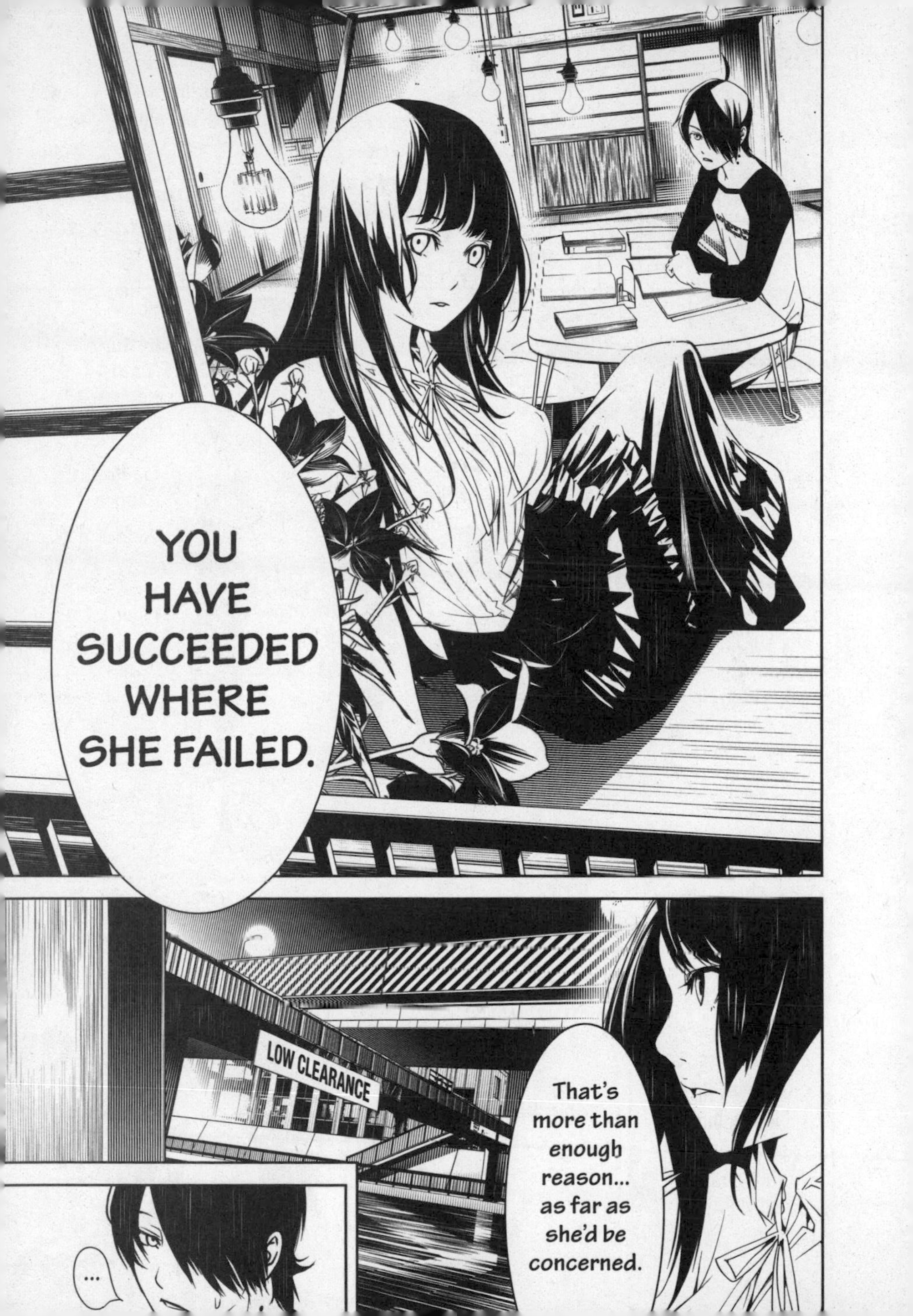
YOU HAVE SUCCEEDED WHERE SHE FAILED.
That's more than enough reason... as far as she'd be concerned.
LOW CLEARANCE
...

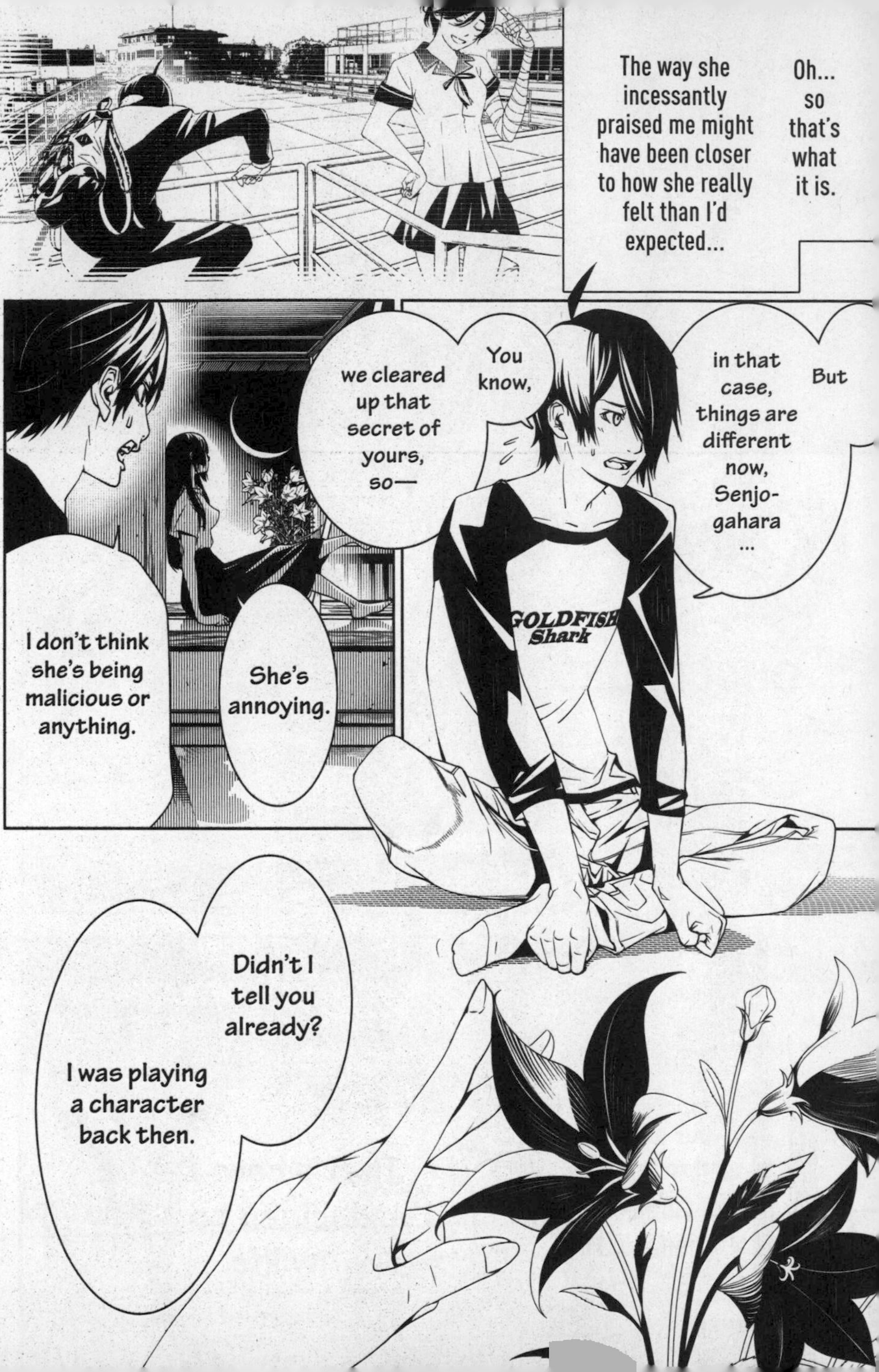
Oh... so that's what it is.
The way she incessantly praised me might have been closer to how she really felt than I'd expected...
But in that case, things are different now, Senjo-gahara...
You know, we cleared up that secret of yours, so—
She's annoying.
I don't think she's being malicious or anything.
GOLDFISH Shark
Didn't I tell you already?
I was playing a character back then.

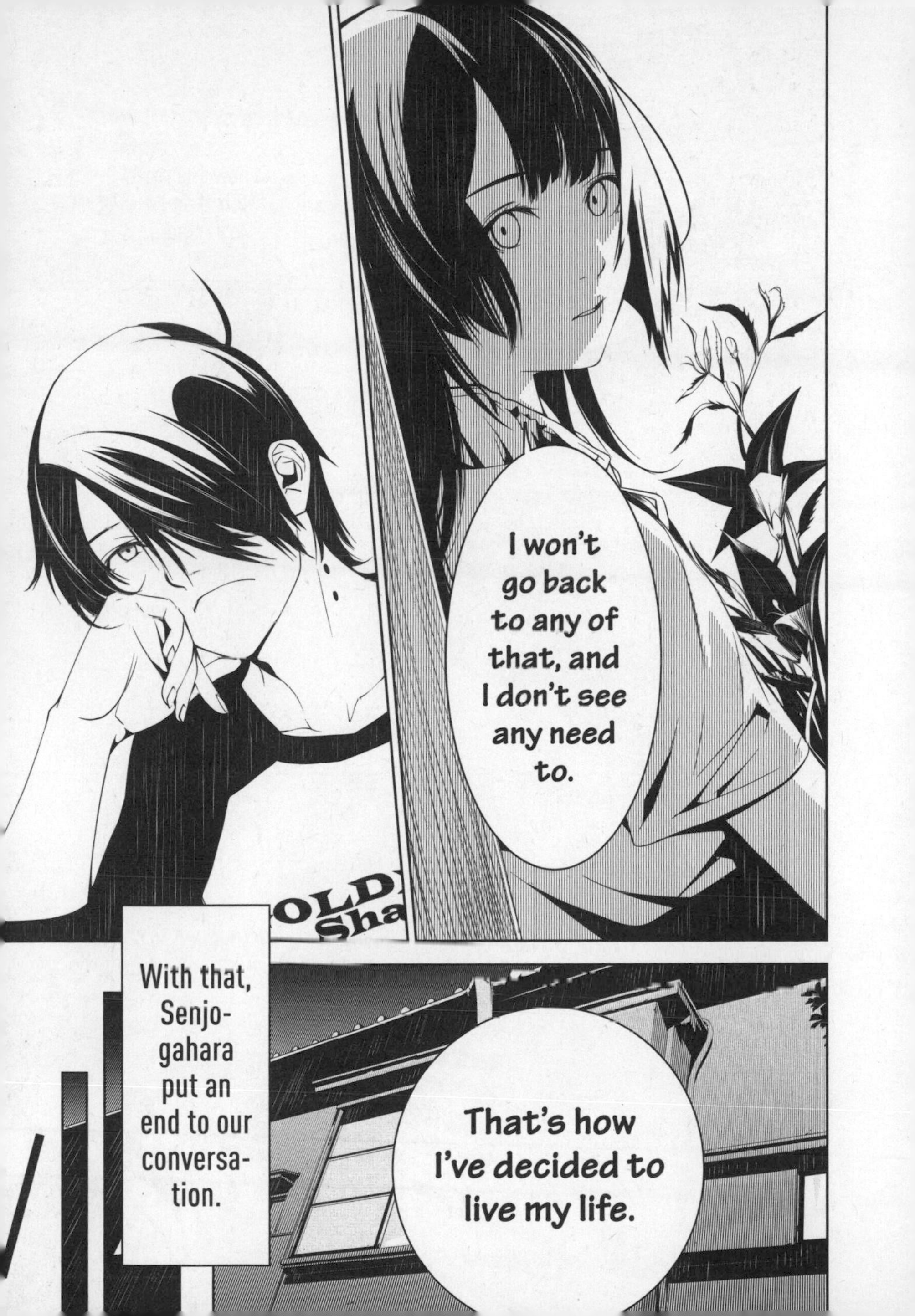
I won't go back to any of that, and I don't see any need to.
That's how I've decided to live my life.
With that, Senjo-gahara put an end to our conversa-tion.

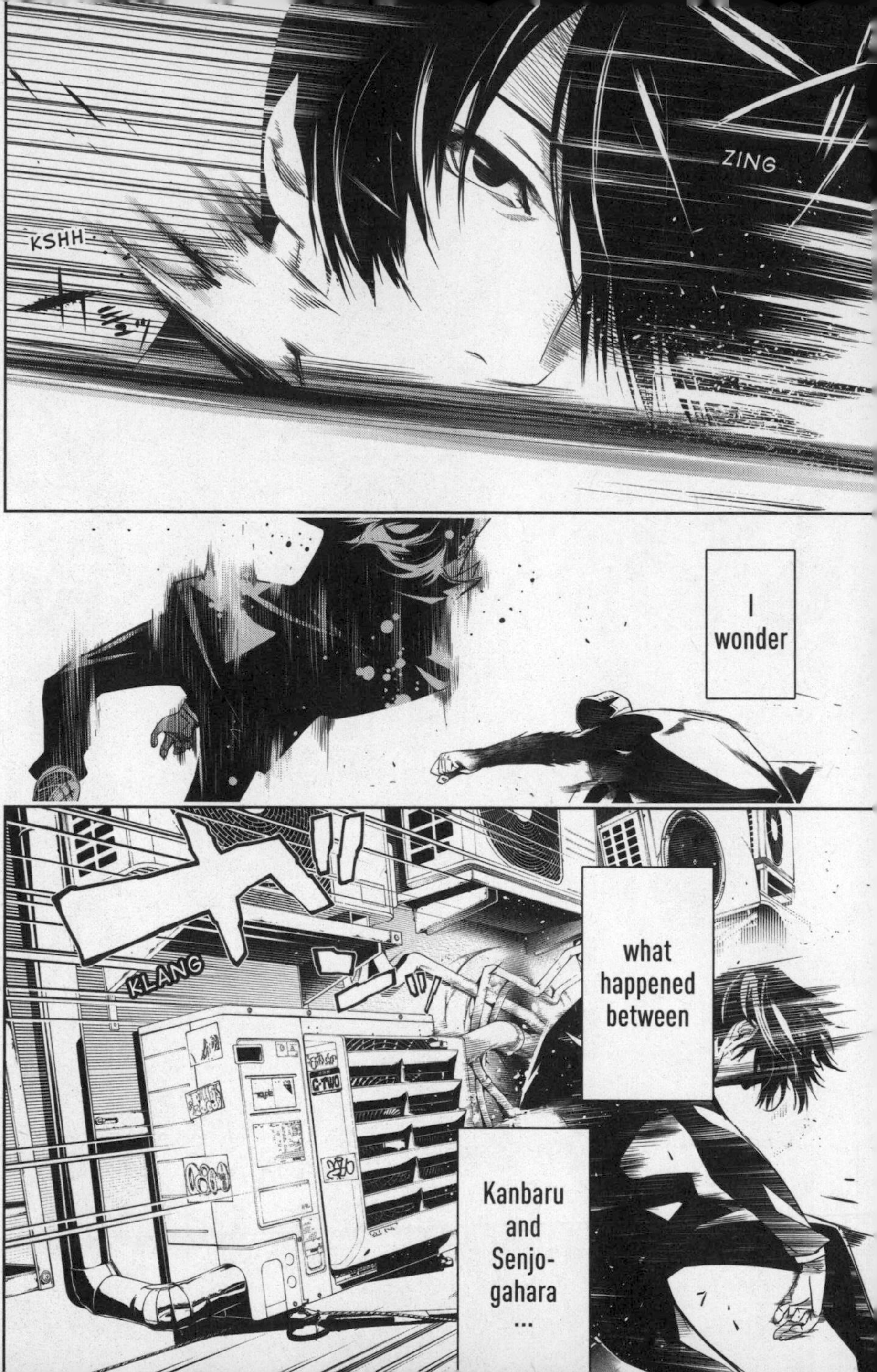
ZING
KSHH
I wonder
KLANG
what happened between
Kanbaru and Senjo-gahara ...

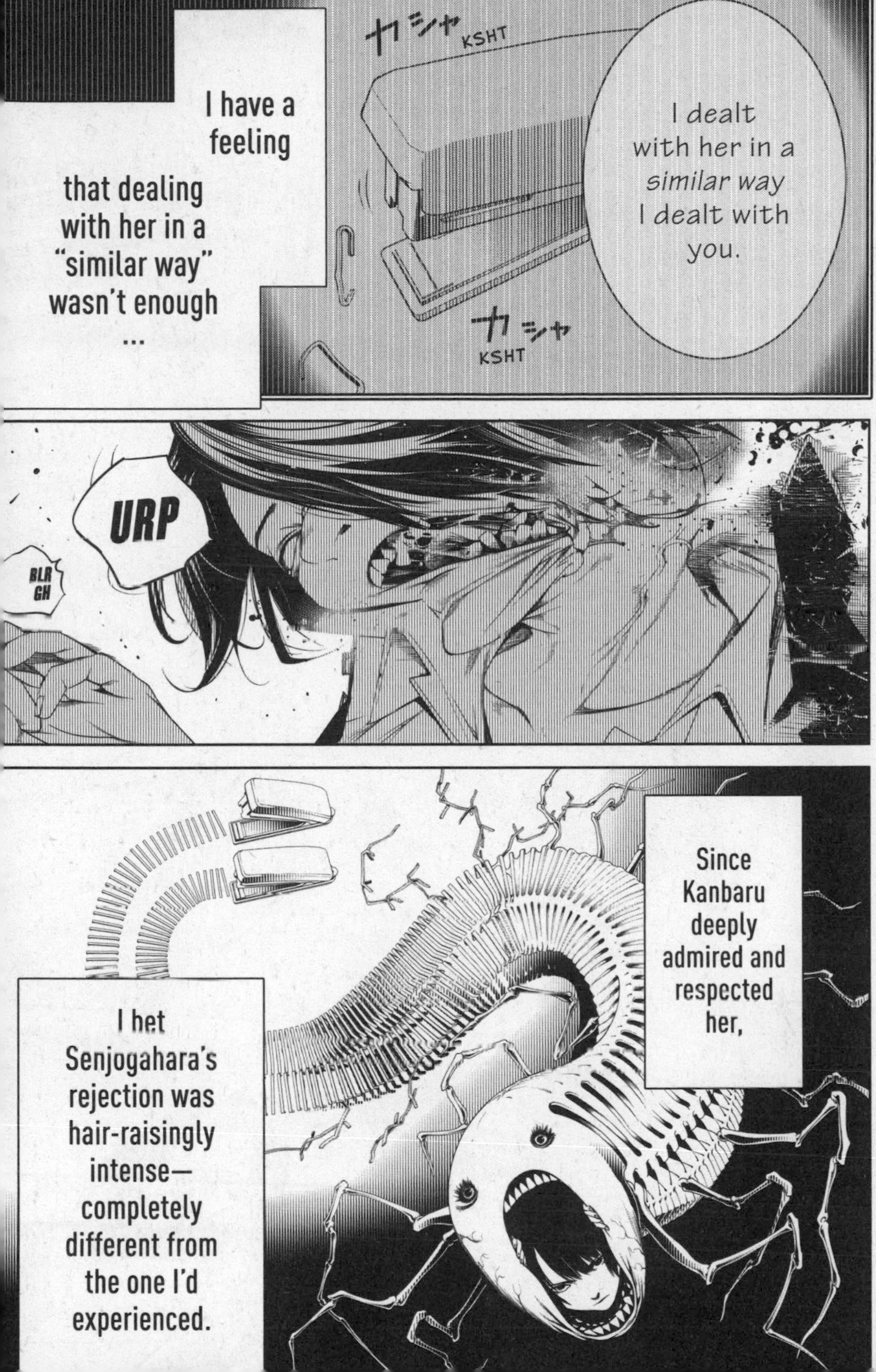
I dealt with her in a similar way I dealt with you.
カシャ KSHT
カシャ KSHT
I have a feeling that dealing with her in a "similar way" wasn't enough ...
URP
BLR GH
Since Kanbaru deeply admired and respected her,
I bet Senjogahara's rejection was hair-raisingly intense—completely different from the one I'd experienced.

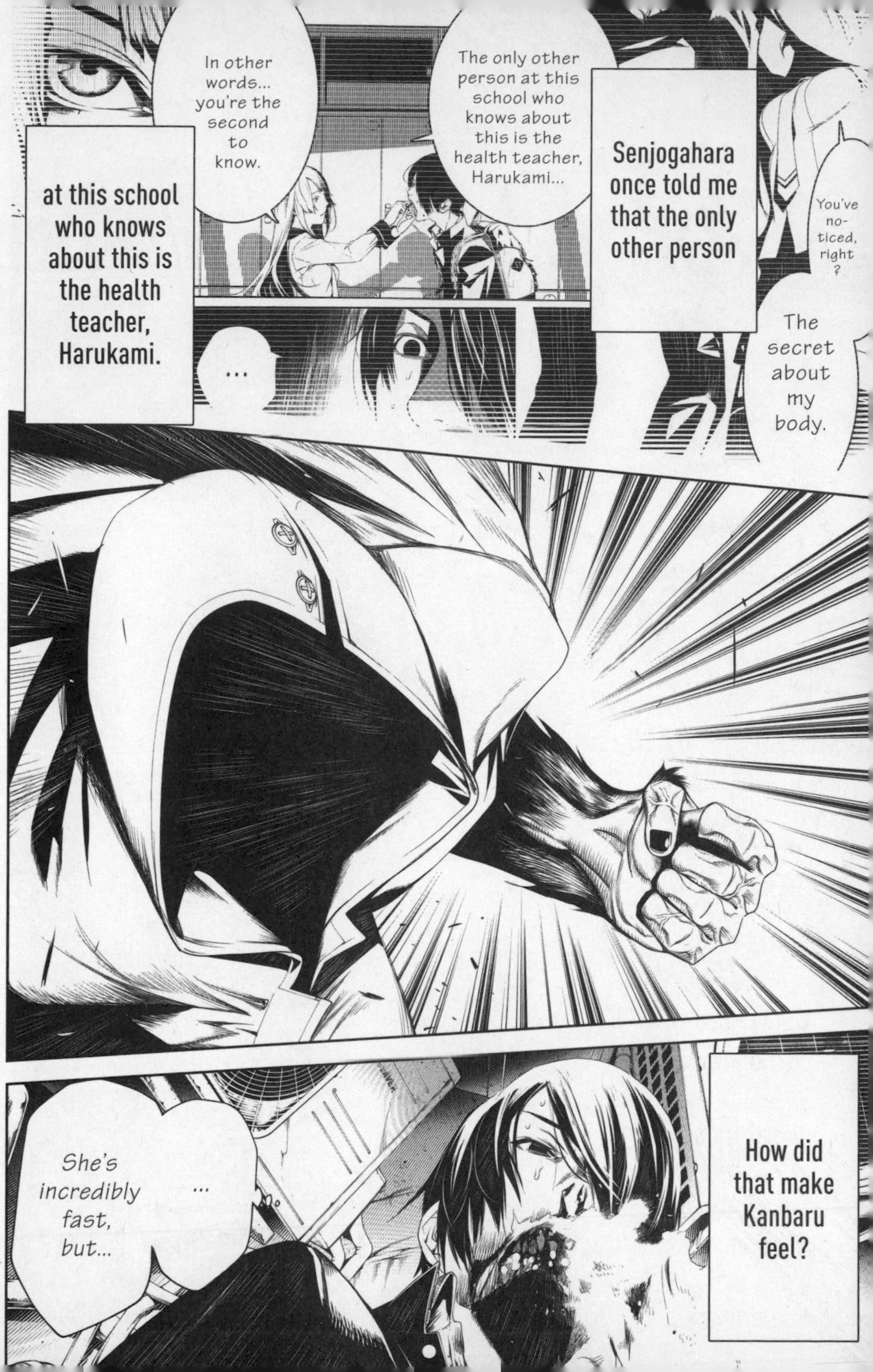
You've no-ticed, right?
The secret about my body.
Senjogahara once told me that the only other person
The only other person at this school who knows about this is the health teacher, Harukami...
In other words... you're the second to know.
at this school who knows about this is the health teacher, Harukami.
...
How did that make Kanbaru feel?
...
She's incredibly fast, but...

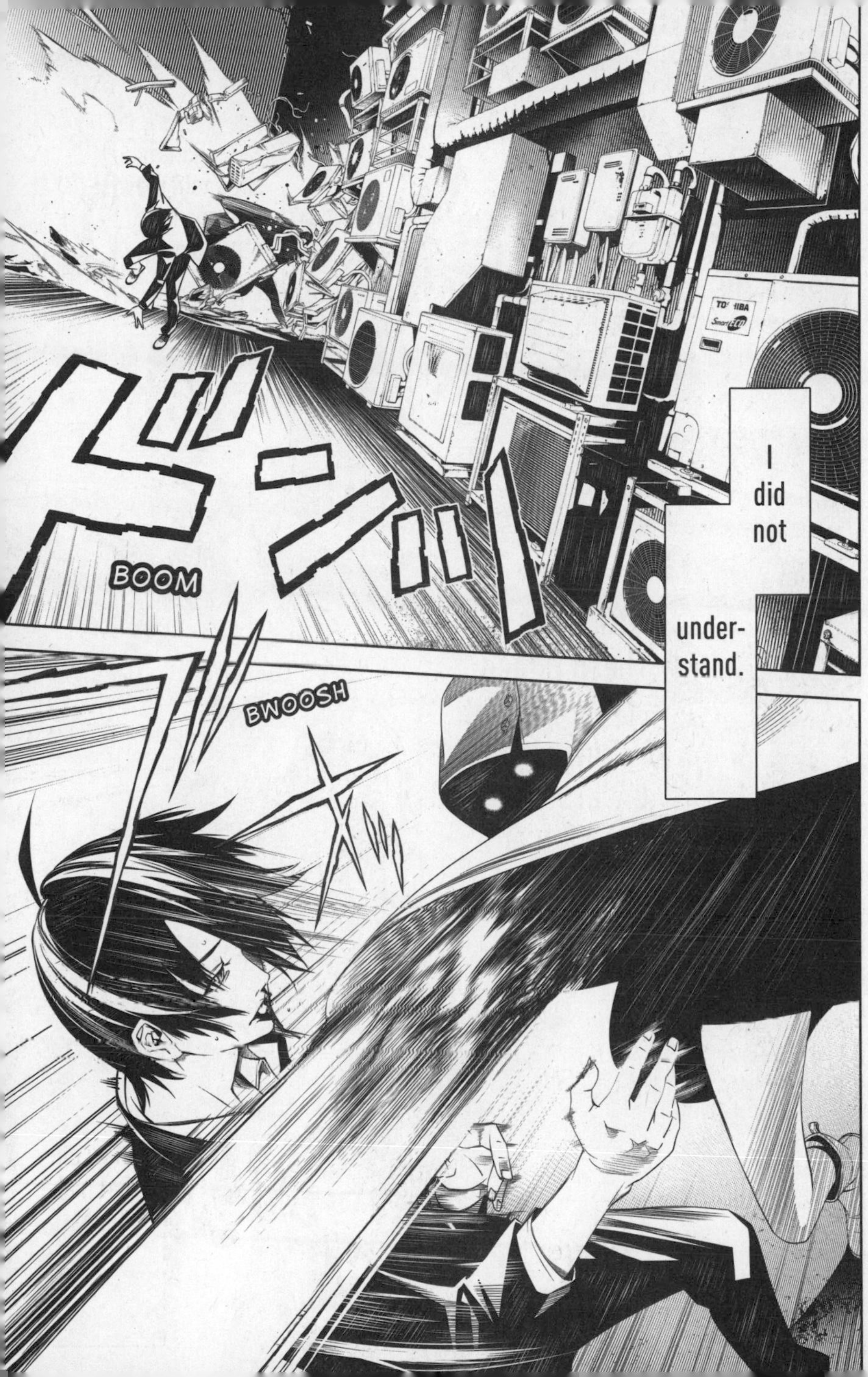
I did not under-stand.
BOOM
BWOOSH

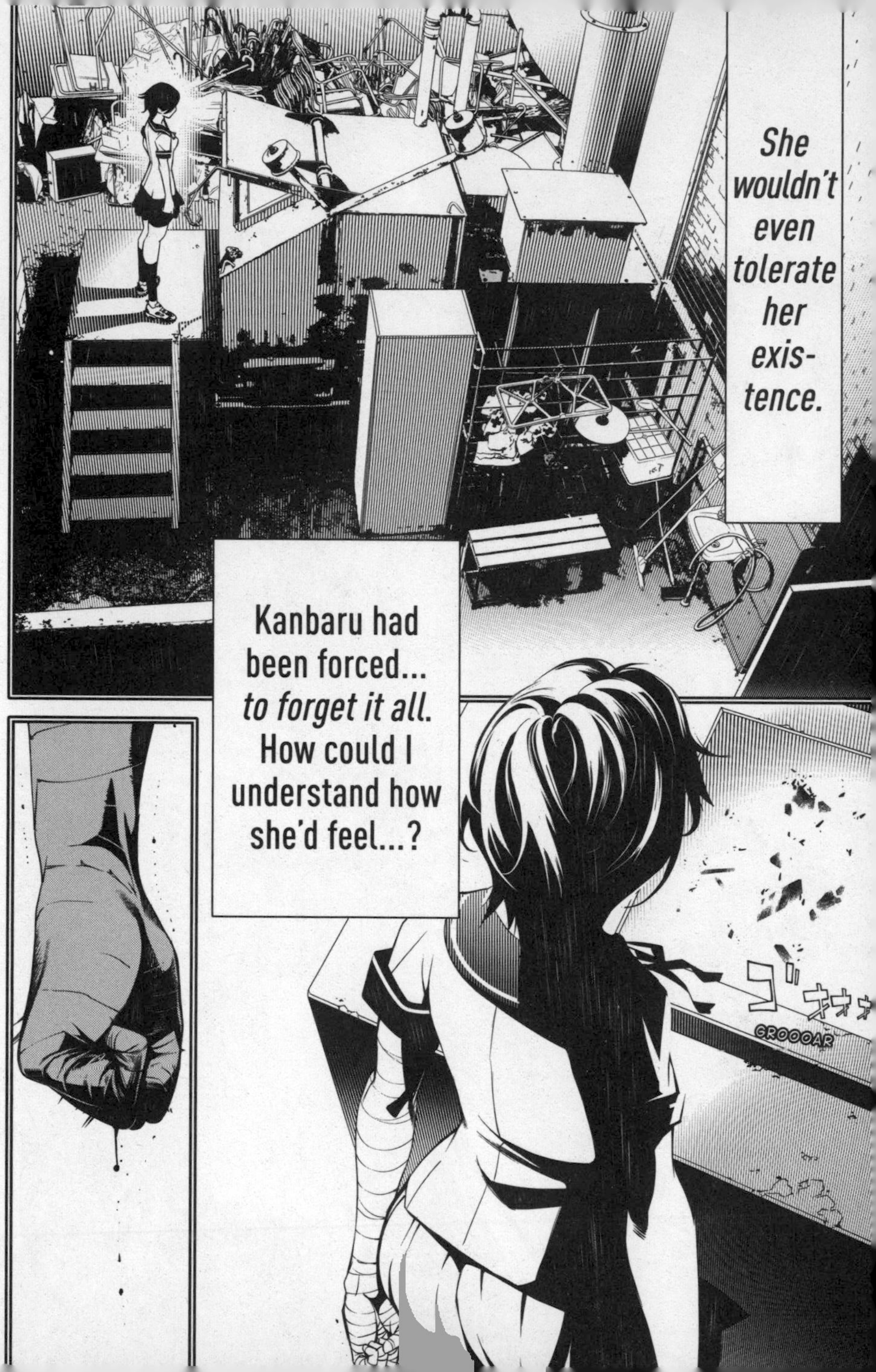
She wouldn't even tolerate her existence.
Kanbaru had been forced... *to forget it all.* How could I understand how she'd feel...?
GROOOAR

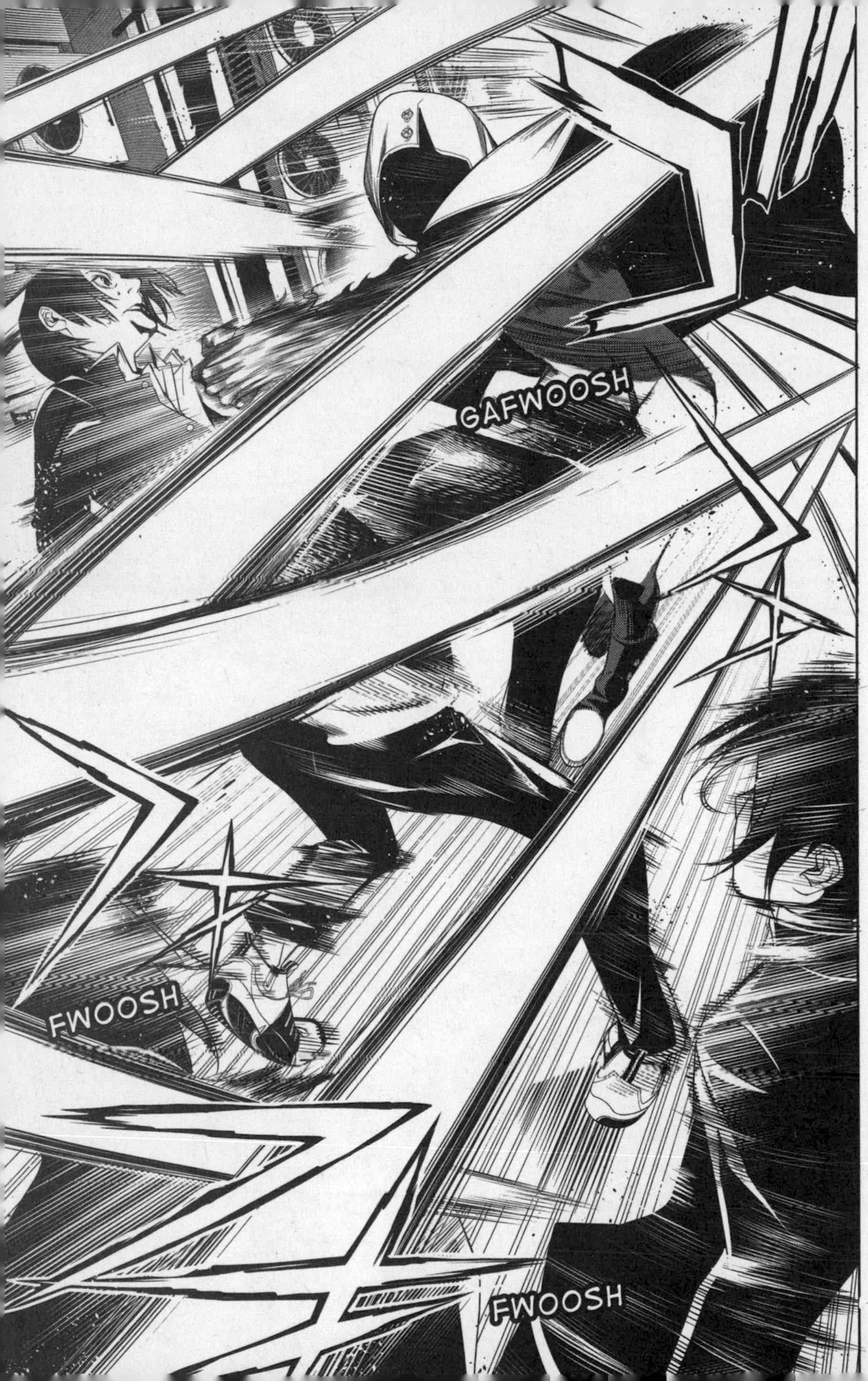
GAFWOOSH
FWOOSH
FWOOSH

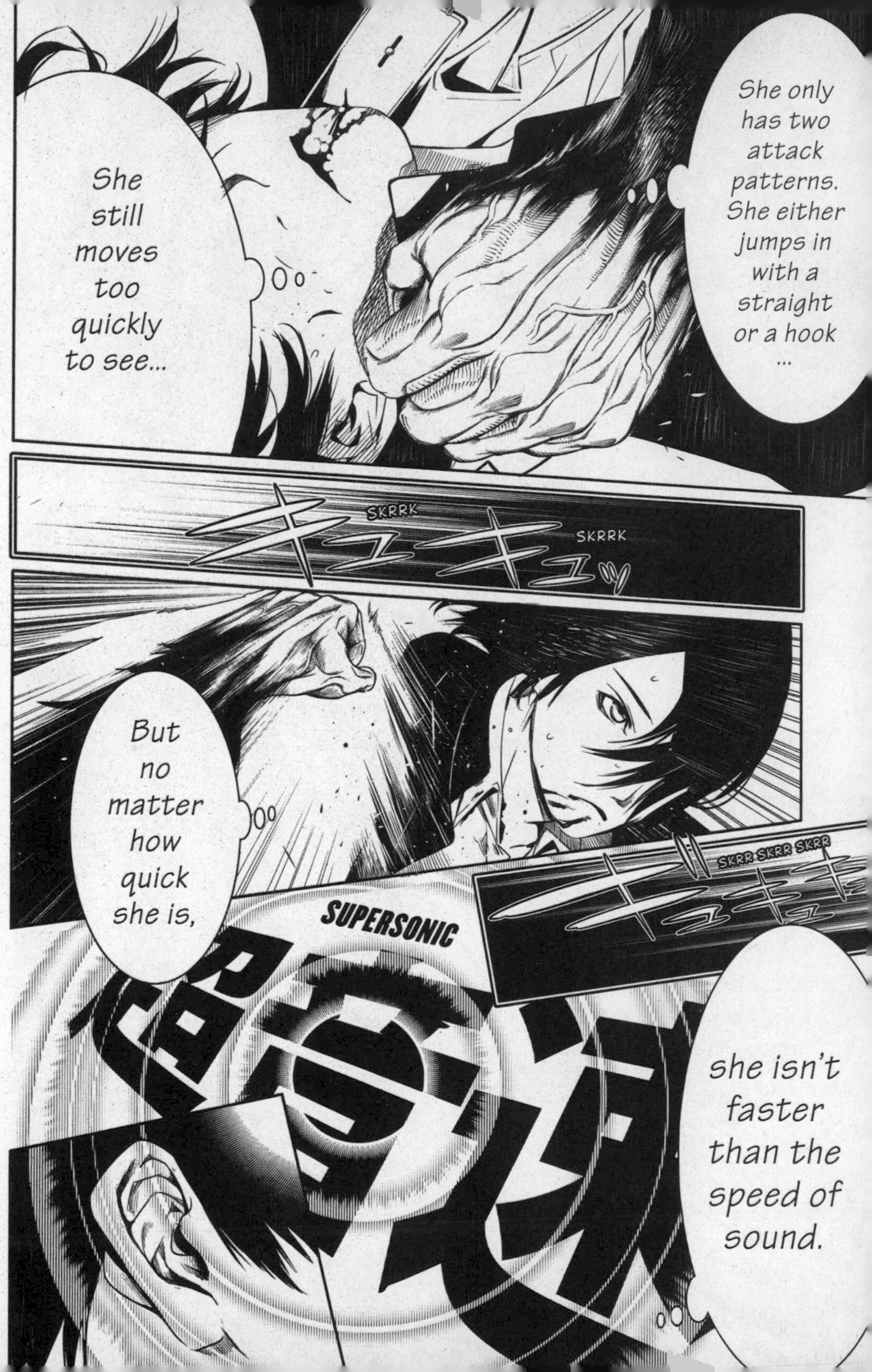
She only has two attack patterns. She either jumps in with a straight or a hook ...
She still moves too quickly to see...
SKRRK
SKRRK
But no matter how quick she is,
SKRR SKRR SKRR
SUPERSONIC
she isn't faster than the speed of sound.

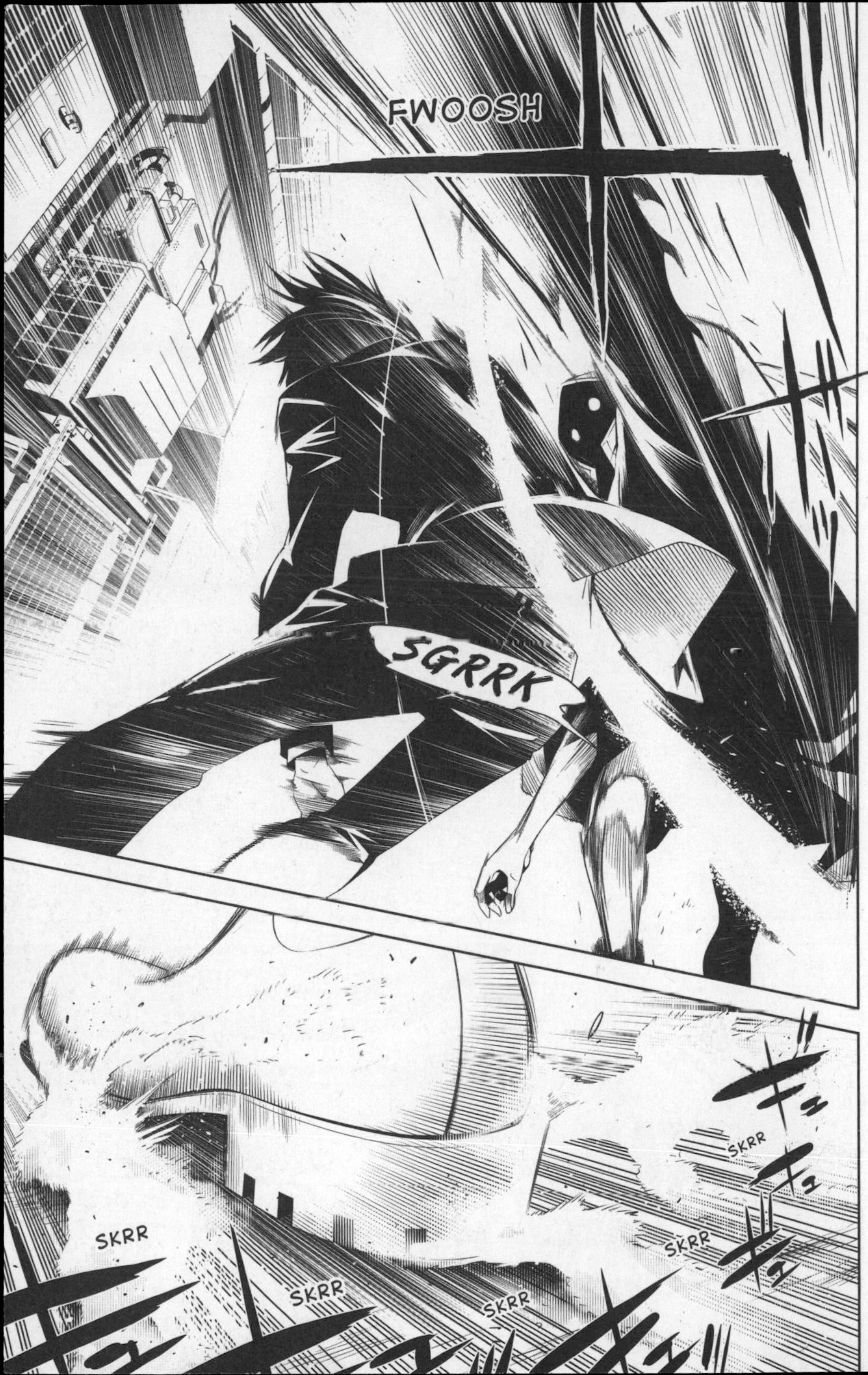
FWOOSH
SGRRK
SKRR
SKRR
SKRR
SKRR
SKRR

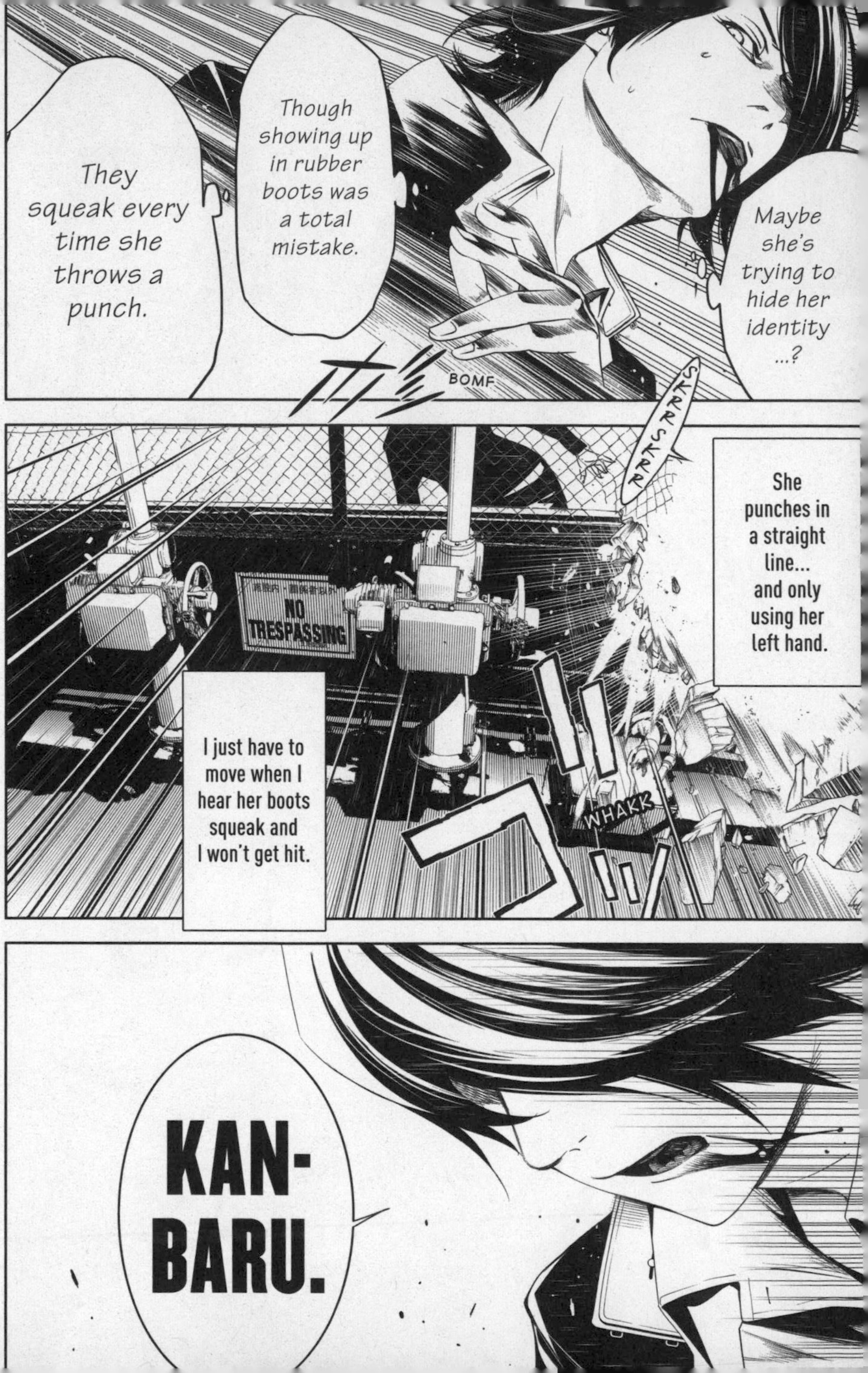
Maybe she's trying to hide her identity ...?
Though showing up in rubber boots was a total mistake.
They squeak every time she throws a punch.
SKRRSKRR
BOMF
She punches in a straight line... and only using her left hand.
WHAKK
NO TRESPASSING
I just have to move when I hear her boots squeak and I won't get hit.
KAN-BARU.

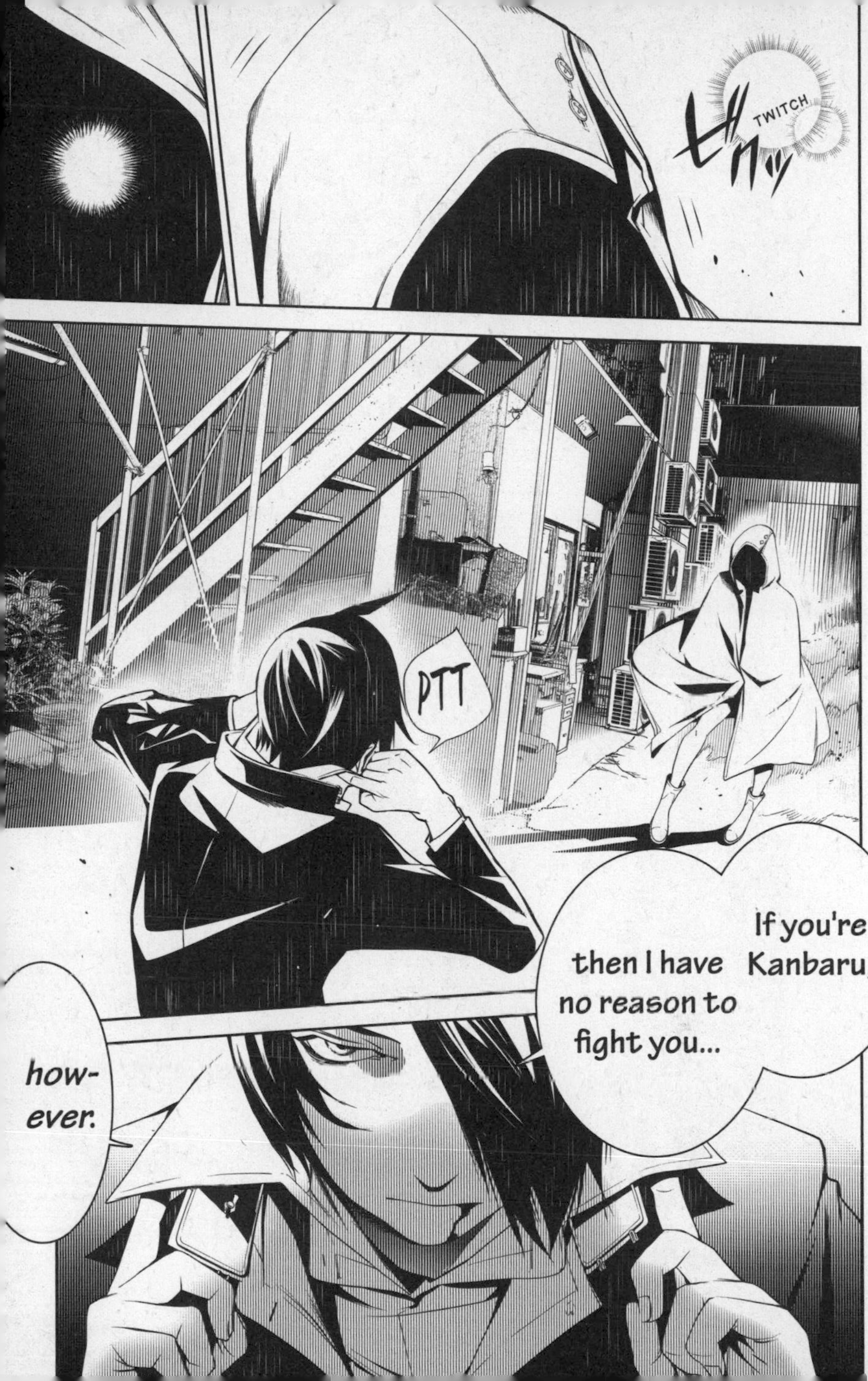
ビクッ
TWITCH
PTT
If you're Kanbaru, then I have no reason to fight you...
how-ever.

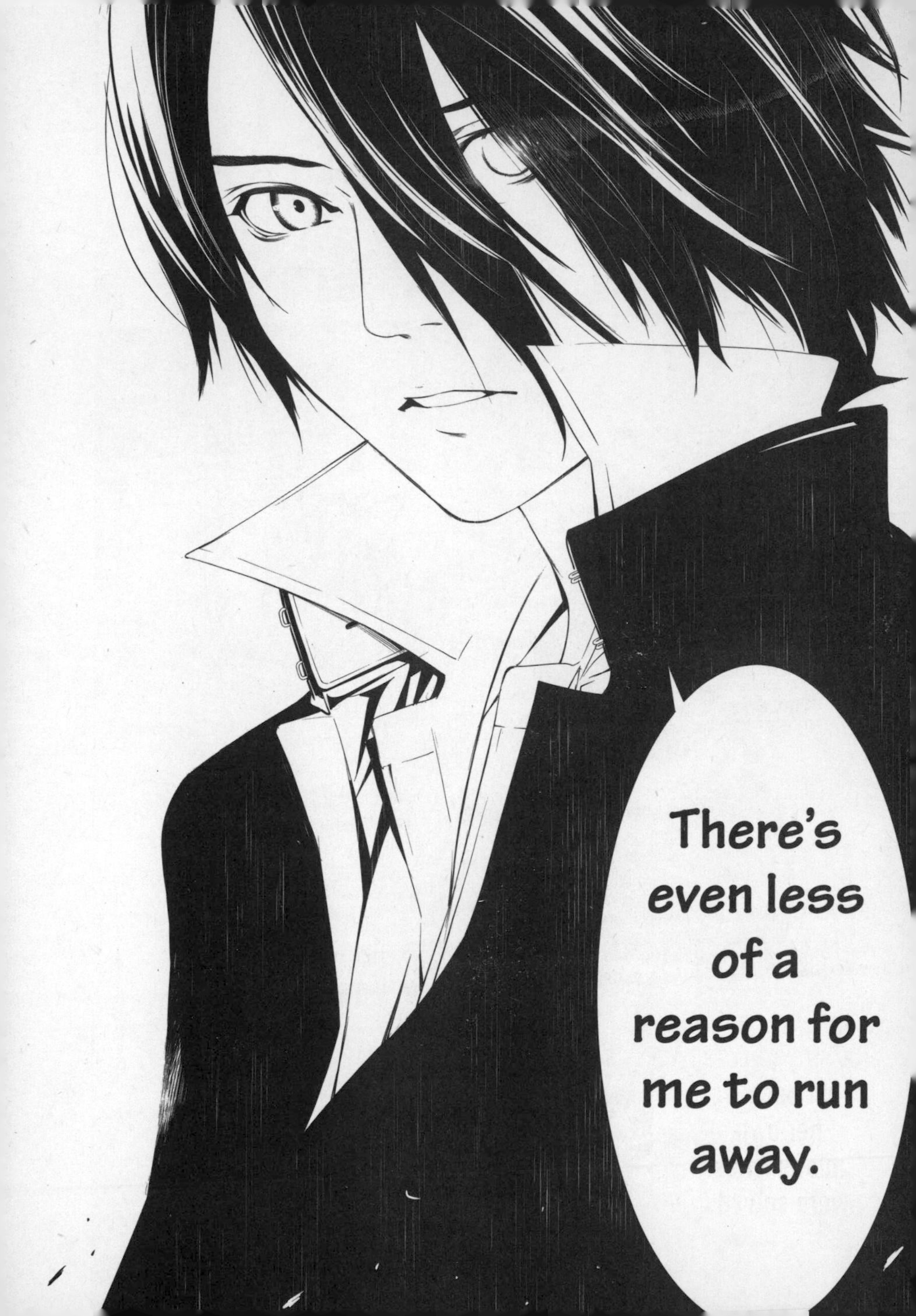
There's even less of a reason for me to run away.

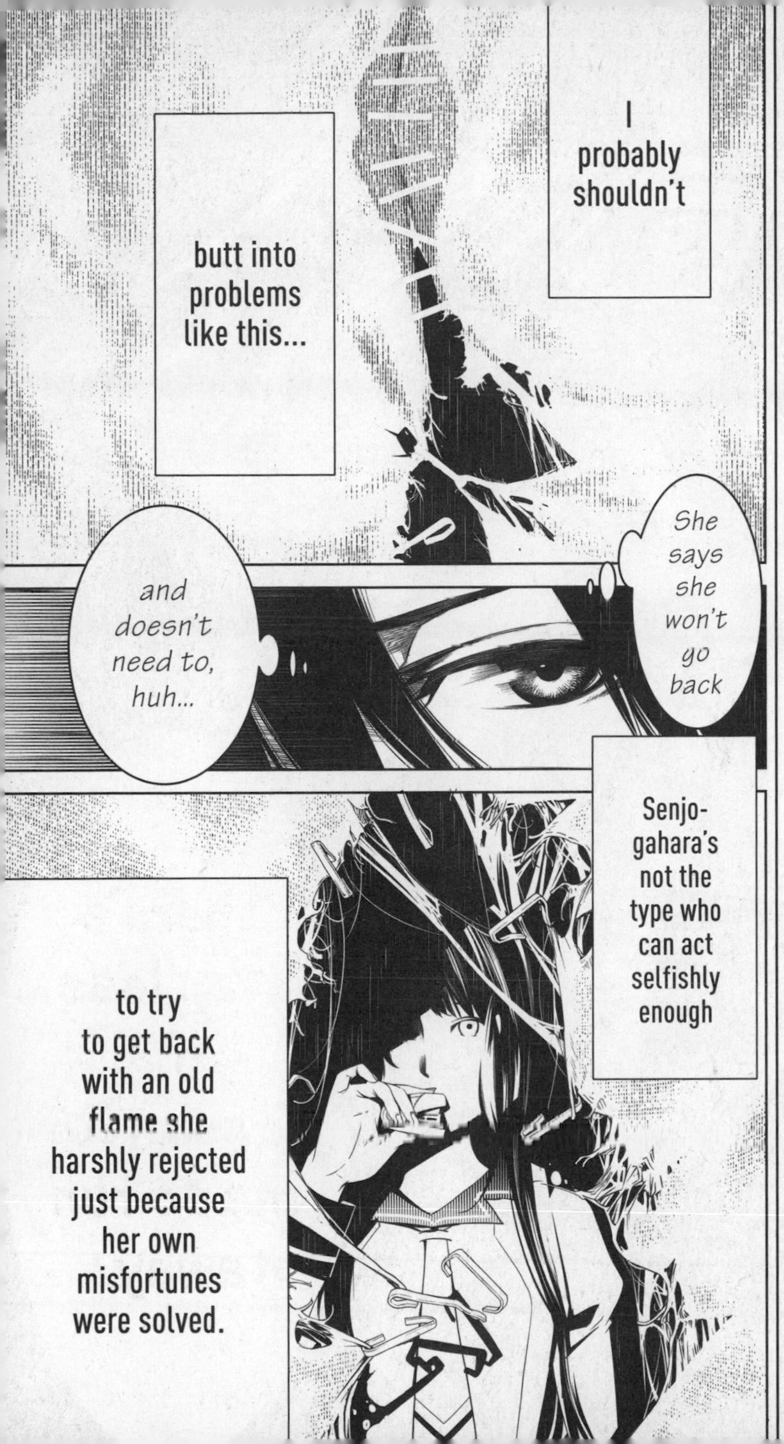

I probably shouldn't
butt into problems like this...
She says she won't go back
and doesn't need to, huh...
Senjo-gahara's not the type who can act selfishly enough
to try to get back with an old flame she harshly rejected just because her own misfortunes were solved.

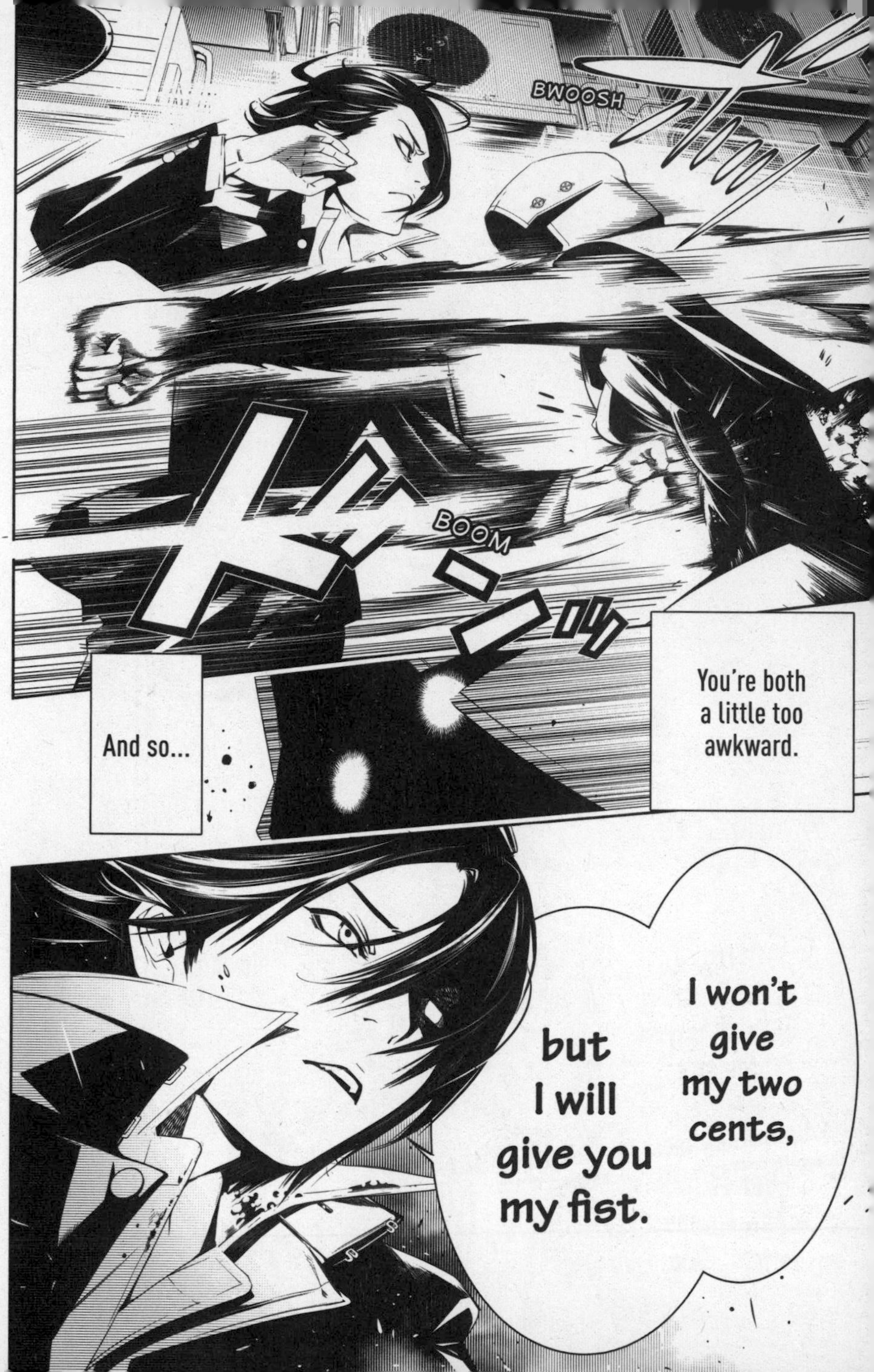
BWOOSH
BOOM
You're both a little too awkward.
And so...
I won't give my two cents,
but I will give you my fist.

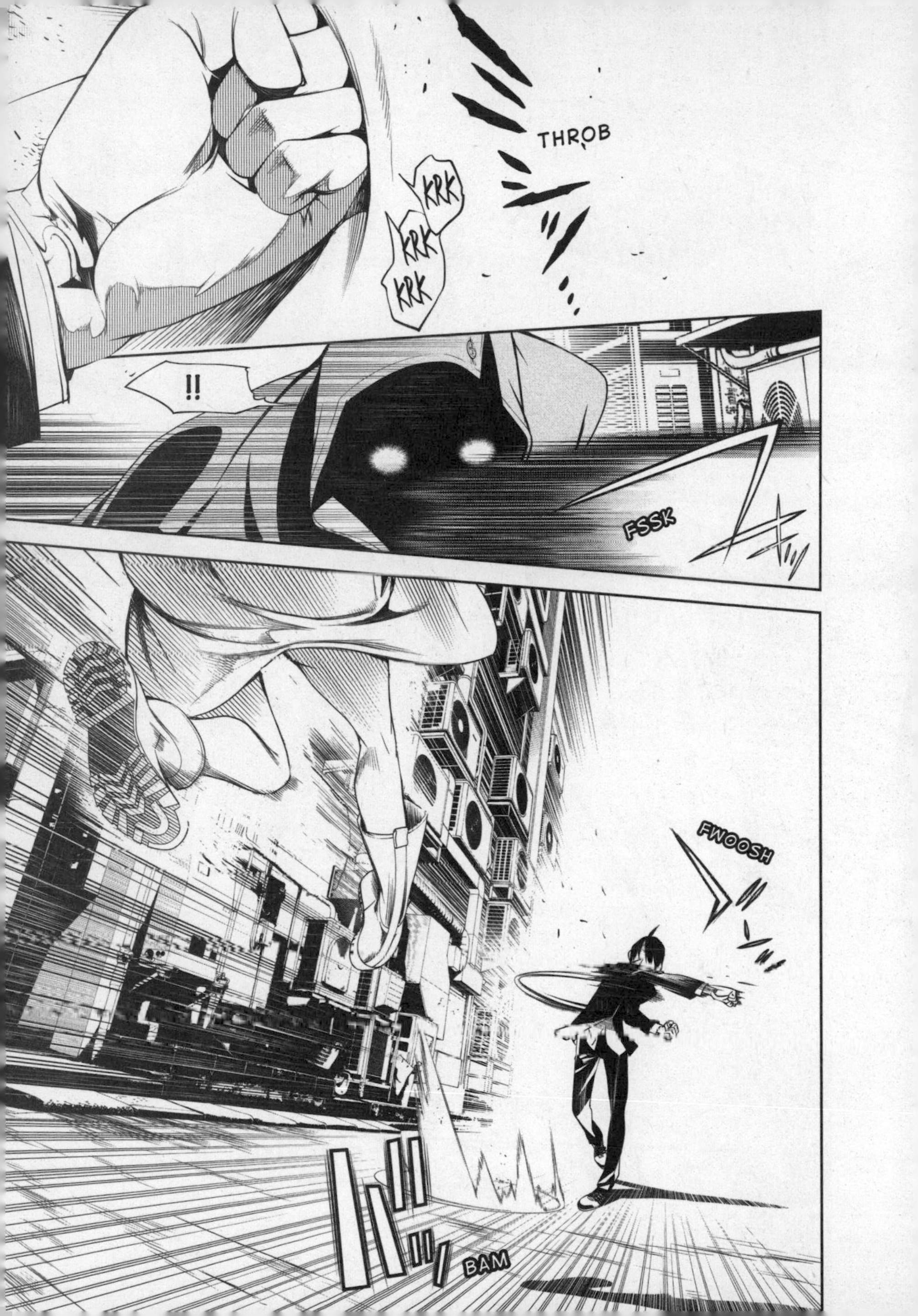
THROB
KRK
KRK
KRK
FSSK
!!
FWOOSH
BAM

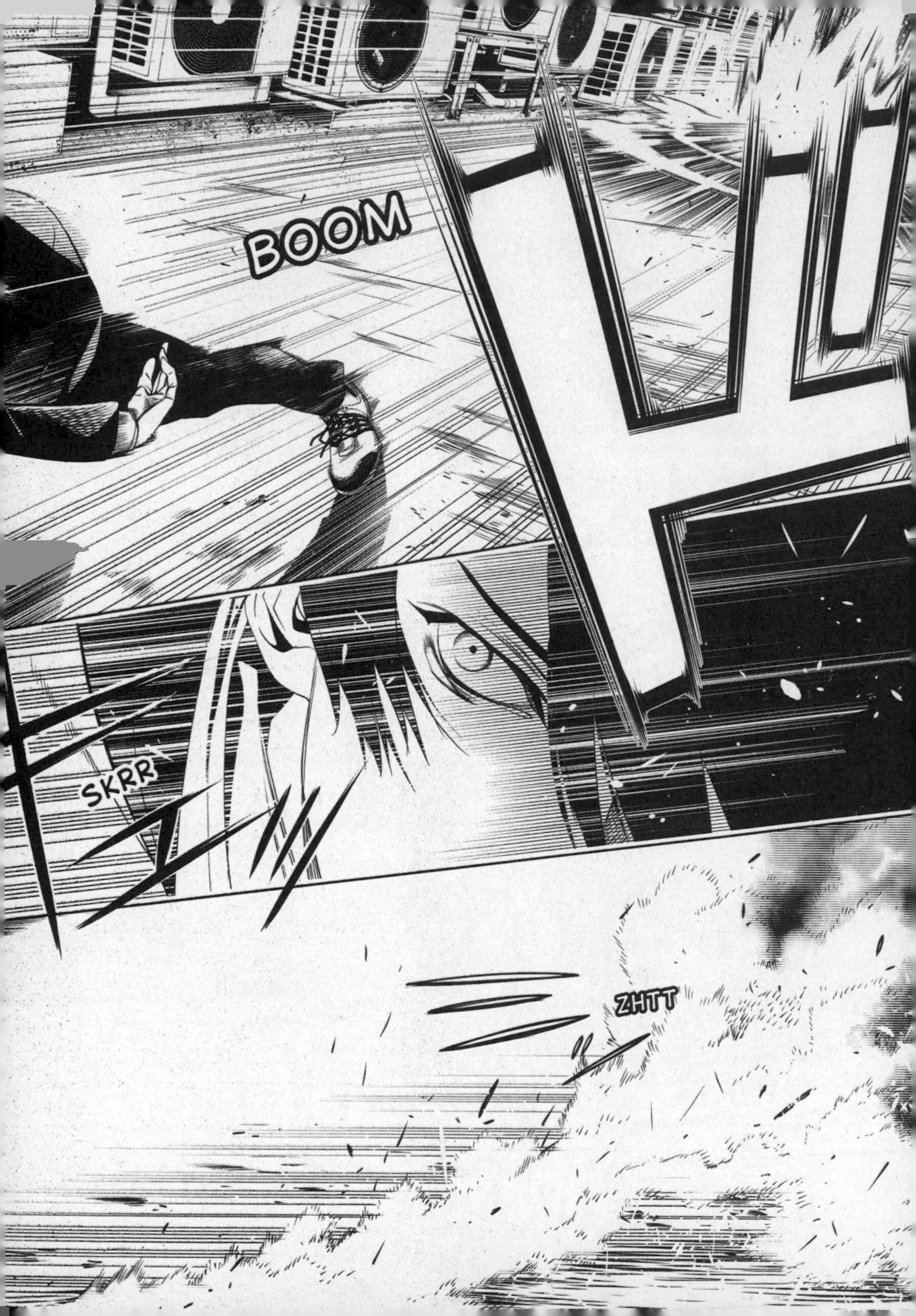
BOOM
SKRR
ZHTT

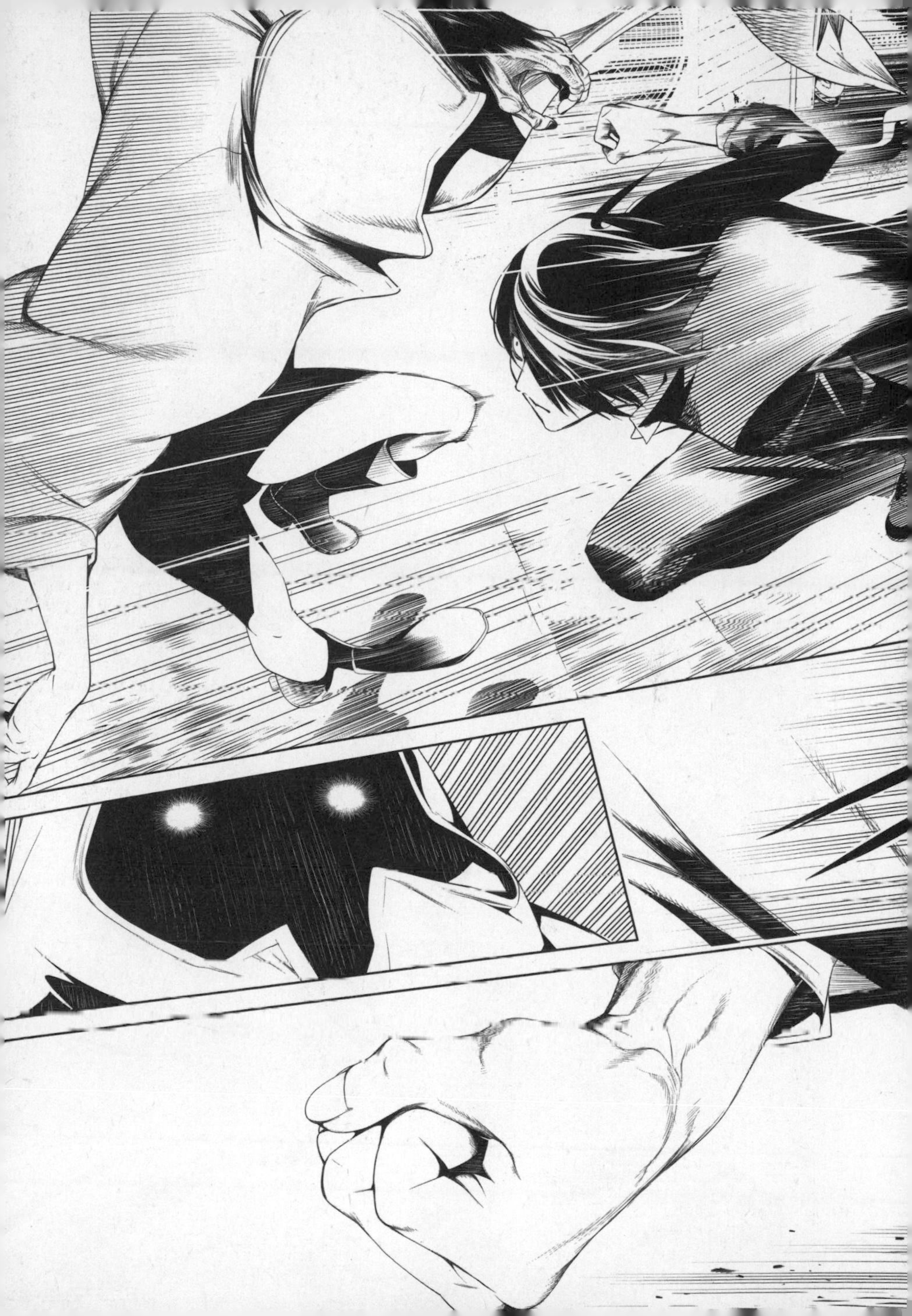

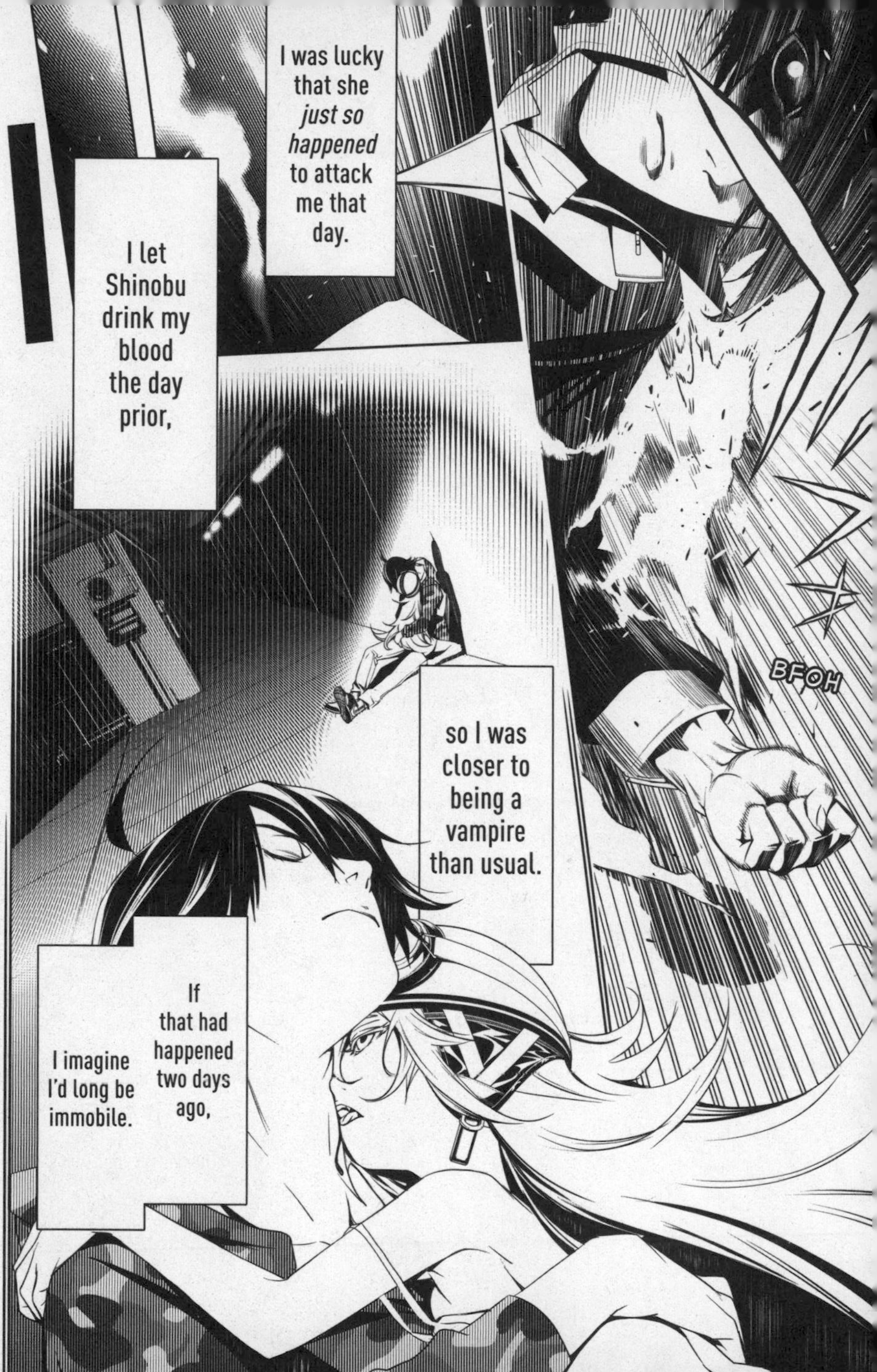

I was lucky that she *just so happened* to attack me that day.
I let Shinobu drink my blood the day prior,
so I was closer to being a vampire than usual.
BFOH
If that had happened two days ago,
I imagine I'd long be immobile.

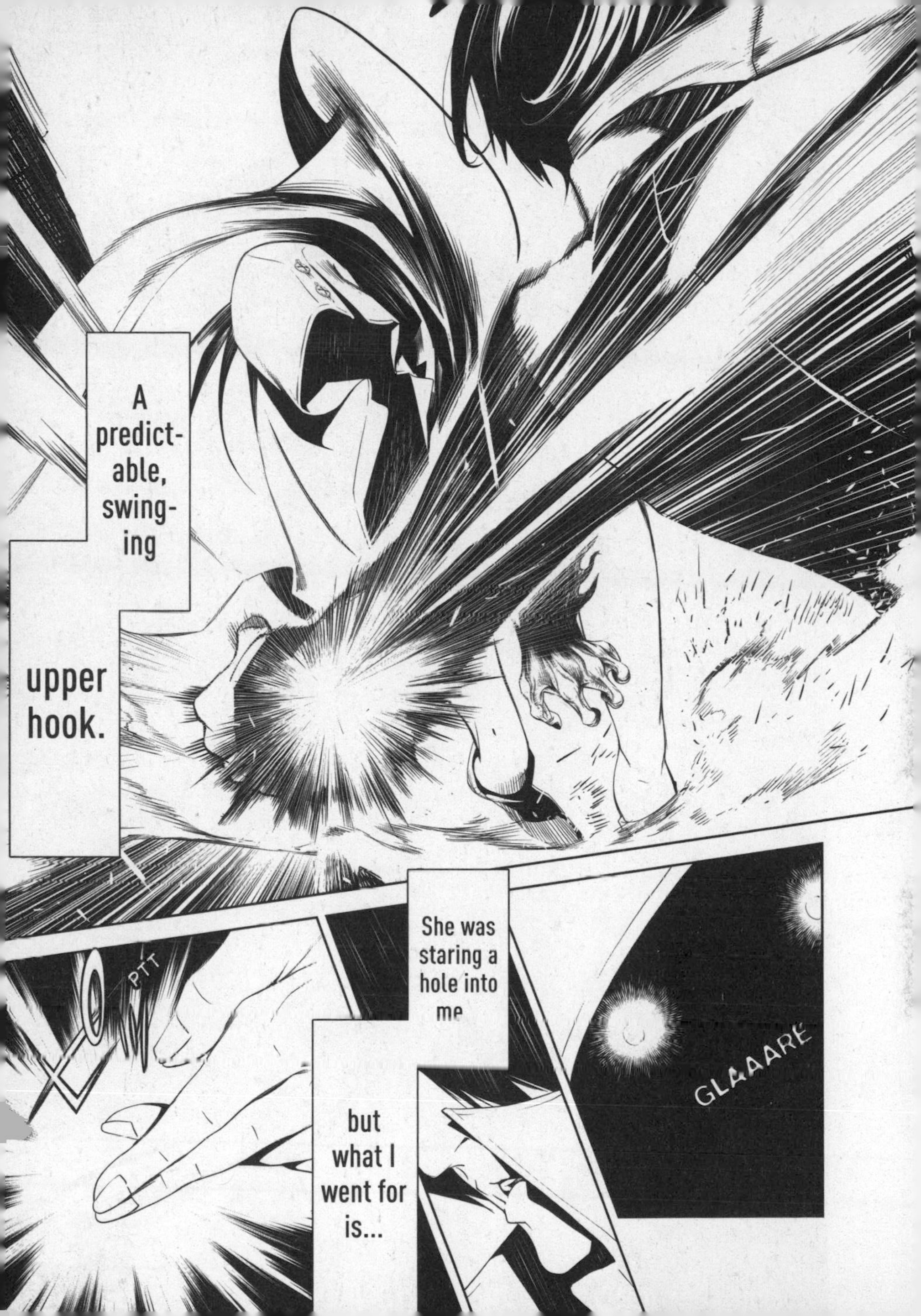
A predictable, swinging
upper hook.
GLAAARE
She was staring a hole into me
but what I went for is...
PTT

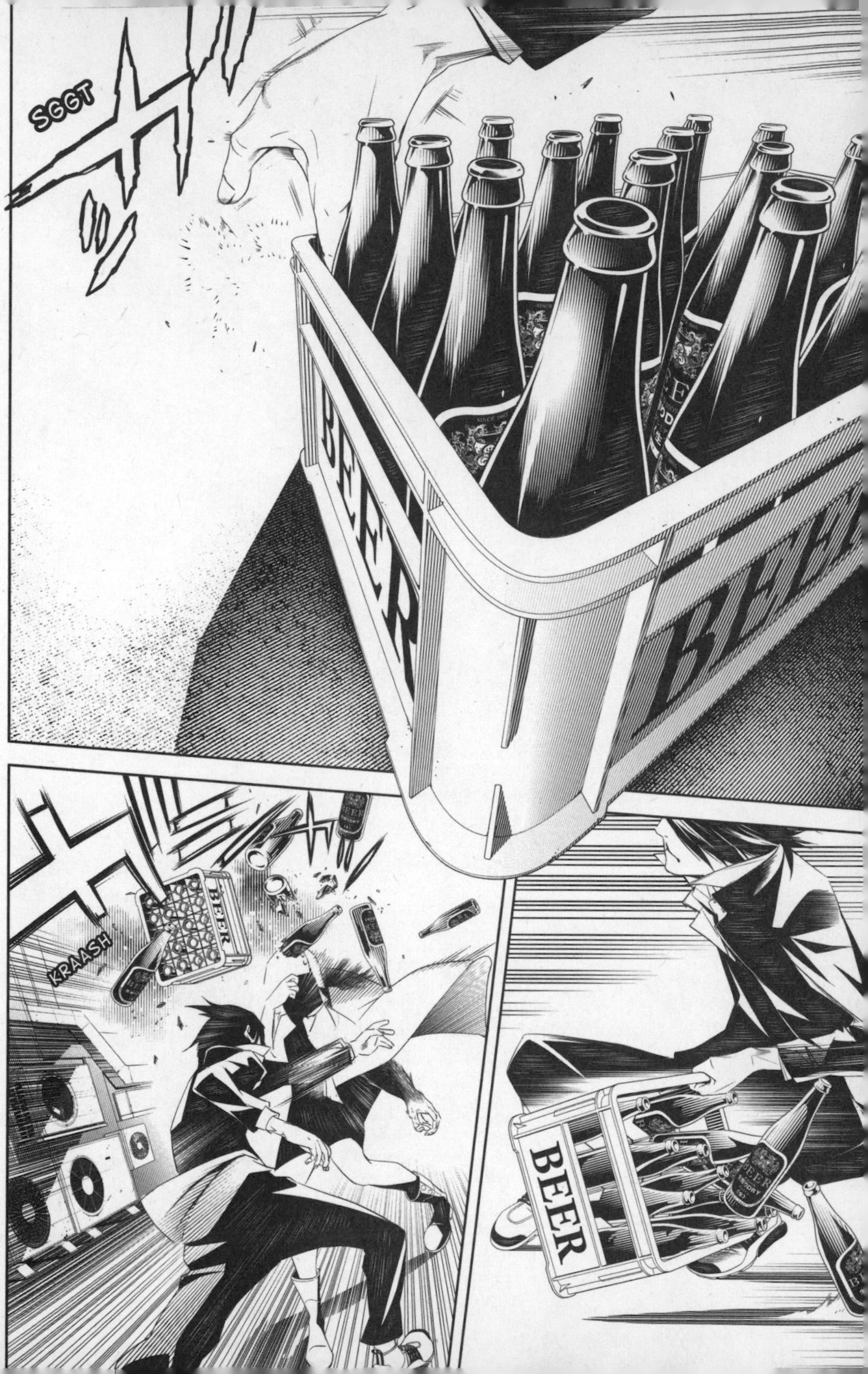
SGGT
BEER
BEER
KRAASH
BEER

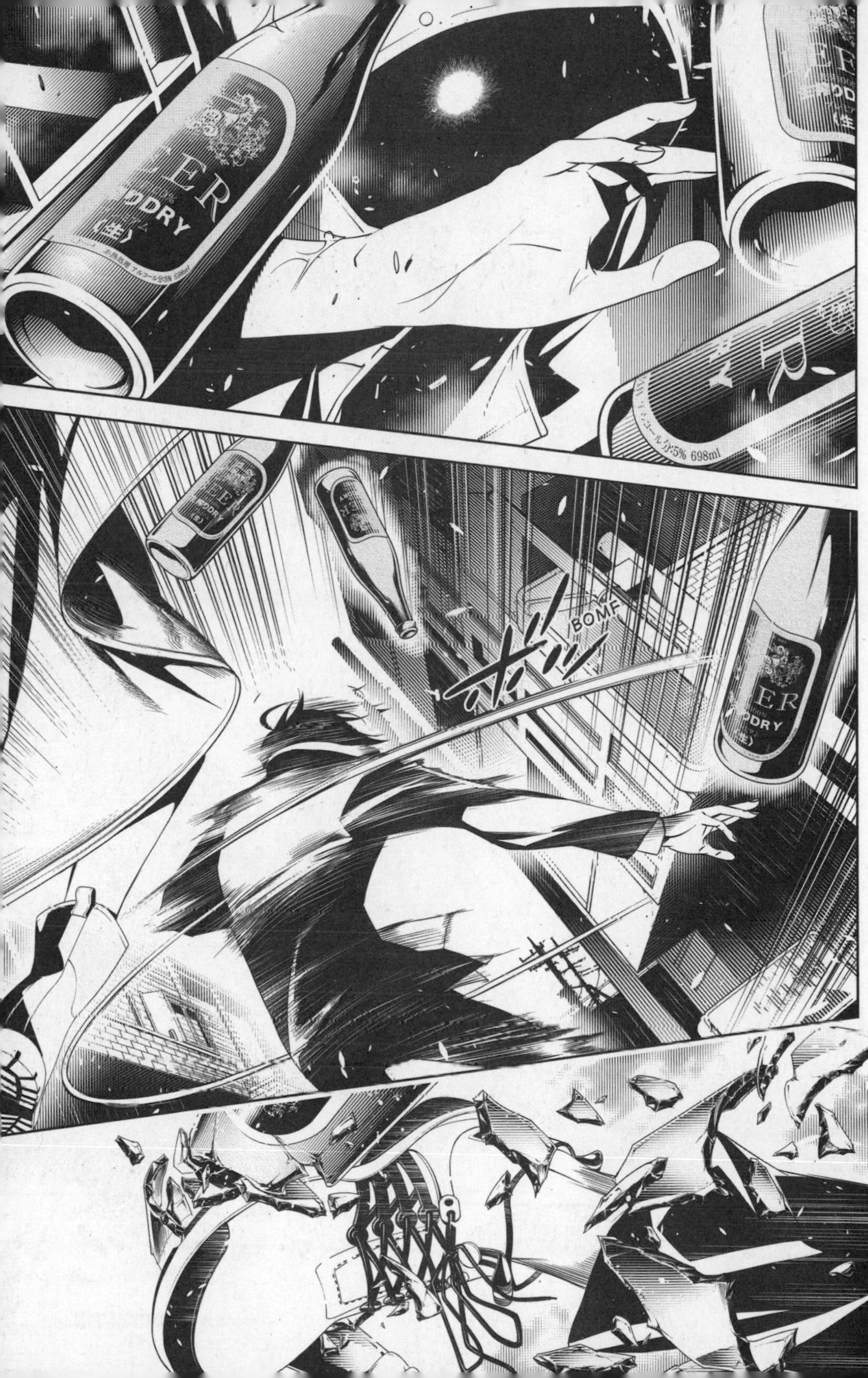
BOMF

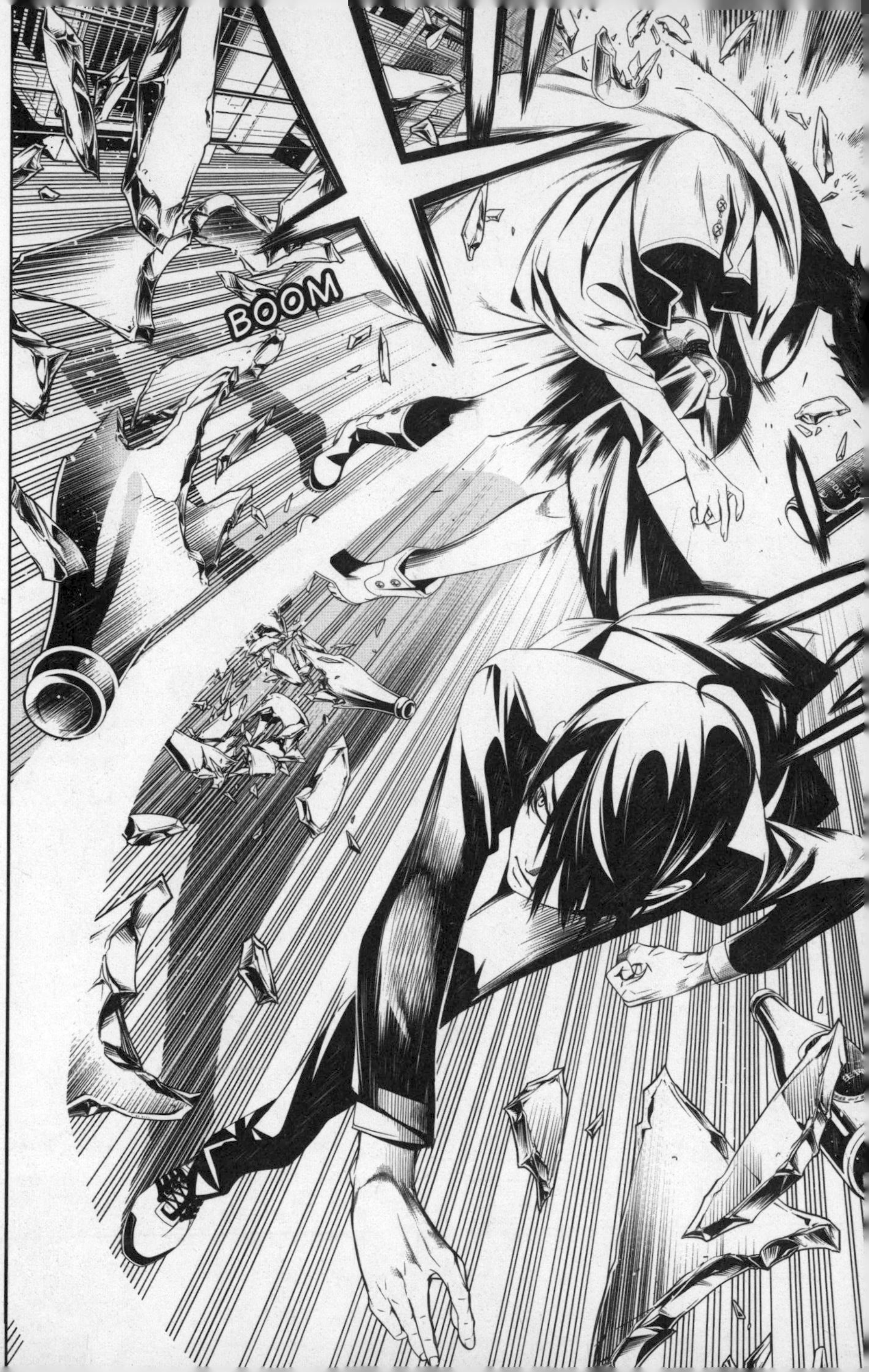
BOOM

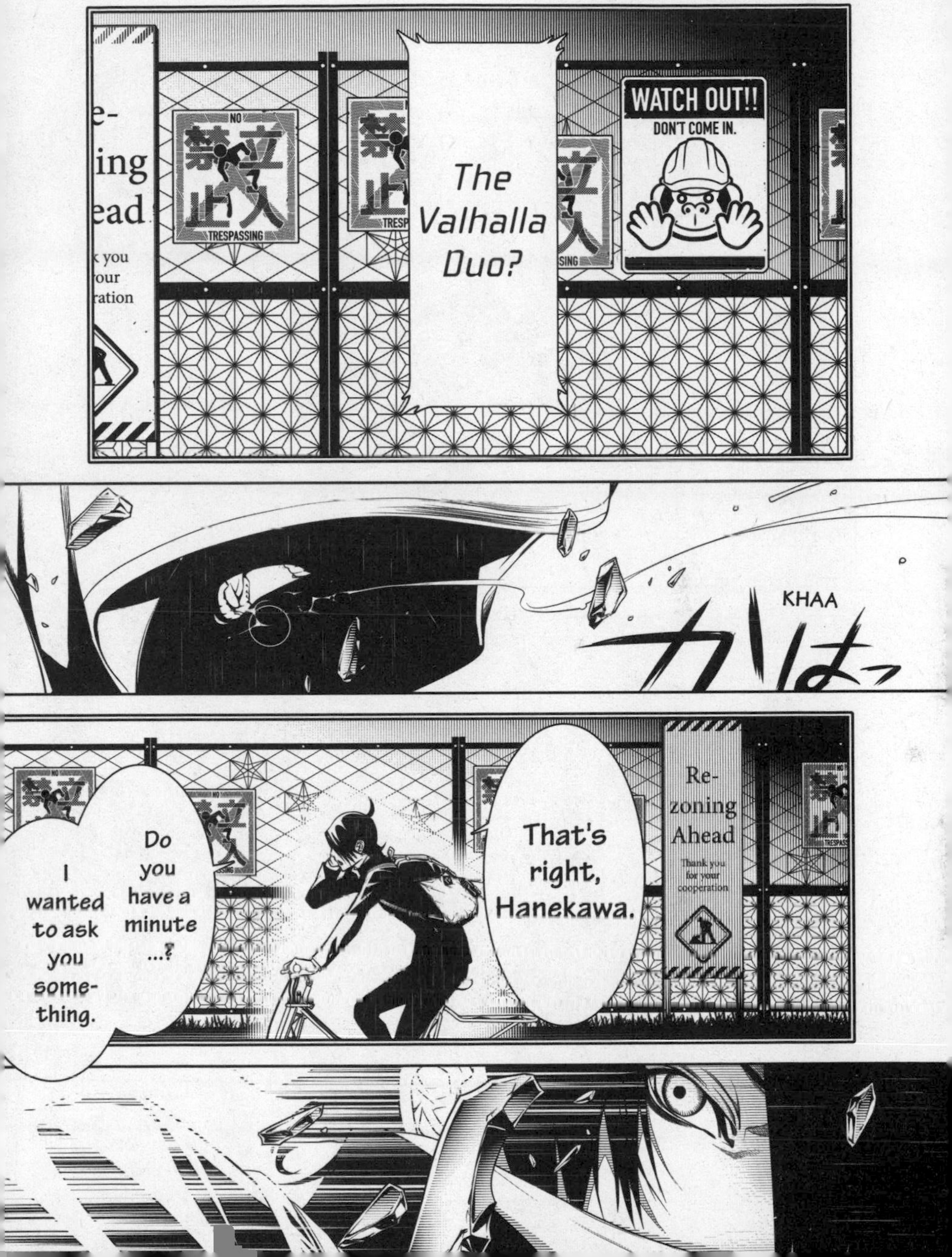
WATCH OUT!!
DON'T COME IN.
The Valhalla Duo?
NO 禁立止入 TRESPASSING
KHAA
カはっ
Re-zoning Ahead
Thank you for your cooperation
That's right, Hanekawa.
Do you have a minute ...?
I wanted to ask you some-thing.

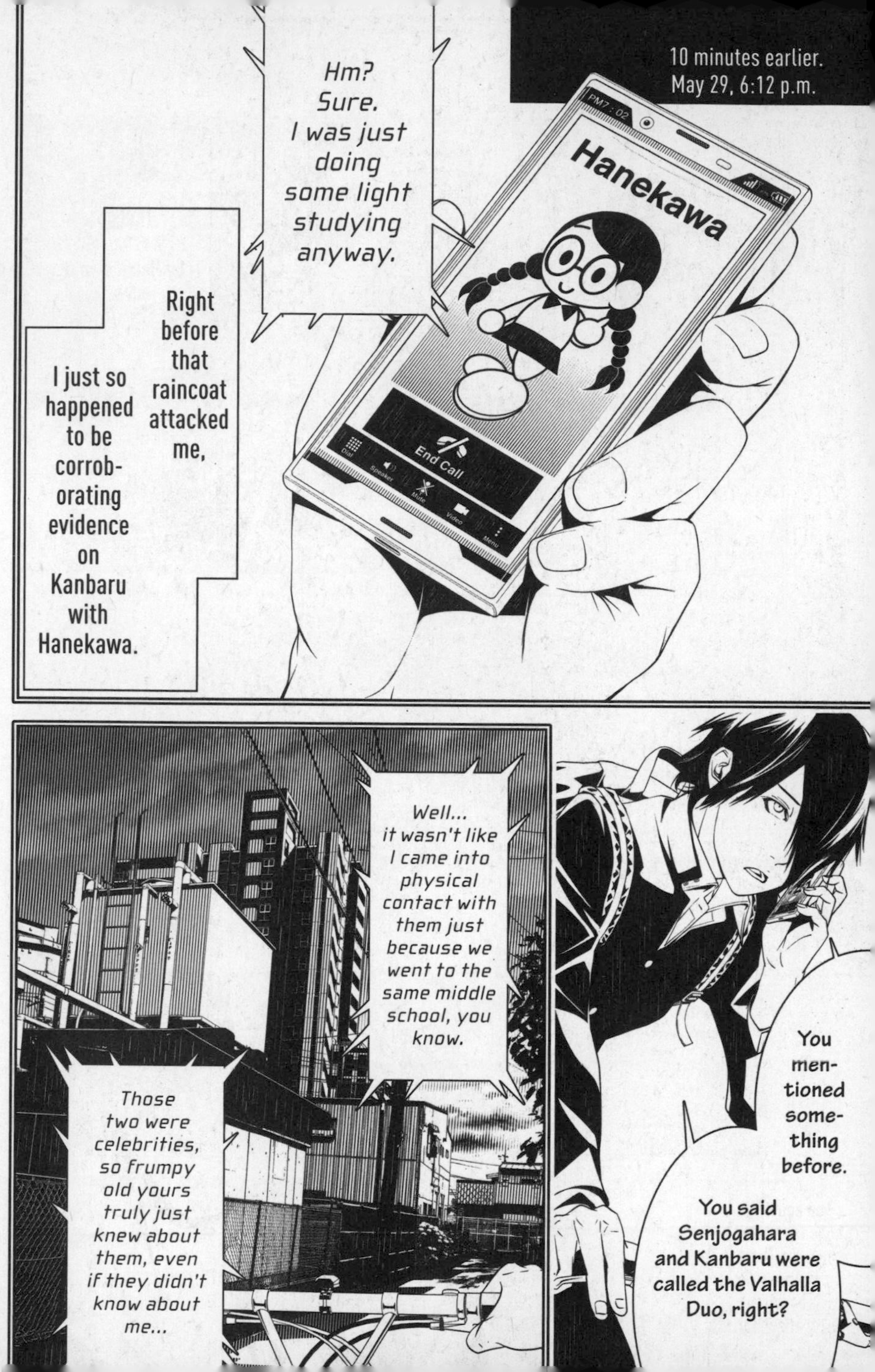
10 minutes earlier.
May 29, 6:12 p.m.
PM7:02
Hanekawa
End Call
Dial
Speaker
Mute
Video
Menu
Hm? Sure. I was just doing some light studying anyway.
Right before that raincoat attacked me,
I just so happened to be corrob-orating evidence on Kanbaru with Hanekawa.
You men-tioned some-thing before.
You said Senjogahara and Kanbaru were called the Valhalla Duo, right?
Well... it wasn't like I came into physical contact with them just because we went to the same middle school, you know.
Those two were celebrities, so frumpy old yours truly just knew about them, even if they didn't know about me...

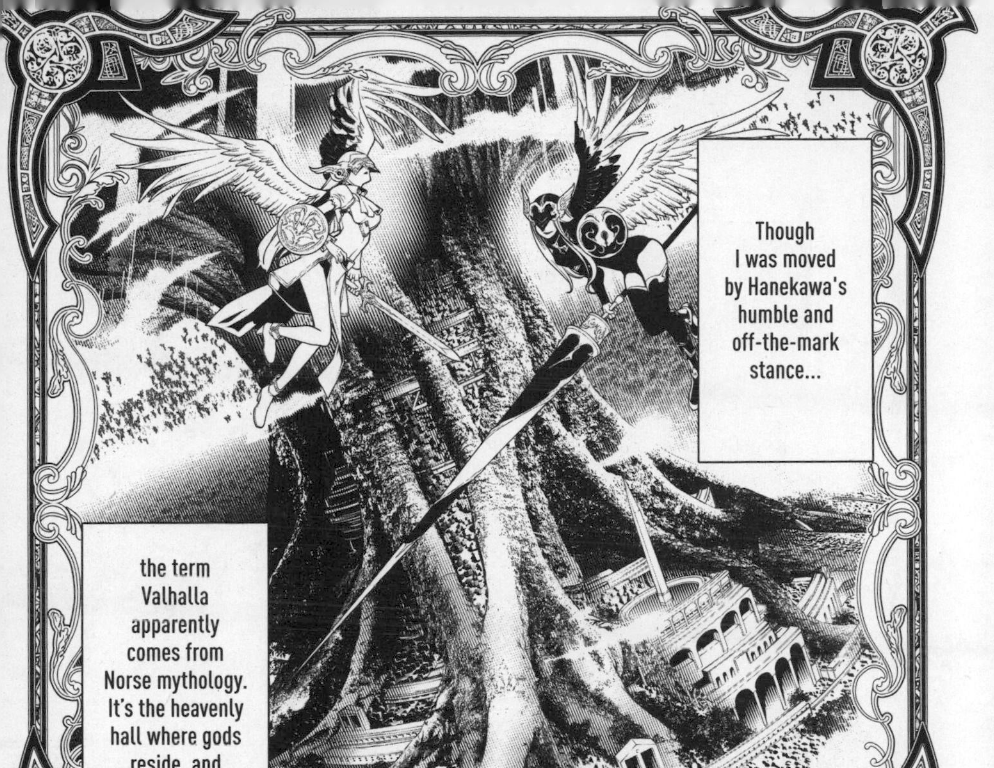
Though I was moved by Hanekawa's humble and off-the-mark stance...
the term Valhalla apparently comes from Norse mythology. It's the heavenly hall where gods reside, and where the spirits of fallen heroes are welcome.

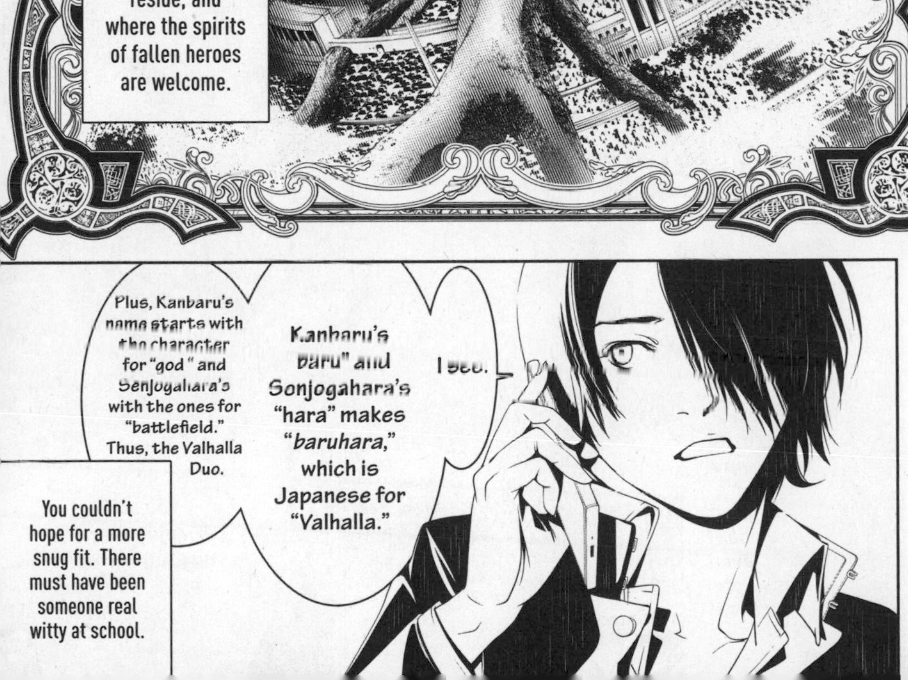
I see.
Kanbaru's "baru" and Senjogahara's "hara" makes "*baruhara*," which is Japanese for "Valhalla."
Plus, Kanbaru's name starts with the character for "god" and Senjogahara's with the ones for "battlefield." Thus, the Valhalla Duo.
You couldn't hope for a more snug fit. There must have been someone real witty at school.

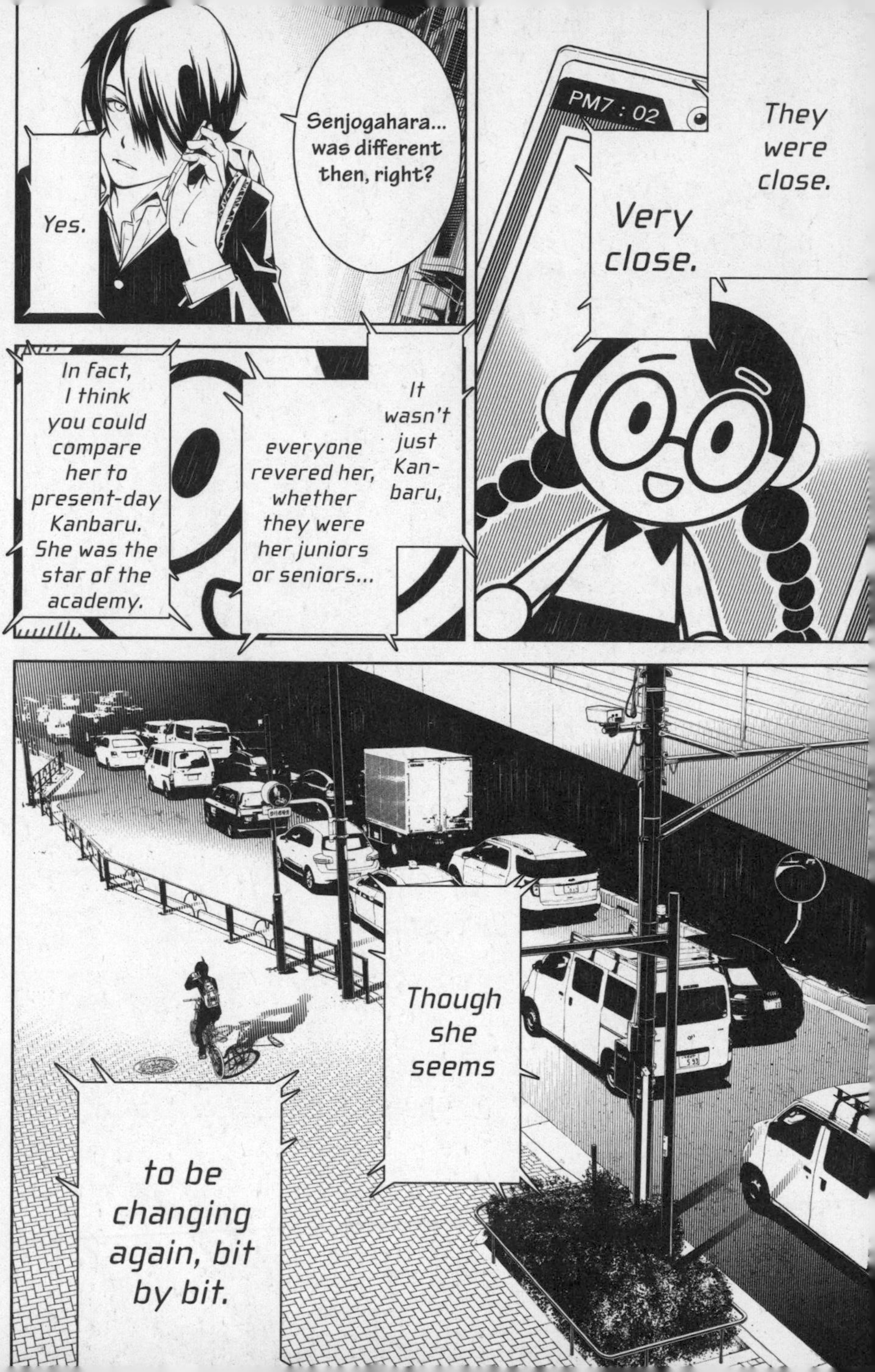
PM7 : 02
They were close.
Very close.
Senjogahara... was different then, right?
Yes.
It wasn't just Kanbaru,
everyone revered her, whether they were her juniors or seniors...
In fact, I think you could compare her to present-day Kanbaru. She was the star of the academy.
Though she seems
to be changing again, bit by bit.

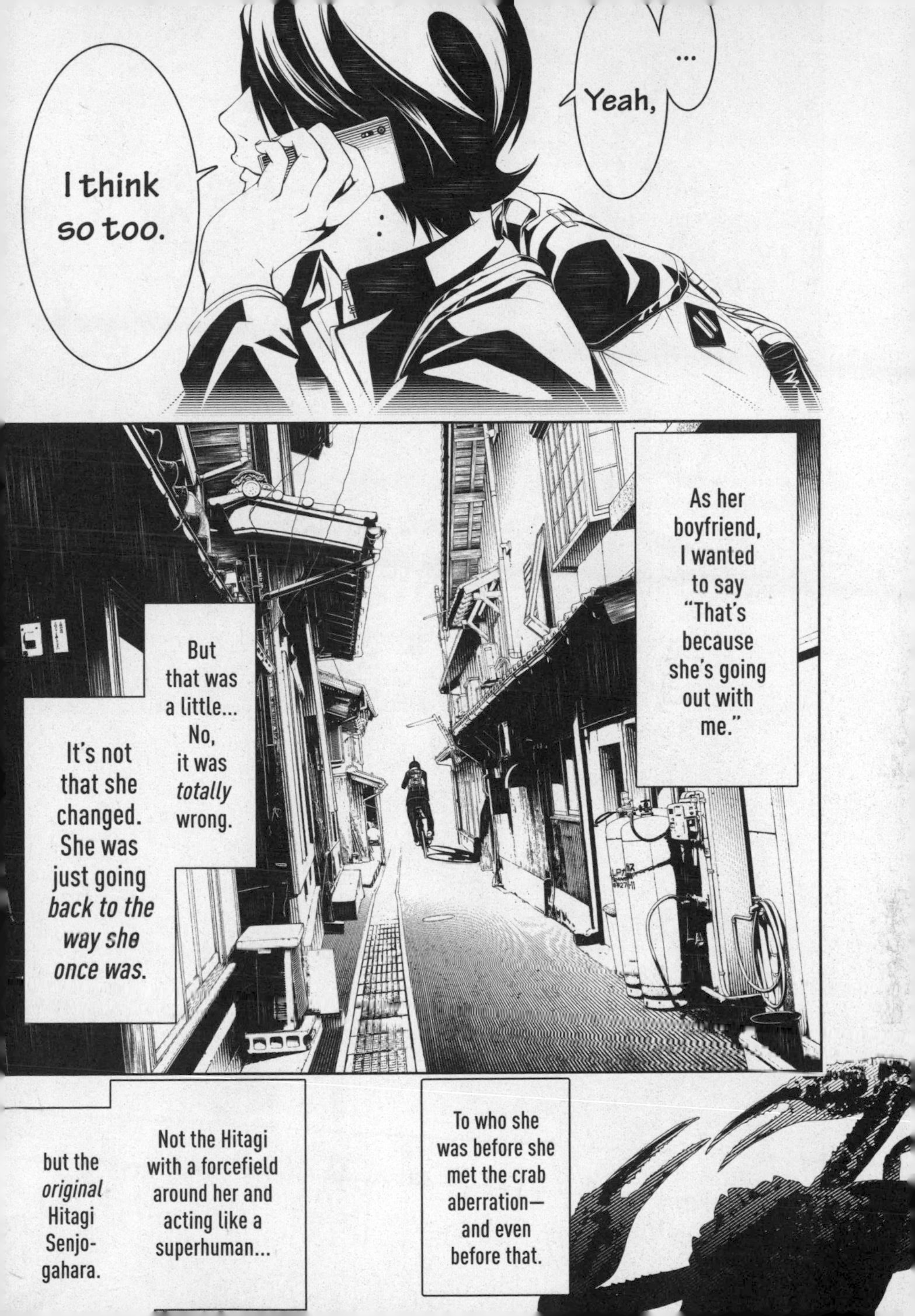

... Yeah,
I think so too.
As her boyfriend, I wanted to say "That's because she's going out with me."
But that was a little... No, it was *totally* wrong.
It's not that she changed. She was just going *back to the way she once was.*
To who she was before she met the crab aberration— and even before that.
Not the Hitagi with a forcefield around her and acting like a superhuman...
but the *original* Hitagi Senjo-gahara.

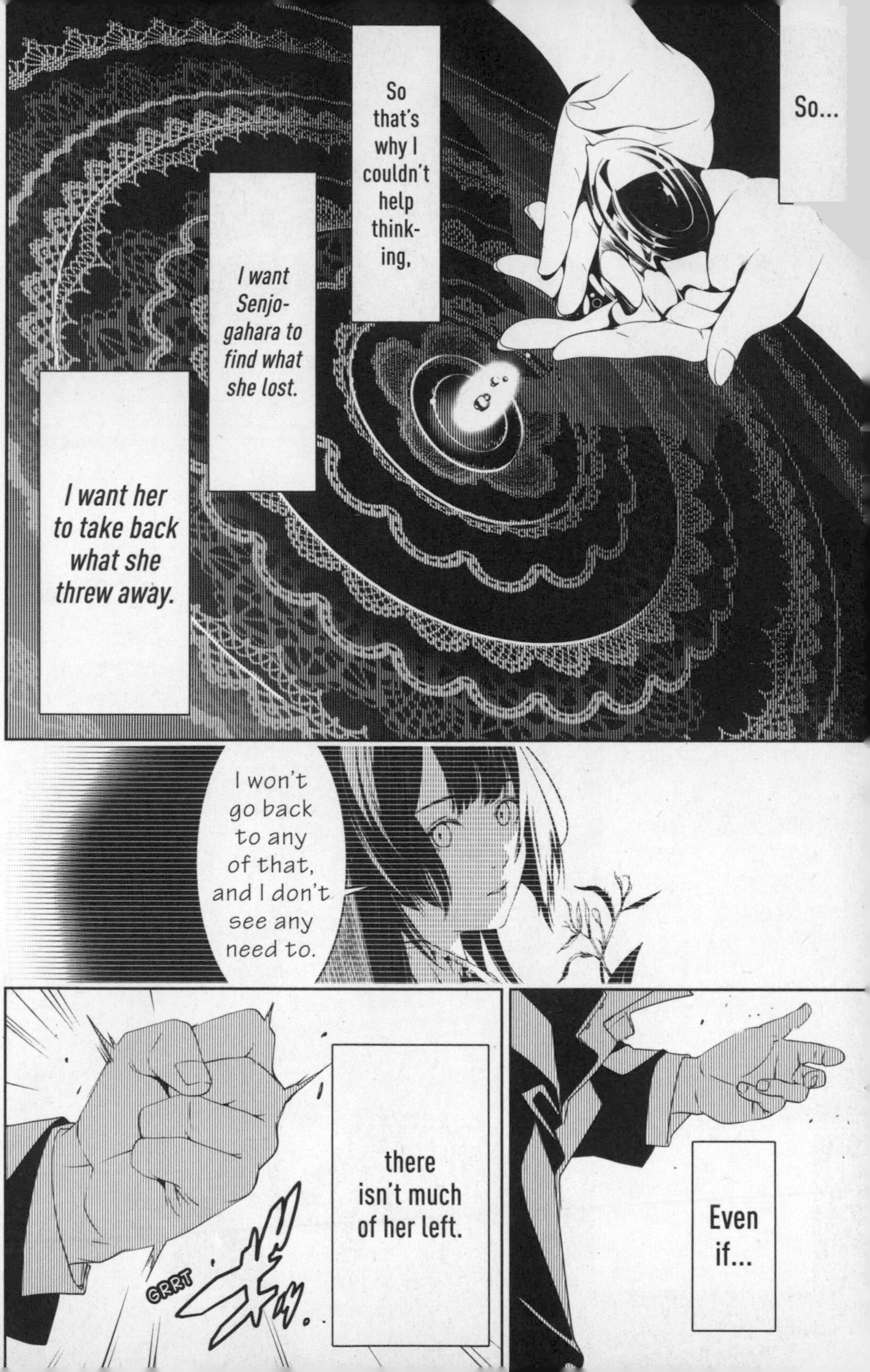
So...
So that's why I couldn't help think-ing,
I want Senjo-gahara to find what she lost.
I want her to take back what she threw away.
I won't go back to any of that, and I don't see any need to.
Even if...
there isn't much of her left.
GRRT

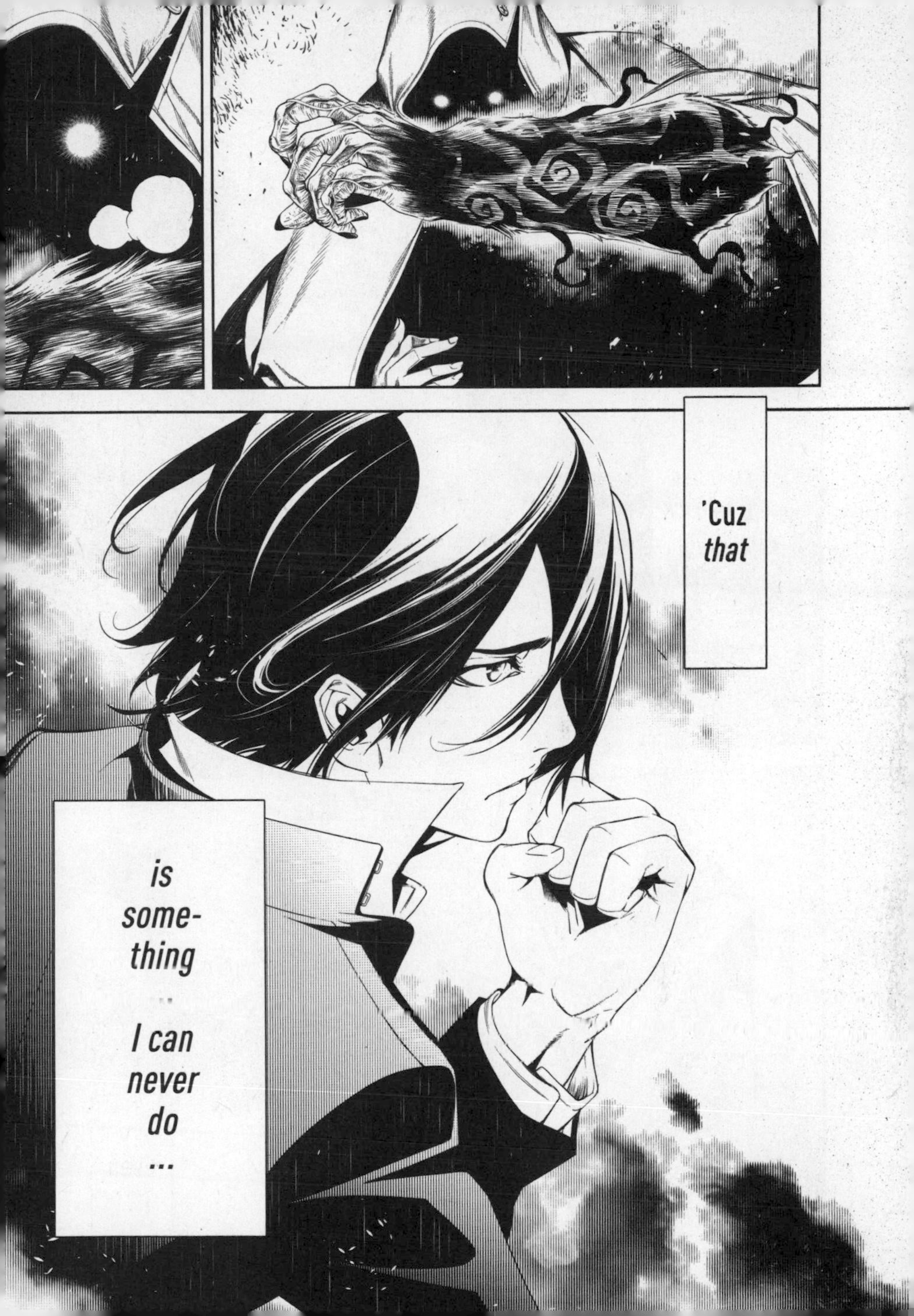
'Cuz *that*
is some-thing... I can never do...

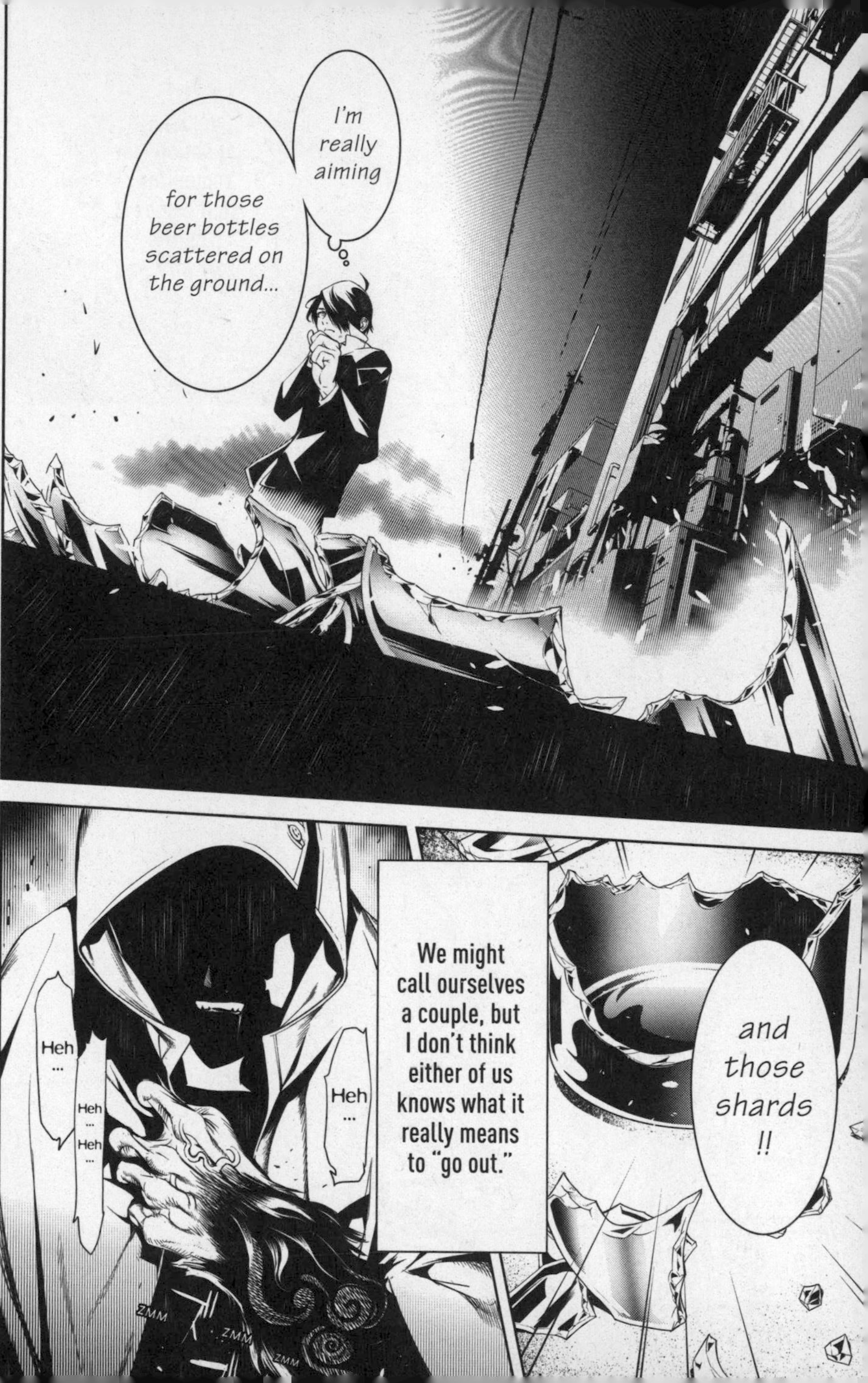
I'm really aiming
for those beer bottles scattered on the ground...
and those shards!!
We might call ourselves a couple, but I don't think either of us knows what it really means to "go out."
Heh...
Heh... Heh...
Heh...
ZMM
ZMM
ZMM

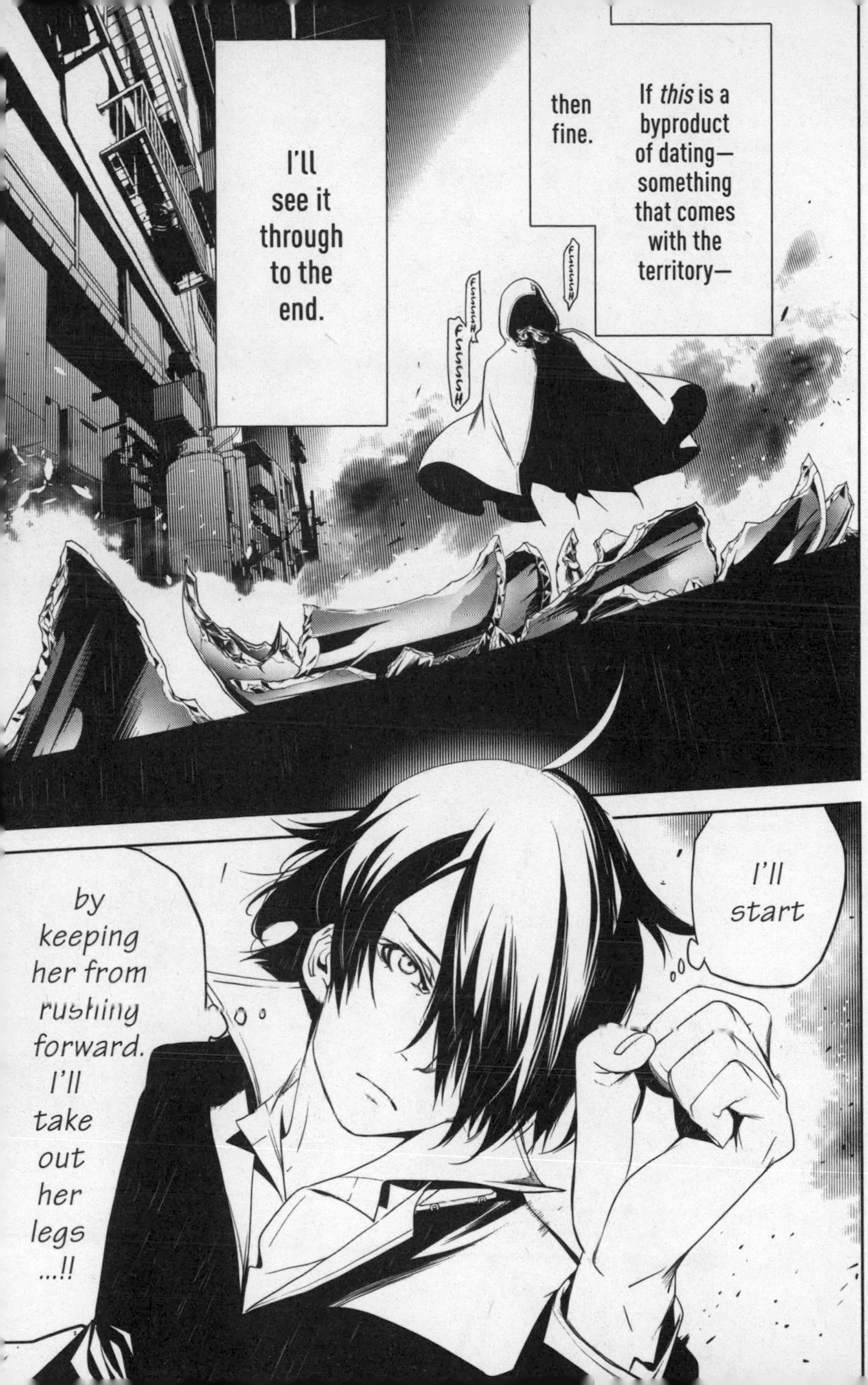
If *this* is a byproduct of dating—something that comes with the territory—
then fine.
I'll see it through to the end.
FSSSSH
FSSSSH
FSSSSSH
I'll start
by keeping her from rushing forward. I'll take out her legs ...!!

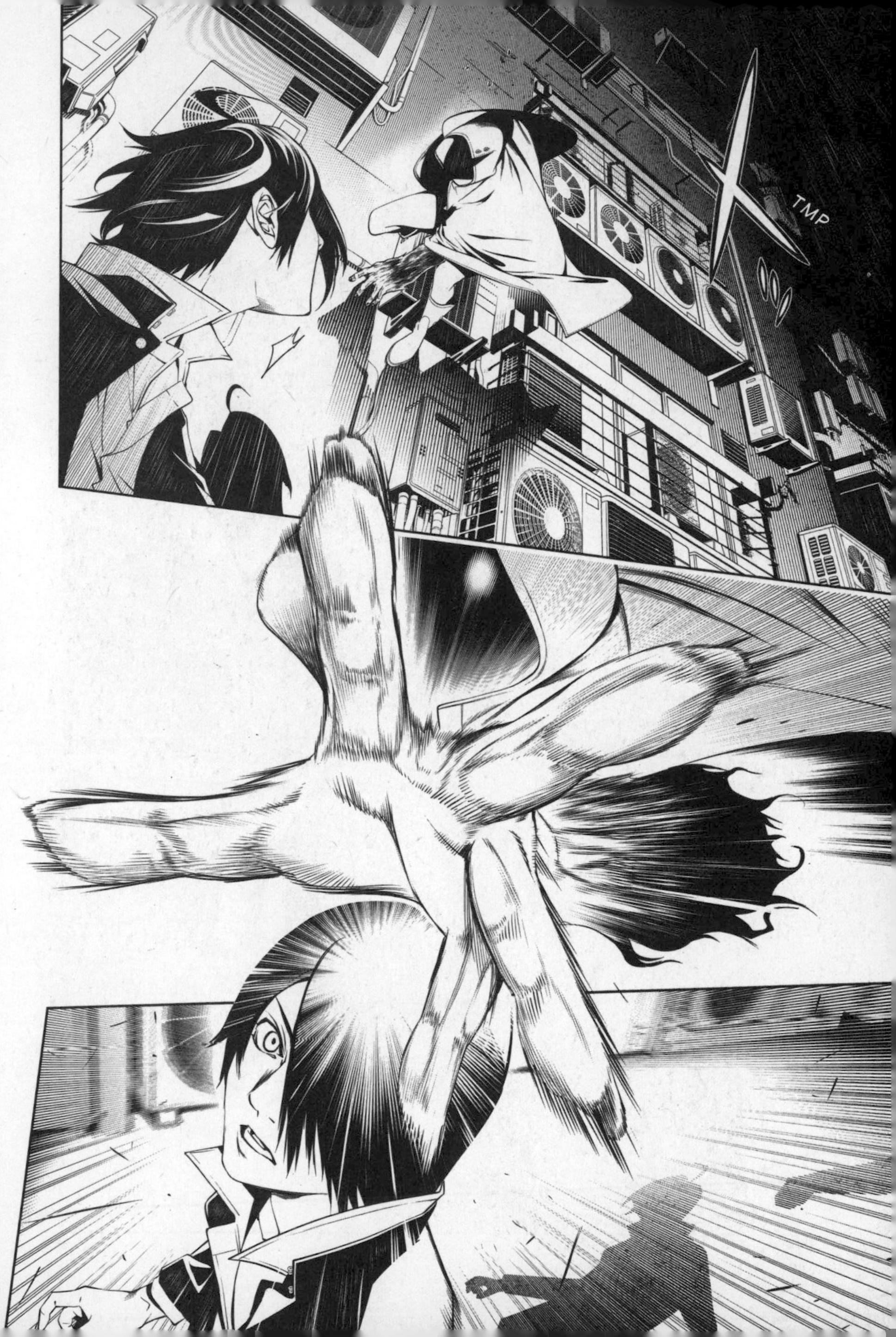
TMP

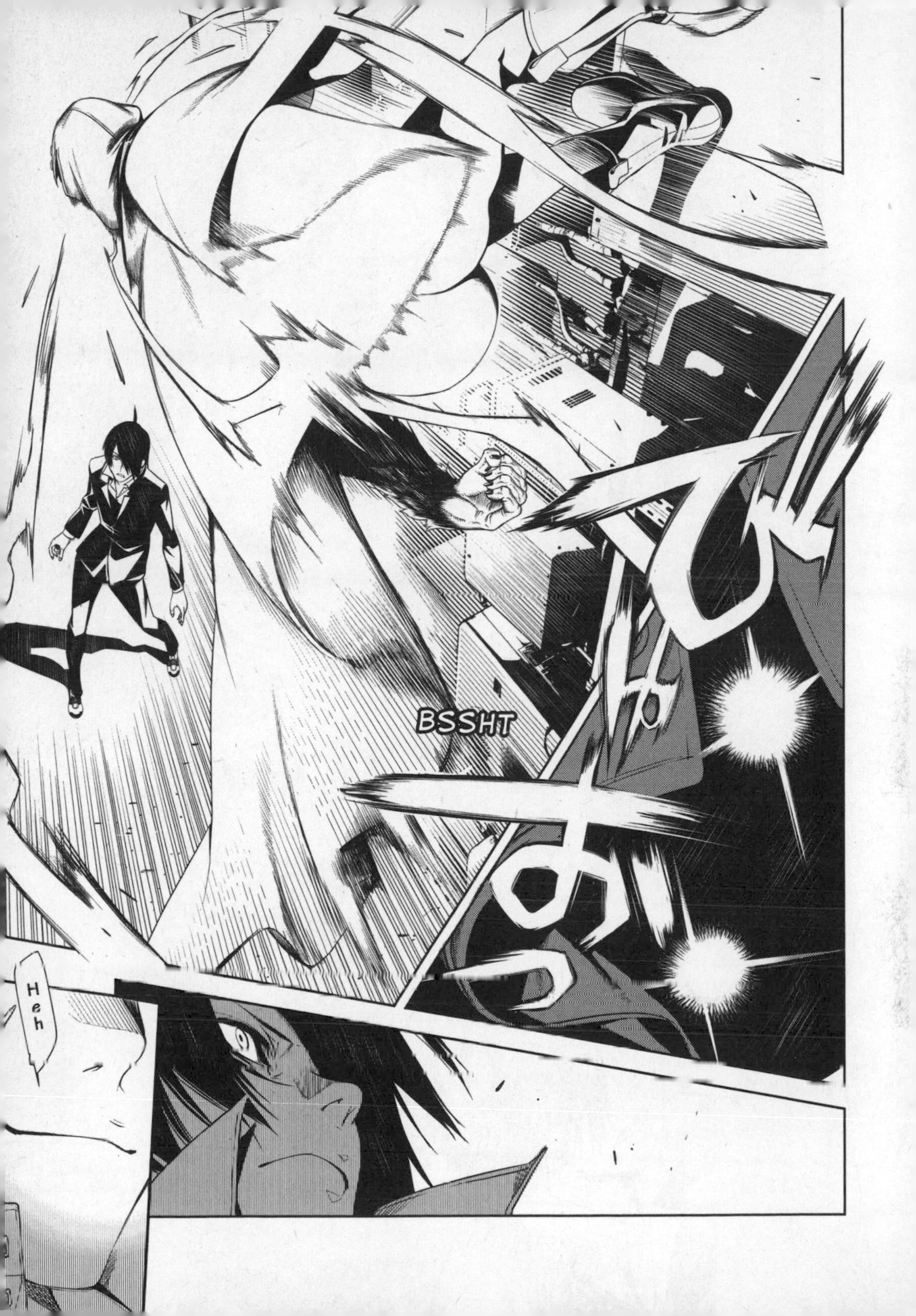
BSSHT
Heh

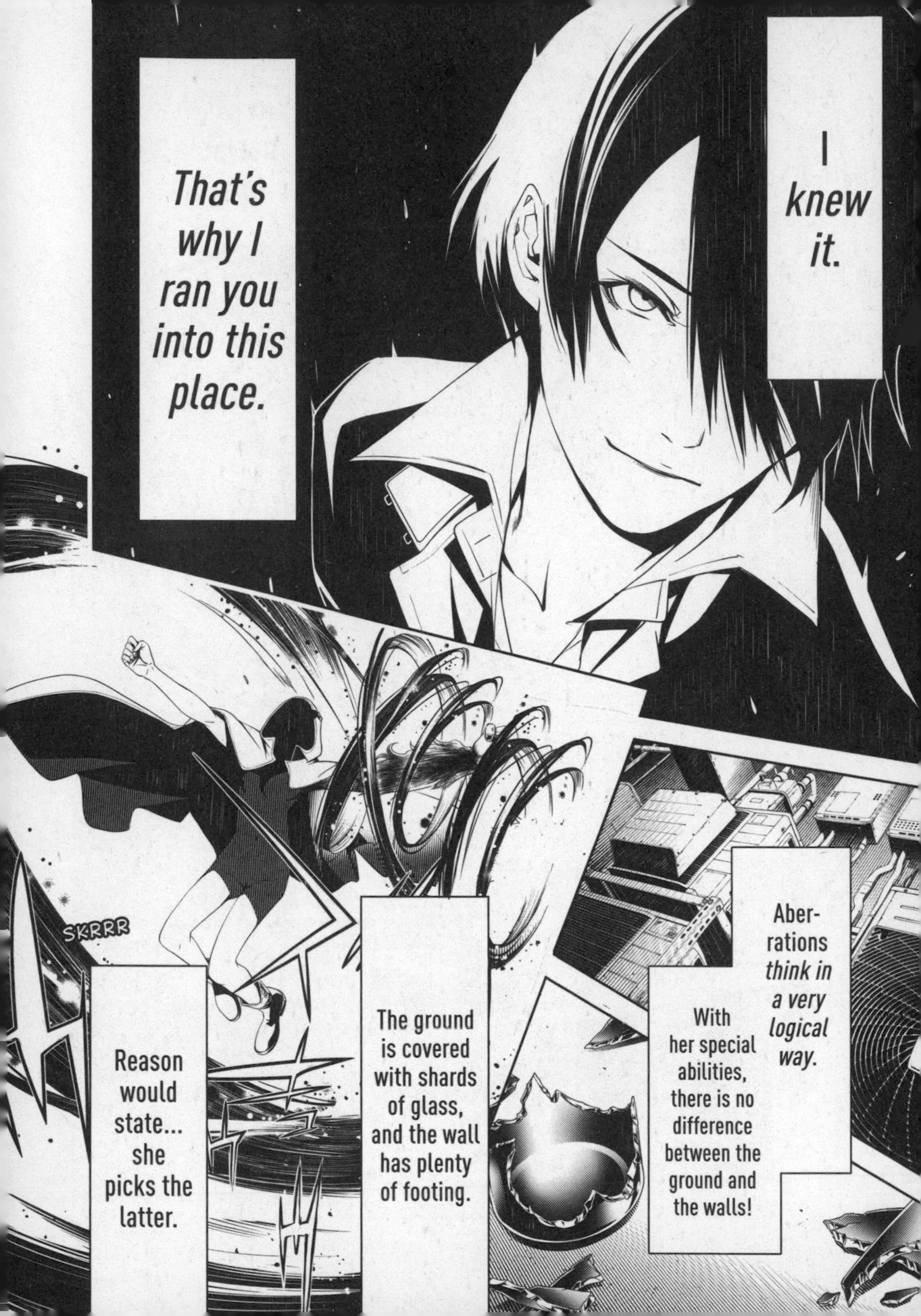
I knew it.
That's why I ran you into this place.
Aber-rations think in a very logical way.
With her special abilities, there is no difference between the ground and the walls!
The ground is covered with shards of glass, and the wall has plenty of footing.
SKRRR
Reason would state... she picks the latter.

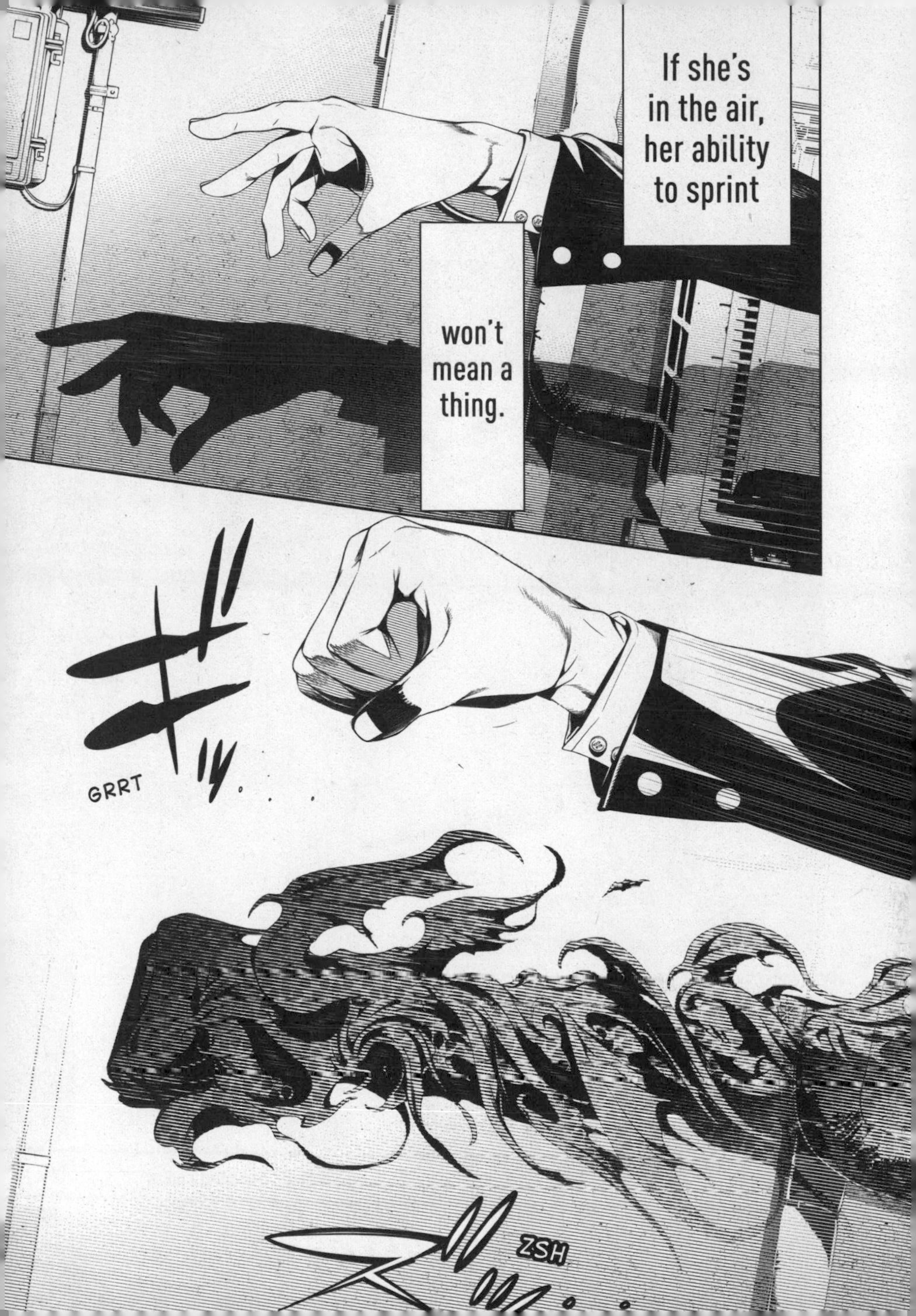
If she's in the air, her ability to sprint
won't mean a thing.
GRRT
ZSH

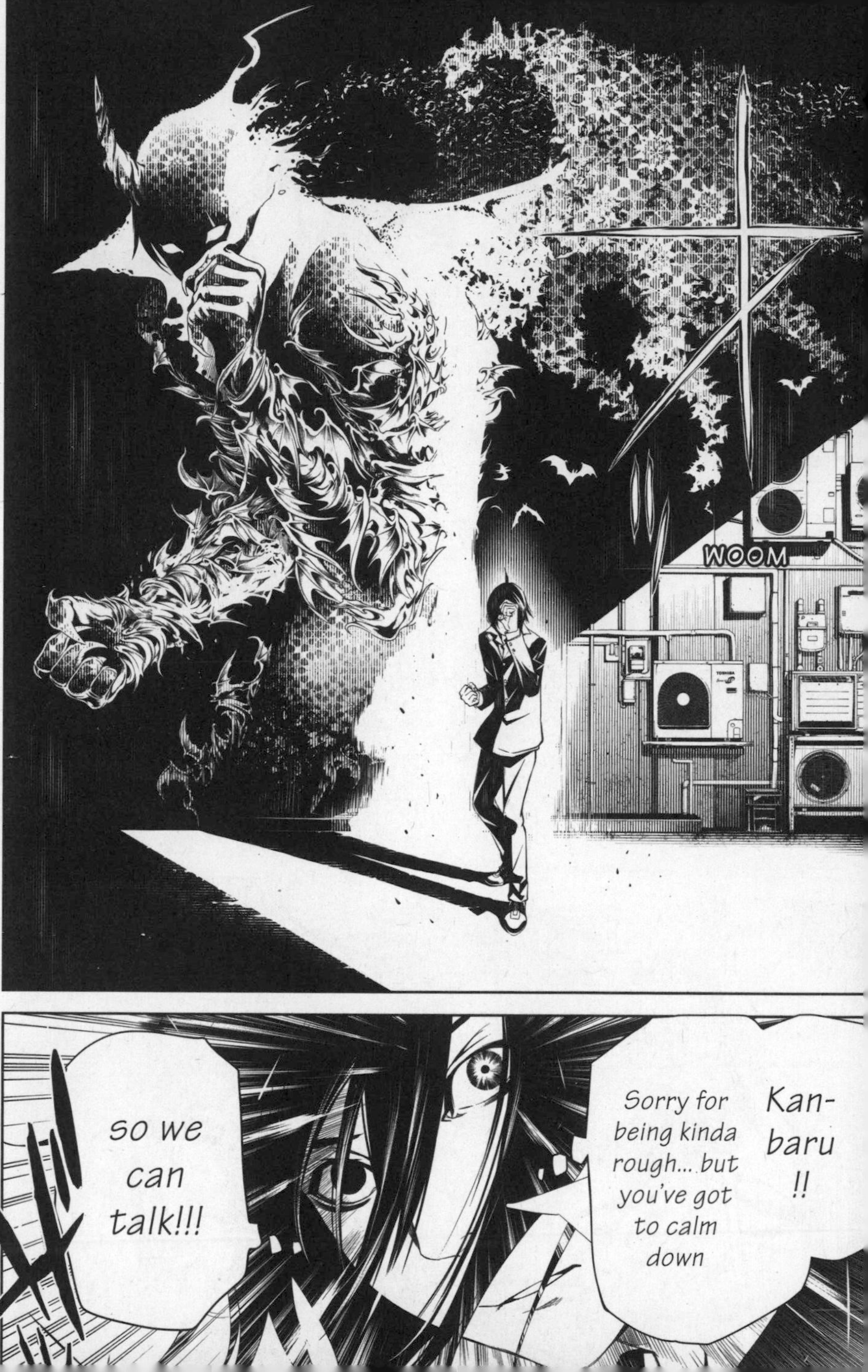
WOOM
Kan-baru !!
Sorry for being kinda rough... but you've got to calm down
so we can talk!!!
ZSH

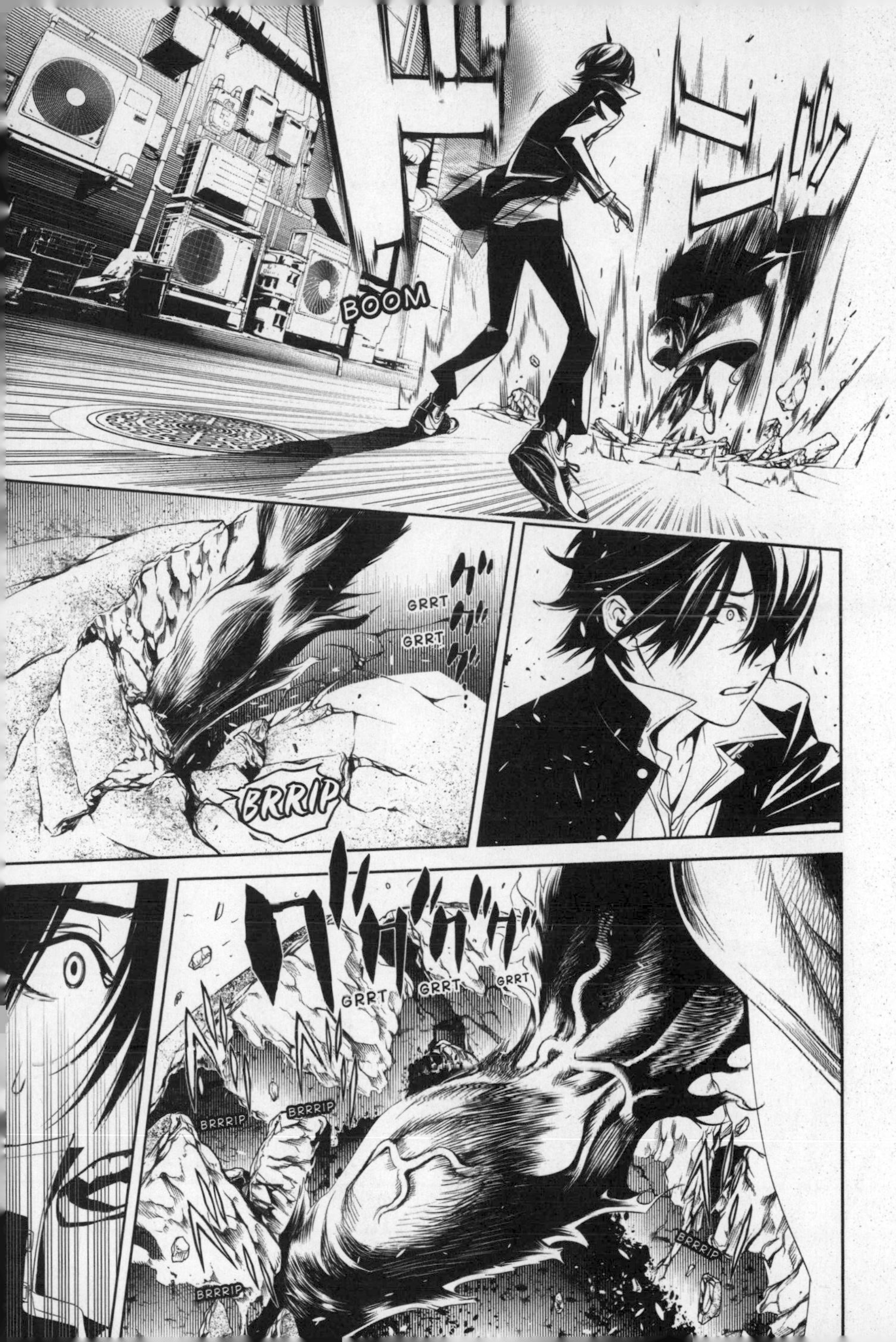
BOOM
GRRT
GRRT
BRRIP
GRRT
GRRT
GRRT
BRRRIP
BRRRIP
BRRRIP
BRRRIP

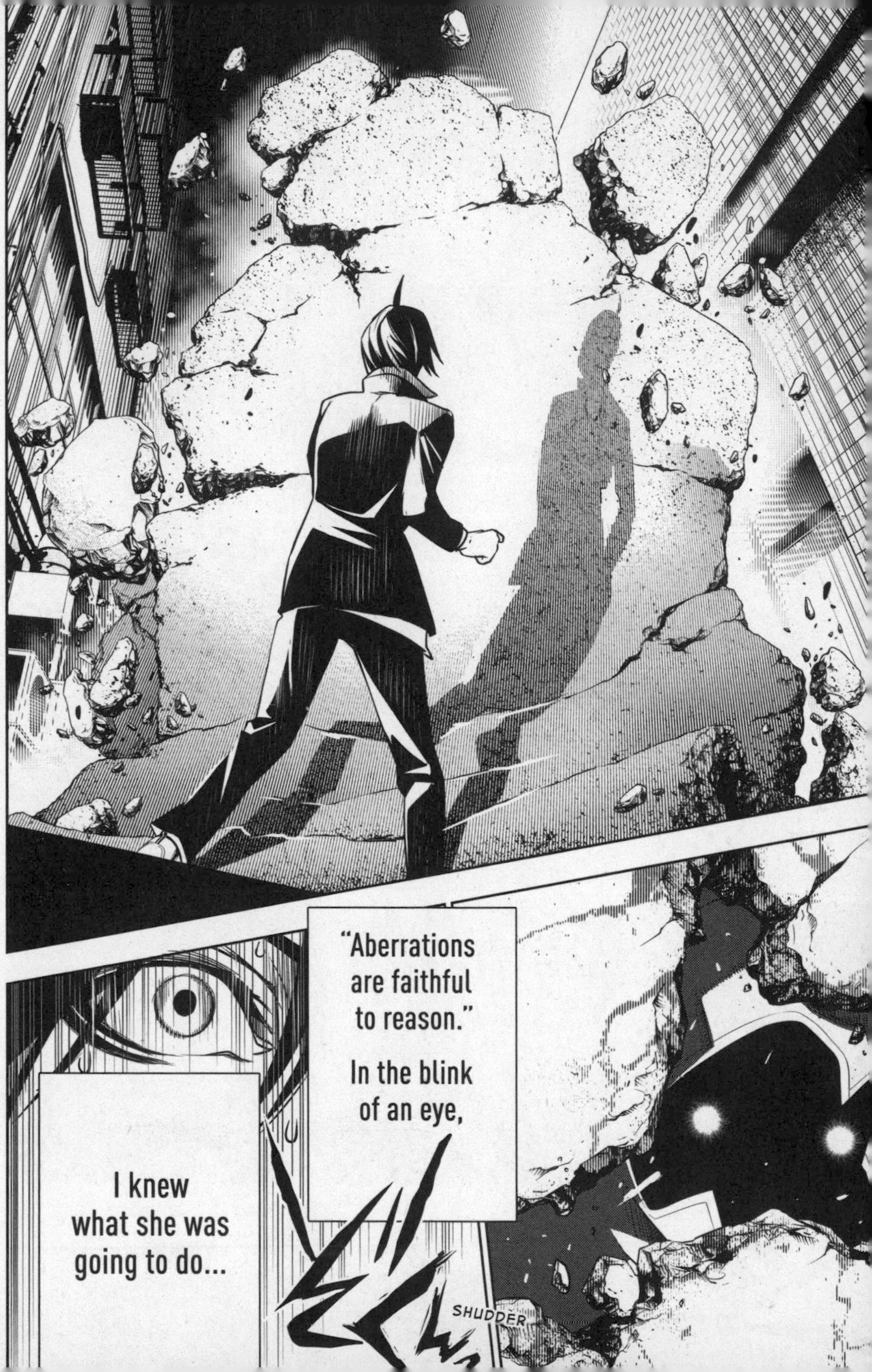
"Aberrations are faithful to reason."
In the blink of an eye,
I knew what she was going to do...
SHUDDER

After all, we're both monsters.

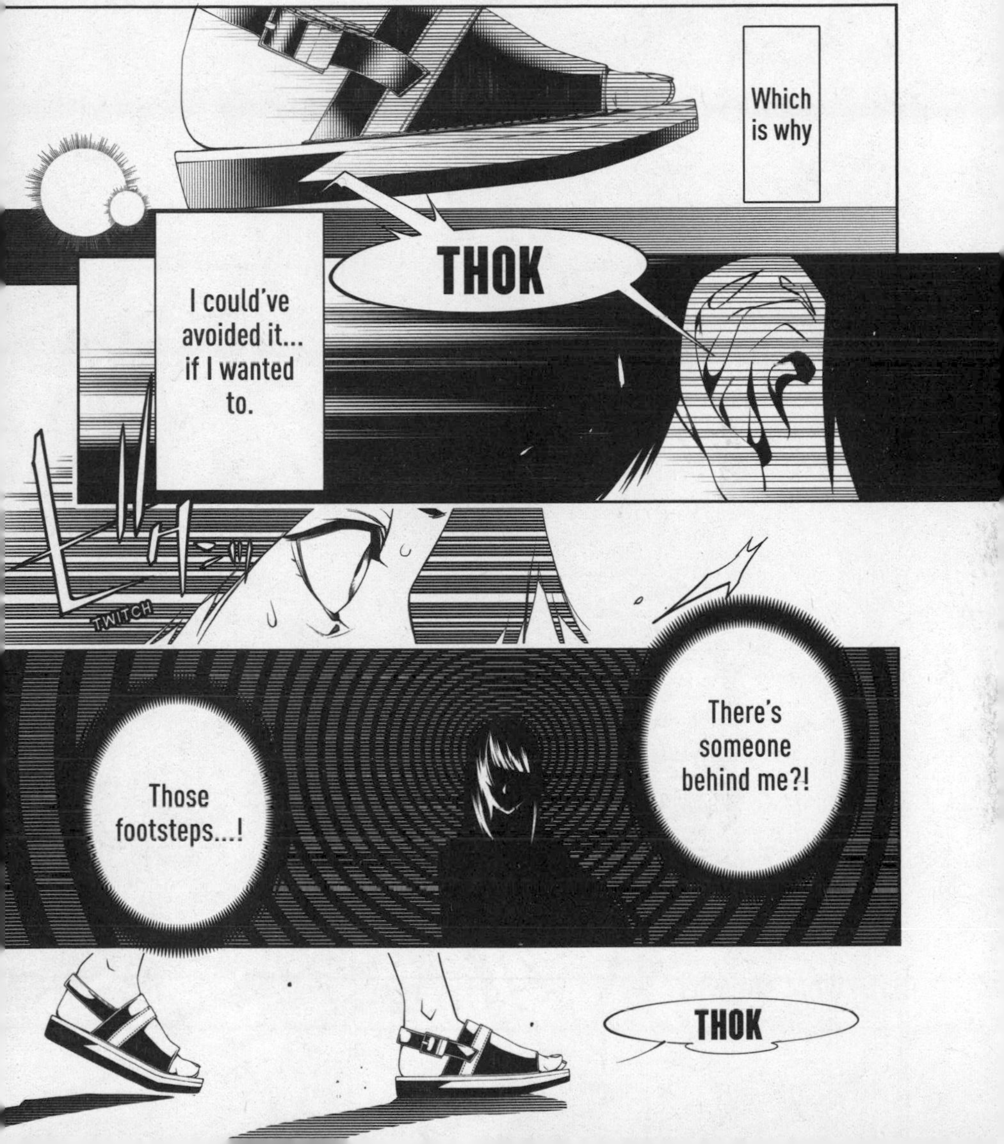
Which is why
THOK
I could've avoided it... if I wanted to.
TWITCH
There's someone behind me?!
Those footsteps...!
THOK

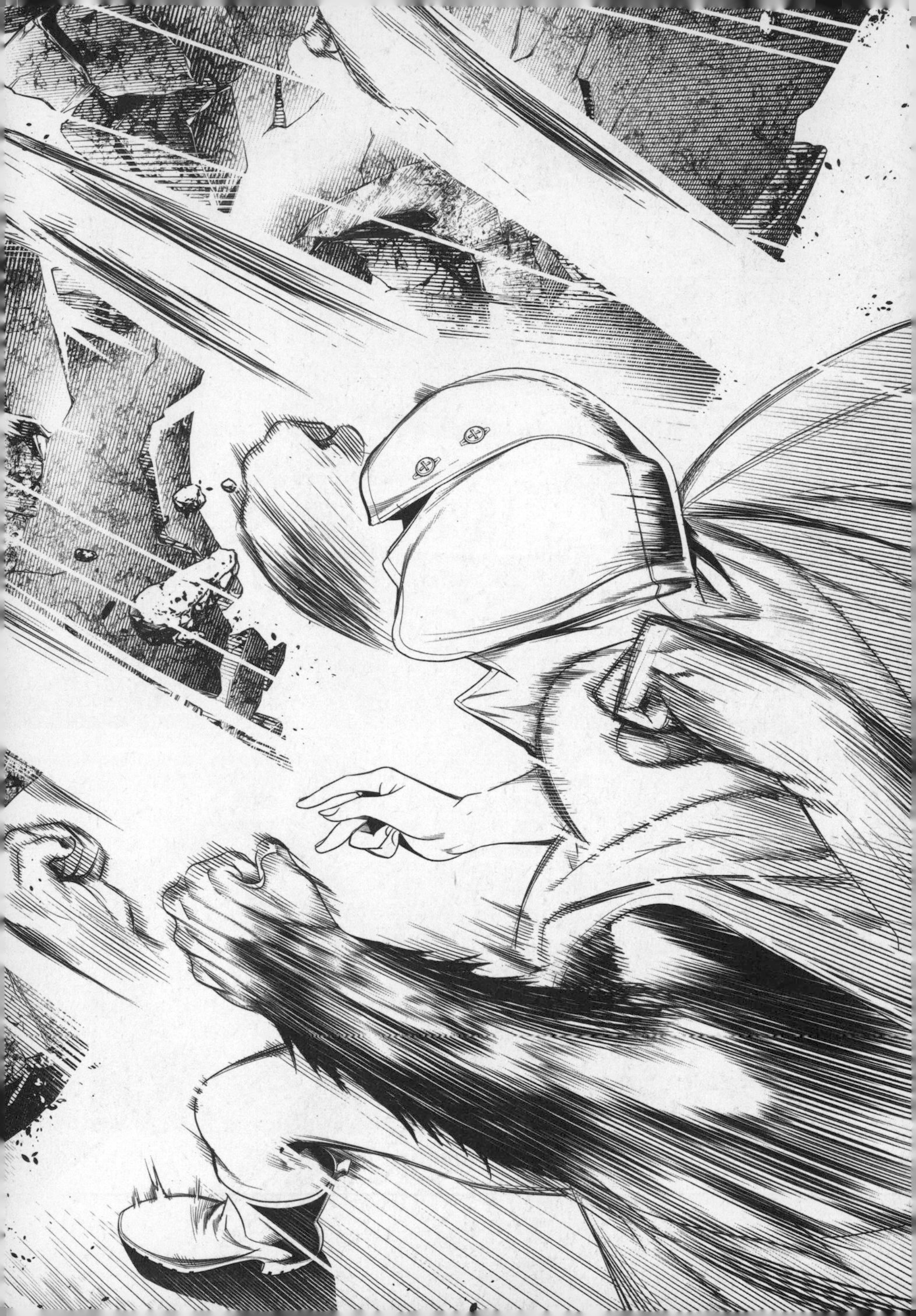

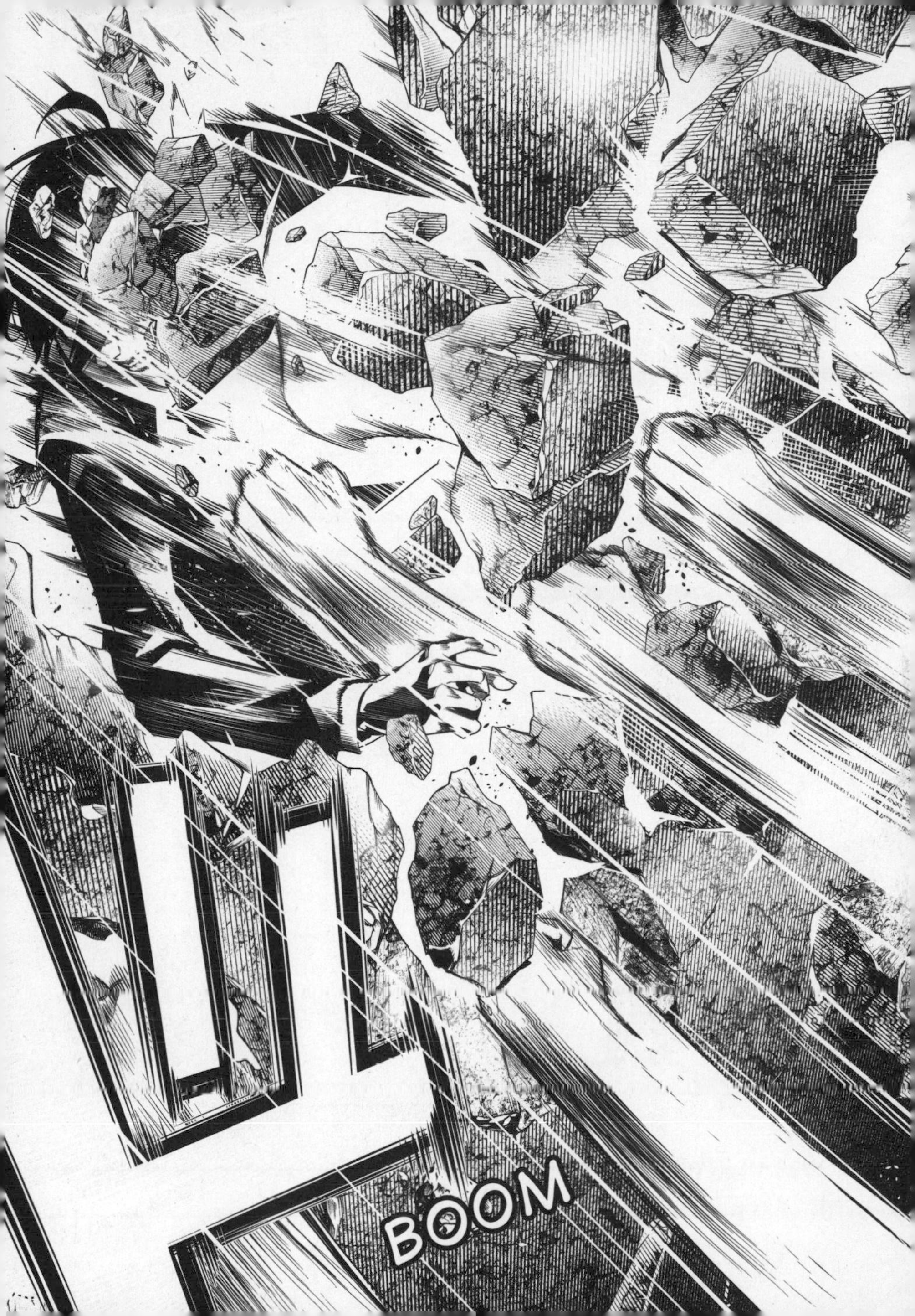
BOOM

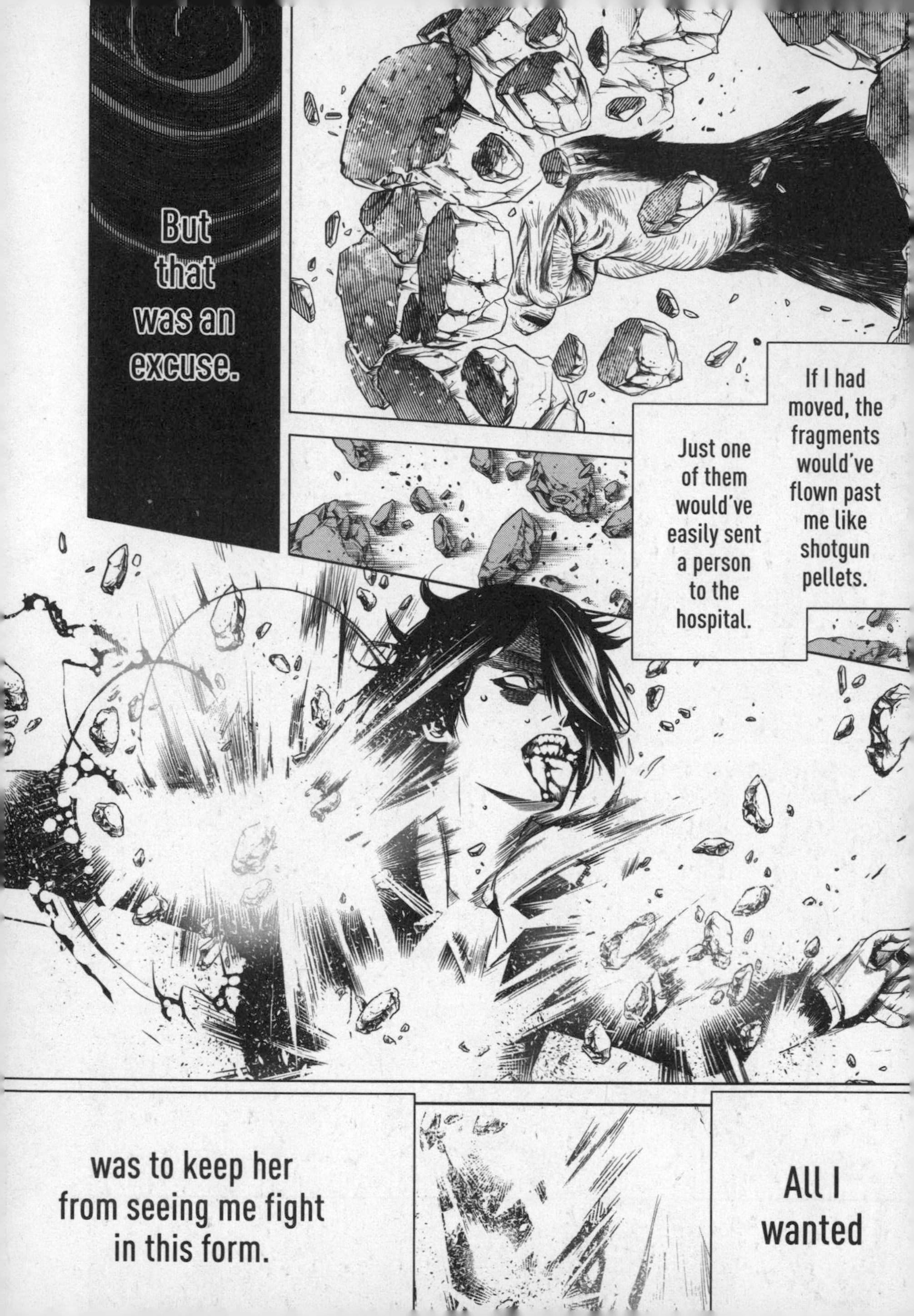
If I had moved, the fragments would've flown past me like shotgun pellets.
Just one of them would've easily sent a person to the hospital.
But that was an excuse.
All I wanted
was to keep her from seeing me fight in this form.

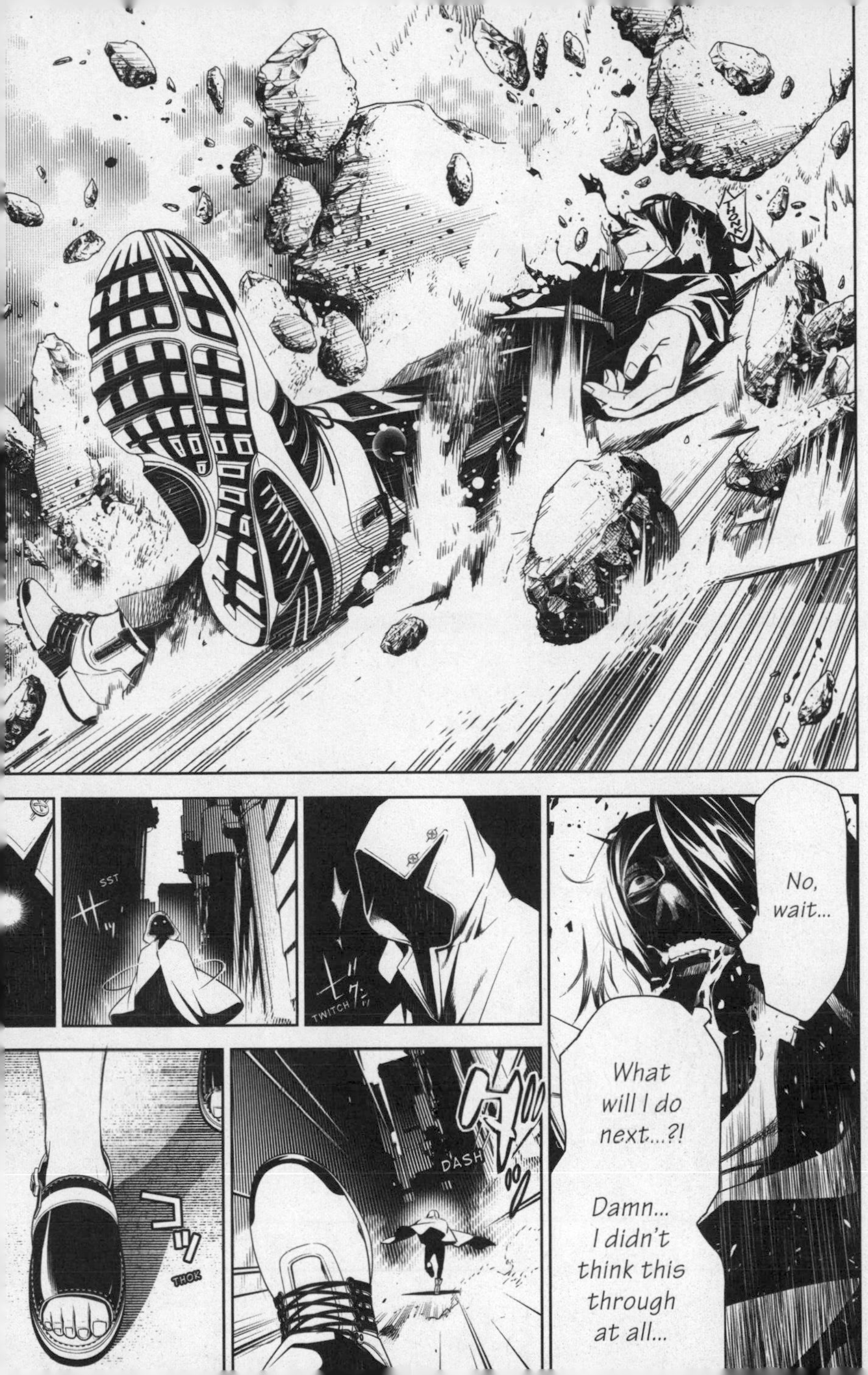
THONK
No, wait...
What will I do next...?!
Damn... I didn't think this through at all...
TWITCH
SST
DASH
THOK

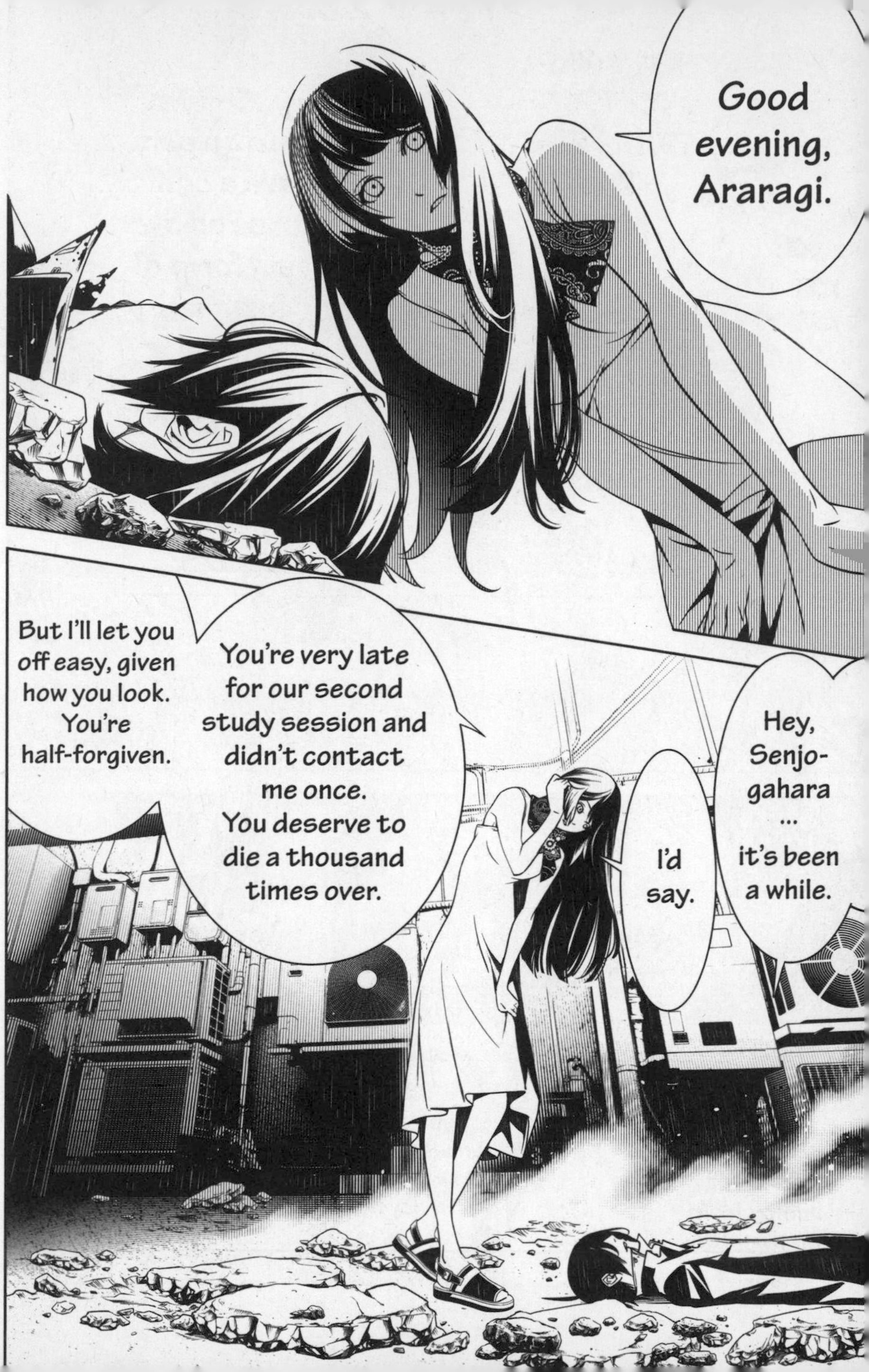
Good evening, Araragi.
Hey, Senjo-gahara ... it's been a while.
I'd say.
You're very late for our second study session and didn't contact me once. You deserve to die a thousand times over.
But I'll let you off easy, given how you look. You're half-forgiven.

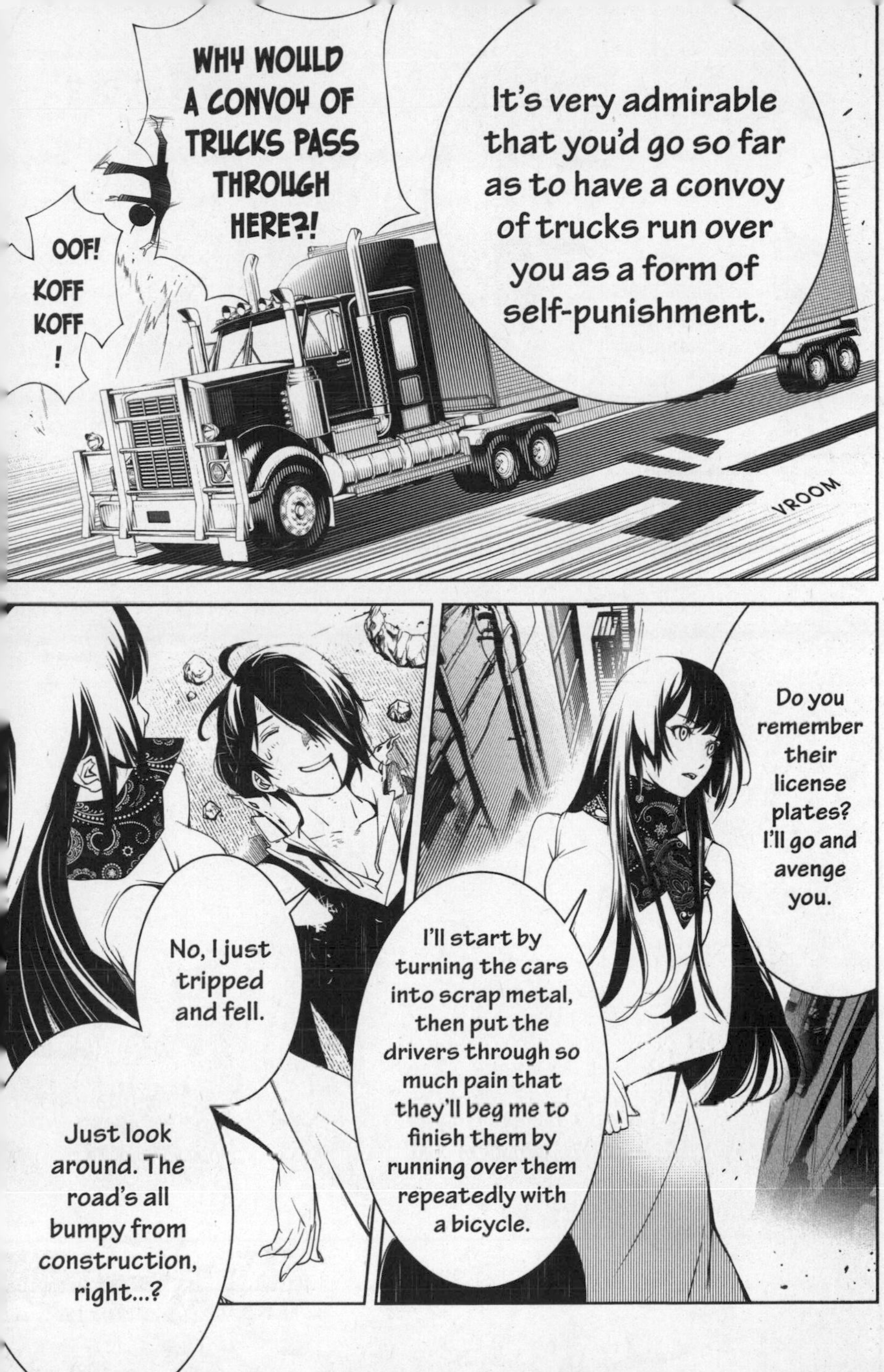
It's very admirable that you'd go so far as to have a convoy of trucks run over you as a form of self-punishment.
WHY WOULD A CONVOY OF TRUCKS PASS THROUGH HERE?!
OOF!
KOFF KOFF !
VROOM
Do you remember their license plates? I'll go and avenge you.
I'll start by turning the cars into scrap metal, then put the drivers through so much pain that they'll beg me to finish them by running over them repeatedly with a bicycle.
No, I just tripped and fell.
Just look around. The road's all bumpy from construction, right...?

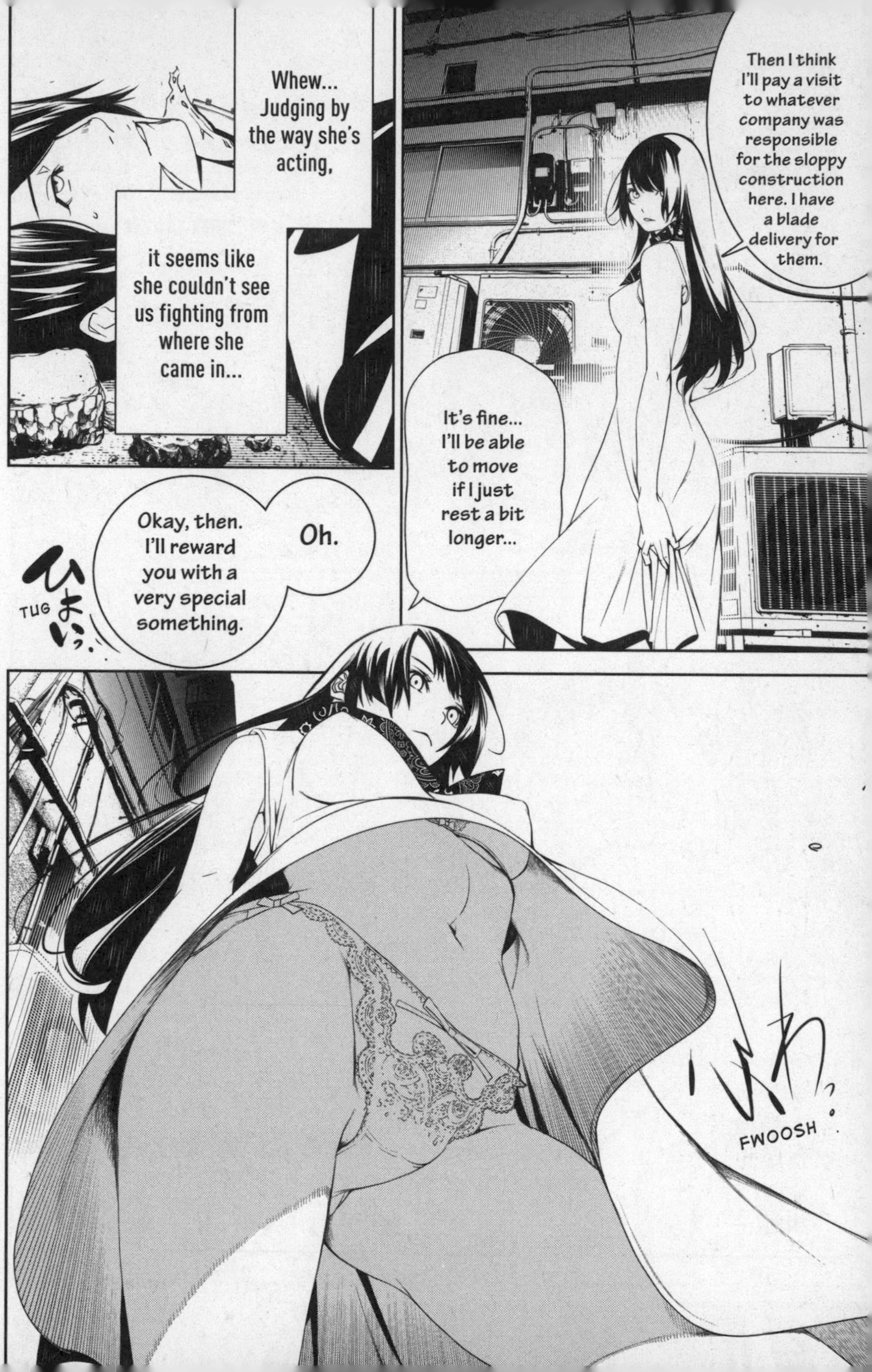
Then I think I'll pay a visit to whatever company was responsible for the sloppy construction here. I have a blade delivery for them.
It's fine... I'll be able to move if I just rest a bit longer...
Whew... Judging by the way she's acting,
it seems like she couldn't see us fighting from where she came in...
Oh.
Okay, then. I'll reward you with a very special something.
ひょいっ
TUG
ぶわっ
FWOOSH

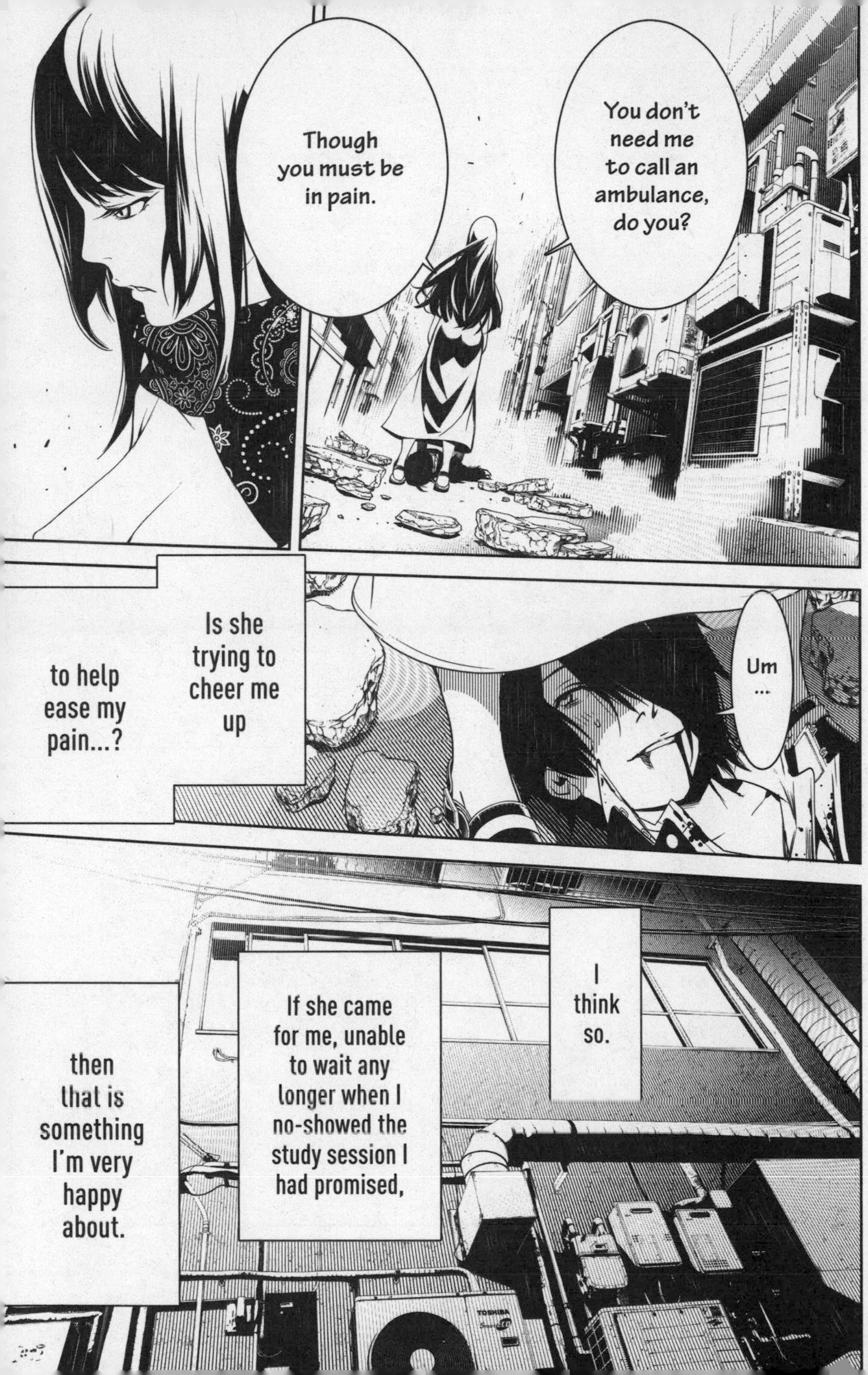
You don't need me to call an ambulance, do you?
Though you must be in pain.
Um ...
Is she trying to cheer me up
to help ease my pain...?
I think so.
If she came for me, unable to wait any longer when I no-showed the study session I had promised,
then that is something I'm very happy about.

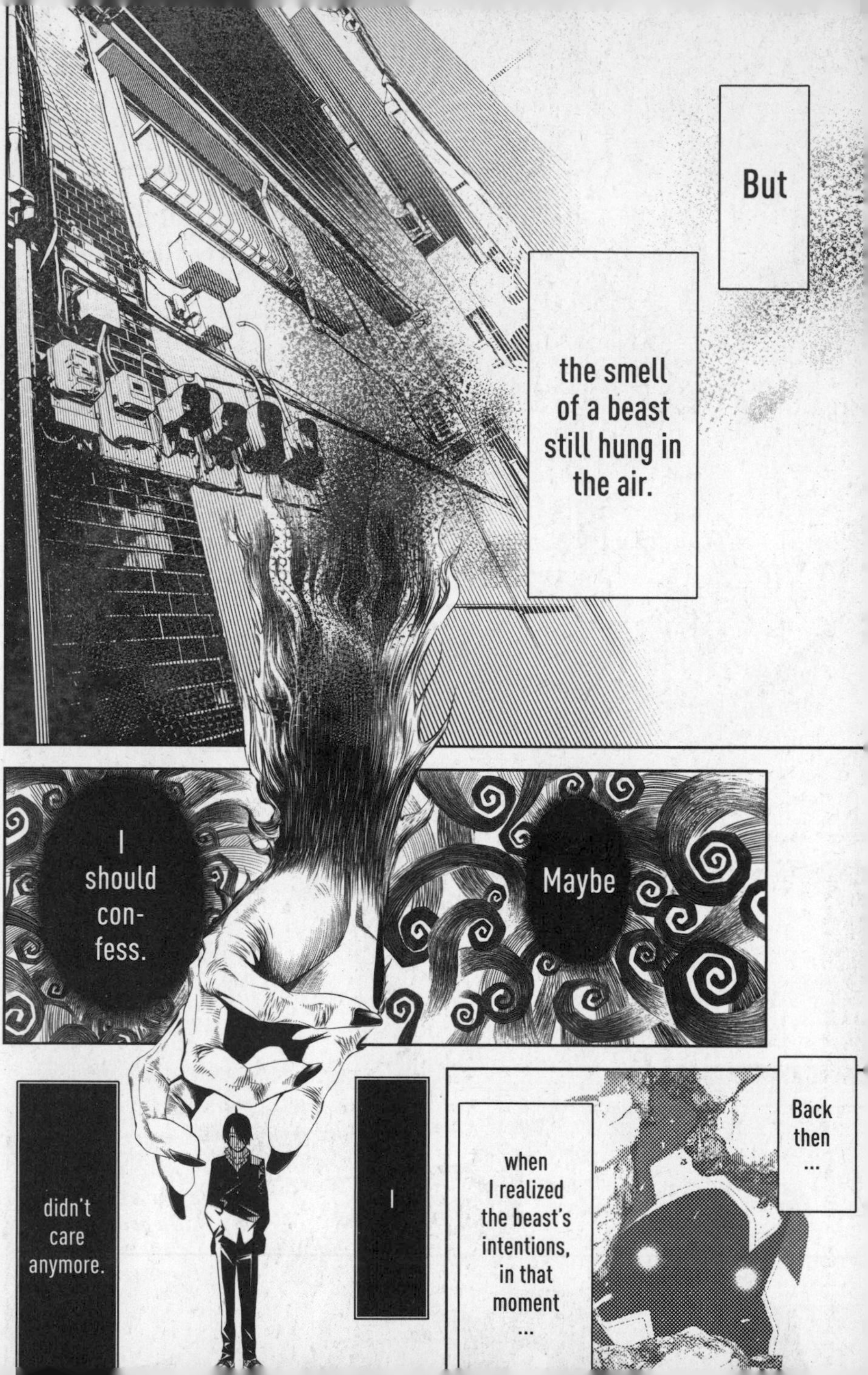
But
the smell of a beast still hung in the air.
Maybe
I should con-fess.
Back then ...
when I realized the beast's intentions, in that moment ...
I
didn't care anymore.

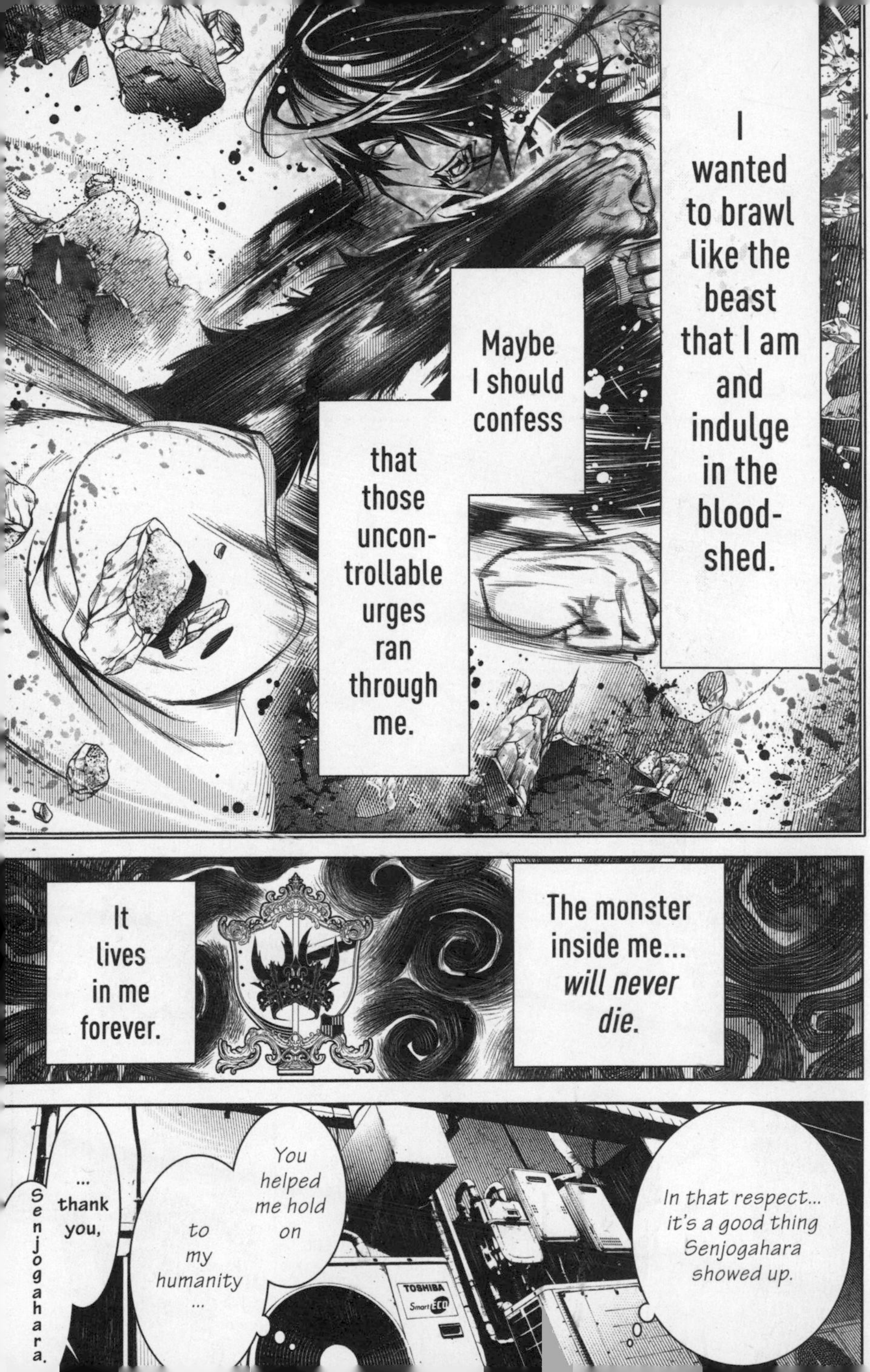
I wanted to brawl like the beast that I am and indulge in the blood-shed.
Maybe I should confess
that those uncon-trollable urges ran through me.
The monster inside me... *will never die.*
It lives in me forever.
In that respect... it's a good thing Senjogahara showed up.
You helped me hold on
to my humanity ...
... thank you,
Senjogahara.
TOSHIBA
SmartECO

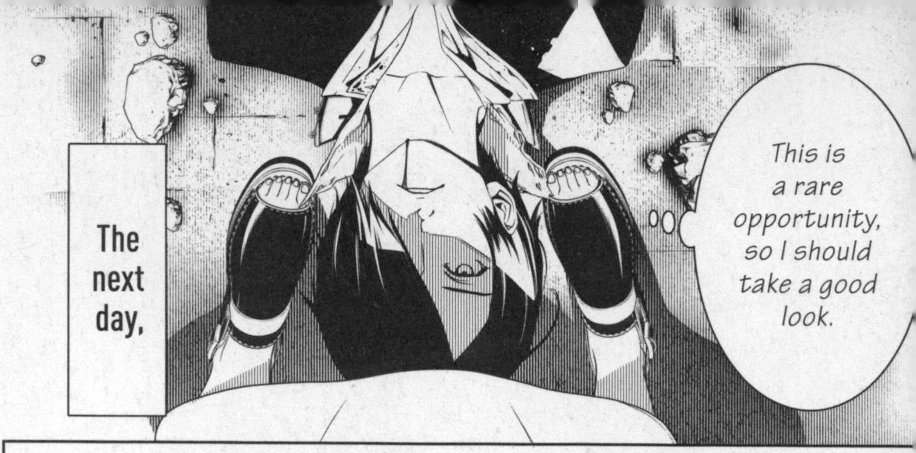
This is a rare opportunity, so I should take a good look.
The next day,
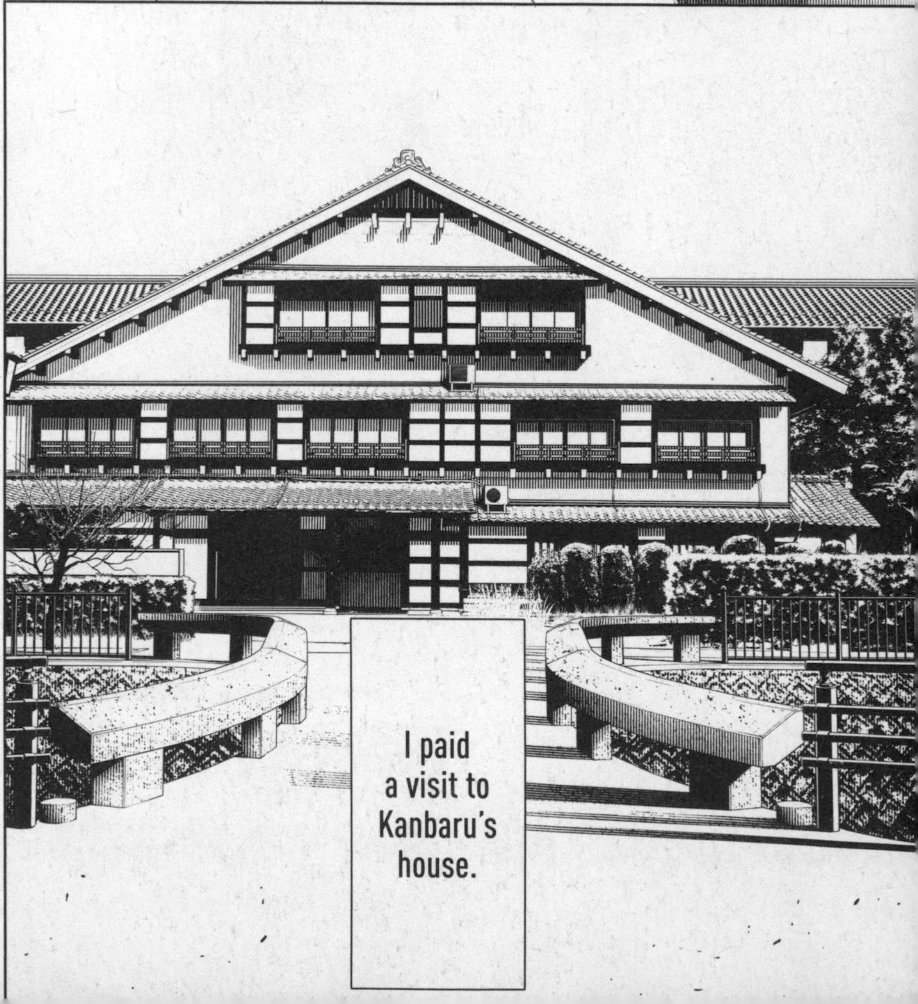
I paid a visit to Kanbaru's house.

Continued in Volume 5

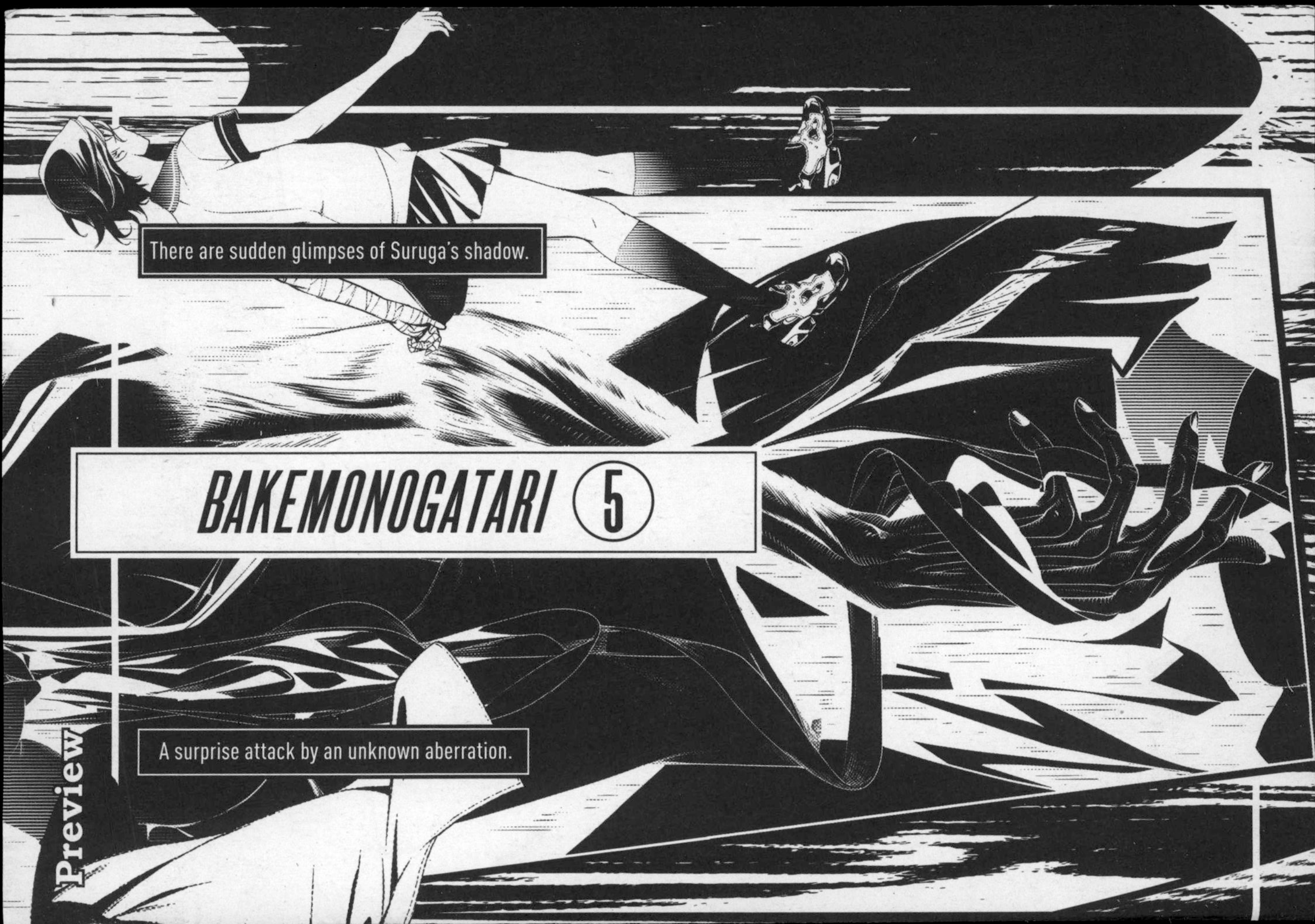
Preview
BAKEMONOGATARI 5
There are sudden glimpses of Suruga's shadow.
A surprise attack by an unknown aberration.